The Green Suit

The

Green

Suit

———

BY

Dwight Allen

ALGONQUIN BOOKS OF CHAPEL HILL
2000

Published by
ALGONQUIN BOOKS OF CHAPEL HILL
Post Office Box 2225
Chapel Hill, North Carolina 27515-2225

a division of
Workman Publishing
708 Broadway
New York, New York 10003

"Deferment" was first published in *The Southern Review;* "Fishing with Alex" appeared in a different form in *Gulf Coast;* "The Green Suit" was printed in *The Missouri Review* and *New Stories from the South: The Year's Best, 1997,* "The Hazeletts' Dog" in *American Short Fiction,* "Succor" in *The Georgia Review,* "Overtime" in *Shenandoah,* "Among the Missing" and "Not Renata" in *The New England Review,* and "Goat on a Hill" in *The Journal.*

Grateful acknowledgment is made to the following: Excerpt from "Makin' Whoopee" by Walter Donaldson and Gus Kahn, copyright 1928, copyright renewed 1955, by Donaldson Publishing Co. and Gilbert Keyes Music, Inc. International copyright secured. All rights reserved. Used by permission. Excerpt from *The Bald Soprano* by Eugène Ionesco, copyright 1958 by Grove Press, Inc. Used by permission of Grove/Atlantic, Inc. Excerpt from "A Coney Island of the Mind #14" by Lawrence Ferlinghetti, copyright 1958 by Lawrence Ferlinghetti. Reprinted by permission of New Directions Publishing Corp.

Library of Congress Cataloging-in-Publication Data
Allen, Dwight, 1951–
    The green suit / by Dwight Allen.
    p. cm.
    ISBN 1-56512-274-7
    1. Baby boom generation—Fiction. 2. United States—Social life and customs—20th century—Fiction. I. Title

PS3551.L39223 G74 2000
813'.6—dc21   00-036243

10 9 8 7 6 5 4 3 2 1
First Edition

For Nancy and George, and in

memory of my father

What can this capricious skin be but a blessing?

—John Cheever, *Journals*

Contents

Acknowledgments

I'm deeply grateful to Nancy Holyoke,
Betsy Amster, and Shannon Ravenel
for the ways each has helped to make
this book a book. Many thanks to the
Wisconsin Arts Board for a grant, and
to Mary Norris and Elizabeth Macklin,
steadfast readers. I'm indebted to my sister
for her encouragement and indulgence,
and to my mother and late father for their
support. Thanks also to Richard Sacks,
Michael Pietsch, Tom Parrett,
Mark Dintenfass, Bobbie Johnson,
Gale Petersen, Dale Kushner, Lisa Ruffolo,
Jesse Lee Kercheval, Heather Aronson,
Steve Finney, Nancy Reisman, Ron Kuka,
Ann Shaffer, and Max Garland.

The Green Suit

I.

Deferment

IN THE SUMMER OF 1970, I spent a lot of time trying to get a girl named Lizzie Burford to sleep with me. I had the idea that we would do it at the Goshen Motor Court, out on U.S. 42, near the county line. We'd lie in each other's arms and shiver as the air conditioner blew and the sweat on our skin dried. I was nineteen, a year older than Lizzie, and I thought about motels the way I later thought about churches: as places you could disappear into and lose yourself. I thought of the Goshen in particular because we sometimes drove past it on our way to or from doing nothing. Once when we stopped at the filling station across the highway from the Goshen, I saw a woman smoking in a lawn chair in the grassy oval where the motel owner had planted zinnias around an old water pump. I asked Lizzie what she thought the woman was thinking about, and Lizzie said, "She's thinking she made a mistake. Or why is she sitting outdoors watching the traffic go by and he's in the room eating beer nuts or something?"

"Maybe she got cold in the air-conditioning," I said.

"Maybe she wanted to hear the insects sing," Lizzie said, reaching for the can of beer between my legs. "And now she's thinking about walking across the highway so she can talk to *him*." She indicated the skinny boy washing bug spatters from the windshield.

"I like sleeping in motels," I said. This was more a statement of fact than a proposition.

"You're so romantic, Peter," Lizzie said, replacing the can of beer.

As I waited for the pump jockey to bring me my change, I saw the woman crossing the highway. She was barefooted. I wondered if the warmth of the pavement surprised her. Lizzie said, "Think of all the wrong boys you could end up with with breasts like hers."

I took Lizzie home and kissed her softly on the mouth and then drove to the Frankfort Avenue White Castle and ate six of those silver-dollar-size burgers in about two minutes.

THE NEXT AFTERNOON, on my way to work, I stopped by Lizzie's house. As far as I knew, I was the only boy in Jefferson County knocking on her door. This was so not only because she was flat-chested and lanky, with bones that hung together in a complex, awkward way. It was so because she had a straight-A kind of brain and often carried herself in a manner that led some boys to imagine that she was standoffish or prideful or touchy or all three. And then there was the matter of her being the daughter of an Episcopal preacher and of failing to behave like the hard-drinking, hell-raising offspring of Episcopal clergymen we all knew. She stole sips of beer from me and did not smoke.

When I entered the house, Miles, the Burfords' black Lab, sniffed me all over, then retired to the library. I followed Lizzie upstairs. We passed the door to her parents' bedroom—the Reverend Burford was at St. Timothy's, Mrs. Burford was at the chiropracter's—and then we passed Lizzie's brother's room. Harry was in Vietnam. He'd been there for about two months.

Lizzie flopped down on her bed and resumed writing a letter to her brother. She wrote him almost daily, on stationery with psychedelic filigree which she'd bought at a head shop. I sat on the edge of the twin, watching her write, watching her long, bare legs move back and forth, slowly, metronomically. I was aware of a dull ticking in my head. I took off my work boots and found a place on the bed beside her. I set my mouth within inches of a vaccination mark on her right arm. She was left-handed, the only left-handed girl in the universe, to my knowledge. Her handwriting was messy, difficult to discern.

"What are you telling Harry?" My breath came back at me off her freckled, summery skin.

"Just things. About my job." Lizzie worked in a Head Start program in the mornings. "How many times Daddy took his glasses off when he gave his sermon."

"How many?" I aimed the tip of my tongue at the pale center of her vaccination mark.

"Seventeen. It was a short sermon." She tucked stray hair behind her ear and then said, "You're cramping my style."

I withdrew my tongue and rolled over on my back. I gazed at Lizzie's ear, the curve of it ending in that soft lobe with its tiny ring hole. I fingered the pack of Larks in the breast pocket of my shirt. Though I was nineteen, a sophomore-to-be at a college in Tennessee, I was by any definition except, perhaps, a technical one a virgin. Once, during my freshman year, I'd gotten near-blind-drunk on grain alcohol punch and found myself on top of a girl from Knoxville, who was also drunk and who kept saying, "Are you in? Are you in? I can't feel you."

I listened to the air conditioner rattle in the window frame. It was ninety-something outside. In an hour, I had to be at my job. I worked on the four-to-midnight shift at a lumber mill off Dixie Highway, stacking boards that came off a planer. It was a summer job, the lowliest at the plant, next to sweeping sawdust. I'd chosen it over an offer to be a gofer boy for a firm of Republican lawyers.

I rolled off the bed and went over to Lizzie's desk and picked up the photo cube that sat on a pile of books. There was a picture of Lizzie and Harry as children: Lizzie in a green, bell-shaped dress that made her look like a Christmas ornament, flashing slightly bucked teeth, and Harry in blazer and tie, his hand on his sister's shoulder. I rotated the cube to a picture of Lizzie in last year's prom gown, her teeth straightened, her shoulders so bare I felt I could touch them below the surface of the photo. I turned the cube again, to a snapshot of Harry in jungle pants and Army helmet, crouched by a small black dog, sandbags in the background; Harry was squinting and he looked quizzical, the way dogs do when they tilt their heads to the side.

And then I studied the picture, taken that spring, of Lizzie as Mary the Maid in *The Bald Soprano*, her senior class play. (She'd gone to a private girls' school that employed an ambitious drama teacher.) She wore a short black skirt with a frilly apron and balanced uneasily on high heels. I thought she looked wonderful, even if she was dressed more like a cocktail waitress than a maid in a proper English home. The photograph was of the moment when she recited Mary's poem for the Fire Chief. Her hands were clutched together at her waist, and her head was tilted upward, heavenward, as if ecstasy had descended on her and left her mouth agape. This wasn't quite the first sign I'd had that she was capable of enrapturement, but it was the most explicit.

I opened the top drawer of Lizzie's desk in the hope of finding I knew not what exactly. The letters I'd written her from college that spring, letters all swollen with praise (some of it borrowed) for the parts of her I'd been allowed to kiss?

"What are you doing in my desk, Mr. Nosey?"

"*Rien.*" I walked across the hall to Harry's room. The blinds were pulled and the windows shut tight. The air felt ancient, as if it were being preserved for Harry to breathe when he came back.

The trophies on the bureau—both for swimming—gleamed faintly. A knotted necktie hung from a drawer knob. On the floor were two crates of LPs, mostly jazz, mostly musicians I knew only by name. Harry was deep, though not in an academic way, judging by his failure to hold on to his student deferment. He had fallen behind at college and then had dropped out and gone to Montreal, where he'd planned to spend the war. But when his draft notice arrived, he returned home. Lizzie said he'd felt guilty.

I put a record on Harry's portable Magnavox and sat in his wide-bottomed armchair and listened to Thelonious Monk play the piano. He played the melody in snatches and then nervously jumped away from it, like a man with a hundred worries. I closed my eyes. I thought of Harry crouching next to the little black dog in the Mekong Delta or wherever he was in that country of which my ignorance was extensive. (Once, when Lizzie read me one of Harry's letters in which there was a description of a sunset, I thought, *There are sunsets in Vietnam?*) Wasn't dog considered to be a delicacy in Asia? The dog and Harry vanished and I saw myself lying naked on crisp white sheets at the Goshen Motor Court, waiting for a woman to come out of the bathroom, where she was washing her feet.

"Do you like it?" Lizzie had slipped into her brother's room and was now sitting on my knees, her hands pinning mine to the armrests. She meant the music.

"Yeah," I said.

"More than Buffalo Springfield? More than Joni Mitchell in her big yellow taxi?"

"Yeah."

"Liar," Lizzie said. "Pants are on fire."

In Lizzie's eyes, soft black islands encircled by blue-gray irises casting changeable light, I saw that she couldn't say to herself that she found me undesirable, even if she could say that I didn't impress her. In her mouth, in the ample fleshiness of it, I saw, or imagined I saw, her willingness to accept my devotions, at least until the end of the summer, when she went away to college. She was going to Chapel Hill on a scholarship.

I leaned forward to kiss Lizzie, but I was in an awkward position and she didn't meet me halfway and I couldn't reach that far—or that high, rather. And so I put my mouth on her more accessible breast, a small wonder beneath her ribbed jersey. I was permitted to let my mouth rest there for a moment, like a child being offered consolation, long enough that I felt her nipple rise in response. Oh, I was allowed certain liberties, to use a phrase that even then was old-fashioned, but Lizzie wasn't going to let go of her virginity easily. She had discussed me in her letters to Harry, and he had told her that you had to be careful whom you entrusted your soul to. At any rate, she wasn't prepared to surrender herself to me "just because you have a boner and I have a vagina it can go into." She laughed when she said that. Her frankness threw me and even made me blush.

When Lizzie pulled away and I lifted my head, I saw the Reverend Burford in the doorway. He was short and gray-haired. There was something molelike about his face, as if he didn't spend enough time in the sun. His forehead was marked with lines that faded out at his temples, like old trails. He looked damp and pale, not nearly as pink as the flesh-colored frames of his glasses. In fact, he had a cold.

"Lizzie, I think it would be better if you and Peter were not in your brother's room." He sniffled, tugged at his clerical collar.

Lizzie rose from my knees and brushed at herself, as if to shed the imprint of me. "We were just listening to one of Harry's jazz records before Peter left."

"It's nice seeing you again, Peter," the Reverend Burford said.

"Yessir," I said, rising from the chair, wondering if the stiffness in my jeans was as evident to him as it was to me. I stuck my hands in my pockets and looked down at my bootless feet.

"I missed seeing your father at the Humane Society meeting the other night," the Reverend Burford said, taking a handkerchief out of his coat pocket. "Please give him and your mother my regards."

"Yessir."

"How'd you get out of the draft, man?" Red and I were pushing a cartload of hardwood from the planing room into a storage area. Or rather I was pushing and Red was guiding me across the rutted concrete floor, down an aisle, where the only light was cast by yellow bulbs in wire cages. It was eight-fifteen in the evening, fifteen minutes until dinnertime.

"Student deferment," I said, sliding my safety glasses up my sweaty nose.

"How come you're doing a dumb-ass job like this if you're so smart?" Red came around to the back of the cart to help me push it the last few feet. He was grinning. The reddish-blond stubble on his chin and around his mouth, the beginnings of a goatee perhaps, looked like sawdust stuck to his face, not quite real. As he leaned into the cart, the muscles in his arms flared beneath a cutoff football jersey he'd worn just about every day I'd known him. Six days, to be exact. Today was the first time we'd had something like a conversation.

"Must be the money," I said, hoping this would pass for a joke.

"Maybe you can buy some pencils and tablets with it," he said. We walked back down the aisle and into the planing room with its high, girdered ceiling and doors you could drive a semi through.

I didn't know how old Red was. His hard, narrow face suggested he was older than me by more than a year or two. But he had freckles around his eyes, some residue from a not-too-far-off boyhood. And his eyes were a mild blue. And his hair—stringy, the color of dried-out red clay—was almost long enough to make me think he might be an ally. There were fewer than a handful of workers in the mill whose hair fell over their eartops.

"How'd you get out of the draft?" I asked.

He removed his right work glove and held out his hand. "The trigger finger doesn't look real useful, does it?" It had been severed at the middle joint. "I can hardly even pick my nose with it." He said he'd cut it in shop class at high school.

He put his glove back on and said, "One more load before dinner." He went down to his work station, singing "Whipping Post," and switched on the machinery. Raw ten- and twenty-foot boards of maple and oak and walnut slid sideways down a canted conveyor and Red guided them into the planer. I grabbed them as they shot across a metal table, all hot and smooth, their grains exposed, and flipped them onto a cart. Red had taught me to use the table as a lever. "It's like dealing cards," he'd said. "Nothing to it." But I still wasn't in his league. When both he and I worked at my end of the table—sometimes a man named Boyd fed the planer—Red did the twice the volume I did. Sometimes Red did a little monkey dance while loading his cart and half of mine.

Red pushed boards toward me at a rate I couldn't keep up with, and in a minute I was buried. I waved at him to stop, but he didn't acknowledge me. He was singing to himself. I started shouting, even though I knew he couldn't hear me through the noise of the planer, which was like ten lawn mowers going at once. I watched a batch of black walnut slide off the table onto the floor. Then the machine stopped.

From behind me came a voice. "Son, if you make any more messes like this, you're going to have to find another line of work."

The speaker was Mr. Root, the foreman, who was known as

Adolph, because he bore a passing resemblance to Adolph Rupp, the University of Kentucky's gruff, jowly basketball coach. Mr. Root was sitting in his foreman's motorized cart, sipping coffee, his head hidden under a cap.

"Yessir," I said.

"I'll get him to quit playing with his pecker, don't you worry, Mr. Root," Red said. He was helping me pick up the boards.

"You be sure you do, Cloverly." That was the first time I heard Red's last name; I never did find out his Christian name, unless Red was it.

Mr. Root departed. "Sorry," I said to Red.

"Some guy I know died in Vietnam because some fuckup in his platoon didn't do his job right." Red glared at me.

"Sorry," I said, though I didn't see the parallel between the jungles of Vietnam and a wood mill in Kentucky.

"Don't worry about it, Joe," Red said, slapping me on the back. Joe, I later figured out, was short for Joe College. "Just keep your pecker clear of whirling blades."

He grinned and I grinned back.

"WHERE ARE YOU AND LIZZIE going tonight, Peter?" Mrs. Burford was tearing up lettuce, dropping the pieces into a wooden bowl on the kitchen table. Some of the pieces were as small as confetti. She was on her second Scotch—second that I'd seen, anyway.

"The movies," I said. "Lizzie wants to see this one by Truffaut that Harry told her about. It's at the Crescent." I glanced out the window above the kitchen sink. Lizzie was playing with Miles while the Reverend Burford tended the barbecue grill. She was wearing a sundress, her arms and legs covered by nothing more than smoky light. Watching her throw a ball to Miles quickened my desire for her. The fact that she threw awkwardly, as if her left arm operated independently of her brain, made her only more desirable.

"Harry took me to some Swedish movie at the Crescent just before he went off to boot camp," Mrs. Burford said. "It was all pain and desolation. With subtitles I couldn't make out half the time." Mrs. Burford stopped tearing lettuce and picked up her drink. The bracelets on her wrist slid and jangled. She was a tall, thin woman, nearly a head taller than her husband. She wore her graying hair in a permanent wave, possibly in the hope that it might divert attention from the signs of disintegration in her face. There was darkness under her eyes, which were like glimmers far out to sea.

I picked at the label on my beer bottle. "Do you like musicals?"

"Musicals?" she said, tilting her head, as if there were something hidden in my question and she were trying to shake it loose. In fact, it was a mindless question, though I did see how it might lead her away from the subject of Harry, who was all but present. There were pictures of him on the refrigerator, though none showed him in military dress. In one taken a couple days before he'd been inducted, he had his arms around Lizzie and a friend of hers named Evie. Their faces were squeezed together like fruit in a bin. Harry's hair was long and it fell into his eyes, but it didn't hide his fear.

"Musicals?" she said again, opening the refrigerator and leaning in. "I prefer them to Swedish dramas, if that's what you mean." She turned around and handed me a large red onion that had slipped out of its skin. "Why don't you cut this up while I go put something on the hi-fi."

She left the kitchen with her drink in hand. Was I supposed to slice the onion into rings or dice it? Was it for the salad or the hamburgers?

I heard the hi-fi needle land on a record and slide across an acre of grooves before settling on a man crooning darkly about an ill wind. I looked out the window for Lizzie. She was standing next to her father, holding her hair off her neck.

Mrs. Burford re-entered the kitchen, the liquid in her glass a late-afternoon color. The music, the solemn voice of the singer and the lush sound of the orchestra, seemed to have made her smaller, overwhelmed her. Then I noticed she'd taken off her shoes.

"I don't suppose you and Lizzie listen to Frank Sinatra much." She took the knife from me and began to dice the two onion rings I'd sliced.

"I hear him on the radio sometimes." With strings swelling behind him, Sinatra sang of having no one to scratch his back.

"I heard him at the Armory in 1941 with the Dorsey band. The place was full of all these young men without dates. Stags, we called them. It was so hot and crowded I could hardly breathe." She looked up from the onions, into, I imagined, the mists of the forties. "Sinatra was just a tough little skinny kid then, a beautiful singer. When he got older, his voice became less beautiful and more interesting. He made this record in 1955, after Ava Gardner left him."

I swallowed the last of my beer. When Mrs. Burford had offered me the beer, she'd said, "If you're old enough to be drafted, you're old enough to drink." I gripped my empty bottle and listened to the record, trying to hear what Mrs. Burford heard. I was a little bit high, which made me receptive. Then I saw Mrs. Burford lift her head from her onion chopping. She was crying, whether from the onions or the music or something else, I wasn't sure.

Mrs. Burford wiped her cheeks with the back of her hand. Then she asked me to take the salad out to the table on the side porch. There was nothing in the bowl besides the shredded lettuce.

I stood under the slowly spinning ceiling fan on the porch and watched Miles run out of the yard in a hurry, as if he'd just caught the scent of something juicier than the Reverend Burford's hamburgers. Frank Sinatra was singing about a man alone in bed. The music seemed gravely wrought, if not overwrought, and I wanted to escape it and go have a cigarette.

When I came back into the kitchen, Mrs. Burford said, "What do you plan on doing if you're drafted?" She was standing at the sink, washing a head of broccoli. I couldn't see her face.

A year before, in the weeks before my eighteenth birthday, I'd had some notion that I might file for conscientious objector status, though I'd barely cracked the books about pacifism I'd gotten from the library and I knew in my heart I wasn't going to cut it as a C.O. And when the time came to make an appearance at the Selective Service Office, I'd gone downtown and said, in effect, "You can have me when you need me." The clerk, a woman with a Rhine-maidenish tower of hair, had smiled at me through coils of cigarette smoke. A few months later, after I'd gone off to college, I'd received my card and my deferment. I was 2-S.

"I guess I'd go," I said. "Probably." I sat down at the table.

"You don't sound very sure of yourself." Her back was still turned to me. Her blouse had come untucked.

I touched the glass that held her Scotch, then glanced at the pictures of Harry on the refrigerator door. Would I have submitted to the government's call and come home from Montreal? Probably.

Mrs. Burford turned around, the head of wet broccoli in her hands, glistening, dripping on the floor. "I didn't hear what you said." She'd dried her eyes, but her face was clouded and dark, as if there were more bad weather on the way.

"I'm hoping I don't lose my deferment," I said. "My lottery number is kind of low." My number was 43.

"You shouldn't do what your heart tells you not to do." She turned back to the sink. "Harry went because he said some poor kid would have to go if he didn't. He was trying to be noble."

If I went to Vietnam, would Lizzie sleep with me as a parting gift? I thought not. She was a girl with principles.

"Maybe you could take the ketchup out to the porch," Mrs. Burford said. "It's in the fridge. And the horseradish. My husband won't eat a hamburger without it."

I found the bottles and carried them through the living room, where Sinatra was singing to the blue sofa where Lizzie and I sometimes sat, me with my boner, Lizzie with a Coke she sipped endlessly, and Miles at her feet. I set the bottles on the porch table and when I looked up, I saw a car stopped in the street, a pale blue Falcon sedan like my grandmother drove, with a woman in a golf skirt and visor standing beside it. She'd hit Miles. I could see his black shape a few yards from her fender. I looked dumbly at Miles sprawled there, in the end-of-the-day haze, and then Lizzie ran by the porch, shouting, and I noticed the way her body moved inside her sundress.

Miles was still breathing. The Reverend Burford wrapped him in a sheet and lifted him into the back of his wood-paneled station wagon, which he'd bought at a discount from a parishioner. Lizzie was weeping, tearing at herself because Miles was her responsibility while Harry was away, and she insisted on going with her father to the vet's. There was blood on her hand, where she'd stroked Miles, and on her cheek, where she'd wiped her hand in despair. Mrs. Burford and I stayed behind. She had another Scotch and then she excused herself and went upstairs to her bedroom and didn't come back down. I helped myself to another beer and drank it on the blue sofa as the light leaked out of the day and I felt my desire for Lizzie wane.

"YOU NEED TO pick up the pace, boy," Red said, "or you're going to get your ass canned." We were on a smoke break, sitting on a bench outside the planing shed, below a huge pile of shavings and other mill refuse. Boyd, who was feeding the planer that night, was sitting apart from us on an overturned bucket, not smoking. It was dark, between ten and eleven.

I was tired and, not for the first time, on the verge of quitting. It gave me pleasure to imagine lying on my bed, listening to Thelonious Monk play the piano, my hand lolling next to a vent that cool air poured through. I could almost hear the air flowing through the duct and Monk doing his odd sprung-rhythm thing. I'd persuaded Lizzie to let me borrow a couple of Harry's LPs.

Red dragged on his cigarette. "You getting laid enough?"

I exhaled smoke and produced a noise like an assent.

"Maybe he's a fairy," Boyd said. Boyd poured the last of a pint carton of chocolate milk down his throat and then let the carton fall to the dirt. According to Red, Boyd was a drifter. He didn't spend any time mixing with others. At dinnertime, he went out to his car with his vending-machine sandwich and chocolate milk and ate there.

"Fairies get laid, I hear," Red said. "They just go at it different."

"You know that from experience, Red?" Boyd pushed down on the carton with his work boot.

"I know that from seeing you and Adolph get it on in the back of that shit-for-wheels Fury of yours. I asked myself: why can't they go to a darned motel if they want to do them things? Wasn't I telling you about that, Joe?" Red jabbed me in the shoulder with the stub of his trigger finger.

I nodded in a way that I hoped might be imperceptible to Boyd and then saw him slowly rise from his seat. Boyd was tall and bony, with an Adam's apple that jutted like a crag. His hair receded from a wispy widow's peak high on his forehead. I estimated his age at between thirty and fifty.

Boyd walked past without glancing our way and went into the planing shed and switched on the conveyor and planer.

"Fucking drifting alky trash," Red said. "Don't pay any attention to him."

A couple nights later, the night we got paid, I drove Red to a twenty-four-hour gas station after work. The tires on his Camaro had been slashed. He punched the ceiling of my VW and swore, telling me what he planned to do to Boyd when he caught him. (Boyd was long gone; he'd disappeared at the six o'clock smoke break, after the paychecks had come around.) The station wouldn't cash Red's check, so I let him use my credit card, and then drove him back to the mill and watched him put the new tires on.

As he tightened the bolts on the last tire, he said, "I know this girl Virgie who has a sister I could fix you up with. I owe you, so don't say no."

I didn't.

I WENT OUT with Lizzie the next night, as planned. She was in a cheerful mood. She'd gotten a letter from Harry, who said that he was doing fine, "just sitting here on my cot, drinking warm beer, and listening to Johnny Cash on the radio in between choppers flying over." He added, "I wish it was Billie Holiday instead of Johnny, but you can't have everything (ha ha)." Lizzie wrote back to say that Miles was doing OK after the accident. The vet had amputated a leg that was crushed beyond repair, but Miles was now able to hobble around and find his way to the pork-chop bones in the kitchen trash.

Lizzie and I went to see *Jules and Jim* at the Crescent and then we drove to a wayside on River Road and sat on the damp ground under a buzzing street lamp and watched the river flow by. We talked about the movie, about how the Jeanne Moreau character was too much for either of the men to handle by himself. I said I couldn't see sharing a lover with somebody else.

"You can't have everything," Lizzie said, laughing. Then she asked me to give her my wallet.

"My wallet?" But I did as she requested.

She went through the contents—a photo of her, the combination to my athletic locker at school, my Standard Oil credit card—until she found what she wanted. She held it up to the light and read my Selective Service number and my Random Sequence number and my classification. Then she folded the card into quarters and put it in her mouth. She let it rest against her cheek for a moment, like a plug of tobacco, before she began chewing.

I watched in silence. I was opposed to the war—or, anyway, opposed to having to participate in it myself—but I'd done little to declare my opposition, aside from taking part in a candlelight march at school. There was a whole army of us, upper-middle-class white boys with draft cards in our back pockets, hoping the war would end before our deferments expired.

"What does it taste like?"

"Like paper with typing on it, except for your signature, which is kind of inky. You want a bite?" She stuck her tongue out; in the juices of her mouth, the card had been reduced to something larger than a spitball.

"No, thanks."

She resumed chewing; she chewed noisily, like a child making a show of her eating.

"You can do time for 'knowingly' mutilating a card," I said. I'd read the fine print on the back.

"Here," she said, leaning toward me. "Be a good boy and swallow." She shoved the sodden wad into my mouth and then kissed me hard. She pushed at the card with her tongue, trying to steer it down my throat, until she started laughing.

I took the lump out of my mouth and put it in my pocket. "I'll tell the draft board my girlfriend ate it," I said.

"Be brave," she said. "Tell them you don't want to fight in their shitty war."

"Would you sleep with me then—before I went to jail, I mean?"

"I'd write you letters in jail." She put her arm around me.

"It doesn't matter. I'm not going to get drafted anyway."

I ARRIVED LATE for Harry's funeral and found a seat in the rearmost pew, next to the man who'd taught Latin to Harry and (later) me in high school. Mr. Becker had also coached the swimming team of which Harry had been captain in his senior year. He shared a hymnal with me and sang enthusiastically, in his emphatic Latin taskmaster's baritone. My eyes strayed from the book to look for Lizzie, but I couldn't see far enough forward through all the dark suits and saucer-shaped hats. I'd not seen her since the night she ate my draft card. I'd been going out with Cheryl, Virgie's sister, the girl Red had set me up with.

When the congregation sat for the reading of the lesson, I saw the back of Lizzie's head. It seemed more remote than I had ever imagined it might become. I listened to the lesson: "Behold, I show you a mystery; we shall not all sleep, but we shall all be changed, in a moment, in the twinkling of an eye, at the last trump." I read, responsively, the even-numbered verses of Psalm 121, and then I went outside and took off my jacket and got into my car.

I lit a cigarette. I looked at the white doors of St. Timothy's, the little flourish of a steeple poking at the pale sky, the hearse driver sitting on a fold-up stool in the courtyard next to the sanctuary. I watched cars go down the street—traffic from another world, it seemed. I remembered that when I heard about Harry's death—he stepped on a mine—I was in the bathroom brushing my teeth, getting ready to go see Cheryl. I listened as the bearer of the news, my mother, talked to me through the door. When she left, I finished brushing my teeth and worried a pimple and then wrote Lizzie a note, which, despite its brevity, I flattered myself to imagine was heartfelt. I dropped the note in the Burfords' mailbox on my way out to Shively, where Red and Cheryl and her sister lived. This was my second date with Cheryl, who sold popcorn at the new Movieland on Dixie Highway. On our first, we'd driven around with Red and Virgie, stopping at an all-night auto-parts store, where Red wanted to look at tachometers, and ending up at a party halfway to Fort Knox. Cheryl had a boyfriend, I found out, who was in Vietnam, and it came as a surprise to me when she took my hand and studied my palm and said, "Don't worry. He won't kill you if we make it."

I saw the funeral parlor driver get up from his stool and a couple minutes later the church's white doors opened and six men hauled Harry's coffin into the sunlight. I saw the Reverend Burford without his vestments—he hadn't officiated—and then I saw Lizzie. She was holding on to her mother's arm, moving unsurely, as if caught off guard by the brightness of the day. She didn't wear sunglasses or a hat, as her mother did. The sun was pouring down on her head, cooking her to her roots, and she leaned against her mother for protection.

I hadn't been the kind of person, I thought, whom Lizzie cared to lean into. What had I had to offer, after all, aside from my worshipful dick, which, like some meddlesome, boorish third party, was always ready to interpose itself? And so, about a week before I would learn of Harry's death, I'd gone out to Shively for the first time. The next day, I'd left Lizzie a note—I was big on leaving notes—telling her I was "seeing" someone else. I didn't expect her to answer, but she did. On legal-pad paper, she wrote, in her jumbly left-handed script, "Happiness is a warm gun, *n'est-ce pas?*"

People got into their cars, and then the hearse, like a great gleaming boat, pulled out into the street and the procession to the cemetery began. I got in line behind the last car, a VW containing Evie and another of Lizzie's friends, but when it turned left, I turned right, toward Shively.

"Don't you know any girls, man?" We were in Red's Camaro, parked across the street from a package store, drinking short boys. Virgie and Red had had a fight, and he was in a dark mood. Cheryl was working at the movie theater. It was barely seven, the package store neon buzzing in the lingering daylight. When I suggested we pick Cheryl up when she got off work, Red said, "Maybe she can sit in the crack"—he indicated the space between the bucket seats—"and jerk us both off." He smirked at me through the bristly fringe of his goatee. "I don't know, Joe. I don't think you ought to get too excited about Cheryl. She'd screw pretty much anything with two legs, which is why I set you up with her in the first place. I could see you were in need."

I remembered Cheryl saying, after we'd made it for the second time, "You're so quick." And then she'd kissed me, as if my being quick hadn't mattered too much. This was two weeks ago, the afternoon of Harry's funeral. We'd driven from Shively to the Goshen Motor Court, and afterward had lain on the stained sheets, watching a game show on a TV whose picture wouldn't stop rolling. The air conditioner produced only warm air, and at some point Cheryl had taken a shower and then had left the room to look for something to eat. When she came back, with barbecue chips and a Moon Pie and two Orange Crushes, I was overcome by hunger for her. "Whoa," she said, but she was under me before she could take a bite of anything.

I looked out the windshield. A man as skinny as a snake came weaving down the sidewalk. He was wearing an unbuttoned, puffy-sleeved paisley shirt and bell-bottoms that were slipping down his hips and a sashlike belt that fell to his knees. I thought he might weave himself right on to the hood of Red's car, but he slid by.

"Thought that was Boyd for a second," Red said. "Dressed up like a dipshit." He pushed in the lighter and reached for his Raleighs, which were wedged between the sun visor and the roof. "So you aren't going to introduce me to any of your high-class girl-friends?"

I'd tried to keep from Red—and Cheryl—the fact that I lived in a wealthy East End neighborhood, a considerable distance from the mill and working-class Shively, as well as from the package store outside of which we were now twiddling our thumbs. I'd always driven out to Shively or, as on this evening, met Red in-between. My economic status had become clear to Red when he'd phoned me, and Willie, the maid, had answered.

"OK," I said. "That way." I pointed in the direction of Lizzie's house.

WE SWUNG BY my house first. My parents had gone out, and I invited Red in, but he declined: "Wouldn't want to dirty the carpet." I got the two Monk LPs that Lizzie had let me borrow and grabbed an unopened quart of Scotch from a kitchen cabinet. When I presented Red with the bottle, he studied the two Scottie dogs on the label and said, "Woof! Woof!" Then he said, "Now show me where the long-legged women are hiding."

We drove out of my thickly wooded neighborhood, across U.S. 42 and over to Lizzie's, where the trees were younger and there was less space between houses. I told Red about Lizzie's brother. I said I didn't know if she'd be in the mood to ride around with us.

"Go ring the doorbell, man," Red said. "I'll cheer her up."

I went up the Burfords' brick walk with the albums. In my note to Lizzie about Harry, I'd said she could call me whenever she wanted. In my arrogance, I'd imagined she might come running to me in her grief. I liked Cheryl, I liked the way she held on to me for those brief moments I was inside her, one hand on my neck, the other at the base of my spine, as if she were guiding me through some country waltz. I liked the frank but uncritical way she gazed at me and the way she said, when a certain C&W singer came on the radio, "Oh, God, I love that man almost as much as my daddy." But I was prepared to give her up in the event Lizzie sought me out—not that Cheryl, if Red was to be believed, would have minded too much. When Harry had died, I'd actually imagined that his hold on Lizzie might weaken somehow, that she might see the usefulness of entrusting herself to me, if only temporarily. It wasn't easy admitting defeat. I liked Cheryl's soft, sweet breasts, breasts between which Moon Pie crumbs could get lost, but I'd set my heart on Lizzie's small, firm ones.

I rang the doorbell and peered through the screen door into the unlighted front hall. I saw Miles lying at the end of the hall, near the kitchen door. He didn't get up. Then I saw Lizzie, halfway up the stairs, gazing at me. Her stillness, the way she sat with her elbow on her thigh and her finger to her lips, startled me. The whole house seemed sunk in stillness, the way a house is when you come back to it from a vacation.

I said through the screen, "I should've come to see you before now."

"Why should you have? What difference would it have made?" She spoke so softly I could barely hear her.

"I brought the Monk records back." Miles was twitching in his sleep, dreaming of chasing a cat on four good legs.

"You can keep them," she said.

I ran my finger around the doorknob. "Where are your parents?"

"Daddy went on some church retreat thing in the Smokies. Mom's upstairs."

I heard a radio—Eric Burdon singing "Spill the Wine." I turned around and saw Red standing beside the car, drumming on the roof. When I turned back and saw Lizzie on the stairs, like a child suspended in some purgatory, her face cradled in her hands, I thought of delivering the apology I'd prepared, or a brief version of it: "Forgive me, Lizzie, for having offered you next to nothing when your brother died." But I was stubborn enough not to, as stubborn as Lizzie had been in her resistance of my charmless attempts to possess her.

"We could go get stoned," I said. "With my friend Red." I nodded toward the street.

"A few nights after Harry died I went out with Evie and got drunk and puked right where you're standing." The recollection of puking where I was standing didn't please her enough that she smiled.

I picked at the mesh on the screen.

"How come you're not out with your girlfriend?"

"She's not really my girlfriend," I said.

"Easy come, easy go, right, pardner?" Red had crept through the dusk to stand alongside me. He'd tucked his football jersey into his jeans.

"This is Red," I said, and Red said, "Hey!" Miles awoke from his dream and scrambled to his three feet and hopped down the hall to sniff us through the screen. Mrs. Burford called from upstairs to find out who was there, and Lizzie said it was just Peter and his friend. Red told Lizzie that he was sorry to hear about her brother, and that he'd had a friend the gooks had killed.

"I played football with this guy," Red said. "We went swimming together all the time at a quarry. Once he bet me that he could stand in this field where grasshoppers were flying around and open his mouth and catch five in two minutes. He won, but he cheated. He had a fucking huge mouth."

Lizzie smiled a little. Eventually she went upstairs to tell her mother that she was going out. She wore tennis shoes and a sundress and rode in the front seat.

RED DECIDED THAT we should go sit on the Big Four railroad bridge and watch the sun go down. The bridge, which was no longer used, wasn't easily accessible from the Kentucky side of the Ohio River, so we had to cross via a downtown bridge and then drive back up the Indiana shore. Even though Red drove as if our lives hung in the balance, there wasn't much left of the sunset by the time we parked—just a few reddish-purple carcinogenic streaks at the bottom of the sky.

"We can watch the stars come out," Lizzie said, almost cheerfully. She'd drunk half a short boy on the way over. Red and I had passed the Scotch back and forth.

"Sounds romantic," I said. A blaze warmed my skull, but it didn't ease my regret for bringing Red and Lizzie together.

"He misses Cheryl," Red said. "The fastest girl in the West." We were walking on the rail bed out to the bridge itself, with its immense steel spans held up by old stone piers. Red was on point, Lizzie was in the middle, and I brought up the rear.

"Cheryl," Lizzie said, turning around to look at me. I glanced downward, at the ties and the gaps between them. I could see the glimmer of the river below. Heights frightened me; in this case, the fear took the top off my buzz and left me grim.

"We went to the Goshen," I said. I didn't say that I'd registered under the names Harry and Lizzie Burford.

"Motel love," Lizzie said.

We walked to the center of the bridge. The evening was mild, and there was a breeze, which seemed more pronounced up there among all the cables and struts and arcing steel. It licked at Lizzie's dress and hair.

Red sang the refrain from that Eric Burdon song and did a spastic boogaloo. He turned to Lizzie and said, "You want to climb up?"

"Sure," she said, as if climbing bridges were as simple as breathing.

"You'll have a much better view of Indiana from up there," I said, struggling to light a cigarette, cupping a match against the wind.

"You can wait for us while we go up," Red said. "Play with yourself or something."

All but the last glow of the day had been sucked from the sky. The lights of downtown Louisville were on, and there was a sprinkling of lights along the Indiana shore. In the growing dark, the bridge seemed to lose its firmness, to become tracery in the sky.

Red and Lizzie went over to the downriver side of the bridge and began to climb a ladder attached to the middle span. Red first, Lizzie second.

I flicked my cigarette away and followed. The ladder rungs were more like hand-holds than steps — narrow U-shaped bars riveted into the beam. I gripped the rungs, flattened my body against the available steel. Lizzie went up slowly. I stayed close, close enough that the crease behind her knee was within reach. I didn't look any farther up her dress. I didn't want to disturb my equilibrium. Fear was a chastening force. Nor, of course, did I look to either side of her.

"Lizzie," I said. I didn't know what I was going to say, but I wanted to hear her voice instead of the wind, the sound of a boat puttering up the river, Red singing the refrain.

She didn't answer.

"Lizzie," I said, louder. "What are you doing?"

"Climbing a bridge. Saying to myself that poem the Maid says in honor of the Fire Chief." She stopped climbing. We were perhaps halfway to the top. My mouth was at the level of her tennis shoe.

She seemed to be quivering, unless it was me—or the bridge—that was moving.

"'The men caught fire, the women caught fire, the birds caught fire, the fish caught fire,'" I recited. "'The fire caught fire, everything caught fire.'" I didn't know I knew the poem until I'd said it.

"You skipped some lines," she said. "'The water caught fire, the sky caught fire, the ashes caught fire.' It's a progression."

"Fucking A," Red exclaimed. He'd reached the top of the bridge.

I noticed that the right rear edge of Lizzie's right sneaker was worn down, a fact of no importance and yet one that struck me as poignant: she was a girl who wouldn't go through life on the balls of her feet.

"Lizzie," I said. "What could I've done to get you to sleep with me?" The wind didn't carry away the self-pity in my voice.

"You could've doped me up and raped me."

"That would've pleased you?"

"I would've been oblivious, but you would've accomplished your goal."

She continued climbing. When she reached the top, she crawled along the beam to where Red was sitting and smoking, his feet dangling over the side. He held her arm as she unwound her long legs and settled herself next to him. He brushed something from her knee—bridge grit, I supposed.

"This is scary," she said. I admired her for her honesty.

"Hold on to me," Red said.

She asked him about his severed index finger and he told her how he'd lost it. "It made me 4-F," he said. "Saved my ass from getting shot off in some jungle."

"Good for you," she said. Her tone wasn't bitter, but she let go of him, folded her hands in her lap.

"Shit," Red said. "Sorry."

I gripped a stanchion and looked outward rather than down. The dark was almost complete. I saw a drive-in movie screen a mile or so beyond the Indiana shore. The figures on the screen were indecipherable, like bug remains on a headlight. Was the sound I'd make when I hit the Ohio River two hundred feet below like *whap? Whump?* But I wasn't going to fall. I was going to crawl back down, slowly, not failing to place my foot where there was a rung.

Fishing with Alex

WHEN MY SISTER was a sophomore in college, in Philadelphia, she fell in love with a sallow-skinned, lank-haired boy whose chief interest in life was the effects of hallucinogens on the neurochemistry of white rats. This was in 1973. Ed was two years older than Alex, and when he dropped her, she came unglued. She left school and returned home to Kentucky. One morning in March, after eating half a grapefruit and casting a cold eye on the saucer of vitamin pills my mother had set before her, she went back upstairs, swallowed most of a bottle of barbiturates, and sat down in the reading chair in my bedroom. By the time my mother found her, Alex was in a stupor; her head lolled, her hands were clammy, her blood was pooling, not moving. My mother, who had been on her way to church to tag items for a bazaar, called an ambulance and got Alex to the hospital, where her stomach was pumped. Later, the doctor put her in Queen of Peace, a columned and porticoed institution that sat on a hill about a mile from the new county zoo. Because the windows to the rooms were sealed shut, it was unlikely that a patient would hear an elephant trumpet or a peacock shriek or a lion roar. But Alex said there was a man in her morning group therapy class who complained that the animals kept him awake every night. As for Alex herself, she heard nothing at night, just a whispering in her head, like a breeze passing through fir trees.

A few days after my sister entered Queen of Peace, I took the bus home from college. My father picked me up at the depot downtown. I asked how Alex was, and he said, "Your mother thinks she might be hypoglycemic." I looked puzzled, and he said, "Something about a low level of sugar in the blood." He didn't tell me what he thought. Three stoplights later, we fell silent. Eventually, he turned on the radio. The car filled with opera—it was a Saturday—and then he dialed around until he got a basketball game. "Now here's something in English," he said.

My father led me into the hospital and up a broad, curving staircase, which I pictured women in long dresses descending, on their way to meet men who wouldn't have resembled me or my father in his raincoat that looked as if he'd slept in it. At the top, Dad remembered that my mother had sent along a sack of vitamins for my sister. He left me at Alex's door and went back to the car to fetch the sack.

My sister was sitting up in bed. Next to her, on the nightstand, was a fish bowl, and above her, on the white wall, was a small plaster crucifix; the bony Jesus, his head downcast, looked as if he'd given his last cry. Alex wore a black shawl over a white blouse that was buttoned to the throat. I'd never seen the shawl. It made her look dramatic, in a formal kind of way, like someone in a painting from another century and another country. Alex had always liked to dress up, and I thought it was a good sign that she hadn't stopped. I didn't know if it was a good sign that she'd tied her hair back, leaving her brow so exposed.

"Don't worry, Peter," she said gamely. "I'm just having a run-of-the-mill nervous breakdown. Isn't that right, fishy?" She tapped on the bowl. The goldfish, the only truly bright spot of color in the room, streaked away. It was a gift from Bobby Tarr, a guy Alex had dated in high school.

"Mom thinks I'm chemically unbalanced," Alex said. "And spiritually at sea. And that I go out with the wrong boys." She looked out the window. It was an erratic mid-March afternoon, full of clouds one moment and bursts of sunlight the next.

"What do you think?" I touched the too-small black beret on my head. I'd bought it at a thrift shop. I'd hoped it would make me look worldly.

"I don't know," she said. "I guess some of my boyfriends haven't turned out too hot." She glanced toward the doorway, as if love might be there, waiting.

I saw a wimpled nun walk past, then another. I expected to see a third—didn't nuns travel in threes?—but she didn't materialize.

I said, "You've had some OK boyfriends. What about Bobby?" Bobby was three years older than Alex; he'd dropped out of college by the time she met him. At the moment, he was the leader of a band called the Tarrdy Boys and clerking in a store on Bardstown Road where you could buy incense and peasant shirts and Tarot cards, among other things.

"Bobby can be nice," Alex said. "But I'm just one of his chicks."

"And Mac?" Mac, whose actual name was Eldon McRae, was my age. Alex had first gone out with him when she was a sophomore in high school and he was a senior. Mac was shy and awkward, except on the basketball court, where he became someone who could make fallaway jumpers with his eyes half-closed. Alex found Mac's shyness appealing—that and his soft, blond, almost feminine looks. Mac felt flummoxed by his shyness, and as a result, he drank more than was normal in our group. When he drank, he sometimes did stupid, shy-boy sorts of things. Once, he tried to pole-vault into Alex's second-story bedroom, using a long metal rod he'd stolen from a construction site. He'd risen briefly into the air, like a pioneer of flight, and then had fallen on his shoulder, dislocating it. Like me, Mac had been a solid B-minus student, and we'd ended up at the same college, a boys-only institution, on a mountain in Tennessee.

"Mac got so bombed sometimes," Alex said, "he missed my face completely when he tried to kiss me." I saw her watching Mac's face float by again.

"Well, anyway," I said, "Mac said to say 'Hi.'"

"'Hi' back." Alex gazed at her fingers, which a flare-up of eczema had reddened, and made a church out of them, loosing silence upon the room. She was burrowing into herself, her nose leading the way. She had the Sackrider family nose. The sharp tip suggested that it would be worth your while to tell her a joke or a story.

"How are the nuns?" I asked.

"*Les zéros?*" She roughened the *r* expertly; she used to practice her French in the shower, bouncing *accents argus* off the tiles. "They're watchful."

My father appeared in the doorway, the sack of vitamins in one hand and a tweed motoring cap in the other. The cap was a Christmas present from my mother, something to make him look more sporty. He was a judge, and as a rule he dressed like one, though he sometimes failed to notice that his dark suit coat didn't match his dark suit trousers. After all, there were motions and petitions to be pondered, precedents to be considered.

Dad told me he was going to wait outside in the car. "I don't want to intrude on your discussion," he said, stooping to kiss Alex on the forehead. "We love you, Moony Tooth." My father had a whole hatful of names for my sister: Izzy Woo, Alexosaurus, Babes, Miss Graham Cracker. The last was derived from Alex's full name, Alexandra Bell Sackrider.

After my father left the room, Alex said, "Dad told me a story about how some East Coast girl had snubbed him when he was in college and how he'd been down in the dumps for days. Then he came back home for Christmas, and he saw Mom at a party, standing under mistletoe."

"Mom under mistletoe? Wasn't she a member of a Trotskyite cell back then?"

"Allegedly," Alex said. "Anyway, Dad kissed her. 'I took the liberty,' was how he put it, 'and I started living again.'"

"Didn't it take Dad about seven years to persuade Mom to marry him?"

"He left that part out," Alex said. The goldfish darted around the bowl, filling the room with its agitation. "I guess he was trying to tell me to hang in there." She pulled her shawl more tightly around her shoulders.

Ten minutes later, when I left Alex's room, it was snowing. It shouldn't have been snowing in Kentucky in mid-March, when green was surging through everything, but there the flakes were, all fat and wet. They fell on my face, like kisses from somebody—an aunt, say—who hadn't seen me in an age.

I found my father in his gray three-on-the-tree Chevrolet Biscayne, a car as unstylish as his old raincoat. He was leaning his forehead against the steering wheel.

When I got in, Dad sat up straight and adjusted his cap. The steering wheel had left a mark on his brow. "I was thinking of that fish Alex caught in Lake Cumberland. Fall of sixty-two. You remember that?"

I remembered our fishing guide, a narrow, dilapidated man named Bristow who rolled his own cigarettes. He was so quiet that he'd essentially finished talking for the day after he'd said "Morning" to you.

"Alex was the happiest girl in the state when she caught that fish," my father said. "A little old crappie. And now she's inconsolable because of this fellow Ned."

"Ed." I watched the snow fall, as thick as a plague of moths. "But I doubt it's just him."

"What else do you think it is?" He pushed his glasses up his nose. Maybe my father loved the world too much to imagine that someone's sorrow could lead her to want to vanish, to forgo the chance to drop a line in the water once more.

I said, "Sometimes you lose your grip and you start sliding down the slope and you can't stop."

"Yes," my father said. "You need something to hang on to when it gets rough." He fired up the Biscayne, turned on the windshield wipers. "Isn't it peculiar, this snow?"

SEVERAL WEEKS LATER, when every dogwood in Jefferson County was in bloom, Alex sat at the table in my parents' kitchen, smoking one of Willie's Salems. Willie, who had worked for our family since before I was born, sat across from Alex, snapping the ends off green beans. There was sunlight in the room, a springtime flood of it. It washed over the cut-glass sugar bowl and the three china monkeys (See No Evil, etc.) on the lazy Susan, over the faint hairs on Alex's wrist, and over the cast-iron pot Willie dropped the beans into.

"Last night I dreamed I was on a Greyhound," Alex said, "and this soldier kept falling asleep on my shoulder. And when I'd wake him, he'd scratch his head and say, 'Excuse me, ma'am, is this the Silver Dog to Bozeman?'"

I thought it was a good sign that Alex was having travel dreams. Since coming home from Queen of Peace, she'd rarely ventured out of the house, except to see her therapist. Once she'd driven to Frisch's Big Boy and ordered a cheeseburger and a shake, but had left before the curb girl could deliver the food. On another afternoon she'd gone with Bobby Tarr and his friend Pipe Cleaner Man to see a show at the planetarium.

"Don't talk to no soldiers on Greyhounds is my advice to you," Willie said. Willie handed out advice without much prompting. She snapped the stem off a bean. "You getting ready to leave us, Alex?"

"I'm just telling you my dream," Alex said. Cigarette smoke hung around her like a cloud, then slid out the window. She looked pale and a bit undernourished, but not without resources. I watched her trying to work out things behind her large brown eyes. A thought sped by; she touched her temple. Another thought, a longer one, it seemed, unfurled itself and lingered near the corner of her mouth, which curled downward.

"What do you think I should do, Willie?" Alex asked.

"Well," Willie said, "if I was you, I wouldn't be sitting here in my bedclothes at three in the afternoon with the sun shining. That's first. And second, I don't know that I'd be fooling with that boy Bobby and his friend, the one that looks like a Halloween skeleton."

"Pipe Cleaner Man," I said.

"He has a good heart," said Alex, who was drawn to socially marginal boys, boys whose brows were unclear, boys who liked to sleep in their labs with their rats and gels. "He can't help how he looks."

"All that reefer don't improve him any," Willie said. "And you neither." Her eyes, bloodshot from too much work or too many cigarettes, aimed daggers at me.

"I wonder what Bozeman is like," Alex said, giving the lazy Susan a push. The three monkeys glided by, two of them clearly grinning.

"Never heard of it," Willie said.

"Cowboys, rednecks," I said. "What would you be thinking of Montana for?"

"Bobby's sister lives there," Alex said. "She's a weaver."

"Cowboys, rednecks, and a weaver," I said, reaching for one of Willie's Salems.

"You can leave your money on the table," Willie said to me, carrying the pot of beans over to the stove. She was short and wide, a formidable squarish shape, like something not easily knocked over, though she walked on the sides of her feet and her white shoes were split at the seams.

"What about New York?" I said to Alex. I was thinking of moving there when I graduated from college, later that spring. "We could go together, find an apartment."

"I hear they got rats as big as suitcases in New York," Willie said. "Rats that eat children." She took an onion out of a bowl on the counter and slipped off its brown jacket.

"New York's too close to Philadelphia," Alex said, looking out the window. Our mother was kneeling at the edge of the garden, her trowel flashing in the sunlight. Hugo, our old dachshund, lay nearby.

"Where would you go, Willie," Alex asked, "if you were trying to think of someplace to go?"

"Walter took me to Chicago once," Willie said, "but I didn't think much of it." Walter was Willie's husband; he worked in a mattress factory and shot more pool than Willie believed was good for him. "When I was a girl, I used to like to visit my Great-aunt Alberta down in Hardin County. She had a horse and some Seckel pear trees. Sometimes she'd wrap the pears in newspaper and stick them in a drawer to let them ripen." Willie pushed chopped onion off the cutting board into the pot of beans. "But Hardin County might be a little slow for you."

Alex rubbed her temple with an index finger; a thought had lodged there, apparently. "Maybe I should be a nun."

"You're just talking," Willie said. "Anyhow, you ain't Catholic."

"The Episcopal Church has nuns," Alex said. We were Medium

High Church Episcopalians, except for my mother, who practiced Episcopalianism but kept her ears open to the teachings of Baptist fundamentalists and Catholic mystics who lived on nuts and berries.

"You got to stay in the nunhouse on Saturday night if you're one of them," Willie said.

"Mac asked after you," I said, blowing a smoke ring that wobbled over the lazy Susan before collapsing.

Alex peered at me through the haze of smoke and sunlight. "How come you keep promoting Mac?"

"He's my friend," I said. "He likes you."

"Is that the boy who tried to fly into your window like he was some kind of spirit?" Willie asked.

"The same," Alex said. "If drunks had wings."

"Yeah," Willie said. "Then they could fly upside down and sing to you like Smokey Robinson."

Alex studied her hands. Eczema had chewed up her fingers, but they still flexed and wandered and grasped. Outside, sunlight washed over the figure of my mother kneeling among columbine and coralbells, Hugo dozing in the abundant green grass. Alex said, "Maybe I'll go get dressed and play some piano."

"PIGS ARE SMART, you know," Mac said. He was telling Alex about Ben Franklin, a pig he'd kept as a pet for most of our last semester in college. We were in a johnboat on a lake east of Bardstown—my father in the bow, Alex and Mac in the middle, and myself in the stern, my hand on the tiller of a six-horsepower engine. It was a hot late-June afternoon, the sky the color of steam, no more than a shred of breeze. None of us had caught anything in the three hours we'd been on the lake. Alex and Mac still had lines in the water, but only my father, who secretly believed that catching a fish could make your blood rush and your soul expand all at once, fished as if he meant it. He was using a green popping plug, something that had worked for him on other occasions. Twenty times, the plug fell out of the sky into dark, weedy water near the shore, and twenty times my father slowly reeled in, flicking his rod now and then so that the open-mouthed lure made a sound—*bup-bup*—intended to excite bass. And twenty times the plug reached the boat slathered in algae.

"Where did the pig sleep?" Alex asked. She lifted her bait out of the water—a night crawler that resembled a knot of blanched viscera—and then dropped it back in.

"He slept in my dorm room in a box, until he got too big. I got him a student ID with his picture on it." Mac grinned. The sun had turned his fair skin a bright pink. His little blond mustache, which he'd worked on for months, was barely perceptible.

"Maybe I should try one of those weedless jigs," my father said. He opened his tackle box and took out a yellow-skirted lure. I saw a hawk cruise the pines at the far end of the lake, then dive out of sight.

"Is that the end of the story?" Alex asked. "I bet not. I bet that pig didn't live happily ever after." She glanced at Mac from underneath her baseball cap.

"I sort of donated him to my cultural anthro class," Mac said. "I gave him to my professor. We were studying hunting cultures and how they relate to animals."

"So then you barbecued him," Alex said.

"Eventually, yeah," Mac said, sighing a little. "But first I had to shoot him and cut his throat. Except I screwed up and missed the jugular. So then the pig gets up all of a sudden, all zonked on adrenaline, and starts flying around the pen in the professor's yard, splattering blood everywhere. And everybody in the class is silent, like this is a secret ceremony or something."

"The class watched you do this?" Alex asked.

"Pig Killing 101," I said.

"Yeah," Mac said. "So the professor and I caught the pig and cut the vein. I needed a keg of beer when it was over."

My father cast his yellow-skirted jig toward a stump, the monofilament gleaming as it arced across the water. It was possible that he hadn't heard Mac.

"What was the hardest part?" Alex asked Mac. Her knee was almost touching his, and she moved it away. "Shooting the pig? Slicing his throat? Or eating him?"

"Shooting him, I guess," Mac said, glancing at me. Mac had omitted from his account the fact that he'd been near tears as Ben Franklin flung himself around in that last mad rush of adrenaline, and the fact that it was the professor who had finally cut the jugular. "You're supposed to shoot him between the eyes. It's cleaner that way. But the pig wouldn't stand still while I was trying to sight him in. He kept moving his head back and forth, like he was on amphetamines, sniffing the dirt. I kept waiting for him to look at me." Mac didn't say that his hand had been shaking and that his first shot had hit the pig in the shoulder.

"If I'd been that pig," Alex said, "I would've looked at you. I would've wanted you to feel all my dying pig thoughts." She stared at Mac.

"Yeah," Mac said, turning away.

Alex reached over and pressed the sunburned flesh above his knee with her thumb. "You're going to fry, if you don't watch it."

My father reeled in his jig, and proposed that we move toward the end of the lake that lay in shade.

We scooted across the water, stirring up a breeze. Mac put a fresh night crawler on his hook and offered to put one on for Alex, but she said she'd do it herself. When I turned off the engine and we began to drift through the shade, my father said, "There's a fish waiting for you here, Moony Tooth."

"If you say so, Dad." Alex tossed her rebaited line into the water, and set her elbow on her thigh and her chin on her fist.

My father's yellow jig flew toward a fallen tree near the shore and the bass that surely slept there.

Mac watched his bobber. "Come on, fish. Bite."

A dragonfly landed on the bill of Alex's cap, its four wings in repose. "I've decided to move to Montana," she said.

My father reeled in his lure, which wiggled like a grass-skirted dancer. I could see him pondering the distance between Kentucky and Montana. He and my mother had wanted Alex to stay in-state for a while, spend a semester at U of K or U of L. "Long enough for her to get her feet on the ground," my mother had said. When I'd argued that I thought Alex had her feet on the ground—I'd still hoped she'd come to New York with me—my mother had replied, "Do you know what you're talking about? Depression doesn't just go away, like the chicken pox. It follows you around, and then one day it's sitting on your chest again and you can't breathe." My mother talked with her face turned aside, as if to spare me some of her indignation. "Can you imagine what it would be like for your sister to fall ill in a desolate place like Montana, where she doesn't know a soul, except for Bobby Tarr's sister?"

The dragonfly flew from Alex's cap. I considered the distance between Montana and New York, and I thought I saw Mac calculating the distance between Montana and Nashville, where he would begin work later that summer, selling pool tables for his father, who owned a chain of billiards stores in the mid-South. Anyway, I saw Mac's pink face darken, as if some slim hope had fled. Alex had a hold on Mac's imagination, the more so since she'd tried suicide. It was as if she knew things now—what pigs felt, why space curved.

"Montana," Mac mused. "Do they have daily mail delivery in Montana?"

"Are you going to write to me every day, Mac?"

Mac stroked the fuzz on his upper lip and studied his bobber.

My father looked out across the lake, which was flat and glaring where the sun struck it. Perhaps he was thinking of the winter he'd spent in Wyoming. He was fresh out of college then. Having been deemed unfit to serve in the Army—his eyesight was unacceptable, he was thinner than a darning needle—and having no good idea of how he should spend his professional life, he took a job at a private school in Sheridan founded by an oilman's wife. Dad had told Alex and me this story at dinner a few nights before. "Oh, it was as cold as Billy Blue," he'd said. "I thought spring would never come. I couldn't wait to get back to Kentucky." When he'd finished the story, Alex said, "I'll be sure to take some warm clothes with me, if I decide to go."

Now my father removed his glasses and cleaned them on his shirt. The lake was still. All the dull weight of the afternoon seemed to lie on it. Then Alex's bobber went under and her rod bent. The line ran parallel to the boat, then doubled back. Her face was intent, as if she were in the grip of a revelation.

The fish she pulled out of the water was a silvery yellow, with dark stripes. It wasn't much longer than her hand.

"A bluegill," my father said. "You saved us from being skunked, Moony Tooth."

"A lunker," Mac said.

"It's not always the size that counts," Alex said, grinning, showing Mac some of her fine, straight teeth.

"That line's older than my grandmother," Mac said, grabbing hold of the fish as it twisted in the air.

"Still applies," Alex said.

Mac wrestled with the hook—it was in deep—until the bluegill squirted out of his hands, landing on the slatted floor of the boat. I picked it up, felt the muscle bunched beneath its scales, then watched it shoot out of my hands. Alex took off her baseball cap and scooped the fish into it. Her loosened hair fell across her face.

"I've got a hook disgorger somewhere," my father said.

"That's OK, Dad," Alex said. "I can do it." She pushed her hair out of her face and bent over the fish, which she held on her lap in the cap. "Don't look at me like that," she said to the fish, working the hook back and forth. When the hook finally came free, she placed the fish back in the water carefully, as if she were setting a vase of flowers on a table.

"Go!" she said.

The Green Suit

Once upon a time — September of 1974, to be exact — I went to New York. I was twenty-three. I'd been out of college for a year. I could read, I could conjugate Latin verbs, I could discuss the contributions of the Venerable Bede to Western civilization, and I could handle a mop and a bucket. The last skill I'd picked up the previous winter in Nashville, where I'd cleaned the offices and bathrooms of people in the music business. This was a night job. During the day, I'd lain on my friend Mac's sofa and read novels and waited for the moment when I'd be ready to go to New York.

As I drove east, I sometimes checked myself in the rearview mirror. I had longish hair and full cheeks from which the baby fat had never quite disappeared. My small, turned-down mouth showed the effect of wanting to be taken seriously. In my eyes I thought I saw something flashing, a twitchy eagerness I'd failed to suppress in my desire to be a person whom life wouldn't burn. When I stopped at the George Washington Bridge tollbooth and looked at myself a final time before entering Manhattan, I saw someone who had drunk seven or eight cups of coffee and smoked a pack of cigarettes between the Ohio River and the Hudson. The thrumming I felt at my temples was almost visible.

I'd made arrangements to stay at my Aunt Vi's apartment on the Upper West Side. Aunt Vi was my mother's older sister, a painter, twice divorced. She had a house out in Westchester, her primary residence, which she shared with two Airedales. I was supposed to get the keys to her apartment from a man named Elvin.

It was after eleven when I found my aunt's building, a brownstone between Central Park West and Columbus Avenue. A man was sitting on the stoop, taking the mild September air. He wore a suit that was a lizardy green. The trousers were flared and the jacket lapels were as big as wings. The suit brought words to mind — *predatory, naive, hopeful* — but none of them seemed quite right. The suit glowed in the sulphurous glow of the street lights, but it would have glowed in pitch dark, too.

The man, who wore a white T-shirt beneath the jacket, didn't look at me as I came up the stoop with my luggage. He was smoking a cigarette. He had thick, dark, wetted-back hair, like an otter, and a pale, bony face that was not unhandsome despite the crooked nose. Under his right eye was a purplish smudge — the remnant of a shiner, perhaps. I thought he might have been in his late twenties, older than me by several years, anyway.

Across the street, two men were shouting at each other in Spanish. Curses flew back and forth, blurring the air.

"I'm looking for somebody named Elvin," I said to the man on the stoop. I remembered that my aunt had mentioned that Elvin was from down South — Mississippi, maybe. "He's a hick just like you, honey," she'd said, "except he's got a lot of mustard on him."

The man picked a piece of tobacco off the tip of his tongue and flicked it away. "You're looking at him, bro," he said.

"You're the building superintendent, right?"

"I guess I am," Elvin said. "I'd rather be the Sultan of Swing, but you got to deal with the cards that get dealt to you, don't you?" He was watching the two Hispanic men; one stalked away from the other and then turned back quickly to deliver an elaborate, gaudy curse. New York was like opera, I'd read somewhere—people in costumes discussing things at the top of their lungs.

Elvin said, "So you must be Violet's nephew. Come to get down in the big city." He smiled and brushed something visible only to himself off the sleeve of his jacket. Where, I wondered, did Elvin go in his suit and his ankle-high black boots that zipped up the side?

"Peter Sackrider," I said, holding out my hand.

"Pleased to meet you." He clasped my hand soul-brother style. "What you got in that box there?" He pointed to the case that held my Olivetti, a graduation gift.

"A typewriter," I said.

"Ah," he said. "Tap, tap, tap into the night, right?" He dragged on his cigarette and then launched it toward the sidewalk. "I used to know this writer who lived in New Orleans. He OD'd or something." Elvin rose from the stoop and looked skyward. He'd been sitting on a magazine to keep his trousers clean. "Looks like we got a big, old, hairy moon on our hands."

I'd seen the moon earlier, driving across New Jersey. It was a harvest moon, the dying grass moon. Seeing it had made me shiver a little. Then it had slid behind clouds. Now, when I saw it again, hanging above apartment buildings topped with water tanks, it seemed no more than an ordinary celestial body on its appointed rounds, a cratered thing shedding some extra light on overlit New York.

"My old man used to say 'Katy, bar the door' when the moon got full," Elvin said. "I used not to believe any of that ass-trology stuff, but I might have to change my mind. I'm feeling sort of werewolfish tonight." He undid the middle button of his jacket.

"You're going out now?" I asked. "It's kind of late, isn't it?"

"Never too late for love, bro," Elvin said. "Never too late for some of that."

• • •

A FEW DAYS LATER, I took a typing test at a temporary-employment agency. Even though I made a number of errors while typing at close to a crawl, it was decided that I was a "pretty good" typist, and the agency sent me off to midtown companies in need of secretarial help. I worked for a direct-marketing firm, a bank, a company that sold gag items such as hand buzzers, an oil company, a cosmetics firm. I wore my tweed coat with the elbow patches and read Faulkner on my lunch breaks. I doused my typing mistakes with correction fluid, hoping I wouldn't be exposed as a charlatan. Late that winter, the agency sent me to a publishing house on Fifth Avenue. I was put in the office of a vacationing editor and given a piece of a manuscript to retype. "Be careful you don't spill anything on the original," an editor, a woman in a black pants suit, said, tapping the top of a Thermos of coffee I'd brought with me. The manuscript pages were faded yellow second sheets; they looked as delicate as dried flower petals. After the editor went back to her desk, I held a page to my nose and sniffed it.

The section of the manuscript I typed was about an American couple traveling in the south of France. She had cut her hair short to make herself look like a boy. He wrote stories in cheap notebooks with sharp pencils. They swam naked in the cold blue sea and drank absinthe in cafés and made love. I had read most of the prescribed Hemingway in school, and I thought that what I was typing now, on an old manual Olympia, must be more of him or at least a very good imitation. I was excited. I was enthroned in an office a half dozen flights above Fifth Avenue, black New York coffee was running through my veins, and sunlight was flowing in the windows—late-winter sunlight that seemed to illuminate the pleasure I felt in being where I was (however fleeting my tenancy was likely to be) and to promise more: spring, love, a life in literature. Now and then, the editor put her head in the door to check on me. Once, when she came all the way into the room, I felt an urge to tell her how much I liked her black pants suit, which was Asian in style and made a little swishing sound when she moved. But I lost my nerve.

A few weeks later, I got a permanent job at a publishing house called Church & Purviance, a sleepy, old-line company. I worked for an elderly editor named Mr. Stawicki, who had a corner of the C & P building all to himself. He was responsible for the house's military history books. He had white hair that streamed away from his mottled forehead—one could imagine him on the deck of a frigate, spyglass in hand, studying the horizon for enemy cutters—and in close quarters he gave off a scent that was a mix of talcum powder, butterscotch candy, and decrepitude. Mr. Stawicki had trouble getting my name right, for some reason that seemed only partly related to his age. He called me Son or Champ or, once, William, which was the name of a nephew of his who sold bonds on Wall Street. "Well, William," he said, "I think it's time for Mr. Powell's morning constitutional." Mr. Powell was Mr. Stawicki's thirteen-year-old Sealyham, whom I was required to walk two or three times a day.

One reason that Mr. Stawicki may have been unable to utter my name was that my predecessor's name, Petra, was close to my own. Mr. Stawicki carried a torch for Petra, who had left him to work for a C & P editor named Marshall Hogue. On the one occasion when Mr. Stawicki and I went to lunch together, at a dark Lexington Avenue bar where both he and his dog were known, he said, following his second Rob Roy, "You know, son, you're a nice boy, but I can't forgive that man Hogue for stealing Petra from me." He pronounced her name with a soft *e* and a trilled *r*. And then he predicted that he would soon be lying in the "dust bed" of history, "along with Max Perkins and that gang." Drinking seemed to make him gloomy.

I got my job at C & P through Mr. Hogue, whom I'd met at a

party at my aunt's house in Westchester. He'd grown up in Louisville with Aunt Vi and my mother, who'd sat next to him in fifth grade. He went away to boarding school, and then to college and into the service, and he returned to Louisville only for the occasional holiday. The time spent elsewhere made him more interesting to the young women of my mother's set. My mother considered it a coup when he asked her to a Derby ball. But he wasn't planning on sticking around. Like Vi, who'd gone to New York to study painting, he was bound for other places.

At my aunt's party, Mr. Hogue and I drank wassail and ate salty country ham on beaten biscuits and talked about the town where we no longer lived. His voice had been swept clean of all but a trace of an accent. He had a tidy grayish beard and close-cropped hair and he wore wire-rimmed glasses. He was tall and thin, like a swizzle stick. He told me that I looked like my mother. I swallowed some wassail, the scent of cinnamon riding up my nose, and said I'd take that as a compliment. Then Mr. Hogue told me that I should come see him whenever I decided to give up the temporary-employment racket. Spaces opened up at C & P now and then, he said. Of course, the pay was dreadful and much of the work was humdrum, but literature must be served, mustn't it? He laughed a small, refined laugh.

In the evening, after I had finished my work for Mr. Stawicki, I went home to my aunt's apartment. The building was near the Columbus Avenue end of the block, the less genteel end, across the street from an empty, paved-over lot where kids played stickball and a man once stood in the rain and shouted out passages from the Book of Isaiah. Aunt Vi had moved into the building in 1959, after bouncing around the Village for more than a decade. For a number of years, she used a second apartment in the brownstone as a studio. Then, around 1970, she decided to move her easels to the countryside. The apartment I sublet didn't receive much light, but the ceilings were high and the claw-footed bathtub was large and the bedroom looked down upon a kind of courtyard that the two Irish sisters who lived below me had planted with vinca and lamium. Sometimes I would see Grace and Betty down there on warm evenings, sitting in matching aluminum-tube lawn chairs, sipping Dubonnet.

Aunt Vi's apartment was sparsely furnished. There was a card table, folding chairs, a metal cot, a worn red velvet sofa that might have passed for cathouse furniture, kitchenware (including several Kentucky Derby souvenir glasses), a small pine desk, and a couple of Aunt Vi's paintings. One was a *nature morte*—a sea bass on a platter, its mouth agape and eye bulging. In the other, Aunt Vi stared at the viewer through large, black-framed glasses. She had a cigarette in the corner of her mouth. Her chin was uptilted, as if she were waiting for an answer to a question. Her skin she'd painted a hazy rose color, the color of smoke mixed with the tomatoey hue that years of drinking produces in some people. The painting was hung above the desk where I sat most evenings, trying to write a story called "The Green Suit." After several months of looking at my aunt looking at me and failing to make much progress with "The Green Suit" or its spin-offs, I decided to cover the painting with a dish towel whenever I sat down at the desk. Covering the portrait seemed less radical than taking it down or moving the desk to the opposite wall, where the dead fish was hung. I imagined that if I removed the picture of my aunt scrutinizing me, I'd be upsetting a certain balance of forces in the apartment.

One reason I had trouble writing was that I had my own crush on Mr. Stawicki's former assistant, Petra Saunders. I sometimes found myself thinking about Petra in the midst of trying to imagine what Elvin did when he stepped out in his green suit. (I'd learned that he sometimes went to New Jersey—"the land of opportunity," he called it—and so I thought of his suit as his going-over-to-Jersey outfit.) Or I would find myself thinking about Petra while trying to light upon the word to describe the complexions of Grace and Betty, who were both tellers at a bank in Chelsea, who both wore white gloves to work. Grace and Betty were going to be in "The Green Suit," a story in which the narrator, a boy from the provinces not unlike myself, is drawn into the peculiar New York life of a man not unlike Elvin. I foresaw the story turning violent at some point—Grace and Betty mugged? Elvin wild with anger? But I was a long way from reaching that point. The distance between where I was and where I wanted to be seemed immense, and I often found it easier to retire to Aunt Vi's dilapidated sofa, where I could give myself up to thoughts of Petra.

Not too long after I'd been hired at Church & Purviance, Mr. Hogue took me out to lunch. Petra came along. "You don't mind, do you?" he asked. We went to an expensive Chinese restaurant. I drank two gin-and-tonics and struggled with my chopsticks and confessed to liking Faulkner and Hemingway. "Faulkner more," I added.

"The big boys," Mr. Hogue said, pinching a snow pea with his chopsticks.

Petra didn't comment on my literary tastes, though I guessed, from the way she sipped her ice water and averted her eyes, that she didn't approve. She was quiet—even, I thought at first, evasive. Some part of her face always seemed to be in shadow, eclipsed by her long, dark, wayward hair or by a hand pushing the hair back. When I asked her where she'd grown up, she said, "Oh, you know, all around. My father was in the Foreign Service." She said this as if it were common for American children to grow up in Rome, Addis Ababa, and Bethesda. When I went back to the office that afternoon, my head full of gin and tea and fish sauce, I got my diary out of my desk and wrote, *Is she stuck-up, or am I* blind? *She doesn't drink—at least not at lunch. She's reading an obscure Japanese novelist—obscure to me, anyway—which Marshall, as she calls Mr. Hogue, recommended. She looks at Mr. Hogue fondly. When she says the words* Addis Ababa, *I think of all those soft a's tumbling around in her mouth. She has a large mole between her collarbone and left breast. She wore a scoop-necked summer dress—blue, beltless.*

One afternoon a couple weeks later, after I'd walked Mr. Powell and returned him to his cedar-scented bed in Mr. Stawicki's office, I went downstairs to the C & P library. Mr. Stawicki had asked me to look up something about a diplomat who had attended a naval conference in London in 1930. By the time I reached the library, I'd forgotten the diplomat's name. The library, which was small and windowless, smelled of orange. Petra was sitting at the table, a handsome old oak piece on which the first Mr. Purviance (so the story went) had once been pinned by an author armed with a penknife. Petra didn't look up when I entered the library. She was reading, one hand lost in her dark hair. Then I saw that hand reach for a slice of orange—it was laid out in sections on a napkin—and convey it to her mouth. The name of the naval conference participant suddenly came to me, or almost came to me, but when Petra looked up, her mouth full of orange, the name squirted away, leaving a bubbly trail in my brain.

"I'm doing research for the Admiral," I said, referring to Mr. Stawicki by his nickname. "For his encyclopedia of warships. The two-volume thing. I can't remember what I was supposed to look up."

"That's a problem," Petra said. She was wearing a plain white blouse and a dark skirt. The mole below her collarbone wasn't visible. With her book and her lunchbox, she looked like a proper schoolgirl. Except that her lunchbox had a picture of Mickey and Minnie on it. I took this to mean that she might have a sense of humor.

"Are you still reading that Japanese guy?" I asked. I waited for his name to surface. "Tanizaki?"

"I finished him," she said. She put another section of orange in her mouth. "Marshall asked me to read this Yugoslav writer to see if we should commission a translation." She held the book out toward me. I came closer. Her fingers and wrists were bare, no jewelry. On the cover of the book, crows or bats were swirling around a man wearing a derby and a clownish cravat. "It's sort of a surrealist satire of life under Tito. This is the Italian translation."

"Does Mr. Hogue—Marshall—send you home with work at night?" My hands were deep in the pockets of my khakis. Though swimming with desire to know what she did when she wasn't at the office, I hurried on to the next question. "Is Mr. Hogue fun to work for?"

"He does interesting books." She put the orange peels and napkin in her lunchbox, which, I saw, also contained a Milky Way candy bar. I found it comforting that she had a vice.

"And you don't have to walk a dog," I said.

"No," she said, latching her lunchbox and getting up from the table. "But I didn't mind walking Mr. Powell. I went all over town with him. I could be gone for two hours and Mr. Stawicki wouldn't say anything."

"He's sweet on you," I said.

"He's kind of lonely, don't you think?" Petra said. "Well, good luck with your research."

After work that day, I walked over to Korvettes to buy a window fan. The weather had turned hot, summer having laid its heavy hand on the city even before May was out. The day's heat was in the sidewalks, in the buildings I walked past, in the sweaty, pock-marked face of the blind man who stood with his tin cup and his guide dog at the corner of Fifth and Forty-eighth, rocking back and forth, like a man taken over by spirits.

When I came out of Korvettes with my fan and began to walk up Fifth Avenue, I saw, a half block ahead, Mr. Hogue and Petra. They seemed not to be walking so much as gliding—as far as that was possible on a crowded sidewalk. At several points, Mr. Hogue, who was wearing an olive-green suit (cuffed trousers, narrow lapels), touched Petra on the arm and guided her around a clot of slow-moving tourists or out of the way of some speeding local. I remembered that my mother had said of Mr. Hogue in a recent phone conversation, "He was quite a dancer in his heyday. All the girls wanted to be led by him. Little did they know!"

"Little did they know what?" I'd asked.

"That he preferred men to women," she'd said. "Haven't you figured that out yet, honey?"

Instead of turning left, toward Sixth Avenue, where I could catch an uptown train, I followed Petra and Mr. Hogue up Fifth Avenue. Where were they going—Petra with her lunchbox and musette bag, Mr. Hogue with his Moroccan leather satchel? Neither lived in the direction they were walking. (Petra lived way over in the East Eighties; once, after going to a movie in her neighborhood, I'd walked by her building.) Perhaps they were going to meet an agent or an author for a drink. Perhaps they were going to an early movie and then to supper at some Turkish or Balinese place Mr. Hogue would know about and then—my mother's assertion about Mr. Hogue's sexual preferences notwithstanding—to a mutual bed. Wasn't it possible that they were lovers, even if Mr. Hogue was old enough to be Petra's father? There was that moment, for instance, outside the tobacconist's at Fifty-fifth, where Mr. Hogue held Petra's lunchbox while she fished around in her musette bag for money to give to a legless man who rolled himself along the sidewalk on a little furniture dolly. And then, after Mr. Hogue returned the lunchbox to Petra, there was the way, too delicate to be fatherly, he touched the small of her back, nudging her toward wherever they were going.

I followed a half block behind, humping my three-speed fan and my briefcase, sweating through my seersucker jacket. At Grand Army Plaza, where I stopped to light a cigarette, I got caught in an auto-pedestrian crosswalk snarl and fell a block behind. I lost sight of my quarry for a minute, and then I spotted them disappearing under the canopy at the Hotel Pierre.

I walked across the Park, toward the West Side, secure in the knowledge that the life I wanted to possess was going to elude me. I saw a man drinking a carton of orange juice while riding a unicyle. I saw some Hare Krishnas crossing the Sheep Meadow in their saffron robes. Then, on a path near the Lake, a man wearing a floppy red-velvet beretlike hat on top of his Afro stopped me and asked for my wallet. He showed me an X-Acto knife, no more than an inch of blade sticking out of its gray metal housing. I gave him my wallet and stared at the carotid artery in his neck, which seemed to be throbbing. He went through my wallet without saying a word. I felt I should say something, and so I asked him if he wanted my fan, too.

"No, I don't want your dumb-ass fan, you dumb-ass bitch," he said. He dropped the wallet on the ground and walked off. He'd taken the cash and a ticket I'd bought for a Met production of *La Bohème*.

I walked out of the Park and up Central Park West. By the time I'd reached the Museum of Natural History, I'd stopped shaking. By the time I reached my street, I felt oddly at ease, as if I could float the final half block, past the spindly young trees whose trunks were wrapped with tape, right on up the stoop, on which Grace and Betty had set a pot of geraniums. I picked a cigarette butt out of the pot, flicked it away, and went up to my apartment. The door was ajar. I heard Aunt Vi's voice, and then I saw Elvin slumped on the couch, smoking.

"Hey, bro," Elvin said. "You're just in time for cocktails." Elvin was wearing a black sleeveless T-shirt and blue jeans. No shoes. The shirt was made of a shimmery material, like his green suit. He was all muscle and bone, and he gave you the impression that he'd done nothing to achieve it, except, perhaps, smoke to curb his appetite. At one time, he'd told me, he'd worked as a mud logger on an oil rig in the Gulf of Mexico and commuted with wads of cash between New Orleans and New York. Before that, he'd been in the Army, but had somehow avoided a tour in Vietnam. More recently, he'd worked as a car jockey in a parking garage in Midtown. Now, he did odd jobs for the landlord to pay off his rent. And occasionally earned beer money by modeling for Aunt Vi.

Aunt Vi came out of the kitchen with a drink in each hand. "I let myself in, Petey," she said. "I hope you don't mind." She gave Elvin his drink and surveyed me through her black glasses. The glasses made her seem both distant and overbearing, like a bird of prey.

"No, I don't mind," I said, setting down the fan but leaving my jacket on for the moment. I didn't consider the apartment to be mine, any more than I considered myself to be a resident of New York.

"I had to come into town to see Dr. Bickel, so he can pay for the addition on his summer house in Quogue," Aunt Vi said, laughing her heavy, nicotine-stained laugh. "The old buzzard would cap every one of my teeth if he could."

I looked around the room, as if some clue to my existence were to be found there. On the mantel above the nonworking fireplace, I saw the wine bottle that I'd not quite emptied the night before while sitting at my desk, waiting for inspiration to blow through me and prickle the hairs on the back of my hand. Beside the sofa, not far from Elvin's bare feet, the dogs that had carried him far from Mississippi, were one blue sock and a packet of newspaper clippings my mother had sent me from Kentucky. On the wall was

Aunt Vi's painting of her ripe, florid self. It was a stroke of luck that I'd taken down the dish towel last night; I'd used it to mop up a puddle of wine.

"You look like you could use a drink," Aunt Vi said.

"You've been working too hard, bro," Elvin said, hoisting his glass. "Take a load off."

"I wouldn't mind having a drink," I said to Aunt Vi. I thought I probably wouldn't tell her and Elvin about my run-in in the Park.

My aunt went back into the kitchen. Elvin said, "I'm thinking of going over to Jersey on Saturday. You want to come?"

"What do you do there?" I asked.

"Study the landscape, do a little recon," Elvin said, blowing a stream of unfiltered smoke toward the ceiling. "Go bowling some-times. See this girl I know."

I wondered if Elvin went bowling in his green suit, or if he took a change of clothes.

"Sounds interesting," I said, not wishing to offend Elvin, who was, after all, the building's super and could requisition me an ex-tra door lock, if I should ever need one.

Aunt Vi returned with my drink, a gin-and-tonic, heavy on the gin, in a Derby glass. The gin went straight to that part of me that wished to lie down, and so I excused myself, saying I was going to change out of my work clothes.

"Sound your funky horn, man," Elvin said, snorting.

"What's that supposed to mean?" Aunt Vi asked.

"It's just a song I used to sort of like," he said, dreamily.

I went into the bedroom, undressed, polished off the gin, and lay down on the cot. I looked at the Monet poster I'd stuck on the wall—a sun-drenched beach scene, flags rippling in the breeze.

"The boy needs to get laid," I heard Elvin say. He made two syl-lables out of "laid."

"I'm sure he'd be touched by your concern," Aunt Vi said.

"When are you going to sit for me again?" Elvin was one of my aunt's favorite subjects. She'd painted him clothed and unclothed — once in repose on a couch, in the manner of Manet's *Olympia*, with a Mets cap covering his genitals. His eyes were near to being closed. "Drowsy Elvin," my aunt called the painting.

THREE WEEKS LATER, a warm mid-June evening, I lay on the same bed, absorbing the breeze generated by my fan. I was wearing basketball shorts and a Shakespeare in the Park T-shirt. Now and then, I heard firecrackers explode. The Fourth was approaching, and every kid in the neighborhood was armed to the teeth. Below my window, in the dim courtyard, Grace and Betty sipped cocktails and discussed the events of the day: the rudeness of a young officer at the bank, the elderly Negro man whom they no longer saw on the No. 11 downtown bus, Elvin's failure to fix a dripping faucet.

I'd been home since about three in the afternoon, having fled the office in the wake of Mr. Powell's death. I'd taken Mr. Powell for a lunchtime walk over in Turtle Bay, where trees provided shade and there was the occasional poodle or Boston terrier for my charge to sniff. On Second Avenue, I slipped Mr. Powell's leash around the top of a fire hydrant and went into a deli to buy a sandwich. Mr. Powell, being old, wasn't frisky, and I expected him to do no more than wait patiently on the curb while I got my turkey on rye. But he stretched his leash and wandered off the curb into the gutter, where there was garbage to be inspected. I didn't witness the accident, but I was told by a pedestrian, a well-dressed man walking a chow, that a cab turning left and cutting the corner close had struck Mr. Powell, that the driver had hit his brakes but then had gone on, perhaps at the urging of his fare.

Mr. Powell had been killed instantly, but as I carried him back to the office, in a black garbage bag that the deli manager had given me, I kept thinking, absurdly, Maybe he's just sleeping. When I'd picked him up out of the gutter, there hadn't been any blood on his thick white coat or his curious, moist nose. However, he didn't stir as I bore him toward his master, and toward, I felt increasingly sure, my own termination. Mr. Powell grew heavier as I rode in the elevator to my floor, accompanied by silent Jimmy, the uniformed elevator operator, who was the most phlegmatic man in New York.

When Mr. Stawicki saw me with the garbage bag, he said, "Please don't tell me that's my dog." I said it was and that I was sorry and that it had happened suddenly and that Mr. Powell hadn't seemed to suffer much, if at all. Mr. Stawicki looked stricken. He waved me out of his office.

I sat down at my desk and wrote him a note of apology, restating (possibly overstating) my remorse at his loss, saying that I planned to look for work elsewhere but would stay on until he found a replacement. I put the note in the In box outside his door. Then I went downstairs, to the main editorial floor, to see Mr. Hogue and tell him about Mr. Powell and my decision to leave Church & Purviance.

But Mr. Hogue wasn't in his office. Nor was Petra in her adjoining nook, though the coffee in her mug was warm. So I went back upstairs, got my briefcase, and walked home, via the Park, where I encountered no muggers, only a violinist dressed up in a bear suit. At the apartment, I put Mississippi John Hurt on the stereo and lay down on the bed. I fell asleep and dreamed about Grace and Betty.

Later, awake, listening to the drone of the fan and the voices of Grace and Betty, I considered the idea of returning home to Louisville and hooking on with my grandfather's brokerage firm and eating high-cholesterol lunches with my father at the downtown club where he played penny-a-point bridge and marrying any one of several young women I knew whose interest in literature was about the same as their interest in ethnography or limnology. This notion occupied me for several minutes—deeply enough that the sound of my door buzzer didn't immediately rouse me. When I did finally go downstairs, I at first saw only Elvin, shirtless, standing in the vestibule, where the mailboxes were. Then, beyond the outer door, on the stoop, I saw Petra, her musette bag over her shoulder. She was leaving. I opened the door and called her name.

Elvin, scratching his flat, bare belly, said, sotto voce, "Hey, man, if she's the reason you bugged out on me, I forgive you."

I hadn't gone bowling with Elvin in New Jersey. I'd pleaded a tight schedule.

"Thanks," I said. I was happy to be on Elvin's good side. I stepped out the door onto the stoop. Elvin remained in the vestibule.

"I was sorry to hear about Mr. Powell," Petra said. She was wearing a white, open-necked blouse and a blue jean skirt.

"Thanks," I said. The stoop felt warm on my bare feet.

"I'm coming from my dentist," she said, "down on Eighty-first. Dr. Fingerhut. This sweet little Austrian. He plays Schubert or Mozart while he's cleaning your teeth. 'Ah, my dear, you haf vut looks like a very sweet tooth. Ve must repair before it becomes a very dead tooth.' Marshall told me about him." She paused, as if to consider her presence on my stoop.

I didn't know what was more improbable: a suddenly chatty Petra or the fact that she was standing near me on a warm summer evening. The air—the grimy, hazy, fume-laden air of Manhattan— seemed almost fresh. There was nearly enough oxygen in it to make your head spin.

"Dr. Fingerhut told me about this Cuban-Chinese restaurant on Amsterdam somewhere," Petra said. "I thought you might be able to help me find it."

"I'll get my shoes."

• • •

WE FOUND THE Cuban-Chinese place, up Amsterdam, in the shadow of a new housing project, but it didn't serve liquor, which, it turned out, Petra avoided only during work hours. We walked back over to Columbus, to a bar called the Yukon, down the block from the Laundromat that I and Elvin and Grace and Betty frequented. I'd watched some baseball in the Yukon, and had even, once, tried writing there. Except for the refrigerated air, there wasn't anything in the Yukon that suggested the remote Canadian Northwest. No pictures of Jack London or sled dogs, anyway.

We sat toward the back, in a booth that had a view of the dartboard. A fat, bearded man and his petite female companion were playing.

"Tell me again how Mr. Powell got killed," Petra said. She'd been in a meeting for much of the afternoon, and had heard about the incident thirdhand.

I told Petra the story, and then I said that I was going to look for work elsewhere and was even thinking of moving back to Kentucky, where I could whittle sticks with my friends. I was hoping, of course, that she would try to dissuade me from the latter idea and give me room to imagine that I could displace Mr. Hogue as her lover. The notion that she was Mr. Hogue's lover continued to flourish in the little hothouse of my mind.

"I've never been to Kentucky," Petra said, turning the frosted glass that contained her vodka-and-tonic. "Marshall talks about spring down there, how pretty it is."

"Yes." I let pass the chance to ask about her relationship with Mr. Hogue. A couple more beers and I might have managed it. "What was spring in Addis Ababa like?"

"It was nice, mild. Addis Ababa is eight thousand feet above sea level, you know." She was looking past me. She laid her hand on my free hand, the one that wasn't gripping the bottle of Rheingold, and nodded in the direction of the dart players.

"Look," she whispered. "On the floor. The bag."

I turned and leaned out of the booth and saw a gym bag under the table that held the dart players' drinks. Then I saw the man, who was wearing a billowy Hawaiian shirt, flick a dart toward the target. The motion his hand made was dainty and precise, as if he were dotting an *i*.

"What?" I asked Petra. She'd removed her hand from mine almost as quickly as she'd put it there. If she touched me again, I thought, that would mean something. I was a boy who required reassurance, an appalling trait to have in a place like New York.

"The bag," Petra said. "It's moving. There's something in it."

I turned again, and saw that there was indeed something moving inside the bag, flexing it this way and that.

"Maybe it's a ferret." I looked at the mole below her collarbone; I wanted to put my thumb on it.

"No," Petra said, firmly. "It's a snake. Those people are snake owners."

I turned around once more. The woman was studying us. She did somewhat resemble a person you might see at a roadside reptile farm—the proprietor's thin-lipped wife, who keeps the books and dreams about running off with the guy who stocks the farm's Coke machine. She had a hard face that was once pretty.

"You don't like snakes?" I asked Petra.

"I don't expect to see one in a bar," she said. "It kind of takes the wind out of your sails."

"I know what you mean." As she finished her drink, I thought I could see her considering whether to take a crosstown bus home or to spring for a cab. If she was going home, that is. In any event, it seemed clear that she didn't wish to spend any more time in the Yukon.

I paid for the drinks and waited by the jukebox while Petra used the Ladies'. When she came out, she stopped to talk with the dart players. Then she came on toward me, the news that she'd been right about the contents of the bag written on her face. She was a person who took some satisfaction in being right.

"It's a python," she said. "A baby python. They have a bunch."

We walked out into the warm, jarring air. The sky was still an hour short of turning the smudgy color that was the local version of nighttime. Yellow cabs were streaking down Columbus. A man wearing beltless, crimson slacks and a shirt of several hideous colors came up the avenue, cutting a wide swath, singing, muttering, nodding violently to himself.

"I guess I'll go now," Petra said. She stepped off the curb and waved for a cab.

"OK," I said.

A cab cut across two lanes and came to a halt a yard or so from Petra's sandaled foot. She didn't flinch. "Don't feel too bad about Mr. Powell," she said. "And don't go home to Kentucky with your tail between your legs." She gave me a quick kiss on the cheek. Its delicate placement reminded me of the way the fat man had thrown the dart.

"What are you reading nowadays?" I asked as she got into the cab, a part of her leg that I'd not seen before becoming briefly visible.

The thought that I was homosexual had, of course, occurred to me—for instance, on those occasions when I'd lain on my narrow, squeaky cot, solemnly holding myself. But if this were true, why did the sight of Petra's thigh, not to mention the touch of her mouth, move me so?

"Proust," she said, pulling the door to. "He's great. You should try him. He'll make you . . ." The cab shot away, like a cork flying out of a bottle, leaving me to imagine what she thought reading Proust would make me want to do. He hadn't been on the syllabus at my college in Tennessee.

I headed back up Columbus. Standing in the doorway of the

Laundromat, smoking, watching the world rush by, was Elvin. He signaled to me. Over his jeans he was wearing what looked like a pajama shirt, V-necked, with red piping. His muscle shirts must have been in the wash.

"Hey, bro," he said, "maybe we can double sometime."

"Double?" I asked, thinking this was street slang I'd failed to absorb.

"Double date," he said. "You and your chick, me and mine."

"Yeah," I said. "Maybe we could do something like that."

ELVIN DROVE UP the Henry Hudson Parkway, slaloming in and out of the Saturday afternoon traffic like a stunt driver — a style that made it difficult for me to concentrate on the long sentences describing the amatory practices of M. Swann. So I put the book down. But watching Elvin drive while he sucked on a joint was too frightening. And looking out the window at the river, sparkling though it was in the July sun, was insufficiently distracting. So I fixed upon the dark, shag-cut head of Connie, who was Elvin's girlfriend and who was not much older than sixteen. She seemed to have a driver's license, anyway; she'd driven over from Jersey before giving the wheel to Elvin. But she was nervous, too — something I thought was in her favor. When Elvin had laid down rubber at the last stop we'd see until we hit the Spuyten Duyvil bridge, she'd said, "My father's going to kill me if you wreck it." To which Elvin had said, "Be cool."

We were going to my aunt's house in the green hills of northern Westchester. It was her fifty-fifth birthday, and she was giving herself a party. She'd invited a great flock of people — artist friends, Village friends, Grace and Betty, my parents, Mr. Hogue, other Kentuckians, her dentist. Grace and Betty declined (they were going to Mystic with a church group), and so did my parents. But Mr. Hogue was coming, and so was the dentist. Petra was supposed to be there, too. I'd asked her, and she'd said yes, though the yes was provisional, dependent on whether she could resolve something in her schedule.

I'd invited Petra to Aunt Vi's party about a week before I was to leave Church & Purviance. One effect of being nearly unemployed was that I didn't feel my usual diffident self around Petra. Anyhow, the sight of her standing next to the copy machine, a cranky, unreliable thing that wheezed and heaved before disgorging paper, had emboldened me. She'd gotten her hair cut quite short; her exposed neck was as pale as a photographic negative. And so I'd asked her for a date, and after she'd startled me with her yes (provisional though it was), I'd also asked if she were no longer seeing Mr. Hogue.

She'd looked at me with her bright, critical eyes for as long as it took the copier to cough up two pages of somebody's five-hundred-page bildungsroman.

"I like Marshall and he likes me, but we don't 'see' each other." Her smile revealed her teeth, which were imperfect. She had a snaggly upper right canine. "He has other interests."

"Ah," I said, which was the sound of my mind opening slightly to receive important information. Air entering the hothouse.

Two weeks later, rocketing up the Saw Mill with stoned Elvin and his barely legal girlfriend, and without Petra, who would get to Aunt Vi's on her own, if a lunch date she had with Ethiopian friends of her father's didn't take forever, I heard myself make a sound like "ah" again. It was the sound of fear escaping from between my teeth. I thought there was a good chance that Elvin would fail to negotiate one of the many curves on the narrow Saw Mill or, if we got that far, one of the many curves on the even narrower Taconic. I thought, too, that there was a good chance that I wouldn't see Petra, even if Elvin didn't wipe us out. She'd made no promises.

Connie passed me a bottle of beer and smiled. She was wearing a retainer, which made her look even younger than she was. She had a pretty mouth with a fleshy underlip, and brown eyes that worry hooded. How had Elvin acquired her, I wondered. Had he been wearing his green suit when they met? I drank my beer rapidly and asked Connie, who was keeping pace, for another. We made more eye contact. Elvin, singing along with a disco number called "Rock Your Baby," miraculously steered us off the Taconic and down a snaky, wooded road to my aunt's house.

It felt wonderful to have my feet on the ground, and after I'd kissed my aunt (who was wearing a huge, brocaded sombrero) and gotten a plate of food and another bottle of beer, I sat down on the grass, under a large sugar maple, next to Beau Jack, one of Aunt Vi's two Airedales. Elvin took Connie to see Aunt Vi's studio, an old implements shed that she'd fixed up. Beau Jack panted as he watched me eat barbecued chicken. It was a hot, breezeless afternoon. The whirligig on top of the studio didn't twitch. Insects crackled. A group of guests sat on the screened-in front porch, under a ceiling fan. I gave Beau Jack a chunk of chicken, and then I saw Mr. Hogue walking across the lawn toward me. He wore long white pants (cuffed) and a blue polo shirt. The heavy July air seemed to part for him. Sweat didn't sit upon his forehead and it didn't mark his shirt. His wire-rimmed glasses caught the light and scattered it.

He settled himself in the grass with his drink, something with a wedge of lime floating in it. "How do you like being retired?" he asked. There was amusement in his eyes. He had offered to help me find a job at another publishing house, but I'd declined, saying I hadn't decided what I was going to do next.

I took a gulp of beer. "Retirement is OK so far. I sleep in and read Proust. Slowly. All those long sentences, you know, that drag themselves across the page like serpents after a meal." I was high and was hoping to get higher. I hoped to see Petra soon, before I peaked.

"Petra is reading Proust, too, I think."

An old wood-paneled Country Squire station wagon rolled up the driveway, crunching gravel. Four men in white shirts got out. Musicians.

"I'm in love with Petra," I said, in a voice that one might use when taking an oath of office.

"I gather you're trying to say you're not queer," Mr. Hogue said evenly.

"No," I said. "I mean, yes, I'm not." I drained my beer and looked toward my aunt's studio. Elvin stood outside the shed, pouring beer down his throat. In the flat midafternoon light, he seemed somehow two-dimensional, tinny: Man with a Big Thirst. I didn't see Connie.

"How would you know that you aren't queer?" Mr. Hogue gazed at me in a kindly, schoolmasterly sort of way.

Was there a correct answer? "I can just feel it," I said.

Mr. Hogue rose from the grass and laid his hand on the ridged trunk of the sugar maple. There were tap holes at the tree's waist. "A young friend of mine told me about a drug he once took— MDA, I think he called it—that made him want to fuck trees. Even skinny saplings excited him. He was out in the woods, you see, trying to get in touch with his soul. And he spent hours, under the influence of this drug, dry-humping anything with a trunk. And he was perfectly happy. Don't you think it's odd that a little chemical adjustment, a jot of this or that, is enough to make you surrender to a tree?"

"You have to watch what you put in your mouth," I said smartly.

"But then a tree is always there for you, isn't it?" Mr. Hogue said. "Well, let me know if you change your mind and want to get back into the publishing business. I won't tell anybody that you killed Stawicki's dog." He smiled pleasantly and walked away.

I DRANK MORE BEER and kept an eye out for Petra while playing croquet with Elvin, my aunt, and Dr. Bickel. With a cigarette clamped between her lips and her sombrero set securely on her head, Aunt Vi drove the dentist's ball thirty yards off the course, into the weeds beyond the edge of the lawn. "Oh, Doctor," she shouted joyfully, "when you fetch that ball, beware the stinging nettle and the wily copperhead!"

The band, which was set up on the other side of the house, played "Blueberry Hill." Elvin sang along and drove my ball into the nettles and fleabane. "Take a hike, bro," Elvin said, and then cruised around the course in a single turn. "It's scary how good I am," he said. "And I'm stoned out of my mind."

The band played a slow blues and I went for a hike. I walked by Aunt Vi's studio, where, through a window, I saw a large canvas of Elvin sitting in a high-backed rattan chair in his green suit; he looked like a small-time criminal dressed for dinner. Then I walked through a field toward a spring-fed pond that was at the back of the property. I'd had five beers, but I could still walk a fairly straight line and identify some of the plants that grew in the field: goldenrod, wild carrot, fleabane. Down in a swale, fifty yards from the pond, was a clump of purple loosestrife. The sun shone brightly and the high grass brushed against my shins, making them itch. I felt a throbbing in the neighborhood of my left eye: pain gathering for a frontal assault. I'd just about given up on Petra's coming. I was looking forward to sticking my head in the water.

There was a swimmer in the pond—three, actually, if you counted Beau Jack and his mother, Cornelia, who were wading in the weedy shallows. The human swimmer was Connie. She was naked as a baby, her white bottom pointed at the pale blue sky. Her head was turned away from me. Then she dove under and when she resurfaced, her black hair sleek and shiny, she saw me. I was standing on the grassy bank, unbuttoning my shirt. She seemed unalarmed by my presence. She'd given me that lingering look in the car, after all, which I'd interpreted to mean: I wouldn't mind it if you saved me from Elvin. Though this reading of things was perhaps nothing more than vanity on my part. I had a habit of seeing sparks where there were none.

"How's the water?" I asked. I put my shirt on the ground, next to Connie's pile of clothes. The dogs came over to sniff me.

"OK," she said. "Cool."

She looked away as I got out of my underwear. Had she seen me trembling, my heart whanging away under my bare chest? Proust: "We do not tremble except for ourselves, or for those whom we love." I didn't love Connie, needless to say.

I waded into the pond, soft, oozy mud sucking at my feet, and then I dove out toward the middle, beneath the sunstruck surface. The cool water gripped me, held me under. I could see nothing. If I kept swimming, I thought, I'd end up on the other side of the world, far from harm.

I came up behind Connie, my mouth inches from shoulder blade and knobby vertebrae. She turned and pushed away from me a bit. Her arms were folded across her breasts. She was wearing a cross around her neck.

"Where'd you meet Elvin?" I asked.

"The Moon Bowl," she said. "In Moonachie. Where I go bowling."

"Do you like him?" I heard the band—the *boom-da-boom* of the bass, an undulant melody from the saxophone. Cornelia caught the scent of something and ran into the field. Beau Jack continued to work the pond shallows.

"Yeah, sure," Connie said. "Except he's kind of crazy, you know." She smiled and I saw the retainer wire across her teeth. "He has this, like, Saturday night special that he bought from this guy at the bowling alley. He got it so he could protect himself from nuts."

"Would he shoot me," I asked, "if he saw us getting it on?" I moved toward Connie. The pain above my eye had increased.

"Don't," she said, backing toward the shore, her hands still covering her chest. I saw the fear on her face, the way her wet, dark hair framed her tightening features. But I said nothing. I half-closed my eyes and lunged at her. Bone knocked against bone as she fell back. Her head went under for a second. I pulled her up toward me. She'd swallowed water and was coughing. I pressed my mouth against hers and tried to insert my tongue between her teeth. She shook her head free.

"I'm sorry," I said, releasing her.

"Go die," she said. She coughed and wiped her mouth against her forearm. She was sitting where the water was perhaps a foot deep. Her breasts were small and waifish.

I turned away and drifted toward the middle of the pond, where the water came up to my chest. I squatted there, in the brilliant sunshine. I heard Connie get out of the water, but I didn't move. I heard Beau Jack's collar tags jangling. I stayed in the water for a long time, watching the skin on my fingers pucker, waiting to hear Elvin's voice. Would he ask me to turn around before he shot me with his Saturday night special? If, for some reason, he didn't shoot me, I thought I might try to resuscitate the story I'd been writing about him.

The sun slipped down the sky and swallows made passes over the pond. I wanted a cigarette and got out of the water. My clothes weren't where I thought I'd left them, however, nor were they anywhere nearby. Connie had removed them, apparently. I walked out into the loosestrife and found one of my sneakers. With the sneaker in hand, I walked back and forth across the field, stepping lightly among the milkweed and fleabane and hairy-stemmed ragweed, looking for the rest of my clothes. After a while, I sat down, using my shoe as a cushion. I was a hundred yards from my aunt's house. I could see people playing croquet, my aunt among them, with her absurd flying saucer of a hat. I could walk naked to my aunt's house now or later. Or I could simply sit here and wait for the turkey vulture, making black circles in the sky to the south, to descend upon me.

Then I saw two figures crossing the field. One was Elvin, his shimmery blue muscle shirt hanging out of his jeans. The other was a young woman wearing a dark skirt and white shirt. Petra. She trotted to keep up with Elvin, who was making tracks, despite being unable to walk straight. They were talking. I heard Elvin say, "I don't know what exactly he did. All I know is what my girl told me."

Petra stopped and held her hand up against the declining sun. Elvin came on. I rose to my feet. I held the sneaker in front of my crotch.

"You look like Mr. Pitiful, bro," Elvin said, squinting, angling his head so that the sun wouldn't strike it so directly. I did not think it was to my advantage that he was wobbly drunk. "But I'm going to hit you anyway. You know why."

I didn't say anything smart or brave. I didn't say anything at all. I just stood there, hiding my privates behind my shoe, looking past Elvin at Petra, wondering where she and her Ethiopian friends had gone for lunch. Wasn't there an Ethiopian dish called *wat*? A hot, peppery dish that made your lips burn? Perhaps she'd had some of that for lunch, perhaps the taste of it was still there on her tongue.

The Hazeletts' Dog

ONE NIGHT IN June of 1979, my mother stepped in a hole near the smoke tree in her back yard and fractured the fibula of her left leg. She had gone outside to look at the moon, my father said when he called me in Ann Arbor the next day.

"I did not go outside to look at the blasted moon," I heard my mother say. She was sitting in the den, at some distance from my father, who was in the kitchen, but she had rabbit ears. "I went outside to turn off the water I'd left running on that pathetic little quince I never should have bought in the first place."

"Well, anyway, the moon was awfully bright," my father said, as if that explained something.

The hole, my mother believed, had been dug by a young dog named Cato, who was spotted like a Dalmatian and stocky like a beagle. Cato had trespassed on my mother's garden before, defiling her pinks and anemones and coralbells. Cato belonged to Hal and Mary Lee Hazelett, whom I'd grown up with. Hal was a reporter for the morning paper and Mary Lee taught Latin at Turnbull, a private girls' school, from which she'd graduated in 1969. In my mother's opinion, neither Hal nor Mary Lee had a clue about how to handle a dog.

"Hal's a smart boy," she said, "even if he is one size too big for his britches, and Mary Lee's a bright girl—she'll talk rings around you in a minute, just like her daddy—but you can't let a dog run wild, for goodness sakes!"

A week later, my father went away to a rail buffs' convention in San Francisco, and at his request I drove down to Kentucky from Ann Arbor, where I was in graduate school, to stay with my mother. It was a couple days before the Fourth, ten days before Skylab would tumble out of its ragged orbit and burn up as it descended through the atmosphere. At a rest stop in central Indiana, a man offered to sell me an "official" Skylab helmet (a hard hat decorated with "Chicken Little Was Right" stickers) as well as drugs and fireworks. I bought some bottle rockets and two joints. I smoked one of the joints before crossing the Ohio River into Kentucky, and then drove past my exit. I'd been looking at the Louisville skyline, its new glass boxes and steel slabs awash in late afternoon sunlight and pollution. Hal had a cubicle in one of those buildings; he was there now, perhaps, smoking unfiltered cigarettes, tapping out a story about the mayor or the board of aldermen. Local government was Hal's beat, one that he considered to be beneath him.

I got off the interstate eventually, and after driving through a run-down section of town (the old Sultan's Gate burlesque theater, which I'd visited once as a teenager, was boarded up, its marquee blank), I found my way back to River Road. A few minutes later, after driving past the River Bluff Country Club (where I had learned to swim and had gone to dancing school and had stolen condoms, with no prospect of using them, from the locker of a distillery executive) and past the low, red-brick buildings of the Burrell School (the Burrell School for Boys when Hal and I and Mac McRae were there) and past a swamp where you would sometimes see herons and elderly black men with fishing poles, and after turning up a hill lined by beeches and sycamores, and then turning again, onto Redbud Lane, the street where I'd spent my first eighteen years, I saw a dog in the middle of the road, chewing on a straw-colored object. The dog, which lay in shade cast by a maple that stood at the edge of Colonel Willborn's property, was Cato, and his interest in my idling Beetle was close to none. He did give me a quick, almost inquisitive look when I moved the car forward a few feet, and then he went back to eating what I now saw was a hat, a wide-brimmed van Gogh–style hat, the kind you might wear in the garden.

I honked at Cato, who shot me another look, and then I saw Mary Lee Hazelett coming down the road. She was wearing blue tennis shoes and had a red bandanna around her neck and what looked like a switch in her hand. Cato jumped up and ran off when he heard her voice, though he didn't go any farther than under Colonel Willborn's maple, where he sat at attention with the hat in his mouth.

"Where'd you get that?" Mary Lee said to Cato, her switch or wand, a leafy shoot of something, vibrating as she stalked him. "Come on, give it to me, now." Cato took off across Colonel Willborn's yard and disappeared behind a hydrangea bush that was as big as a cloud.

Mary Lee stuck her head in the window of the passenger door. The day's sun had caught her square in the face, it seemed; her cheek reflected it back, heated the car an extra degree.

"I don't know what to do about that dog," she said, leaving the formalities to hang in the air. "I think your mother believes we should give him a nice home on a far planet. I made Hal take him to obedience school, but he—they—flunked out. Hal couldn't resist arguing with the trainer." Her eyebrows rose the tiniest fraction in disapproval.

"It's a well-known fact that dog trainers are crypto-fascists," I said.

"Yeah. So, how are you doing, Peter? Aside from looking like you just inhaled an acre of dope, I mean. I see you didn't bring your girlfriend with you. What was her name? Roberta?"

Sometimes when I listened to Mary Lee talk I had the feeling of being caught in a downpour with no cover in sight. But it wasn't an unpleasant feeling, once you got used to it, being peppered by her questions or by whatever else was on her mind. She didn't necessarily require you to keep up your end of the conversation.

I'd known Mary Lee for years. We'd gone to kindergarten together and had made doily Valentines for each other. We'd been confirmed at the same altar rail by the same bishop. I'd taken her to a Christmas dance, and yet, despite the familiarity forced on us by the narrow, intersecting paths we moved along, we'd had, in the summer before our senior year in high school, a kind of romance. At any rate, I'd worked up a desire for her, this pretty girl who was both affable and remote. Her interest in me hadn't run as deep. I was anxious, conformist, sex-mad—ordinary, in a word. Or so I feared she saw me. Nevertheless, she'd let me kiss her one night while we sat on the warm hood of my father's Biscayne, and kiss her again on another night when we were down by the river. Hal had been present on the second occasion. I'd put my hand on Mary Lee's breast, and she'd pulled her mouth away.

"Renata was her name," I said. "Not Roberta." Renata had come home with me from Ann Arbor the previous Christmas. I'd taken her to Colonel Willborn's caroling party, and she'd had a good time. She'd drunk the colonel's ninety-proof eggnog and had sat with Hal on the antique settee in the hall, taking drags off his cigarettes. But then at a Christmas afternoon gathering, my half-soused Aunt Helen had made an anti-Semitic remark, something about how her "Jew plumber" had been overcharging her. Renata, a Jew, had been appalled by my failure to respond to my aunt's comment.

"Renata's in Ann Arbor," I said. It didn't seem necessary to say that I no longer saw her.

"I guess you'll just have to find yourself another sweetheart," Mary Lee said, tapping me on the shoulder with her switch, her wand, her teacher's ferule.

"I guess I will," I said. Why hadn't I noticed until that moment Mary Lee idly stirring the air in the car with that leafy little shoot of whatever it was? Well, because, while gripping the gearshift knob and listening to her talk, I'd been gazing at her face. There was a smudge of dirt on her forehead, above the dusky crescent of her eyebrow, which shaded the pleasant but not quite fathomable pool of her hazel eye. There was dirt on her cheek, too.

"You look like you've been working," I said. The leaves on the flickering shoot were elliptical, toothed, pale underneath.

"I'm taking out the pussy willows by the porch," she said. "I want to put in lilacs. Hal, being oppositional by nature, prefers rhododendrons. You want to be the swing vote?"

"I like them both," I said.

"Coward," she said, grinning.

I looked up the road and saw Cato, hat in mouth, trotting past my parents' driveway. Then Cato took a left, into their yard. Mary Lee saw this, too, and pulled her head out the window and whistled, ring and index fingers between her lips. She produced a long, swooping, come-on-home-now note that caused two feeding doves to flutter up from Colonel Willborn's yard but didn't bring back Cato.

"Your mother is going to murder me," Mary Lee said, sticking her head back in the car. "Me and Cato both, I swear."

"I bet she wouldn't mind knocking off Hal, too," I said. "Wipe out the whole lot of you at once." There was a dime-size hole in Mary Lee's faded blue T-shirt, just to the right of her heart. What would she do, I wondered, if I attempted to put my index finger through that hole? Swat me with her switch?

"She might have to send out a posse to find Hal," Mary Lee said. "He's not around much. He's always saying how much he hates his job, but he never stops working at it." With her switch, she tapped me on the hand that was gripping the gearshift knob. "I should get going. You might want to suck some mints before you kiss your mother. And put on your sunglasses, if you have any. I'll tell Hal I saw you and your big pupils."

"Watch out for spaceships falling from the sky," I said.

"I always do."

I drove up the road past Hal and Mary Lee's small white house (small, that is, by neighborhood standards), and then turned into my parents' driveway, where Cato was stretched out, hatless, pondering his next move.

I WAS SITTING with Willie at the kitchen table the next morning when my mother entered the room on crutches. "Has anybody seen my hat?" she asked. "My gardening hat?" She had looked for it in the garage, she said, where she kept her gardening things. She wanted to do some weeding. Nobody had pulled a weed in days. She could almost see the place going to seed from where she was standing.

Since my mother's question seemed to be directed more toward Willie, who at that moment was peeling a cucumber, than toward me, and since I didn't know that the hat I'd seen Cato eating was in fact my mother's, and since I only dimly recollected having ever seen my mother in a straw hat, I didn't answer. I was reading an article about Skylab in the *Independent*, Hal's paper. A statistician for NASA had estimated that the probability of any particular person being injured by falling Skylab debris was one in six hundred billion, no greater than the likelihood that you'd be hit on the head by a meteorite during a lifetime of walking under the skies.

"No, ma'am, Mrs. Sackrider," Willie said. "I haven't seen that hat since you were last wearing it, back before you hurt yourself." A strip of cucumber skin slid through the peeler onto the cutting board. Willie was making cucumber soup for Colonel Willborn's Fourth of July party the following day—a party at which everybody in the neighborhood, both the sober and the intoxicated, would put his hand over his heart and recite the Pledge of Allegiance.

"I can't imagine where it went to," my mother said. She was scowling, racking her brain. In her view, it seemed, inanimate objects had legs; they ran off, leaving her bereft.

"Shouldn't you be resting your leg?" Willie said.

"I bought that hat at a drugstore down in Biloxi," my mother said, still standing. "You remember when we were there, Peter? We went to Beauvoir and you bought one of those flat-topped infantryman's caps."

I didn't recall the cap. But I did remember buying a plastic statuette of Robert E. Lee astride Traveler. It had been on my bureau for a number of years, along with a plastic figure of Willie Mays. Mays still stood there, like an idol, forever making a basket catch.

"I put the hat away when we got back," my mother continued, "and I didn't see it again until this spring, when Willie and I were cleaning out Alex's closet. How it got there I couldn't say." She opened the refrigerator, as if the hat might be *there*, then closed it. "You're going to put watercress in the soup, aren't you, Willie?"

"I always do," Willie said, expelling air out the side of her mouth. Willie was wearing new glasses, big tinted aviator-style spectacles, which seemed to be designed to put distance between her and whoever was talking to her. Earlier that morning, when I'd picked her up at Winn-Dixie, where the bus from Dickeytown had dropped her, she said, when I asked her how she was doing, "To tell you the truth, hon, after I get through at your mother's some days, all I want to do is lie on my bed and smoke a cigarette with the air conditioner blowing on my head. Except I quit smoking three weeks ago yesterday, which is why I'm fatter than ever, and I can't hardly afford to turn on the air with this energy mess we got."

"The watercress gives it a little bite," my mother said, still on her feet, her crooked toes peeking out of the plaster cast. When my sister and I were children, Mom sometimes permitted us to inspect her feet, which years of wearing narrow, pointed shoes had nearly ruined. Her corns, those horny mounds of epidermis, fascinated us.

Willie diced the cucumber, the knife tapping against the cutting board. My mother touched her hair. "I could've sworn I left that hat in the garage," she said.

"It'll turn up," I said. "The world is full of lost hats waiting to be found."

Willie gave me a sideways look.

"I'll help you find it in a minute," I said. I was reading another article about space—space garbage: dead satellites, bags of frozen waste jettisoned by astronauts, pieces of rocket engines, paint chips, wrenches, toothbrushes, all of it orbiting the earth, mucking up the heavens.

"I'll manage," my mother said. She turned herself around on her crutches and hobbled out of the kitchen.

"Whyn't you go help your mother find that hat?" Willie said, getting up from the table. Once, when I was a boy, I'd made a face at Willie behind her broad back, and she'd said, "I got eyes in the back of my head, you better watch it." She went to the stove and peered into a pot of broth.

"I saw Cato chewing on a straw hat the other day," I said. "It's a goner, I believe."

"Aw-oh." Willie knocked a spoon against the lip of the pot, and then got two potatoes off the counter and brought them back to the table.

I looked out the window and saw my mother propelling herself across the yard, past the smoke tree, with its hazy pink feather-dusterlike blooms. She had a white visor on her head.

"Mom sure does like to garden," I said.

"It keeps her busy," Willie said. A peeled potato, as smooth as a river stone, lay before her. Then she went to work on the other one. "You're going to have to go buy me some peaches. I got to make a pie after I get through with this."

I watched my mother lower herself to the ground, to a weeding position, a maneuver that required her first to seat herself on a limestone boulder, a kind of garden bench, and then to slide to the grass. In the course of doing this, she looked my way. To what should I have attributed my desire to remain seated in the air-conditioned breakfast nook with the newspaper while my mother performed one-legged stunts in the July sun?

"Oh, boy." Willie saw Cato before I did—bounding through the hedge that separated my parents' yard from the Seybolds'. Cato ran toward my mother in a way that suggested he was happy to see her. My mother grabbed a crutch and waved it at him, like a lion tamer with a chair. Willie got up and opened the side door, and when she did, I heard my mother shouting, "Go on, you dumb dog, go on home." And when Cato saw Willie bearing down on him, he did go away, fleeing back through the hedge, like an unwanted spirit.

"Hey." Hal was on the phone.

"Hey."

"How's your mother?"

"Cooling her heels, for the moment." She was in the den, her leg propped up on a hassock. *Madama Butterfly* was on the record player.

"I hear she thinks I'm an irresponsible pet owner," Hal said.

"Yep." I heard Madama Butterfly sing the word *dolor*, drawing it out gently. "She might forgive you if you bought her a new fake snake and shipped Cato out."

"Snake?" The sound of typing, a burst of it, came across the telephone wire.

"She had an inflatable snake in the garden that was supposed to scare away bunnies. It's missing and she suspects Cato."

"Cato is afraid of snakes," Hal said. "Real ones, anyway."

"I didn't tell Mom that Mary Lee and I saw Cato eating a straw hat. Mom's straw hat, it looks like." Willie, I saw through the breakfast nook window, had gone outside; she sat in a lawn chair, under the tulip poplar, drinking a Coke.

"DOG INDICTED FOR BEING A DOG; WILL PLEAD DOGGISHNESS," Hal said, in a banner-headline kind of voice. He banged out something on his typewriter—a little explosion of facts, naked verbs and unadorned nouns. Or so I imagined.

"What are you writing?"

"Two city officials, two double-knit bozos in the Public Works department, went to New Orleans for a convention, some useless meeting, and charged the taxpayers for poontang, among other things. I have a good source inside Pubic Works, as we say down here in the newsroom. Can you hold on for a minute?"

The music swelled, kettle drums were beaten, and Madama Butterfly, crazy with grief, stabbed herself in the throat. Willie came into the kitchen and dropped a joint on the table. She'd found it in my shirt pocket when she was doing the laundry.

"I nearly smoked it just now," she said. "But then I thought, What if it makes me feel all nice and funny, you know? I might become a marijuana addict. I might have to retire from working." She cackled and walked out of the kitchen.

"Guess who I saw the other day?" Hal was back on the phone.

"I give up."

"I'll give you some hints," he said. "The person in question used to coach football at a boys' school on River Road. He now works for a carpet-cleaning firm, in a managerial capacity, I believe. On game day, he wore one of those houndstooth hats, just like the King of Alabama, Bear Bryant. After he led us in a pregame prayer, he'd say. 'Let's put our hats on, men, and go to war.' And then we'd go pound the shit out of the boys from the School for the Deaf or the School for the Blind or some other suitable opponent. Didn't you score a couple touchdowns against the deaf guys?"

When Hal and I were juniors, Harris Diehl had arranged for the Burrell School for Boys to play the School for the Deaf. I'd scored three touchdowns. The next summer, Hal had quit the team.

"Where'd you see him?"

"At the Dairy Dip, over off Bardstown Road," Hal said. "I was having a postcoital cone with my mistress when he walked in." He chuckled. "Can you hold on again?"

What was I supposed to make of that remark? If Hal was screwing somebody on the side, why did he feel obliged to tell *me* about it? We'd known each other for a long time—we'd gone through twelve years of Burrell together—but we hadn't exactly confided in each other. If we'd confessed anything of importance, we'd done it while scratching our butts, so to speak.

My mother came into the kitchen. She looked as if the music had borne her off somewhere, someplace ethereal, not rich in oxygen. She listened to music as if messages meant for her were encoded in it. "Whenever I hear the end of that opera," she said, "I wonder why she doesn't stab that scoundrel Pinkerton instead of herself."

"Good manners?"

"I suppose." She opened the refrigerator and got out a tall glass containing her health drink. It was murky, full of substances

I didn't know the names of. She took a sip and said, "Who're you talking to?"

I was holding the receiver away from my ear. "Hal. I'm on hold."

"Please tell him I'd be grateful if he kept that dog of his tied up and out of my yard." She took another sip of her health drink. Her cheeks had brightened already. "I'm serious."

"Take it easy, Mom," I said. "Give it a rest."

"I will not give it a rest, and I will not take it easy." She set her glass down on the counter. I waited for a storm, the rush of words, my sins and the sins of the world to rain down on me. But the storm didn't come. She went over to the sink and occupied herself with an African violet on the windowsill, pinching off dead blossoms.

"Want to play tennis tomorrow?" Hal was back. "I have the day off."

Hal was a lob-and-chip-shot artist, a dinker. I rarely beat him. He ran everything down. "OK," I said. What else was I going to do tomorrow?

I hung up and looked at my mother, whose back was to me. I studied her shoulder blades, sharp birdlike things, under her shirt. When I'd hugged her, upon my arrival the day before, she'd seemed thinner than ever, her bones like kindling. But she wasn't thin to the point of fragility. She'd always been thin—fiercely thin.

"You couldn't ask your friend to restrain his dog, do that one simple thing for me?" On the profile of her face, the downslope of her jaw, I read the question: What would it cost you to show me love?

"No," I said. "I couldn't."

ONE MID-AUGUST NIGHT IN 1968, the summer before my senior year in high school, Hal and Mary Lee and I drove around

town in my mother's station wagon and drank beer. We drove aim-
lessly, along River Road, past Cox's Park, which was filled with
automobiles, their taillights twinkling.

"Lot of fornication going on tonight," Hal said. He rode in the
far-back seat, which faced the opposite direction. He hung his feet
out the window, and in between chugs of beer shouted things.
"Nixon sucks!" "Humphrey sucks!" "I hate Bobby Goldsboro!"
"No, no, go not to Lethe, neither twist wolf's-bane . . ."

"Show-off," Mary Lee said, not really disapprovingly.

We approached a KingFish restaurant that was supposed to
look like a paddle wheeler. "No, no," Hal shouted, "go not to
KingFish, neither eat its fishy fish sandwich . . ."

We drove out into the countryside, down Rose Island Road,
and parked at a boat landing, which had a strip of beach next to it.

Hal wandered off. Mary Lee and I sat on the beach—more dirt
and debris than sand. A houseboat floated downriver, spilling
voices. The air was cool and damp, but I was warm: a couple of
quarts of beer had dilated my blood vessels. I put my arm around
Mary Lee's waist, my hand under her shirt. Mary Lee pointed to
the sky, which was clotted with stars, and picked out Cassiopeia.
"You see the W sort of lying on its side?"

I saw Hal at the other end of the beach, at the river's edge. He
was naked, his arms folded across his chest. I kissed Mary Lee on
the cheek and then on the mouth, an act that seemed neither to
surprise nor please her. She gave me her mouth, more or less, but
when I lay my hand on her breast she asked for a cigarette. Mary
Lee was the kind of person who smoked one or two cigarettes a
week.

Hal had waded into the river up to his knees. His wiry body
shone above the black surface of the water and seemed almost to
emit light. Mary Lee watched him. I gave her a cigarette and then
began to take off my clothes.

I nearly fell down trying to get out of my shorts. Beer sloshed in my head. Then I was as naked as I'd ever be. "You coming in?"

"No, thanks," she said, looking up at me, smiling. "I wouldn't go into that river even if you stood on your head and sang 'The Star-Spangled Banner' in pig Latin."

I sprinted toward the water, wanting only to launch myself as far out as possible. Before the water closed around me, I heard Hal sing, "O aysay ancay ouyay eesay . . ."

THE NEXT DAY, Hal's father, an attorney at an old Louisville firm, drove his son and me out to a Baptist church camp near Fern Creek. The Burrell School for Boys had rented the camp for a week of football practice. We slept in bare pine-plank cabins, eight boys to a cabin. We ate meals and watched grainy films of last year's games in a shedlike hall in which you could smell the sweat of Saturday night revivals. As one of the captains of the team, I was sometimes asked to say grace before meals. Hal took to calling me "Reverend."

I was one of the captains because the pickings were slim at Burrell, a small school. I wasn't a fool for football, but there were moments when something seized me (I hesitate to use the word *spirit*) and I played with what Harris Diehl, who knew every phrase in the coach's manual, called "reckless desire." Whatever this thing was—the wish to land on the injured list and be nursed by sympathetic women? mindless anger?—it rarely took hold of Hal, who, though not unathletic and not uncompetitive, played football only because football was what you did at Burrell unless you were crippled or so skinny and frail-looking that you had an excuse for running cross-country.

During afternoon practice on the third day of camp, Harris Diehl made a group of linemen run laps for failing to do a drill correctly. "Run till you puke," Diehl said.

One of the linemen was a boy named Ben Panitz, a classmate of Hal's and mine. Ben was a chubby boy, awkward and slow, though he was not slow to anger. He'd fought back when he was teased, as he had been when he first arrived at Burrell, a wary twelve-year-old Jew whose satchel contained Ian Fleming novels and boxes of cinnamon Red Hots. One day when he was set upon in a hallway, he cleared space for himself by spinning wildly with his satchel extended. The dark blaze of his face caught us, tormentors and bystanders alike, off guard, and we left him pretty much to himself thereafter. Around tenth grade, he acquired a nickname—Fillings: his father was a dentist—and he occasionally showed up at beer parties. Sometimes Hal and Ben sat together in study hall and shared Ben's Virgil pony.

While the linemen ran laps, I practiced passing to my receivers, among whom were Hal and Mac McRae. Diehl watched me—and the linemen—from a squat. A ballcap shaded his face, even his outthrust chin. "Set your feet, son," he said to me, after one of my passes sailed over Mac's head. "Don't be floating around in the pocket like goddamn Tinkerbell."

Then Diehl began to yell at the linemen, and more particularly at Ben, who was bringing up the rear. "Run, boy," Diehl shouted. "Move your fat Hebrew ass before I kick it!"

Ben, whose silver helmet reflected the broiling August sun, who ran no more easily than a drunk in armor might, looked toward Diehl but kept moving. Hal caught my eye, then glanced at Diehl; the word *dickhead* formed on Hal's lips. Diehl, who was still down in his coach's squat, who was now chewing on a blade of grass, said, "OK, receivers, run those routes right." Then he swiveled ninety degrees and yelled at Ben, "Run, Panitz! Or I'll call your mama to come fetch your sorry ass."

When Ben came staggering past us again, he said in a surprisingly clear voice, "Go fuck yourself!" Diehl rose out of his squat, stopped Ben, and told him to repeat what he'd said.

Ben made up a story: Hal had been laughing at him, so he'd sworn at Hal.

Diehl turned to Hal and said, "Is that correct, Hazelett?"

Hal toed the ground with his cleated shoe, pulled at an armpit strap on his shoulder pads. "Yes," he said.

"Don't lie, son. It'll make you feel terrible in the morning."

"I'm not lying."

LATE THAT NIGHT, Hal came into my cabin. I was reading a book of Ferlinghetti poems that he'd lent me. My flashlight was the only light in the cabin; everybody else was asleep.

Hal sat down on the edge of my bunk. He pushed his dark hair, long by Burrell standards, off his forehead. "Fillings and me are walking out in five minutes," he said. "You coming?"

He'd told me in the shower after practice that he was going to quit the team and write to the Burrell board of trustees and expose Diehl as an anti-Semite and a "fascist prick." If I quit, too, Hal had said, it would mean more, because I wasn't known as a trouble-maker. "Everybody thinks you're this nice boy who hardly makes a peep."

I kept my flashlight trained on the book. *Don't let that horse eat that violin cried Chagall's mother.* Hal had circled these lines with a blue ballpoint and written in the margin, "Let him eat it."

"How are you going to get home?" I asked.

"We'll call Fillings's brother when we get to the highway." The church camp was two miles off the highway, down a dirt road. "Or Mary Lee. She'll come get us. Put your shoes on, Reverend."

I looked at Hal's face, its planes distinct even in the darkness. There wasn't a lot of meat on him. Where flesh might have been, there was a sort of righteous glow. He looked more like somebody in the ministry than I did, except around the mouth, which was small and ironic.

I said, "Are you going to leave Diehl a note or something?"

"You mean, like a thank-you note? 'Dear Adolf, Thanks for the memories. Good luck in the upcoming campaign.' Get serious, man."

When Hal looked at me then, I thought I saw something surge in him, like light or electricity. He lifted his hand and for an instant I actually thought he was going to strike me. We'd gone a while since we'd last fought—seventh grade, when we got into an argument about why the Confederates hadn't won at Gettysburg. "Because they were stupid, like you," he'd said.

But Hal didn't hit me. He merely swiped at a firefly as it passed over my bunk.

"Are you chickening out?" He'd missed the firefly.

"I never said I was going to quit tonight."

"Can I have my book?" He held out his hand.

I gave him his book, and he walked out of the cabin. As he passed under my window, he said, "Sieg heil!"

ONE RAINY SUNDAY afternoon that fall, I was driving through Cherokee Park with a girl named Melinda Gray when I saw Hal's father's car, a big cream-colored Buick. It was parked by the side of the road, and as I drove past, I saw Hal and Mary Lee, like apparitions behind the fogged-up windows. I made a loop through the park, and then pulled off, maybe twenty yards behind the Buick.

There was space between Hal's and Mary Lee's heads. Smoke came out of the driver's window. Perhaps they were smoking pot and discussing Camus. (Hal had just written a paper on *The Myth of Sisyphus*.) Perhaps Hal was counting the freckles on Mary Lee's neck. Perhaps Mary Lee was looking at—laughing at—the hickey she'd raised on Hal's neck, a mark I'd see at school the next day, a dark reddish oval peeking above his shirt like a sun ascending.

"What are we doing here?" Melinda inquired. She was a sophomore at Turnbull, the girls' school that Mary Lee and my sister attended. Melinda and I had gone out together twice that fall, had drunk beer and made out in the car and on her doorstep. But being with me in the daylight seemed to make her nervous, as if she could see whatever it was that was jumping beneath my skin.

"I don't know." I asked Melinda if she wanted to get something to eat.

"OK." She got a cigarette out of her purse and pushed in the dashboard lighter. She was wearing a pale shade of lipstick, Sunday-afternoon-in-the-car lipstick.

"White Castle? Nine for ninety-nine cents."

"You like those things, those maggotburgers?"

"I do," I said, pulling out into the road. Hal had stuck his arm out the window. He was waving at me—his fingers were moving up and down—while he was also kissing Mary Lee, his head on top.

HAL AND MARY LEE broke up that winter. Something Mary Lee had done had made Hal jealous, and in his distress he'd burned a book of poems she had given him—e. e. cummings, I think—and had sent the ashes to her in the mail. (The ashes had come gift-wrapped, and Mary Lee had used the paper to return to Hal the Tim Buckley album he'd given her.) This exchange seemed to suggest that they wouldn't give each other up easily, and in the spring, a few weeks before graduation, they got back together again. I watched all this from a respectable distance, while growing accustomed to the whorls of Melinda Gray's ears.

During the school year Hal and I had avoided each other as much as was possible, but at the prom, at the River Bluff Country Club, Hal had put his hand on my head, a gesture that seemed almost fatherly, and said, "Let's get ripped." He and I and Mary Lee walked out to the golf course and sat down in a sand trap and smoked a ball of hash. (I'd left Melinda on a sofa in a back room of the club; she was already too drunk to walk.) Mary Lee took one toke and lay back in the sand. "That's enough for me," she said. Would she float off in her long shimmery formal dress, like that untethered bride in the Chagall painting? No, I thought, she was too sensible to do something like that.

I watched a pair of wide-skirted trees—spruces, maybe—turn into whirling black shapes, like upside-down funnels. Hal put his tuxedo tie between his nose and lip, giving himself a mustache. "Now, repeat after me," he said. "The earth is not flat and Harris Diehl is a fascist pig." I laughed until my stomach hurt, until I staggered off into the embrace of those whirling black trees and peed.

MARY LEE WENT to college in Boston and Hal went to an "experimental" school in Massachusetts. For a while, they rode the buses between Boston and the Connecticut River Valley—Hal reading Marcuse and Gramsci and scratching his new beard, Mary Lee reading Ovid and fiddling with the peace button on her sweater. Then, in his sophomore year, Hal did a for-credit "work semester" at a lumber town in Maine. He worked in a pulp mill, wrote a paper about class divisions, and slept with the ex-girlfriend of a forklift operator. When he came home that summer, he told Mary Lee that they shouldn't tie each other down. He quoted Nietzsche to her, something about the enslaving idol of love.

Mary Lee transferred to Vanderbilt. My school was only a hundred miles away, and on one occasion when I came up to Nashville, I stayed with her, on the floor of her dorm room. I remember lying there, on a rag rug that she'd bought at a crafts fair, listening to her talk a blue streak about Martin Buber (she was suddenly interested in theology), thinking that all her talk about I-ness and Thou-ness did not conceal her loneliness very well, wondering if it was her loneliness or mine that made me want to bury my face in her neck. When I asked her if she ever heard from Hal, she said, "That bastard?"

Four years later, in 1976, Hal and Mary Lee were living together in an apartment off Bardstown Road. ("I saw them at that play I told you about, the one about Vietnam with all the vile language," my mother wrote to me. "Dad said Hal looked like a Mexican bandit, with that long droopy mustache of his.") Mary Lee was teaching Latin by then, and doing volunteer work at a halfway house downtown. Hal was a cub reporter at the *Independent*, a job he had obtained after being turned away by several larger and more distinguished dailies. This had wounded Hal, but not humbled him. He regarded the *Independent*, which was owned by a Rockefeller Republican named Rucker, as a place through which he would pass on his way to an interview with Sartre or Castro. His attitude nearly got him canned, but Rucker, with whom Hal's father sometimes played bridge at a men's club, intervened. By 1978, when Hal married Mary Lee, he'd been taken off the crime beat and assigned to cover city government, a move that didn't impress him.

"I'm going sideways into oblivion," he said to me at a party the night before his wedding. He was half loaded, his face as florid as a sunset.

"You're only twenty-seven," I said.

"I'm fucking ancient," he said. "I've got a wife and a Vega, and we're about to buy a house. What kind of fertilizer spreader do you think I should get—the drop or the broadcast kind?"

CATO WAS LYING under the front bumper of Hal's Vega, out of the sun, his eyes open, I guessed, only because it was his duty as a dog to keep tabs on whatever or whoever was foolish enough to be moving through the morning heat. I was sweating after walking the fifty yards from my mother's house. Mr. Mercury, the thermometer-shaped weather figure who occupied the upper-left-hand corner of the *Independent*'s front page, had been shown wiping his brow with one hand and waving a flag with the other. It was the Fourth of July. The temperature was supposed to reach ninety-eight.

I knocked on the door, peered through the screen into the hall and the dimness beyond. When I was a boy, Hal and Mary Lee's house had been occupied by Frank Willborn, a bachelor cousin of Colonel Willborn's. When he died, the house, which had not been kept up, was rented to a young Episcopal preacher and his wife, and then sold, after she had triplets, to Hal and Mary Lee. Mary Lee had planned to fix up the house—strip the floors, replace the rotting windows, do some painting. There was, in fact, a gallon can of primer on the front step, its lid winking in the sunlight. In the meantime, bugs could come and go as they pleased through the rips in the screen door. I saw a bee bump against the mesh, then slip inside.

I knocked again. Mary Lee came from around the corner, holding her hands away from her body, almost as if she were balancing herself. Something silver gleamed in her hair. When she came closer, I saw that her hands were speckled with bits of dough. There was sweat on her upper lip.

"I'm making some things for the Colonel's party," she said. "Come on in." She turned and walked back down the hall. Her feet were bare, and so was her back. She was wearing a halter shirt that was tied at the nape. Like a boy running a stick along a fence, I followed her spine down to the top of her cutoffs as I trailed her into the kitchen.

"Are you going to the party?" she asked.

"I wouldn't miss it." I laid my tennis racket on a chair.

"Is your mom going?"

"We'll see." I'd left my mother in the air-conditioned dark of her bedroom, a bit dazed by a pill she'd taken during the night to ease the throbbing in her leg. She was waiting for my father to call from California, where he was riding antique trains. When I'd told her that I was going to play tennis with Hal, she'd said, "Well, I hope you win." Then, before I left, she asked me to put something on the stereo for her. More Puccini. "You can turn it up," she said. "I like to be able to feel it down to my toes."

Mary Lee took a ball of dough from under a tea towel and kneaded it, turning it as she pressed on it with the heel of her hand. The dough began to shine.

"I'm supposed to braid this eventually," she said. A drop of sweat fell on the dough.

"Braid?"

"You divide the dough into strands, after you let it rise for however long and after you punch it down and after you say a prayer. Then, my undomesticated friend, you braid the strands."

She smiled, information having been transmitted from teacher to pupil. I looked at her clavicle, at the shadowy spot at the base of the her throat between where the bones met. I looked at the eggs bobbing in a pot of boiling water on the stove—she was also making deviled eggs for the Colonel's party. If I stuck my hand among the eggs and recited something from Keats (the would-be subject of my would-be dissertation), would she set aside her dough and pull me to her?

Well, I was foolish but not insane. And what, really, did I want from Mary Lee? For her to abandon Hal and run away with me to Ann Arbor, to my graduate student apartment, which, as it happened, was one flight above an adult bookstore? Or for her simply to look at me in a particular way and say, "Boy, what a guy you are! I never *knew*."

The bee that had entered the house ahead of me was flying around the kitchen, making passes at a jar of mustard on the counter, then at an open-mouthed carton of milk.

"Where's Hal?" I asked.

"Outside," she said. "Digging up pussy-willow stumps. I couldn't get them out myself."

"I'll see if he needs help."

I walked down the hall and into the living room. A floor fan turned slowly, ruffling newspapers that lay on the sofa. Quantities of information had been consumed here. There was even a French paper, an exotic among the native varieties, which lay on a table, under an ashtray. I picked it up. *"Skylab Tombera le Onze Juillet." "Où Sont les Amis du Shah?"*

Then I heard a thudding sound, followed by a stream of *Fuck!s.* When I looked out into the yard, I saw Hal, in gym shorts and work boots, swinging an axe at a stump. His swings were rapid, closer to chops than full windup swings. It occurred to me that he'd be tired when we played tennis.

I went outside through the screened-in porch. Hal had put down the axe and lit a cigarette. There were six pussy-willow stumps to be removed. The bush farthest from the porch had been stripped of its leafy upper branches but not of its main stems. It looked like a hat rack.

Hal's back was pink, a brighter shade of pink up near his right shoulder, where he had burned himself as a child and had a scar that was roughly the shape of Kentucky on a map. Until he was thirteen or fourteen, he'd kept the scar covered, wearing a T-shirt when he went swimming. Later, when he learned that girls wanted to touch it, that it made him more interesting than the rest of us, he exposed it.

"Hey," I said.

"Hey." He vented smoke through the black veil of his mustache. The mustache looked like a burden in the heat.

"I can't believe the roots on this thing," he said. I looked at the hole he'd dug around the stump, the web of roots. The ones he'd severed were pinkish-white at the tips, an inside-of-the-mouth color. "And there are five more of these fuckers."

"Mary Lee wants to plant lilacs?"

"So she says." Hal tossed his cigarette away, then picked up the axe. He straddled the hole and slashed at a root. "In the meantime, I'm trying not to cut my peter off."

A rabbit hopped across the yard, then stopped, as if alarmed — a sunstruck bundle of fur and nerves.

"What did Harris Diehl have to say for himself when you saw him at the Dairy Dip?"

"Nada." Hal had cut through a root, and was now working on another one. "I didn't talk to him. He was too busy eating ice cream, probably thinking about what he was going to say at the next meeting of Aryan People United. I don't think he would've recognized me, anyway. Could you hand me that shovel?"

I gave Hal the shovel. Then I saw Cato coming around the side of the house at a trot, his tail slowly swishing. The rabbit saw Cato before Cato saw it, and the rabbit took off for the yard next door, the Stringhams'. Cato raced off, too, suddenly as peppy as a dog in a Saturday morning cartoon.

Hal glanced toward Cato, who was barking ecstatically. Then Hal stuck the shovel under the stump and tried to pry it up. The stump moved but didn't come free.

"She's a dental hygienist," Hal said. He was addressing the stump.

"Who's a dental hygienist?"

"The girl, woman, I told you about on the telephone," he said, not looking up. "For whom I have forsaken the honorable estate of matrimony." He pushed down on the shovel and a root popped. "She scrapes tartar off people's teeth. She has red hair and a scar on her upper lip which she got when Derwin Rogers shoved her off a jungle gym in 1958. In Shepherdsville. Derwin went to Vietnam and is now working for the phone company."

"Ah," I said.

Hal tried prying the stump from another angle. I looked at his muscled back and remembered the day when we were in seventh grade and fought over why the Confederates lost at Gettysburg. (We'd just had a formal classroom debate about the Civil War; I'd been among those who defended the losers.) Hal had been elusive and quick, hard to keep pinned down. There wasn't much to latch on to beneath his clothes. (We'd wrestled in our coats and ties, the Burrell school uniform.) Even when I finally got him down on his back—when I suddenly found myself sitting on his chest, holding his arms down, bleeding on him from my nose, yelling at him to apologize (for calling me stupid, though I didn't say so)—I felt certain that he could slide out from under me whenever he chose, that he could pitch me aside in an instant.

Hal had pried the stump loose of all but one root. "Can you chop that sucker for me? Can you see it there?"

I saw Cato come loping back across the yard. The rabbit had escaped, it seemed.

"Are you going to tell Mary Lee?" I picked up the axe and swung it. The root wasn't much thicker than my thumb, but the blade was dull, and it took three swings to get it through.

"You wouldn't, if you were in my position?"

"I'm not in your position," I said.

Hal lifted the stump out of the hole—knobby, dirt-encrusted, whiskery, it looked like some inscrutable object in a bad dream—and set it down next to Cato. "Mary Lee and I will have to discuss who gets custody of Cato, won't we, Cato?" The dog didn't look at Hal; he was scouting the yard for more wildlife, his tongue dangling.

Hal wiped dirt from his hands onto his shorts. "You want to play tennis now or bag it? I'm burning up."

"Let's play now," I said.

• • •

MY MOTHER SAT in a wicker armchair on Colonel Willborn's broad porch, a porch that was made for Fourth of July parties, a porch from which you could fly several flags, if you chose,
though Colonel Willborn, secure in his patriotism, had hung out
only one. My mother's leg rested on a red leather hassock that
Colonel Willborn had brought from his study. "There you are,
dear," he'd said, patting her on the knee. She'd smiled. She smiled
again when he fetched her a glass of iced tea, with a sprig of mint
from his own garden.

"That's the loveliest smell," my mother said. "But if you don't
watch out, mint will take over your garden."

"Oh, I like to grow enough of it to smell it from afar," the
Colonel said, politely.

Aunt Helen, my father's sister, pulled up at my mother's chair,
a drink in one hand and a Kool 100 in the other. She wanted to
hear the story of how my mother broke her leg. "Don't spare me
any of the gory details," she said, making a low, raspy sound that
was possibly a chuckle.

"Well," my mother began, "Henry and I were watching a TV
show about Bing Crosby when I remembered that I'd left the water running on a quince that hasn't grown one blessed inch since
I bought it from this man who also sold me two pitiful-looking
azaleas. Anyway, I went outside and turned off the water. And then
I decided to take a walk. The moon was so bright I could just
about see the blue in the veins of my hands. I felt transparent. It
was the queerest sensation."

"Just a second, dear," Aunt Helen said. She went over to the
porch railing, near where Colonel Willborn and I were standing,
near where the flag hung unstirred by any breeze, and stubbed out
her cigarette in an ashtray.

Colonel Willborn was asking me whether Tennyson was still
taught in the university. He had asked me this question on another

occasion, and had then recited "The Charge of the Light Brigade," marking its cadences by tapping me on the arm. There had been a fleck of something in his white mustache—a food particle, maybe—and it hadn't fallen out during his recitation.

I said that the Tennyson authority at Ann Arbor had died recently. He'd been struck down while riding his bicycle out of the parking lot of a doughnut shop.

Aunt Helen asked my mother who her orthopedist was. I had missed the moment, apparently, when my mother would describe her ankle rolling over as she put her foot down on what she had reason to believe was solid ground near her smoke tree. I'd missed the denouement, too: her cries for my father, who had fallen asleep in front of the TV, and her eventual rescue by Vern Seybold, her neighbor, who had happened to be outside.

"Dr. Brock," my mother said. She shooed a fly that was buzzing around her glass of iced tea.

"Well, if you have to see a doctor," Aunt Helen said, "you might as well see a handsome one like Brock."

I asked Colonel Willborn how his book on observation balloons was coming. Though he was not in actuality a colonel, he had served in the First World War, as a lieutenant in a trench-mortar platoon. This and the fact that he was a military history buff were enough, in the imagination of somebody, to bestow on him the title of colonel.

"I wrote the three-hundred-and-twenty-seventh page just this morning," he said, cheerfully. "I wonder where my granddaughter ran off to. I promised her one of these if she would lead us in saying the Pledge of Allegiance." He fished a Susan B. Anthony dollar out of his Bermudas.

Vern Seybold put a suntanned arm on the Colonel's shoulder and said, "A Carter quarter, eh, Colonel? Give the pump boy one of these for a dollar's worth of gas and he'll ask for three more."

Out in the yard, I saw two small boys circling a hackberry, knocking on the trunk with sticks, as if the tree contained a secret that it was bound to yield. Then a firecracker went off, and the boys sprinted toward the back of the house, as if summoned.

I looked at Mary Lee, who was talking to Mrs. Willborn at the other end of the porch. Mrs. Willborn was inspecting the swelling on Mary Lee's upper left arm, where a bee had stung her earlier in the day, when she was taking a nap. She'd put wet baking soda on the sting hole. When I'd told her that I'd seen the bee that had stung her flying around the kitchen that morning, she'd said, "That bee died. I swatted him. The one that got me was his buddy or something."

Mary Lee had come to the party without Hal, who had gone downtown to his office after we played tennis. He'd beaten me, after trailing 1-6, 0-3. At that point, he'd removed his T-shirt, soaked his head with water, and said, "This is it, Pedro. This is your stop." He continued to hit me his usual stuff—dinks and lobs, junkballs that died in the red clay—and, as if on cue, I began to pound the ball into the net and over the lines. I started to mumble to myself. At one point, in what I suppose was an effort to turn the tide, I asked Hal how Mary Lee would react when he told her about the hygienist.

He picked up my blue Tigers cap, which I'd taken off at the beginning of the third set to change my luck, and put it on his head. "She probably won't kiss me," he said, "and she probably won't spike my milk with Drano. Something in between, I'd guess."

"You think she'll forgive you?" I picked at the strings on my wood Dunlop. I needed a new racket.

"Who ever really forgives anybody? If forgiving is forgetting." Hal took off my cap and adjusted the tab so that the cap was one size larger. Then he put it back on. "I can't say I ever really forgave you for not standing up to Harris Diehl."

"That was over ten years ago," I said. "Jesus."

"That's my point," he said. He tapped the net with his old Kramer. The burn scar on his shoulder looked livid. "Have you ever forgiven me for taking Mary Lee from you?"

"You didn't take her from me. I never had her."

"If you say so," Hal said. "Your serve."

I WENT INTO the Colonel's house to get my mother another glass of iced tea. The hall was cool. There was a vase of flowers on the table next to the settee, where Hal and my ex-girlfriend had sat the previous Christmas. A clock the shape of Napoleon's hat ticked ponderously. I went into the kitchen. Bernice, the Willborns' help, was sitting at a table, reading the paper, her coal-black cheek in her palm.

"Happy Fourth of July, Bernice."

"Yessir," Bernice said. "You need something?"

"I can get it, thanks." I got my mother's tea and a beer for myself, and then went into the dining room. On the table were cold chicken and Benedictine sandwiches and Willie's cucumber soup and a flag cake. Mary Lee's deviled eggs were gone, and all that was left of her braided loaf of bread was a heel. I ate the bread and a chicken wing and a piece of Willie's peach pie. I ate the pie while watching a fly go from dish to dish like a single-engine puddle hopper.

A dark-haired boy entered the dining room, the heat of the day on his solemn face. He was one of the boys who'd been circling the hackberry, one of the Stringhams' grandchildren. He filled the pockets of his shorts with cookies and departed. Some portion of the light in the room seemed to go with him. I heard voices on the porch, everybody saying the Pledge of Allegiance, the words coming in clumps of three and four. Then I heard a shriek, a "Lordy!" When I got out to the porch, I saw Cato sitting in front of my mother, his black nose glistening, his speckled brow furrowed, as if he were waiting for her to clarify something. Mary Lee was holding Cato by the collar. Next to the hassock on which my mother's leg rested was a dead rabbit; its head was missing.

My mother had her hand near her heart. Mary Lee tugged at Cato's collar and dragged him off the porch.

"Will somebody get rid of it, please? Peter?" My mother looked at me as if I were somehow responsible for the corpse.

News of the dead rabbit had traveled back to the kitchen, and Bernice appeared with a dustpan and whisk broom.

"All you need to do now," Aunt Helen said, blowing smoke upward, "is skin it and throw it in a pot with some rosemary."

"I'd like to skin that fool dog," my mother said.

"I ate roasted *lapin* in a trench near Saint-Mihiel," Colonel Willborn said. "It was tough as nails. Made me appreciate the corn willie."

I pushed the rabbit into the dustpan with the broom. Its weight surprised me. I had an idea that it would be mere fluff, as light as air. Without its head it seemed phantasmal.

"The garbage barrel is around back, sweetie," Mrs. Willborn said.

I walked around the side of the house with the rabbit, holding the dustpan out in front of me like an offertory plate. The sunlight had dimmed; storm clouds were piling up to the west. The cookie thief and his friend were crouched in the driveway, flanking a bent-over figure in a red T-shirt. Hal. Laid out before them in a row were a coffee can, an aluminum pie plate, and a straw hat, the one that, judging by its tattered condition, belonged to my mother. Hal was unwrapping a pack of firecrackers.

"We're about to conduct a scientific experiment," Hal said. "What you got there?"

"A former rabbit. Cato caught it and brought my mother the remains. Laid it right at her feet."

"Cato can be so thoughtful sometimes." Hal put the pack of

firecrackers underneath the coffee can, arranging it so that the fuse was exposed to the air.

The cookie thief touched the rabbit with a finger. "Why did Cato eat the head?" he asked.

"Maybe he didn't eat it," I said. "Maybe he just chewed it off. Where'd you get the hat, Hal?"

"My assistants found it over there behind the garage," Hal said. He had put another pack of firecrackers under the pie pan, and now he put a third pack inside the hat, pulling the fuse out through a rip in the crown. "What we're going to do here, in case you haven't figured it out, is see how high each of these objects will jump when you light a bunch of firecrackers under them. My friend Robbie proposed the experiment."

Robbie was the other boy. He had light hair that stood on end, almost like pins in a cushion. "It'll be cool," he said.

Hal rose from his knees, wobbling slightly. "Whoa," he said. He took his cigarettes out of his shorts.

"That's my mother's hat," I said. The cookie thief gave me a funny look, as if he found this assertion odder (or perhaps less interesting) than the fact that I was holding a decapitated rabbit in a dustpan.

"I remember now you told me about the hat. Cato stole it, right?" Hal lit a cigarette. "I can see that sentiment is about to get in the way of science. I'll tell you what. I'll trade you the hat for the bunny. What do you say, boys? Shall we see if the rabbit can jump without its head?"

Both boys glanced at Hal but said nothing. Hal took a long drag on his cigarette. As he sucked in smoke, his narrow face seemed to narrow further, and some part of him I liked seemed to fade from view.

Hal watched me as I leaned down to pick up the hat and tried to keep the rabbit from sliding off the dustpan. I felt like a busboy.

"Get any work done at the office?"

"It's hard to say," Hal said. "You're not being very festive, Pedro."

In my head, I leaped on Hal, ground his face into the pavement, ignored the pleas of the boys to let him up. What I actually did was walk toward the garage, hat and rabbit in hand, and utter a halfhearted "Fuck you." One of the boys giggled.

I slid the rabbit into an empty trash can and then placed the hat over the corpse—the magician's assistant disposing of a butchered trick. Firecrackers popped. I watched Hal stagger around, jerk himself this way and that, as if he were a TV cowboy being pumped full of lead. "They got me, boys," he shouted amid the explosions. "Long live the revolution!"

"Long live the revolution," the two boys yelled, not quite in unison.

WHEN THE RAIN STOPPED, I told my mother I was going to take a walk. She was watching a music program on TV—Leonard Bernstein in a white jacket, tossing his head like a wild horse. "Lock the doors, please," she said.

The air was even thicker than it had been twelve hours earlier. Water dripped from trees, and vapor rose from the pavement. I heard fireworks in the distance, and saw, over toward the river, a fizzle of red sparks. The sky was cloudy, starless. Whatever was beyond the clouds—meteors, planets, wayward spaceships—was only to be guessed at.

I lit the joint Willie had saved from the laundry, and walked down Redbud Lane. In my pocket I had two of the bottle rockets I'd purchased in Indiana. Perhaps I'd shoot them off.

The Hazeletts were burning up electricity, but I didn't see Hal or Mary Lee. I walked on down the road, past Colonel Willborn's house, which was dark, except for a porch light. The flag had been taken down. In the morning, the Colonel would raise the flag again and write the three-hundred-and-twenty-eighth page of his book on observation balloons.

A frog squatted at the edge of a puddle in the road. As I watched the frog think its frog thoughts, riffle through the maps imprinted on its frog brain, and consider where to hop to next, rain began to fall again. I heard thunder, and then I heard, nearby, a car accelerating, the engine rattling badly as it rushed toward its limit. I turned my head slowly, in the manner of a stoned person who has been looking at a frog for too long, but it was soon enough to see that the car hurrying toward me was Hal's Vega, that it didn't have its lights on, that the thing sticking out the passenger window was Cato's head. I felt the angry sucking whoosh of the car as it went by me—the same instant that I saw Cato's muzzle and Hal's profile, as sharp as a face on a coin. He was looking straight ahead, aiming for I knew not what. Some moments later, I felt the rain on my skin, saw the taillights of the Vega come on, saw the frog squatting at the edge of the road. The frog had jumped.

Walking back up the road through the drizzle and Hal's exhaust, I felt that there must be more air than was natural between my feet and the road. I looked at my sneakers, saw them touch the pavement periodically, saw them mount the front steps to Mary Lee's house, saw them halt in the front hall, not far from a rawhide dog bone as big as a clown's bow tie. I called out Mary Lee's name, dilating the double e so her name would stretch around corners. I heard a fan spinning, the refrigerator humming. Mary Lee wasn't in the kitchen, or in the living room, where the fan spun, or on the porch. I looked into the downstairs bedroom that she used as an office. Above her desk was a map of the Roman Empire at the time of the Punic Wars, and on the desk was a picture of Hal with his back to the blue Aegean, his arms upraised in a Nixonian V. They'd gone to Greece on their honeymoon, barely a year ago.

I walked up the stairs, a hand on the banister, which was sticky in the humid air. I remembered climbing these stairs as a boy one Sunday after church—Colonel Willborn's cousin had invited us for lunch—and finding, in a room at the end of the hall, a half dozen parakeets in cages that hung from ceiling hooks. The birds were blue and green and yellow, and they were jabbering like mad, and I thought that it might be interesting to release them from their cages. But it was only a thought. I was a cautious child, not the sort of person who would turn other people's birds loose. Instead, I looked at a magazine published by a naturist society— naked people playing volleyball and eating corn on the cob at a picnic table.

At the top of the stairs, I turned right, away from the room where the parakeets had been. I knocked on the door at the end of the hall.

"Mary Lee? It's Peter." I put my ear to the door but heard nothing. Why would she have shut her door? "Mary Lee? What're you doing?"

"Reading. What're you doing here, Peter?" If she felt any alarm at my presence, she hid it. There was a hint of irritation in her voice—I'd interrupted her reading, perhaps—but there was nothing to suggest that her husband had just left the house in an apparent rage or that I had arrived just as suddenly. Except the closed door.

"Are you OK?" What would I see if I looked through the keyhole?

"I'm trying to decide whether I should teach Catullus to my fourth-year students. How would they react to this, do you think? 'O you fruit Thallus, softer than a little furry bunny, or a baby goose's marrow, or a teensy little ear lobe, or an old guy's limp prick.' He wrote that in catalectic iambic tetrameter, an unusual meter for him."

I ignored her question. "What did Hal say to you?"

"When?"

"Just now. Before he drove away like a lunatic with his lights off and missed hitting me by the length of one hair approximately."

"He said he was going to the store to buy cigarettes and a carton of milk. We're low on milk." Had Hal not told Mary Lee about his dental hygienist, or was she simply pretending that all was well, refusing to admit to me that she'd chosen the wrong boy to be in love with?

"Are you OK?" she asked.

"I nearly got squished five minutes ago and now I'm talking to you through a door." My tongue felt thick. I was squatting, having descended to that position almost without noticing it. My eye was at the level of the keyhole, but not square with it.

Mary Lee said nothing. The keyhole was a circle on top of a truncated triangle. A bald woman in a long, flaring skirt was one way of looking at it. Or a nun, simplified.

"What if I stayed here," I said, "until Hal comes back. From visiting his girlfriend."

"You should go home, Peter," she said.

I heard a click—a lamp being turned off?—and I felt myself move sideways and, in violation of whatever decency I still possessed, put my eye to the keyhole. The click notwithstanding, a bedside table lamp was on. Mary Lee was sitting up in bed. The light fell on her legs and on the book splayed on her thigh and on her hands folded at her waist. She was wearing a white T-shirt that stopped just below her crotch. She was looking at me or, rather, at the door behind which I crouched, unable to get up and go away. I felt that she saw me more clearly than I saw her. In her gaze, in the set of her mouth, was contempt: I was less worthy of pity than a dog whimpering to come in. And then she sat forward and pulled the T-shirt over her head and said, "Is this it, Peter? Isn't this all you want from me?"

"No," I said, rising quickly from my crouch, reaching for the doorknob to steady myself. Coins and a bottle rocket spilled from my pocket and clattered on the floor. "No," I said again, walking away, leaving the mess where it had fallen.

WHEN MY AUNT HELEN DIED, in May of 1991, of lung cancer, I drove home for the funeral. I was living in Wisconsin with my wife and our three-year-old son. We'd moved there from New York. I was a full-time househusband, and I was happy to have the funeral as an excuse to leave my duties and the still unthawed ground of Wisconsin.

I didn't get home often, and when I did, I didn't often see old acquaintances, at least not on purpose. Once, in the mid-eighties, I'd run into Ben Panitz at the hospital where my mother had gone for knee surgery. Ben was a hematologist. He looked very much like the wary, chubby boy who had hauled a satchel through Burrell's drab halls, except that now he had a bristly mustache and a beeper. His tie was askew and he was distant.

I'd seen Mary Lee from afar a few times in the early eighties, before she sold her house. I saw her pushing a mower across her lawn and I saw her at Winn-Dixie, holding cantaloupes to her nose, testing them for ripeness. I watched her until she found the melon she wanted. A few years later, I sent her a Christmas card, a photograph of my new plump son in red pajamas and an elf's cap. I thought the picture of Louis would redeem me in her eyes, somehow. I sent the card to an address in Nashville, where she was supposed to be living with her former Buber professor. But the card came back, chewed up, looking as if a dog had tried to open it.

I saw Colonel Willborn at the service for Aunt Helen. He was using a walker. He was uncertain who I was. I told him that I had a copy of his book on observation balloons—it had been privately printed—and he said, "Isn't that nice!"

After the service, I drove downtown to the offices of the *Lip*, an alternative weekly. Hal Hazelett was the editor. The paper was in a dowdy section of town, not far from the old Sultan's Gate burlesque theater, which was now a former disco, and next door to Victor's Costumes & Notions. A mannequin wearing a Ronald

Reagan mask was dressed up in an astronaut's suit, an arrow through the helmet, a "Me Worry?" sign at its feet.

I hadn't seen Hal in a dozen years, not since the night he nearly ran over me. I'd sent him a wedding invitation, but he hadn't bothered to regret. At some point, I'd heard that he'd taken a leave of absence from the *Independent* to go to Nicaragua to write a book about the revolution. Then I'd heard from my mother that he'd been fired from the *Independent* and had joined A.A. "Not that it's improved his disposition much," she said. "I saw him the other day at this place on Frankfort Avenue, where I was having lunch with my prayer group, and he looked right through me, I swear."

Hal was busy when I arrived. I took a seat in the gray-carpeted reception area, beneath a satellite photo of Louisville, and read an article in an old issue of the *Lip* entitled "War Fever in Big Lou." A lawyer, a man who had been one grade ahead of Hal and me at Burrell, was quoted as saying, "I think we should bomb the bejesus out of Baghdad."

When Hal didn't emerge from his office after thirty minutes, I asked the receptionist, a young woman wearing a tie-dyed T-shirt that looked like astral matter flying apart, if I should come back later. She put down a copy of *People* and said, "It's up to you."

"Do you know what he's doing?"

"He's writing something. He has a deadline." She looked me over. I was still in my funeral clothes, minus the tie. "You're a friend of his, didn't you say?"

"We went to school together."

"I'll go take a peek," she said, and walked off down a hall. I stood by a window from which a section of the river was visible between buildings. I saw the Palmolive soap clock on the other side, on the Indiana shore. When I was a child, the clock, with its huge glowing dial, had seemed as profound as the moon. Now, of course, it seemed otherwise.

Hal came down the hall, trailing cigarette smoke. His mouth was concealed by his graying mustache, but he was unable to hide his annoyance. Work, the burden of being a journalist, lay heavily on his shoulders. I saw him trying to estimate how much of his time I was going to take.

"Hey," I said. My heart beat fast, like a dog waiting for a pat, a kindness, a bone.

"Hey," he said.

Succor

I was walking in my landlord's woods—fifty acres of mature up-
land broadleaf forest, all of it posted and none of it for sale, as he
liked to say—when I saw a man sitting on a windfallen tree. He
wore a dark blue jogging suit. His hair was black and shiny, like a
grackle's feathers, and it raced away from his forehead. He sat
straight-backed, palms on thighs, chin tilted up, as if to better receive the sunlight that passed through the budding maples and
ashes. It was a mid-March morning, cool and breezy, but not so
cool that you couldn't smell spring awakening under the mats of
damp leaves.

Now and then, people from Loomis, the detox facility down the
road, wandered onto my landlord's property, and I thought that
this man, sitting so erectly on the fallen tree, might have come
from there. Perhaps he was meditating, listening to the sound of
the traffic on the Taconic, a half mile to the east, or to the cardinal
singing *What cheer, what, what, what.* He sat perfectly still, and
yet his stillness seemed effortful, as if he were trying to suppress
some disturbance within himself. I don't know how long I
watched him before he turned his head toward me.

"Good morning!" he said. This greeting had the ring of a
proclamation.

"Good morning." I stayed where I was, amid a cluster of maple saplings.

"Well, we agree," he said. "I might go further and say it's a beautiful morning." He had a large voice; it ate up the space between us. "But then I'm partial to sunlight. Sunlight is a natural mood enhancer, if you know what I mean."

"You from around here?" I asked. He didn't sound like a native; it was the way those *I*'s hung in the cool air, like Southern vowels come north.

"If you mean, have I escaped from the drunk farm down the road, the answer is no." He crossed his legs. He was wearing blue canvas sneakers and no socks. "Though my ex-wife once recommended I spend some time there."

I assumed that meant he was local, if not necessarily native, but I didn't pursue the distinction. The walk I'd begun minutes before seemed to have come to an end, and I wanted to return to the house—to my one-year-old son and his baby-sitter, whose voices had driven me outdoors in the first place.

"I used to live nearby." He indicated west with his head. "By the Bible college." I knew the college; it was there, in fact, that Claire and I had found the baby-sitter, Martha, who now spelled me a couple of days a week, long enough that I could fiddle at writing. "In the settlement, my ex-wife got the house and the dogs and I got the Saab that just died out on 144. You can see it through the brush."

I couldn't see the car from my position, but I took his word for it.

"I was on my way to the barbershop when the goddamn thing conked out," he said. He scratched his face. "So then, you see, I thought I'd try to calm down, and I found this seat in Mr. Trempleau's woods. I'm the kind of person who ignores posted signs."

"You know Trempleau?" My landlord built strip malls around the country. He was known locally for underwriting a campaign to get taxpayer-funded condoms out of the schools.

"I know *of* him," the man said. He rose and moved toward me. He was short, perhaps five-eight. His jogging suit concealed his weight.

"Larry Hale," he said, gripping my hand. I didn't grip back. I looked at his face—the pouches under his watery blue eyes, the long, doggy nose, the wide mouth, the more-than-overnight stubble growing on his cheeks and in the creases around his mouth. The lines in his forehead, which his slicked-back hair brought into such startling relief, suggested a man who took some pleasure in feeding his despair. I guessed that he was somewhere between fifty and sixty.

"And you are?" He smelled faintly of cologne—yesterday's, possibly.

"Peter Sackrider."

"Peter Sackrider, Peter Sackrider," he said, practically chanting it. "It sounds like a literary name, almost."

Was he suggesting that it was made up? I pushed aside a clump of leaves with my sneaker. I was ready for spring; it couldn't come too soon.

"So you're either a trespasser like me," Larry Hale said, "or you're one of Trempleau's friends."

"I'm his tenant."

"But not his friend. Nor a button-down Republican, if appearances are any guide. Which they aren't, always."

I wore an old sweater and jeans that had been roomy before I gave up smoking. My hair was on the long side; in fact, I hadn't had it cut since leaving my magazine job in the city, shortly before Christmas.

"Would you mind if I used your telephone? I should see about getting my car towed."

He watched me hesitate. But I'd been raised to be polite, and while I sometimes regretted being so, I wasn't often able to turn away from panhandlers or windbags or distressed souls. I was a soft touch, though not really a nice one.

As I led Larry Hale back through the woods, he whistled a few bars of something cheerful from another era. Was it "On the Sunny Side of the Street"?

"You play golf?" Larry asked. We were at the edge of the woods, next to a stand of staghorn sumac, within view of Trempleau's pond and, fifty yards farther on, the house my wife and I rented.

"A little." I heard a peeper calling from the pond and another responding and then there was a great swelling of sound: hundreds of male frogs fluting, their throat sacs ballooning as they laid claim to patches of mud and water.

"I have my clubs in the car," he said. "I was hoping to go to that range up the Taconic and hit a few after I visited my barber." He slewed into a golfer's stance. He bent his knees and wiggled his hips and took a phantom swing, then pretended to follow his shot into the feathery, almost-spring-blue sky. "When you hit one cleanly, it's as sweet as sex."

I said nothing, not wishing to encourage him. I'd played enough golf to know what he meant, but I thought the comparison was imprecise.

"Close, anyway," he said, and walked over to the edge of the pond and squatted there. I saw a rip in the seat of his pants, a slice of white underwear. The frogs were trilling wildly.

"That's a rapturous sound, don't you think?"

I looked toward my house, a caretaker's bungalow that Trempleau had built from a kit some years ago. Was it safe to bring Larry inside with my child and our Bible college baby-sitter? Well, I had to admit that I found it difficult to resist a man who was so unguarded in his response to spring peepers. I loved their sound too. It unloosed something in me.

A breeze came up and ruffled the pond, momentarily hushing

the peepers. Larry rose from his squat and seemed to wobble as he did. He walked toward me, the nylon of his jogging suit making a little rustling sound. His face was pale, drained of color. He looked ill. "I wonder if I might trouble you for a glass of water." He put his hand on my arm. "The medication I take makes me dizzy sometimes. And dry mouthed."

I didn't ask him what the medication was, but he told me anyway. "My doctor has me on some experimental antidepressant whose name I couldn't pronounce even if my tongue wasn't sticking to the roof of my mouth. It's supposed to smooth me out, you see. And then I take something for my prostate, which plays havoc with my sex life." He smiled; his teeth were lusterless but straight.

We walked across the yard, past the vegetable plot that I'd failed to turn over last fall, past the hammock I'd just strung up, past the cat snoozing in the sunlight. I took Larry into the kitchen and poured him a glass of water, and then I went to find Louis and Martha. They were on the futon in Louis's room. Louis was asleep, though his fisted hands suggested he hadn't gone gently. Martha was next to him, reading a textbook, underlining passages with a yellow marker. The room smelled of diaper-rash ointment and poop. I gave Martha a "just checking" wave and she waved back. She had milkmaid's skin and long brown hair that was parted down the center of her head. My wife said she could imagine Martha dressed in one of those bonnets that tie under the chin, churning butter. She was from a small town upstate; her father owned a Christmas-tree farm. She was competent and handy. Once, when I was trying to fix a leaky faucet, she told me I'd bought the wrong kind of washer. "You need an O-ring, Mr. Sackrider."

I pulled the door shut. Larry, having satisfied his thirst, asked to use the toilet. I showed him the bathroom and sat down at the desk in the bedroom across the hall and looked at the insertion point blinking on my computer screen. I was working on a piece of Sunday-supplement fluff about a man who carved shorebirds out of basswood. The sentences I'd written sat there like fat geese waiting to be shot.

I listened to Larry Hale move his bowels. This—gaseous sighs and explosions mixed with groans and, once, "Oh, sweet Jesus!"—went on for an eternity. I went back out to the kitchen, but I could hear him from there, too.

I looked up *Larry Hale* in the phone book and found two *Hale, Lawrences*, both of whom lived in neighboring villages. One lived at an address that also had a children's phone and the other at a place called the Sleepy Hollow Arms.

Larry flushed the toilet and then turned on the sink tap. Above the flow of water, I heard him singing. It sounded like a tune from the liturgy—"For you alone are the holy one"?—something I'd mumbled halfheartedly on those occasions when I went to church. When he emerged from the bathroom, he said, "Now that I've put my troubles behind me, I can get on with my life." He grinned.

"You want to call the wrecker now?"

First, he called his barber. While he was talking, jiggling the keys in his pocket, Martha came into the living room to get her purse. He put his hand over the mouthpiece and said, "Good morning!" His face suggested that the room had just filled with the most amazing sunlight.

Martha looked at me as if to ask if Larry was a friend of mine and then said, "Hi."

"I'm sorry I didn't get to speak with your bride more," he said later, when I led him outdoors.

"She's the baby-sitter." Did he actually think Martha, who was almost twenty years younger, was my bride?

"Right," Larry said. The chimes Claire had hung in the crab-

apple tree tinkled in the breeze. "Well, thanks for giving me succor." He held out his hand. "Perhaps we can play golf sometime."
He headed down the driveway, all loose and jaunty inside his jogging suit. Over his shoulder, he said, "I'll call."

That night Claire informed me that a favorite necklace of hers,
a little silver Byzantine cross she'd bought in Ravenna many years
ago, was missing. The clasp had broken that morning, when she
was getting ready to go to work. She'd left it in the bathroom. I
said, "We'll find it," not wishing to alarm her and say that a strange
man had been in our house.

On Good Friday, which in that year (1989) fell at the
end of March, I drove into Haverskill to do some shopping. Claire
had given me a list: Pampers, toilet plunger, liquor, lamb for
Easter dinner. On the way back, I was supposed to pick up Martha,
so that Claire and I could go out to dinner with some of her academic friends. She taught French and Italian at a private school in
the north Bronx.

The sky was a mousy color and rain was in the air, but the tulips
planted at the base of the war memorial were blooming, standing
at attention like soldiers in busbies. And there on the bench, fac-
ing west toward the railroad station and the river beyond, was
Larry Hale. He was wearing his navy-blue jogging suit and had a
briefcase alongside him.

I parked at the other end of River Street, in front of the Spotted
Dog, a downscale bar, not the kind of place that, despite its prox-
imity to the railroad, drew commuting attorneys or magazine edi-
tors. I walked past the bar's glass-brick windows and went on to the
market, where I bought a three-pound leg of lamb. I assumed this
would be more than enough to feed Claire and me and my Aunt
Vi. I bought fresh mint—or as fresh as it could be after having
been shipped a thousand miles north. I thought I'd make mint

juleps for my aunt, a fellow Kentuckian, who believed in having at least one stiff drink a day. I bought bourbon at Camilli's and a plunger at the hardware store, then carried the load back to the car. It had begun to rain. Larry was leaning against the yellow-brick facade of the Spotted Dog, unsheltered from the drizzle, briefcase in hand.

"Buy you a drink?" he said. "A Good Friday pick-me-up?"

The idea that I wouldn't see Larry again after our meeting in Trempleau's woods hadn't occurred to me. Every time the phone had rung over the past couple of weeks, I'd imagined it would be him—though why would he call if he'd stolen Claire's necklace? I'd dreamed about him, and once, after spending an hour or so with Louis at the war memorial watching the trains come and go, I'd driven toward Grevey's Landing and found the Sleepy Hollow Arms, a former tourist court on a bluff above the river, just up-stream from the nuclear power plant. An old, pale green Saab—Larry's, apparently, resuscitated—was parked in front of a cabin topped off by a large television aerial. On both sides of the cabin were parasol-shaped clotheslines, one of which was festooned with underwear.

"I'm on my way to the barber's," I said weakly, realizing mid-sentence that I wasn't going to lose Larry with this fiction.

"It wouldn't hurt you to lose a little weight up there," he said, touching his own hair, which shone with droplets of rain. His cheeks were cleanly shaven, though this only seemed to expose his haggardness further. Was it pity or a lack of courage that led me to decide that I wasn't going to ask Larry about Claire's necklace?

"I'm starting to look like a derelict or something," I said.

"Frowzy, maybe," Larry said.

I shifted the packages in my arms. I remembered that I was supposed to buy Pampers.

"You're going to Aldo's, I take it," Larry said.

"Yeah." There were a couple of unisex salons in the village, but only one barbershop.

I put my packages in the Corolla. We went back up River Street, past the war memorial, past the hippie crafts shop and the used-book store presided over by a crank and his throw-rug-size cats. Walking with Larry, whose pace would have seemed leisurely even if it hadn't been raining, I had a memory of being ushered to the barbershop by my father when I was old enough to go by myself. My father's slow, Southern dad's pace as we walked from the car to Mr. DuPree's four-chair shop concealed his determination to see that none of the hairs hanging over the rims of my ears should go unclipped.

I said, "I used to get my hair cut in the city at an Israeli shop. In the Diamond District. By a woman named Dani."

"I used to go to the barbershop in the basement of the Waldorf," Larry said. "But that was an expense I had to give up, along with dry cleaning." He held the door to Aldo's open for me; his eyebrows rose solicitously. *"Per piacere."*

It was warm inside, much warmer than the mild, damp air outside. An electric heater hummed in the corner and gave off a fried-wires smell that mixed with the aroma of cigarettes and hair-treatment chemicals. A man was seated in a barber's chair, his chin on his chest.

"Aldo," Larry said, shutting the belled door hard, jarring Aldo from his nap. "I brought you a customer. Time to rise and shine."

"I am rising," Aldo said, dismounting from the chair, smoothing his barber's white tunic, adjusting his steel-rimmed spectacles. He was a short man, like Larry, though he was also thinner, springier. He seemed to skip most of the intermediate stage between sleep and wakefulness. "Please," he said to me, holding his hand toward the padded, red-leather throne he'd just gotten out of. I climbed on, feeling like a child.

Larry sat down across from me and placed the briefcase on his knees, then folded his hands on top like a commuter settling in for the ride.

"This is my friend Peter Sackrider," he said. "He rescued me the other day when my car broke down."

"You should sell that jalopy," Aldo said. "Buy American." He gave me his hand, which was moist and warm. "Pleased."

"You have ten thousand you can lend me, Aldo?" Larry popped the latches on his briefcase. "Dollars. Not lire."

Aldo shook out a sheet and let it float down around me. He fastened it at the nape. "You should work for me, Larry. Be a barber. I'll make you a partner. You can write your books at night."

Larry took a medicine bottle out of his briefcase and unscrewed the cap. He swallowed the pill—for his head? prostate?—without a lubricant. "I'm an old horse, Aldo," Larry said, "and you know what they say about old horses."

"That they should be put out to stud?" Aldo wrapped a scratchy collar around my neck.

"Ho ho," Larry said. He latched the briefcase and set it on the floor.

"What do you write?" I asked.

"Trash mostly, though not exclusively or intentionally." I noticed the Southern slant in his voice again, *trash* having been drawled to where you could almost detect a scent. I also noticed that he hadn't told me what he wrote.

"You ever see the ad for that soda drink called Thwack?" Aldo asked, combing my hair, trying to find the part. "Where you hear this voice say 'Polly wants a Thwack! Polly wants a Thwack!'? And then you see this pretty girl in a parrot suit on a trapeze and a man flying toward her with a six-pack of the stuff? Larry wrote that."

I hadn't seen the ad or heard of the drink.

"The product bombed," Larry said. "It wasn't the first I handled that bombed. I was shown the door by some young asshole in suspenders and a Road Runner tie."

"You get severance pay?" I thought Larry had fallen rather hard for a big-time New York advertising man, but perhaps he was omitting some key facts.

"Not enough," Larry said.

Aldo flexed the scissors rapidly. "You want me to trim it to the top of the ears? Or more?"

"Top," I said.

"Maybe his wife likes it long," Larry said, getting up from his chair and walking toward the back of the shop. The rip in his jogging pants seemed to have widened. He had exchanged his old blue tennis shoes for espadrilles, which added a Continental touch to his dilapidation. He disappeared through a doorway.

"You see Larry a lot?" I asked Aldo.

"I cut his hair and we play a little golf."

"He lost his job just because of that soft-drink ad?" I assumed he must have made other errors along the way, not necessarily creative ones.

"Larry doesn't like to wear suits. He's *anticonformista*, you know."

My hair slid down the sheet, collecting in a trough at my belly. The idea of getting my hair cut short suddenly appealed to me. It would be *anticonformista* — or different, anyway. I thought it might please Claire, too. "You can cut it short," I said.

"Short like my putting green?" he said, thumbing the receding silvery filaments that lay on his skull in a kind of arrowhead pattern. "Or not so?"

"About like your putting green," I said boldly.

I listened to the sound of the clippers, the buzz of the electric heater. Then I heard the toilet flushing, and when that subsided, voices speaking Italian. Larry's Italian was fractured but ardent. The other voice was a woman's. Perhaps it was Aldo's wife's.

Larry returned, bearing a small tray, a tea towel draped over his arm. "Your mother prepared a snack for us, Aldo." On the tray were three juice glasses and a bowl of Ritz Bits. From his briefcase Larry produced a bottle of ouzo. "Just the thing for a gloomy Good Friday afternoon, don't you think?"

Aldo abstained, but I took a glass, and before I'd swallowed half of it, I'd agreed to play golf with Larry on Saturday afternoon. (Aldo begged off; he had to drive his mother somewhere.) Aldo handed me a mirror, and I observed the back of my head as the ouzo washed through me like a bitter home remedy. Then he turned the chair around, and I saw that even though I'd been relieved of a lot of hair I still had my face. More of it, in fact. My forehead, exposed now like something long beneath a rock, seemed wanton.

"You look like a new man," Larry said. He was pretending to swing a golf club; he was already into his second ouzo. "Like somebody I used to know."

"Jack Nicklaus before he let his hair grow out? Fat Jack?" A year or so before, when I smoked thirty cigarettes a day, I'd been thin.

"No. Somebody from long ago. Some boy I knew in Baltimore. A drinking buddy."

"You're from Baltimore?"

"Kentucky. Versailles, Kentucky. Just down the road from Paris." He said those names with a heavy mid-Kentucky accent, to let me know, I gathered, that he was only formerly a hick.

When he asked where I was from, I said Kentucky too. I didn't want to be from the same state as Larry, but in this case I wasn't able to tell a lie.

"I don't hear any Kentucky in your speech at all," Larry said.

"It comes out when I go back."

"A chameleon," Larry said. "Well, damn."

• • •

CLAIRE SAT ON the edge of the bed in her underwear, holding her little Byzantine cross, which had been returned with the fastener fixed. According to Martha, Larry had come by the house while Claire and I were out to dinner. Martha's arms were full of Louis when she answered the door. She said she'd recognized Larry right away—the pallor, the black, stiff hair, the grubby jogging suit. She said he smelled of booze. And when he'd handed her a small brown envelope with the necklace in it, he'd pressed his thumb into her wrist, at the pulse point, and told her that she reminded him of a girl in a painting, a Dutch farm scene. He said the painting was in the Metropolitan. And then Louis, as if sensing Martha's fear, had started to cry, and Larry had stumbled back out into the rain.

"I'm trying to figure this out," Claire said. "You let this guy, this Larry Something, use the phone and he steals my necklace and then two weeks later he brings it back with the clasp repaired?"

"Apparently." But I was a little puzzled, as well as a little drunk.

"How come you didn't tell me about him?" One of the camisole straps had slid off her shoulder. She was a small-boned woman, with beautiful black, curly hair that she kept short.

"I didn't want you to worry about it," I said, gazing at the ridges of her collarbone beneath her olivey skin. Back when she was a tomboy living in suburban Chicago, she'd fallen out of a birch, from which she could see Lake Michigan, and fractured her collarbone. The cross, with its flared arms, would lie in the hollow where the ridges met. The cross didn't have any religious significance for Claire—she was a lapsed Catholic—but it reminded her of a moment of happiness she'd had on one of her first trips to Italy. This was long before me.

"The man with a thousand secrets," Claire said, repeating a line she'd used before.

"A thousand and one. I saw the guy again this afternoon, in the village."

"On a stool in the Spotted Dog?"

"On a bench by the war memorial. Dozing. Dreaming fucked-up dreams, I'm sure." I went into the bathroom to get some Tylenol. I couldn't help observing that my eyes were bloodshot, the tip of my nose seemed to be inflamed, and my freshly clipped head looked like a bad decision. Once upon a time, I thought with the requisite self-pity, I was handsome and slender as a prince, suitably employed, a commuter with a *Times* in his satchel, and now I'm as puffy as a toad.

I got Claire's diaphragm out of the medicine cabinet—a new one, which she'd yet to try out; the old one had somehow sprung a leak—and went back into the bedroom with the device on my head, like a baby yarmulke. "Well, anyway," I said, "you got the necklace back. The guy even fixed it for you."

"And scared the bejesus out of poor Martha." She pulled up the strap of her camisole and went to the dresser, where she placed the cross and her eyeglasses. It was raining still; it pattered among the rhododendrons by the bedroom windows. I could smell the heavy earth in which they grew.

"Martha was OK about it," I said, defensively, removing the diaphragm from my head. I held it out to her, like something I'd found on the beach. "Here. I brought you a gift."

She gave me a weary look. "Who's going to get up at the crack of you-know-what?" Our son was an early riser.

"I'm your man." I undressed and lay on the bed. What was the thought process (if any) that had led Larry to return the necklace he'd stolen and then had had repaired (unless, of course, he'd fixed it himself)? At what point had guilt overtaken him? Why hadn't he just stuck the necklace in the mailbox or, if he felt compelled to make a show of his guilt, given it to me at the golf course tomorrow? Did he know that Claire and I were going to be out? While sipping ouzo at Aldo's, had I mentioned something about having to fetch a baby-sitter? If he'd come to the house simply to gaze at Martha and her milky, upstate farm-girl's skin, why had he brought the necklace?

Claire was astride me. I saw past her small breasts to her throat, her upraised chin, her sharp, serious nose. The way her head was turned slightly to the side suggested a lack of interest. But her hands were gripping me under my rib cage. I thought of Larry pressing his thumb into the tendons of Martha's wrist. I thought that if you tried to kiss a girl like Martha—if you were someone other than Larry Hale, that is—she would shut her eyes right away, as if in prayer, so that she could concentrate.

"All done, my speedy one?" Claire said, lowering her mouth to my ear.

"Yeah." My mouth was in her black hair, my hands on her hips. She'd proposed having a child for each hip, but I'd balked. "Sorry."

"*Fa niente*," she said. "Fuzzy." She kissed the top of my head.

"I invited Martha to Easter supper," I said. "She's not going home, for some reason."

"Just so you don't invite Larry the burglar." She rolled off me and pulled the sheet over herself.

"Why would I do that?"

"Only the sandman knows." I felt her body receding, withdrawing into itself. The rain continued to fall, plodding and mournful. I heard Trempleau's bluetick barking in his kennel. I thought of Martha lying in her dorm bed, unsure of what to make of the specter coming at her through the rain in her dream. I thought of Larry sitting in his underwear in his tourist-court shack, the lights blazing and the TV babbling, trying to remember if he'd taken that experimental antidepressant he couldn't pronounce.

● ● ●

I DROVE UP the Taconic to the Holly Tree Public Links. I didn't really believe that Larry would keep our date, and I wouldn't have known what to say to him if he had. ("Thanks for returning the necklace you stole"? "Thanks for not raping my baby-sitter"?) But the sunshine and the sky, purged of all but blue, made me feel blithe, so I waited for him outside the pro shop, watching men in two-toned FootJoys and slacks the color of Easter eggs take their turns on the first tee. Eventually, I went over to the driving range. I hit off a soiled plastic mat until I'd raised blisters on both hands. A few balls I hit squarely, and they flew in ideal arcs. I recalled Larry's opinion that a cleanly struck golf shot was as pleasurable as sex, and I thought again that he was off. Golf was harder, and the bliss that flooded you after a good shot could vanish the next moment, when, full of yourself, you hit the thing no farther than the piece of sod you ripped from the fairway.

I put my clubs in the Corolla and drove into Haverskill, where I had a grilled cheese and a beer at the Spotted Dog. I half-expected to see Larry there, trolling the gloom with his briefcase full of medicines and sheafs of whatever it was he wrote. Crappy mysteries? Pornography? Villanelles and sestinas? I ordered another beer and watched Fred Couples amble up a Florida fairway with the care of someone determined to hide his ambition from the world. I listened to two middle-aged women at the bar tell the bartender, also a woman, stories about their former husbands.

I went out into the sunshine. I had a mild, one-and-a-half-beer buzz, almost enough to impair my judgment. I could have gone home and lain in the hammock with my son and breathed my beery breath on his chubbiness. I could have started work on another Sunday-supplement article. But instead I got in my car and drove up along the Hudson toward the Sleepy Hollow Arms. I was going to tell Larry to stay clear of my family. At least, that's what I thought I was going to do.

Larry's pale green Saab was parked in front of his cabin; it looked more or less roadworthy. On a metal chair by the cabin's front door—a seat from which you could contemplate the broad, glistening Hudson and the stacks of the nuclear power plant—was a fuchsia, recently purchased from a local hothouse, judging by the price tag on the basket handle.

Larry didn't answer the door when I knocked, so I went around the side, past the clotheslines on which a single pair of men's briefs was clipped. Larry was in back, seated before a typewriter that was on a card table. The table also held a glass of water and a transistor radio that was playing an opera, possibly *Tosca*. Larry had shed his jogging suit and was wearing a T-shirt and Bermudas. The sun made the sheet of paper in the typewriter seem very bright.

"It's Peter Sackrider," Larry said, typing. He was using an IBM electric, which produced a militant rat-tat-tat that nonetheless sounded a bit antique. He'd run an extension cord through the bathroom window. "Come to have a word with me about a certain matter, I bet." He wasn't a pure touch typist; he watched his fingers strike the keys. "If I may just finish this paragraph."

I stood in the shade next to a propane tank, my hands in my pockets. Larry typed and a tenor bellowed his passion. I felt foolish standing there, but I wasn't able to move. I felt as if I were stuck inside somebody's sloggy dream, though whether it was mine or Larry's, I couldn't have said.

"How do you spell *sesquipedalianism?*" he asked. "As in, 'He was guilty of a multitude of sins, including sesquipedalianism.'" He turned down the radio.

I spelled it, obediently, like a child called upon in class.

"It's a five-dollar word, I know, but it's the *juste* one in this case."

I played with the tees in my pocket. "You must have forgotten our golf date."

"It slipped my mind," Larry said. He switched off the typewriter and turned in his chair, a dining room kind of chair. An imitation French piece? Perhaps it was one of the bones tossed to him in the divorce settlement.

"I woke up feeling like holy shit this morning," Larry said. "I could just about hear my eyes creak in their sockets when I moved them." He rubbed a dark cheek. "I borrow the image from Robert Penn Warren, a fellow Kentuckian, who, like you and me, left the dear old South for the chilly Northeast."

I remained silent. I thought there was a good chance that Larry would offer a confession. That was his style, after all.

"I was driving through your neighborhood last night," he said, "after an impromptu meeting with my ex-wife concerning some payments I'm behind on. Two of my children are undergoing expensive private educations at East Coast schools, and it's my duty, according to the court, to bankroll the sense of superiority that they acquire, or have affirmed, at these places. Anyway, I thought I'd stop by to see if you wanted to tip a few with me down at the Spotted Dog." He smiled. "May I get you a drink? I have everything you can imagine, even a collector's can of Thwack."

"No, thanks," I said. "I'm interested in the necklace, the cross — why you took it, why you returned it."

"I don't know what you're talking about," he said evenly.

"When you came by my house," I said, "you gave our baby-sitter my wife's necklace, which was stolen from our bathroom the day you and I met. You gave Martha the necklace while squeezing her wrist and telling her some bullshit about some painting."

Larry shifted in his chair, seeming to wince as he did. Perhaps, in addition to all his other problems, he had lower-back discomfort. "Some of what you describe is accurate enough," he said. "I don't recall what exactly I said to your Martha, though I do remember being moved by her beauty — the simple youth and unworldliness of her—and I suppose I got carried away to the extent that I grabbed her wrist. In fact, I'll admit that I would've liked to have plunked her right on your doorstep. But I didn't, as you know. And neither did I return this item you say I stole. Theft is one crime I haven't been accused of in a while. Not since 1948, when I stole a pack of firecrackers from Mr. Greenwell's in downtown Versailles."

"Well," I said, studying the black plastic garbage bag stuck in the Cyclone fence at the edge of the motor court property, the sun shining on it as intensely as on the river or the sheet of typing paper.

I looked back at Larry. He sat erect with his hands folded in his lap. All his weight was concentrated there, in his paunch, and in the pale, heavy loaves of his thighs. His shoulders and chest were narrow and his hairless shins tapered, piglike, to rather delicate-looking ankles and small feet in espadrilles. His stillness, his level but not quite smug gaze, made me look away again. I imagined he could see into me. I thought he was waiting for me to admit that we had things in common. Maybe he thought I'd keep him company as he pissed away his life here by the edge of the Hudson.

"Well," I said again.

"I wouldn't steal your property," Larry said.

I didn't know whether to believe him, but I accepted his repeated offer of a drink, perhaps out of politeness or thirst or a desire to see the interior of his cabin. Certainly I was thirsty. I tried the Thwack, a lemon-flavored cola that seemed to bore into the fillings in my teeth. Then I joined Larry in having a bourbon. I observed myself sinking into the sofa, which was covered with a bleak plaid material. We talked about books and fatherhood and Martha and Kentucky. Larry proposed we get together on Derby Day, and I hemmed and hawed. I saw how disappointed he'd be if I simply said no.

I PULLED THE car over near Trempleau's woods, a hundred yards short of the road that went up to his house and mine. Some of the maples had started to leaf out; they looked gauzy.

"Why are we stopping, Mr. Sackrider?" Aside from my son's pediatrician, a bow-tied old-school sort, Martha was the only person whom I regularly saw who addressed me as *Mister*. She said it without irony, as if age alone had conferred status on me.

"I need to ask you a question," I said. "About Friday night." I looked at the checks in her green-and-white cotton dress. It was a bit faded—something handed down, perhaps.

"I know what you're going to ask," she said, shifting the purse in her lap, looking forward. It was a breezy, somewhat overcast Easter, the sun a bleached disk with an enormous ring around it foreshadowing (I assumed) rain.

"It doesn't matter really," I said, ready to withdraw the question I hadn't yet asked, thinking that I saw her soft chin begin to crumple. "We feel you're an excellent baby-sitter. We like you very much. We'll just forget about the necklace." The *we* was editorial—I hadn't mentioned to Claire my meeting with Larry or the conclusion I'd come to that it was Martha who had pinched the necklace. Claire would've gotten rid of Martha.

Martha turned away, disappearing behind her hair, which fell straight as a curtain to her shoulders. She directed her words toward the far corner of the dashboard. She rambled and cried and some of what she said I didn't catch. I heard her say that it had taken her only a minute to repair the clasp on the necklace. It was a simple fold-over clasp. She was good at that kind of thing—fixing stuff, close work. Her father had taught her how to take an engine apart and put it back together again. She hadn't stolen anything since sixth grade, when she and this other girl, Donna, ripped off a bottle of cough syrup that Donna's brother had said would get them high. She was going to give the cross back, put it in the mailbox or something; she'd bought the manila envelope for it. She didn't even know why she'd taken it; it was just there, on the toilet top, and she wanted to feel it against her skin. Then this guy, this creep—it was here that she began to cry, as she hadn't on Friday night, when describing Larry's visit—came to the door all boozed up. He picked at the screen with his long fingernails, like a cat wanting in. And all the time he was asking her personal questions. And then he came in—she didn't say why she'd admitted him; Larry told me he'd asked for a glass of water—and grabbed her wrist and started saying more things.

"He was saying this weird stuff about that painting." She pushed her hair back and mopped her wet face with her fingers. "And then he said the reason you hired me was so you could, you know, have intercourse with me."

"My wife and I hired you," I said, aware that my hand hovered near her shoulder, like a moth considering whether to put its tiny mouth in the fabric of her dress. Or was it the larva that ate cloth?

She looked at me from behind her hair, like a child peering around a door, hoping to divine the drift of the obscure adult talk in the next room. I saw that her crying had darkened her skin. I looked down the road and recalled that Larry, after plying me with bourbon and showing me framed photographs of his two daughters (National Merit Scholars, glowing with achievement) and a slender literary magazine that contained a piece of his fiction and proposing that we spend Derby Day together, had asked if I had any interest in seeing a sex film he'd bought with his literary earnings. ("I'm joking," he said. "The film cost me sixty-five, plus shipping and handling, and I got only thirty dollars for the story.") He said there was a fair amount of offbeat activity in the film, in case that might offend me. About two-thirds of the way through the movie, during a bondage sequence that was as solemn as a court proceeding, I announced that I needed to get home. Larry laughed. He said he'd be seeing me soon.

"I hope you didn't believe that guy. Larry. I know he frightened you." I saw a dog come zigzagging out of Trempleau's driveway, followed by a couple. It was Trempleau himself and his young wife and their bluetick, out for an Easter walk.

"You won't trust me anymore," Martha said, starting to cry again. "I should've just quit. I don't know what I'm doing here."

I put my hand on her shoulder, careful not to touch skin or hair. But I could feel her beneath the dress.

"Let's just forget about it," I said. "Start from scratch." I saw Trempleau's dog nosing around in the ditch, where a few months from now there would be chicory and Queen Anne's lace and purple thistle.

"You won't tell?" She looked at me directly. Did the glimmer I saw in her damp brown eyes signify anything beyond a conjunction of light and tears, a simple optical event? Was there cunning in her gaze? And then her hand, her left one, the one not tangled in the strap of her purse, floated up out of her lap and took mine and held it near—but not on—her breast.

"No," I said. "I won't tell." I let my hand linger in hers and I even closed my eyes for a moment, as if waiting to be kissed, as if struck blind. When I opened them, I saw Trempleau approaching, his gray head cocked as if trying to determine whether the people parked adjacent to his property were likely to be trouble.

"DID YOU BRUISE or crush the mint leaves?" Aunt Vi asked, removing her nose from a pewter julep mug I'd received as a wedding gift.

"I just sort of stuck them in there," I said. "Along with the Old Croak and the New York State tap water. And the extrafine Domino sugar." In my own mug, I'd gone a bit heavy on the bourbon, which may have explained why the mint sprig that brushed my nose smelled so faint.

"If you crush them," my aunt said, extracting a cigarette from her carpenter's jeans, "you get a bitter flavor, I'm told. Not that it makes a damn bit of difference to me. It's the liquor I'm partial to." She laughed her coarse, precancerous laugh and waved away smoke from the barbecue grill. "I like that girl you have, Petey. Martha."

My aunt was the only person in the world who called me Petey. It made me feel little, as if I should be in the grass hunting for doodlebugs.

"She's good with Louis," I said. They were at the other end of the yard, heading toward the pond. Martha was holding Louis's hand as he attempted to walk on his chubby, unmuscled legs.

"I'd be interested in getting her to sit for me." She took a puff of her cigarette and advised me to turn the lamb.

I turned it, poking at its charred and puckered skin, and wondered if Aunt Vi would ask Martha to pose nude. Claire had posed for my aunt and had not quite forgiven her for the result, which, in Claire's opinion, made her look gawky and unhappy.

Aunt Vi went into the house to help Claire prepare the supper table. I listened to their voices as they discussed this and that—an off-Broadway show Claire had gone to, a New York artist Aunt Vi despised. I listened to the peepers fluting raucously, as if their pondside habitations were under siege. There was no trace of the sun now; the sky was as gray and bristly as sharkskin. At church that morning, kneeling at the communion rail, I'd prayed to a God I hadn't much believed in since I was a child. "Watch over me," I muttered, looking down at the tan bucks on the preacher's feet. "Keep me out of trouble."

I nudged the lamb with a long-handled fork and thought how much I would like to have a cigarette to go along with the bourbon. I brushed marinade on the meat, and when I looked up, I saw Larry coming through the breezeway between the house and garage. I was no more surprised by his appearance than I would've been to discover that the wart that was on my palm when I went to bed at night was still there in the morning. Nonetheless, I felt my jaw clench, my pulse quicken.

He was wearing a summer sports jacket over a T-shirt. He carried a plant in a hanging basket—the one I'd seen yesterday outside his door. It was clear from the way he walked, veering wide around Louis's stroller, that he was loaded.

"I smelled meat burning from a long way off," he said jovially. "Happy Easter!" He handed me the fuchsia, with its gaudy and prolific blossoms, the price tag still dangling from it.

I didn't thank him, nor did I ask him about the scrape on his forehead, which a Band-Aid didn't entirely cover. Perhaps he'd fallen while hunting for the hair coloring among the bottles of pills and tubes of ointments and topical creams that filled his tiny bathroom. Apparently, he'd found the coloring, for his hair was black as obsidian. He'd found his razor, too, but liquor or illness or both had spoiled the effect.

"I have some guests," I said, setting the plant on the ground. I glanced toward the pond and saw Martha there, with Louis in her arms. Louis had decided to see the world from aloft.

"I went to church this morning," Larry said, walking over to the hammock and abruptly lowering himself into its ropes. "In his sermon the priest started out with a piece of wisdom from *The Gospel According to 'Peanuts'*, some easy-to-swallow bullshit for the irregular churchgoer. And then he told a story about a bishop who was on his deathbed, about to cross over. And how a fellow priest had wondered at the bishop's calm and asked him if he wasn't the least afraid. And the bishop replied, 'How could I be afraid when my Father owns both sides of the river?'"

Larry paused, as if to consider the bishop's answer; his position on the hammock was awkward, half seated, half reclining. "Later, when I was out in the churchyard, watching children running around in search of plastic eggs, I thought, But who owns the river, who owns that old deep, roiling passage between His two properties? Isn't it the river, just the thought of having to swim it, that makes us piss our pants? Death drives us to distraction, doesn't it, Peter Sackrider?"

Larry lay back in the hammock, put his head on the striped pillow. I thought unkindly how nice it would be if the pillow had an antimacassar.

I saw Martha coming back across the lawn with Louis wriggling like a fish in her arms. He wanted to get down again. I said, "I think it would be better if you left, Larry."

"I wonder if I might beg a drink off you." His voice was thin; perhaps his oration had worn him out. "I have a terrible thirst."

"It's really inconvenient for you to be here," I said. How was it possible to be gracious without also being (in this case) stupid? I lacked the finesse (or courage) to see my way through the pile of complications that Larry had set down before me. What was I to do but say, finally, *Leave?*

"Forgive me, Peter Sackrider." He massaged the bridge of his nose with thumb and forefinger. "I'm having a dizzy spell. The trees look like whirling dervishes. Or something like that."

"Here," I said, handing Larry my julep mug. There was a drop of bourbon in the melting ice and mint. "Then you need to go."

Martha was standing on the other side of the grill, holding Louis's hand. She could see Larry—the parts of him that weren't submerged in the hammock, anyway.

"That's not very generous of you, Peter Sackrider," Larry said, looking up from inspecting the mug's contents. "After the good time we had yesterday watching that fuck flick and drinking and talking that serious man talk." Larry raised his voice as he saw that he had an audience besides me and Martha. Claire had come out onto the porch, a serving spoon in hand. Aunt Vi was beside her. I wondered if she was sizing him up as a potential artist's model.

"And you telling me," Larry went on, "how you lack the backbone not to betray in five seconds everything you supposedly love. And you, Peter Sackrider, saying how you're just a bag of shit and lust and cowardice!"

"That's not what I said." While drinking with Larry, I had confessed to weaknesses, but I hadn't used the phrase "bag of shit."

"Rough translation," Larry said, shaking the julep dregs, then tilting the mug toward his mouth.

"Who *is* this?" Claire called. "What's going on?" Louis had gotten away from Martha and was playing with the marinade brush, painting the side of the grill.

"I'm his friend," Larry said.

I took the brush from Louis and pulled him away from the grill. He started to cry. "Don't worry," I said to Claire. "Larry's leaving."

But he wasn't. Larry lay suspended between trees, the julep mug on his chest, his mouth wet and hungry looking.

II.

Overtime

THEY'RE ALL OUT there in the sunshine, smiling for some man's camera, except for Peter's baby, who's crawling in the grass, talking to the chiggers. Judge and Mrs. Sackrider are in lawn chairs, the Judge in an ice-cream suit that he must have been hiding all these years, Mrs. looking like a butterfly that just landed—a butterfly that's got fifty summer dresses and can't decide until the last minute which one to show all the other butterflies and little white cabbage moths. Thirty minutes ago, she was in her robe, knocking heads, saying to me "Willie, this" and "Willie, that" and "Willie, the tablecloth's got a stain on it, we can't use it." She has her hands in her lap now, all peaceable and sweet. Peter has his hands on his mother's chair, like he's trying to hold himself in place, like he can think of better things to do, like get a drink from Mr. Edward, who is setting up his table under the poplar, where he won't bake in his starched white jacket. Alex already has a glass of something in her hand. She stands next to her brother in a silver dress that would keep you awake like moonlight if you were trying to sleep in a room with it. Though it might take more than that to keep her husband from going off to stand on a corner and smoke a cigarette. He's long and thin, toothpicky, not much of a mixer. Every so often his mouth pops out from under his mustache, like a fish rising to bait. Alex married him in a hurry, after the first one went out the door looking for somebody who'd want to conquer wild rivers with him more often than she did. He was a hairy one, that first one, black beard like some prophet, big shoulders. This new one, Rick, is more of an indoors man, Alex claims, but if I was a prophetess, I'd say he wasn't going to be in a lot more Sackrider family photos. But then Peter, a boy who never seemed like he'd be faithful to much more than his own shadow, is still with Claire. Sometimes a baby works like glue, at least for a while. And then there are Judge and Mrs. Sackrider, forty years to the day together in the same bed that I've made up ten thousand times easy, her closest to the door with that special silk pillow for her neck, him next to a night table piled up with railroad timetables and books and the Baby Ben alarm clock. I was there just about the first time they messed that bed up. Mama sent me over; she was still working for Judge Sackrider's mother then. I was twenty-four, six years married, three babies hopping out of their cribs and crossing the street to get into Mr. Collins's Concord grape vines. I remember seeing the new Mrs. Sackrider's face one July morning. She looked like she'd woken up crying, or else her eyes had been bitten by bugs, and I thought, Well, I'm not going to be working here for long. I got that wrong—you can look at me now and tell how wrong I got that.

THE OTHER DAY, Judge Sackrider was delivering me to Winn-Dixie, where the bus picks me up and takes me on out to Dickeytown. Sometimes he drives me all the way home, usually he doesn't. We were aiming for the six-thirty bus, but we were running late, because Mrs. had me working late to prepare for the children's arrival. She was in a state of excitement, having me vaccum this, swab that, put those plastic safety plugs in sockets so Peter's child wouldn't electrocute himself.

The Judge was driving his little Cavalier like it was Sunday and he was out for a ride on the River Road, cooling himself. This was how Walter, my husband until he disappeared, mostly drove too, like his old LeSabre was a pleasure boat. The only times he ever drove fast with me in it was when he picked me up at the Sack-riders in the evenings. Sometimes he'd have to wait a while for me to come out of the house—I'd have to finish cooking something, empty trash cans, change out of my uniform that I wasn't going to wear in public—and when I got in the car, the light all but gone from the sky unless it was summer, he'd be about to climb out of his skin. He'd snap off the radio, put the car in gear before my door was shut, and tear off down the road, until I reminded him where he was, children and dogs and who knew what else stirring in the dusk. I'd say, "At least you could turn on your lights, so we could know what we're hitting when we hit it." He wouldn't say any-thing. There was only his big neck rising out of his work shirt, which had "Walter" stitched on it in yellow threads just in case anybody he'd been working with at the mattress factory for twenty, thirty years didn't remember who he was, his face still and stern, like it belonged on a penny. He'd be like that the whole way home. Sometimes he'd just drop me off, not wait around for me to make him supper, his first word in twenty minutes being that he was going down to Jim's, the market, to get himself a sandwich. Of course, Walter wasn't one for talking much, even when we were driving in the car on a Sunday afternoon and there was nothing to be angry at. Now and then I'd catch him singing—or humming, more likely—and I'd say, "What's that nice noise?" and he'd say it wasn't anything I should bother about. Can you miss someone's si-lences? Sometimes I miss Walter's—when I'm not thinking how he drove the LeSabre with all our savings to some casino on the Gulf of Mexico after he said he was going to visit his cousin in Pascagoula and do a little fishing. I said, "You need to go all the way to Mississippi to go fishing? What's wrong with Kentucky

Lake?" He said, "You don't know anything about fishing." It was forty days ago that he left.

I missed the six-thirty bus by five minutes, at least. There wouldn't be another one for an hour. "Maybe we can catch it," Judge Sackrider said.

So we chased after it, up 42, down Burleytown Road, past the shopping center where there used to be corn, past the state hospital for the infirm that's still red brick with ivy climbing up it. We didn't see the bus, didn't even smell a fume.

Judge Sackrider said, "I guess I might as well take you on home, Willie." We were about two miles from Dickeytown, as the crow flies.

"Yessir," I said. "I'd appreciate that."

The Judge took his time and we got caught by a train at a crossing. He watched that freight inch by like he was wishing it was going slower than it was, so he could study it even closer. He was counting cars, I believe—a white-haired man who rules over some big court downtown. After the caboose passed, he said, "You know, Willie, the railroads are going to do away with cabooses. Rear-end devices, they call them now." He chuckled.

He turned at the A.M.E. church, down a road the county hasn't seen fit to improve since I started walking. It's got holes you could bury someone in. Walter always drove around them like a snake gliding, wanting to save his whitewalls. The Judge hit one that made my purse leap off my lap. "Pardon me, Willie," he said. He took the corner slow onto my street, which used to be dirt with ruts and is now gravel with ruts. We went past Aunt Betty June's and were a shout away from my house when I saw a man sitting on my porch. For about two seconds, I thought it was Walter, having hauled himself up from the Gulf of Mexico somehow. I already had it in my head what I was going to say to him: he could sleep on the back porch with Venus, the dog. They'd have some privacy there. But the man was somebody I didn't know, somebody stocky and dark-complected like Walter, but with a thinner face, younger. He was sitting in a cast-off wicker chair Mrs. Sackrider gave me. Walter always preferred the porch sofa that glides on rails.

Judge Sackrider commented on the morning glories climbing my fence. "I see you've been beautifying, Willie," he said, though they or something else had been there twenty summers at least. He didn't notice the man on the porch, or maybe he thought the man was part of the scenery. He got his wallet out of his trousers and asked what he owed me.

I told him, but he could find only forty in his wallet that would hardly stay shut unless he sat on it. "Can we give you the other ten tomorrow, Willie? You'll be coming tomorrow, won't you?"

"Friday," I said. Tomorrow was a day of rest. Walter Jr., my youngest, was supposed to come by in the morning with his electrician friend and fix my air conditioner, if it could be fixed. Then he was going to take me over to Kroger's. I never did learn how to drive. I leave that to others.

"The children'll be home on Friday," Judge said. He was looking up the street. There were two boys coming down it, shorts drooping to their ankles.

"Yessir," I said. "I'll be glad to see them." I opened the car door, felt the hot air come get me even before I'd swung my legs out. I didn't see anybody on the porch then; there was nothing there except for chairs and the sofa and two pots of petunias and a broom. I stepped out of the Cavalier, heard the Judge say "Have a good night, Willie," saw the two boys slouching through the heat, shooting me a look like the weather and everything else was my fault, heard a dog bark (Venus, probably, on her chain in the back), and still didn't see any man on my porch. Maybe I'd conjured him. The Judge went off slowly, eyes open for more slouching boys. I looked into my mailbox and found two bills and an invitation from an insurance company, all addressed to Mr. Walter Minton. Or maybe, I thought, the man went into the house when I wasn't watching. Call me a fool, but I don't always lock it.

"HEY, WILLIE," ALEX SAYS, sticking her head in the sliding door. "Come and get in the picture."

"I'm busy." I'm putting beaten biscuits and slices of ham on a tray. I'm trying not to eat the ham.

"Let the caterer do that. What'd Mom hire a caterer for? We need you to be in a family picture."

"I don't need to be in any pictures, thank you." They're busting up out there anyway. The photographer is bent over his black bag. Peter is chasing his baby down toward the yellowwood tree that smelled so sweet just a few weeks ago. Alex's husband is off having a smoke, like an Indian in his tepee. The Judge is out of his chair, and Peter's wife is brushing something off his coat. Mrs. is blazing a path for the house, with more instructions for me or the catering lady, probably. The catering lady is in the dining room, perspiring through her dress, even though the AC is on full.

"You shouldn't even be working today," Alex says, coming all the way into the kitchen. "You should be in your nice clothes, drinking wine with me." She gives me a squeeze, then pinches a piece of ham.

Mrs. stops on the patio, inspects her hibiscus that has blossoms as big as parasols, then takes a little detour to check on Mr. Edward at the bar. "Your mother sent me an invitation, engraved and all, and a couple weeks later she asked could I help her out. So here I am. You can see me in my nice clothes when I'm laid out at the funeral parlor."

"Oh, Willie," she says. Then she tells me how young I am, in *spirit*, while diving into the ham again.

I slap her hand away, put sprigs of parsley around, and carry the tray, silver, engraved with all four of Mrs. Sackrider's initials, and heavy as a bowling ball, into the dining room. The catering lady is there with her helper, a pink-skinned man in a bow tie, arranging what she brought—dips, slab of salmon, salads, cheeses, marinated mushroom caps that look like drawer pulls. Alex gets a look from the lady when she sticks her nose into a bowl of something.

Back in the kitchen, Alex says something sharp about the caterer, loud enough that you wouldn't have any trouble hearing it in the dining room. She's in the food business herself, where she lives, out in Oregon. She's never been shy about saying what she thinks. She and her mother are always getting into it.

She offers to fetch me a drink. I order a Coke.

"No wine?"

"I'm on duty. Don't be tempting me."

Alex goes out and Mrs. comes in. She finds things to correct wherever she looks. She tells the dog to hush its barking, then wonders if I should put him down in his pen in the basement. "Everybody'll be here in a minute," she says.

And here they come, like Mrs. ordered them up, trooping across the yard in their seersucker jackets and polka-dotted dresses and sun hats. Most of them huddle in the shade under the poplar, near Mr. Edward's bar. I see Mrs. Durham, who's in Mrs. Sackrider's prayer group, shaking Peter's hand. I see Dr. Price, the Sackriders' vet, give Alex a big hug. (Mrs. said to me once, "He likes dogs, but he prefers women.") Standing in line, waiting for his own hug, is somebody Alex used to ride around in cars with when she was a girl, a boy named Mac who looks the same except his hair is thinning. Once, I recall, he tried to vault himself on a pole or something into Alex's bedroom, two flights up—didn't make it. Behind him is another well-wisher. Alex's husband is down the hill, in a chair under the beech, close enough to the woods that he could talk to all the copperheads and deer that live there.

Sometime later, Alex finds me in the basement with the dog. "I smelled your smoke," she says, handing me my glass of Coke. I quit smoking before Walter left town, then started up again.

"This don't taste right," I say, sipping. "What'd you put in it?"

Smiling, she tells me that Mr. Edward put a drop of rum in it.

"I don't usually drink it this way. I like my Coke straight. But I forgive you and Mr. Edward both."

The dog, not much more than a puppy, scuffles around on the newspaper in his pen, whimpers. Alex says, "You miss Walter?"

"If you can miss a skunk, I might miss him a little. Maybe." I've smoked my cigarette down to the filter, so I put it out. I try to limit myself to ten a day. That was number seven.

"Forty-five years is a long time." She goes to unlatch the dog-pen door.

"Not as long as forty-six," I say. Digger—that's his name, little brown dachshund—runs up the stairs on his inch-high legs. "You're going to get me in trouble."

"How come you think he left you?" She had a lot of questions as a child: How come we got to eat liver every Monday night? How come we have to die? How come God made snakes? Who says carrots are good for your eyes?

"What he told me was he was going to visit his cousin in Pascagoula. And do some fishing. He didn't tell me he wasn't coming back." I feel the rum conspiring to keep me in this chair for the rest of the afternoon, but I stand up. "Got to go to work," I say.

"You think he might have a lady friend?" The orchid on her dress looks a little floppy—too many people have been hugging her.

"He might have, until he gave all our money away to those robbers at the casino. He'd be lucky to have a dog friend now."

THE EVENING I saw that man sitting on my porch, I went across the street to Mr. Collins's place. Mr. Collins has a little house, clapboard, indoor plumbing (which not everybody in the neighborhood, even though it's 1990 A.D., has), glider on the porch, redbuds in the yard. The grape arbor is gone, but he has a garden out back which he is always giving me squash and melons from. He never had a wife that I know of. His sister lived with him for a while, but then she died. He worked at some white men's club downtown for years. Sometimes he came over to my house to watch *I Love Lucy* or the Cleveland Browns on Walter's color Sylvania when it was new. Sometimes I went over to his house to use the phone. Walter was against phones for a long time—for TV but against phones.

After I knocked for a while, Mr. Collins came out of the dark back of the house. He's over eighty, a little slow afoot. He invited me in for some iced mint tea. He'd just made it. He's a small, light brown man, smooth scalp except for a fringe of cottony hair. He's always polite, no matter whether you catch him in his Sunday clothes or a T-shirt with holes in it. He knew about Walter being gone of course—he's got eyes and ears, like everybody else on the street—but he never said anything about it, except to ask me if I needed anything.

I declined the tea, and then I asked if he would mind walking with me into my house. I said I'd noticed something suspicious. I was having all kinds of thoughts by then: maybe the man on the porch was some sort of bill collector or loan shark Walter owed money to and he was going to take possession of my house and everything in it.

"Well," he said, "we could call Mr. Pike." This was the policeman. "Except he might have to shower and shave and eat his supper before he could make it all the way over to Dickeytown, where the colored folks live. So let me get my hat."

We went across the street, Mr. Collins in his T-shirt and backless house slippers and flat little roadster cap, going about one mile an hour. I was thinking I should've found somebody less wispy to help me out, in case we ran into trouble, but it turned out Mr. Collins had armed himself when he grabbed his hat. He took a pistol out of his pocket when we got up on my porch.

"You have one of these, Willie?" he asked, holding it in his palm like it was a caterpillar or something that had fallen there from a tree.

"No, sir," I said. Venus had started to bark again. Venus is a hunting dog Walter never got around to training. All she can do is bark and eat. "Walter used to have a shotgun, but he sold it."

"I never used mine except once," Mr. Collins said. "Got him, too—this old woodchuck who was eating my garden up."

I opened the door. Mr. Collins went in first, tipping his cap down half an inch, holding the pistol along his pants leg. The house wasn't any different from when I'd left it in the morning, aside from the air being stiller and hotter. There, on the hall chair, was the stack of shirts I'd ironed for Walter Jr. last night and the lightbulb I wanted him to put in the upstairs hall. There was the dent in the couch where I'd sat after I got done ironing Junie's shirts, where I watched some murder show on the TV and talked to my eldest up in Ohio. She said, "You and Daddy never went anywhere, maybe he just had to get away for a while."

"Awhile?" I said. "He's been gone forty days. His cousin hasn't seen him since he went to the casino to give all our money away. They never even went fishing."

Mr. Collins whistled a little, a soft nothing, like you might do in your sleep.

In the kitchen, the door to the back porch was open a bit. "Maybe you didn't shut it tight," Mr. Collins said. The screen was hooked, so maybe I didn't. I opened the screen and yelled at Venus to hush. She lay down in her worn place in the shade.

Mr. Collins said, "You think the intruder might have gone upstairs, Willie?" Polite but doubtful. He'd put his firearm back in his pocket.

"Well," I said. "Maybe I was seeing things." In my mind right then, the man was as clear as day: fine white shirt, hands folded in his lap, dark serious face. Like he was sitting in judgment in that wicker chair, waiting to tell me all my wrongs. "I don't want to keep you any longer. I appreciate the company."

Mr. Collins had his handkerchief out and was dabbing at his neck. His T-shirt had a blot of perspiration on it right above where his stomach began to rise into a nice country loaf. "You sure you don't need me anymore?"

"No, you go on." I thanked him, watched him latch the fence gate behind him and cross the street in his slippers.

I would've accepted his firearm, had he offered it. But he didn't, so I went and unchained Venus and brought her inside, which I wouldn't ever let Walter do, unless there was a blizzard or something. I said, "Let's see you hunt, even though you got a fancy name and don't know how." I urged her up the stairs. She sat on her haunches, looking at me like I was a fool. "Go on now," I said, giving her a tap behind her dusty ear. Then all of a sudden she flew up, like she'd caught a scent. I let her patter around some before I climbed the stairs.

There was nobody in the children's old room for Venus to bark at or me to see, nothing in the bath, either, except a dripping faucet. My bed was the way I'd left it (made), the air conditioner was still filling the window, doing no good, Walter's one suit was still hanging in his closet.

I turned the oscillating fan on to "High" and lay down. At around ten, I fixed myself some macaroni and cheese for supper, and gave Venus a cold frankfurter with her kibble. She acted like she'd love me forever.

• • •

THE JUDGE IS giving a speech out on the patio. He looks all tidy in his ice-cream suit and his white hair combed off his forehead and his necktie still riding tight against his Adam's apple despite the heat. He's telling a story about Mrs., his mild voice competing against a million insects buzzing and Digger yapping at something out in the yard and Peter's child squirming and complaining in his mother's arms until she carries him inside, past me standing on the kitchen doorstep with my glass of champagne that Alex brought me for toasting. "You must be hoping to get me drunk, girl," I said. But I haven't touched it; I'm not much of a champagne drinker.

The Judge says, "I courted Libby for five years—six if you count the time between when she said yes and when we got married." Mrs. is fanning herself with her hat; she looks somewhat worried. "And you know how I finally got her to succumb?"

"There's a word," Peter says to Alex. Brother and sister are standing side by side, two feet from me.

"Tell us, Henry," a tall gent in a madras jacket booms. His head looks like the sun has been beating on it. His wife pulls on his sleeve.

"Well, she was in the hospital," the Judge says. "A couple nights before, we'd been at a dance and she got sick on me, sick as a dog, and I started to wonder if my old charms had worn off. Unless it was you, Ned, cutting in on me once too often that made her react that way." Ned is the sunburned man. He guffaws. "But the truth is that her appendix was inflamed and had to be removed."

Mrs. is fanning herself faster now, turning her head to see what Digger's barking at. Maybe she doesn't want to be lying on that hospital bed, waiting.

"So I walked over to the hospital one afternoon," the Judge says, "from the law office, where I'd been sleeping in the library, pretending to do research."

"All rise," somebody says. "The Honorable Henry L. Sackrider is in court."

"Well, yes," the Judge says, pondering this announcement or joke or whatever it is. "I was kind of in court. I had a bouquet for Libby."

"That you bought from the hospital florist," Mrs. says, halting her fanning. "For a dollar fifty."

"A dollar fifty went a long way in 1949." Some people are laughing.

"We're waiting for the punch line, Dad," Alex says. But her brother isn't. He's walked off down the yard, to where Digger is making a racket.

"I'm getting there, Moony Tooth," the Judge says kindly, though not looking in Alex's direction. "So there she was, on the hospital bed, in her hospital gown, as pale as the palest dawn. I had her where I wanted her, see. The only problem was that her mother was sitting alongside her."

"I bet you told her a joke and made her incision hurt." A man's voice comes from over by the garden, where the sun is hitting. "And you kept telling her jokes until she was in so much pain you said you'd stop only if she agreed to marry you."

"That's the low road, Ralph. I leave that to you and your associates at Axton & Armstrong."

"You better hurry up and get to the end," Mrs. says to the Judge. "Everybody's champagne is getting warm."

"You're hanging fire, Judge," somebody says.

Peter comes back up the hill to the patio with Digger wriggling in his arms. Peter looks paler than Mrs. must have looked lying on her hospital bed.

"There's a copperhead down there that's as long as a goddamn car, excuse me, Willie," he says. "Digger had his nose in its face almost."

I know that snake, or his cousin, anyway. I saw him sunning himself on the driveway one day this spring, when I was wheeling the garbage out to the street. Twenty-four hours later, Walter told me he was going fishing down to Pascagoula. A few weeks later I saw that snake or his cousin under the wren house that hangs outside the kitchen window; he was waiting for lunch to fall out.

Peter hands me the dog and takes my glass of champagne. It seems like a fair trade. I don't care to be outside anymore, in the vicinity of copperheads. I take Digger on in the door—his little brown body is vibrating, like he's still got the smell in his nose—and put him in front of his water bowl. I hear applause—the Judge must have figured out a way to get the Mrs. to say "Yes" to him. Mrs. starts up with her speech, and I go down into the basement to have a smoke. Number nine. I'm so tired I can hardly finish it. Sometime later, I come blinking up into the lights and Mrs. saying, "Why, Willie, I didn't know you were still here."

ALEX AND RICK take me home. Alex drives her father's car. Rick sits in the back, reading one of the mess of old magazines that the Judge keeps forgetting to deliver to the Veterans Hospital. The sun has just about sunk. Alex drives slow, at sight-seeing speed, pointing things out to Rick. There's the house where her friend Rose grew up. She and Rose were the first girls in their class to own white go-go boots, she tells him. "You remember them, Willie?"

"Sure," I say.

She points out the water tower that boys used to dare each other to climb and the place where the house was—it's gone now, all subdivided—where her invisible friend lived, some man I used to have to set a place for at the dinner table, back when Alex was in pigtails, before she got her go-go boots. (I didn't allow invisible people at my dinner table; sometimes I didn't allow visible ones.)

Then, not too long before we cross the tracks into Dickeytown, she goes by a dead-end road that was a Lovers' Lane for the white children.

"It was bumper-to-bumper on Saturday night," she says.

"I never could get laid when I was a teenager," Rick says, like I'm not in the car. "I must've been living in the wrong state."

"Must've been. Though most of the boys here who said they got laid were lying. Where'd you go, Willie?"

"Where'd I go when?"

"When you went spooning with your boyfriend." We go bumping over the tracks. "When you were sixteen."

"I don't think I'm going to answer that question," I say. We go past the elementary school, where some black boys are playing basketball in the dusk. Up ahead, Mr. Pike sits in his policeman's car, eating a candy bar, listening to his motor run. Usually he's on the other side of the tracks; maybe he got lost.

Alex turns onto the unpaved road and hits the same hole her daddy hit a couple nights ago. We go by Aunt Betty June's, bats or swallows or something chasing around above the rooftop. It was right along here, in the dirt road, that Walter said to me, "Well, I guess you got to marry me now." He was all hot from playing baseball, a Sunday afternoon game, married men against unmarried. He was eighteen, barely old enough to be among the unmarried. Sweat was making paths in the dust on his cheeks. I might have wished he was more handsome, more of a smiling person, but I was glad he had a job and all those fine muscles, because I was pregnant. I wasn't going to tote that baby all by myself. So I told him how I was as we walked by Aunt Betty June's, honeysuckle past blooming, trumpet creeper climbing up a big ruin of a tree that's now a stump where my aunt sets out a pot of geraniums. I said, "It looks like we got a child coming." And he kept walking, his bat on his shoulder (he could hit, for sure), his eyes forward, and saying that line, "Well, I guess you got to marry me now." As if there'd been a time when he'd been down on his knees, begging. And I said, "I guess I might, if it's all right with you." And he said, in a whisper almost, the birds nearly drowning him out, "It's all right."

There's a light burning in my bedroom. I'm hoping it was left on when Walter Jr. and his friend came over to work on the air conditioner, if they did, two days after they promised they would. I can't think of any other reason for it to be shining.

"You want to come in?" I say to Alex. "I'll make you some coffee."

Husband and wife have a conversation, and he says he needs more cigarettes (my filtered ones don't suit him) and some ibuprofen because he has a headache from drinking wine in the sun and talking to people who kept asking him what kind of work he does out there in Oregon. "There was this old guy, Vern Somebody, who decided we were soulmates because he works in public relations just like me. 'Well, goddamn, isn't that just like fate kissing you on the forehead,' he said. Whatever that means."

"Don't be so crabby," Alex says. "Go buy your pills."

When he drives off into the almost darkness, toward Jim's, Alex says, "I think I let him get me pregnant. I ought to know for sure in a couple weeks."

She stands on the porch step in her silver dress, looking no more pregnant than a bud vase, while I hunt in my purse for my key. I locked up when I went out this morning.

"What kind you want?" I ask. "Boy or girl?"

"The kind that sleeps through the night and doesn't cry a lot."

"One of those imaginary babies?" When I open the door, I feel the dark lean into me and put its hot breath on my neck. And then I notice that there's no light falling down the staircase, not a trickle. So, what'd I see up there—a moonbeam?

"Yeah, I'll take one of those smart, quiet, self-cleaning ones, if you please," Alex says. I find the light switch. The stack of Junie's shirts is still on the chair. Didn't I call him last night and tell him for the second time to come get his wash and fix my air conditioner, and didn't he say, "I'll be there tomorrow, Mama, I been busy"?

The kitchen is the way I left it in the morning. Probably that's the same fly circling my basket of onions. I open the back door and call to Venus. I hear her chain rattling, see something rise up from the dirt into a dog shape. I've let her stay inside with me the last couple of nights, on the floor by my bed.

"Your house looks good, Willie," Alex says. She means it as a compliment, but you'd never catch her living here in her silver dress. Or in any other outfit either.

I thank her and get the can of coffee off the shelf, get the per-colator going. She looks at pictures on the walls, asks me questions about what this daughter's doing, who's that person, is that Walter Jr. in his baseball uniform?

"No," I say, "that's Senior. Way back when." I pass that picture every day—his ballcap pulled down low like it was hiding some-body with fire in his eyes, lips sealed, "Giants" stitched (by me) across his chest—but never do anything about it.

"I still have all these pictures of my first husband," Alex says. "There's one where we're on this beach on the Colorado River, and we're naked as jaybirds and we're squeezing each other and the light is beautiful and everything. Six months later, we're di-vorced."

I give her a cup of coffee and pour myself one.

"Is this decaf, Willie? I hope."

"Yes, ma'am."

I give her the milk carton and watch her pour. I notice that her fingers are pink and scaly, like she has a rash. When she was a child, her skin would flare up with one thing or another. I was al-ways putting ointment on her, telling her to hold still.

"You remember Mac?" she asks. "One of my high school boyfriends? The one who drank like a fish and tried to pole-vault into my bedroom window?"

"I saw him, yeah."

"His wife dumped him, and then he quit drinking and became a born-again Christian. But he's still the same guy—cornsilk hair and baby cheeks, still sells pool tables for his dad—except he believes Jesus died for our sins."

"I keep hoping He did, too," I say, hearing a knock on the door.

AFTER THEY DRIVE OFF, I sit on the porch and smoke number ten. I watch the lightning bugs go about their business, listen to a car rolling up the street, playing rap music loud enough to rattle the dead. It gets Venus going for a while. Then the night turns quiet again, just bugs ticking, the floorboards on my porch stretching as the air cools down. Over at Mr. Collins's, there's one light on, hardly enough to read the newspaper by. He likes to save on electricity; he still doesn't own a TV.

It startles me a little when I hear a voice call me, nothing solid attached to it. "Willie? That you, Willie?"

I see a body taking shape out in the street, just beyond my fence. "Who's that?" I think I know but I don't want to say.

"It's Walter." The body has a hat on its head.

"No, it's not. He went away to Mississippi and died there. His family don't even mourn him. His dog never heard of him."

"You smoking again, Willie? That'll kill you."

"Ho ho," I say, lighting number eleven, one to grow on. "Ha ha."

Among the Missing

COME SEE MY DAD'S FISH," Eric Wunsch says, standing close enough that I can smell his candy-scented breath. He is six, the youngest of three boys. He has a sharp, thin nose and blue eyes that you can't see to the bottom of and dirty blond hair that sticks up in tufts, like prairie fescue. His ears are small and sweetly curved, like those of a woodland spirit. He is slight, no heavier than a few bones packed in excelsior. He runs around with my son, Louis, though Louis will sometimes abandon him for another child.

"What kind of fish did your dad catch?" I ask, trying to keep annoyance out of my voice. Before Eric entered, I was grading exams for my Italian 103 class and listening to a recording of *La Bohème* that I got at a yard sale—a scratchy mono recording, circa 1950. By the end of Act I, my house had emptied. First, Louis went down to the Wunsches', and then Peter, my husband, left to search the neighborhood for his bike. It was stolen from our garage last week, the day before Easter, when the air was briefly warm and it looked as if spring might be taking root in our part of Wisconsin.

Eric describes the fish as "big ones, bigger than Cassius." He points to our elderly cat, who sits by the window, still as a picture,

gazing out. Spring is in retreat. Two days after Easter, snow fell—
like fallout from the Resurrection, one of my colleagues said—
and blobs of it remain on the ground.

I say, "Maybe I'll come see your dad's fish a little later." I hold
up an exam and smile. I want to hear Mimi sing her last, bedrid-
den aria.

Eric stands his ground. He puts his hands behind his back and
dips his head, like a butler awaiting further instructions. We both
look at his feet, which are bare, in defiance of the weather, and as
white as eggs under refrigerator light. I look at the vents in the
knees of his trousers. All of the Wunsch boys go around half in tat-
ters. "I don't sew," their mother, Liz, once said to me, as if it were
a point of honor with her. "My husband ties a nice trout fly, but he
wouldn't stoop to sewing on a button."

Eric's candy-scented mouth hangs open a little. The inside is a
shade of blue not found in nature. I feel myself giving way. I ask if
he wants something to eat.

He says, "OK" and follows me into the kitchen. I ask if Louis is
still at his house.

"He and Tim are playing," Eric says. Tim is the middle Wunsch
boy, a second-grader, a year ahead of Eric and Louis. "They
ditched me."

"I'm sorry. It's hard for three friends to play together, isn't it?"
However, I recall seeing all three happily peeing in the snow in
Mrs. Lauterbach's yard a couple days ago, making intricate designs.

"Tim's a big jerk. I'm going to cut his wiener off with my dad's
knife." Eric tries to stare me down, then pretends to study a coffee
stain on the counter.

"I bet it won't be long before you and Tim are friends again," I
say, giving Eric two juice-sweetened cookies that my husband,
who has taken to minding his calories, purchased.

Neither my prediction nor the cookies seem to lighten Eric's

mood. I say, "Well, let's go see what your father's fish look like."
Act IV of *La Bohème* will have to wait.

I go into the back hall to get my coat, a black, quilted, ankle-length thing that I bought in New York when I was pregnant with Louis. It's a bit grungy, having gone through three New York winters and four Wisconsin ones. I pull my scarf out of a pocket and with it a season's worth of flotsam: ATM slips, candy wrappers, something I clipped from *La Repubblica*, yellow Post-its, a piece of a carrot that has gone all soft and rubbery. The carrot doesn't surprise me, but a note on one of the Post-its gives me a start. It says, "Wassup, docta? When we gonna burn down da casa, tu ed io?" (Is the note supposed to go with the carrot?) The handwriting is unfamiliar to me, but the mix of Italian and MTV English suggests it's from one of the males in my Corso Intensivo. I think of their faces at 8:00 A.M., glazed and uneager, studs and rings decorating their ears and noses and eyebrows, and then I feel something ripple through me, a pulpy thought: I'm desired by somebody twenty years my junior.

I empty the contents of my coat pockets into the garbage pail—all but the mystery Post-it, that is. I hear Eric go out the front. I see him pattering across the unthawed lawn, windmilling his arms, as if he's about to launch himself.

I knot my scarf and step outside. Eric shoots down the street, into a breeze from the northwest that has a whiff of cow pasture in it. I don't see anybody else, except for Tom Heckman, who is on a ladder, inspecting the cedar-shake roof he put on his new two-car garage. Tom, a retired professor of geology, built the garage last spring and summer, mostly during the evening hours. He rigged up floodlights to illuminate his work. One August night, when Peter and I were in bed and Tom was pounding nails, Peter got up and yelled out the window, "We're trying to sleep here, Tom, for Christ's sake." Actually, neither of us was trying to sleep. We were reading, hunkered down in our pools of lamp-light. His and Her pools. Seeing Peter at the window in black bikini briefs that I had no previous knowledge of stirred me. (As a rule, he wore boxers.) When he returned to bed, I got on top of him, pinned him. He accepted me the way a piece of wood accepts a nail.

I walk down the street toward the Wunsches', heckled by barrel-chested crows who have staked out garbage that has escaped from the Lauterbachs' can. Eric has disappeared into his house, a pale yellow frame in need of a coat of paint. The storm door, hanging by a hinge, flaps in the wind. Even before I mount the front steps, I hear music—something fast and brutal that Silas, the oldest Wunsch child, probably put on. Silas is on the verge of thirteen. He shares a room with an iguana, a snake, a parrot from the jungles of Africa. When he ventures out into the world, he hides himself in hooded sweatshirts and oversized camouflage jackets and stocking caps.

I decide to go around to the kitchen door. I walk past Liz's border garden, dollops of snow lying among last year's stalks of sedum, and then around Dennis's dented blue pickup to the fenced-in back yard. The fence is for Vukie, the Wunsches' Irish terrier, who likes to wander. For the moment, Vukie sits next to the picnic table, watching Dennis clean fish.

As I lift the loop of wire that keeps the gate closed, man and dog look up at me simultaneously. It strikes me that Dennis, with his long face and scruffy, outdoorsman's beard, resembles Vukie.

"Welcome to the funny farm," Dennis says. I assume he is refer-ring to the music pouring out the back of the house through the open kitchen door—that and the voice (Liz's) that's not quite lost amid the grinding guitars and a vocalist (female, I think) scream-ing "Lick my eyes, I'm on fire."

"Eric told me I had to come see your catch," I say, watching

Dennis slide a knife along the silvery-black back of a fish that is the length of his forearm, if not the thickness. Dennis has the forearms of a person who digs holes for hundred-pound root balls. He owns a landscaping and tree-trimming business. He is dressed as if he lives in a southerly planting zone—short-sleeved shirt unbuttoned to his sternum, bare feet.

"What kind is this?" I ask. The knife pokes out near the anal fin and then edges toward the tail.

"Lake Michigan coho. Caught it over by Racine. Got a couple rainbows, too." He invites me to look in the cooler on the bench. I open it and see three large fish with vapor trails of pink on their silvery sides. At the bottom is a sandwich bag full of milky-pink roe. One of the trout was carrying a load.

"Very nice," I say. "Have you seen the boys—Tim and Louis?"

"Can't say I have." Dennis cuts the fillet away from the rest of the salmon and holds it in his palm, as if to assess its weight. The flesh is rosy pink. Then he puts the fillet in a bucket of brine. "But I admit I haven't been looking."

The music has been turned down a few notches, and I can hear Liz's voice now, loud and clear. "Don't you swear at me, Silas Wunsch, or I'll put you and your stinking lizard down in the basement and lock the door." Liz is a small woman who seems delicate at first glance, but her voice is big enough to turn heads a block away. Maybe all the hours she spends tiptoeing around at the sleep disorders clinic—she's some sort of research assistant—make her want to shout when she gets home.

"I'm trying to listen to my music, Mom," Silas says, in a brittle voice. "Tim and Louis are annoying me. Jesus Christ on a stick."

So, I think, Louis is inside, listening to someone demand that her eyes be licked, *subito*.

"Silas just hit puberty, doing about ninety miles an hour," Dennis says, cutting the other fillet away from the coho's rib cage.

"Well, it had to happen sometime. Is he still interested in nature, his animals and all of that?"

"You'd have to ask him," Dennis says. Something flickers along his cheekbone. Then it skitters away, like a mouse through a hole.

In my pocket, I feel the sticky-backed Post-it that bears the proposition from one of my students. Which one? Ian, the red-haired boy with the nose ring? Aaron, the black-haired boy with the nose stud?

Dennis takes one of the rainbows out of the cooler and lays it on the table. The house has become quiet. The music has been turned off. I look up and see Liz out on the second-floor minideck—a rickety little platform, inadequately railed in. She is wearing a silky black knee-length bathrobe and black slippers. Liz is the nonconformist in the family, the only one, anyway, who could be accused of dressing up.

"Hi, Claire," she says, though it isn't me she has stepped outside to speak to. "You here for Louis?"

"Only if he's a bother." The truth is, I wouldn't mind getting a glimpse of him before I leave.

"Three's a crowd, four's a riot," Liz says. "I'd invite you in, except first I need Dennis to help me wash out Silas's mouth."

Dennis doesn't look up from his filleting.

"Dennis?" Liz stands with her hands on her hips. Bare-legged under her robe, her blond hair wet and untidy, she looks like a gal doing her best to hang tough.

"Be with you in a minute," Dennis says. He glances my way. "You like some fish for dinner? I was thinking of smoking these guys, but I could give you a piece now, if you want."

"Now sounds good."

A slender, blond boy appears in the doorway behind Liz. Silas's blondness outshines his mother's and his brothers'. He seems to quiver beneath it, as if angry at having to show himself out here in the fresh air.

"If you tell Dad," Silas says to Liz, "I'll tell him about you."

Liz says nothing. But when he bolts into the house, she follows, calling his name.

"Looks like things are going to hell around here," Dennis says. He wraps a fillet in newspaper and hands it to me. A door slams. Dennis rises from the picnic table. His shirt hangs out of his jeans. There is something silvery scattered in the thickets of his beard. Fish scales? Does he know what Silas knows about Liz? What does Silas know? Dennis's eyes, soft brown but half-curtained, don't clarify anything.

"Maybe I should fetch Louis for you," he says. "Before the shit hits the fan big-time."

I walk around to the front to wait for Louis. I lean against the rear of Dennis's truck and, for no reason that I know of, recall standing at the Information Booth in Grand Central Terminal, with Louis, who was six months old, strapped to my back. We were waiting for Peter, who was coming from his office on Forty-third Street. (He worked for an in-flight magazine; a couple months later, he quit to become a househusband, a career he still pursues, more or less, while keeping an eye on the stock portfolio he inherited from his grandfather.) We were going to take the train out to Westchester and look at a house that was for rent. As Louis and I waited, we watched the airfoil-like tabs on the Arrivals and Departures board spin. An express, then a local, left without us. A man with a green scarf tied around his head like a babushka stood before us with his palm out. He gave off an odor of sweat mixed with ruination. I gave him money and moved away. At last, I saw Peter descending the Vanderbilt Avenue stairs, forty-five minutes late. He was wearing a plaid hunting cap, the kind Holden Caulfield wore, and a car coat, now quite ratty, which had once belonged to his grandfather. There was something forlorn about Peter then, some sadness that was almost adolescent in the intensity of its expression, which may have accounted for his tendency to run late. But he brightened when he saw Louis, whom he'd brought a gift, a frog puppet whose long, red paper tongue shot hungrily from its mouth.

Silas bangs out the front door. I say "Hi," but he ignores me, a lady standing in the cold with a slab of fish. He heads up the street, cowled like a monk in a sweatshirt. I go up the front steps and peer in. There's an overturned basket of laundry in the hall. I call Louis's name. "Time to come home, honey." I hear Silas's parrot gabbling. Then I see Dennis coming down the stairs—his naked feet, his grubby jeans, the billow of his stomach pushing against his half-buttoned shirt. He stops before he reaches the bottom.

"The boys went out the back," he says, gripping the banister. Even in the dim light of the hallway, I can see that he is rattled, that something is pulsing under the skin above his beard.

"OK," I say. "Thanks for the fish."

"You bet."

I'M DRILLING A HOLE in the floor of the side porch. It's here, next to the kitchen door, that I'm going to affix the boot scraper that Peter gave me for my birthday, last week. The boot scraper is in the shape of a hedgehog, all stiff black bristles except for its snout. Peter ordered it from a catalog. It's a nice boot scraper, as boot scrapers go, but I think I would've preferred a book or some racy underwear.

As I screw the hedgehog's wooden base into the floor, Peter lies in the hammock, reading. It is mid-May, two weeks past the last frost. The lilacs that grow near the porch are close to blooming, and there are flowers on the sweet woodruff in the border. In celebration, I'm as barefooted as a Wunsch, two of whom are in the house with Louis, making savage noises. School is out—for me, anyway. (The children have a couple more weeks.) All I have to do is turn in my grades. I'm giving a B to the boy who slipped me the hip-hop mash note. This may be one grade below what he actually deserves, since he aced the final; only the past-perfect subjunctive tripped him up. But he missed as many classes as he attended, and in those he did attend he observed near absolute silence. His name is Adrian. I saw him once outside class, in a College Avenue pub where I go to play pinball. (I love the way the balls rocket up the chute into that carnival world with its corny flashing lights and thumper-bumpers and pop-up targets.) He leaned on the machine, a vintage Bally, momentarily obstructing my view of the ricocheting ball. He was handsome, almost beautiful, even with the two-day-old stubble on his face, even with the rather frightful Moe of the Three Stooges haircut. He had a ripe, fleshy, just-shy-of-corrupt mouth, like one of Caravaggio's boy models. I knew without asking that he was the author of the note.

After I have secured the boot scraper to the floor, I notice that the door, when opened by a hurrying child, will strike the hedgehog's snout about halfway through its arc. I can move the scraper now, or I can go inside and get a drink and think about moving it later. I go inside and drink a can of fizzy water while standing at the kitchen sink, from where I can see Peter, or some of him. What I can mostly see are his hands, which hold a book above the edges of the hammock. He has nice hands—small, feminine, unmarred, except for the cicatrix at the base of his left thumb and a wart on his right palm. He doesn't do much in the way of manual labor. He isn't any good at fixing or tinkering or building, all those nuts-and-bolts things that men do because their fathers taught them how to. But when I married Peter, I knew I wasn't getting somebody who could repair a leaky tap. So what does my husband do with his hands? He prunes the lilacs after they bloom, and in the fall he rakes leaves, raising a blister or two, and chops firewood. He scrubs the bathroom now and then. He punches in numbers on his calculator. Every so often he goes to the early-bird service at St. George's and swallows the Host that the minister lays in his palm. He shows Louis how to hold a split-finger fastball. In the days before Louis, Peter would sometimes sneak up from behind and put his hands on me. And then we would put our smoky mouths on each other. But neither of us smokes anymore.

And of course his hands grip books. He disappears into books, like a boy into a cave. Peter may look like a bump on a log, a loafer, a ne'er-do-well, but there he is—reading, picking his way through the dark toward what he hopes will be an explanation, something as simple as a pictograph, dreaming of writing books in which spelunking boys like himself might wander happily, though doing this, he has figured out, takes work.

Out in the living room, Louis and the Wunsch boys are discussing anatomy. Their voices are low and conspiratorial.

"Your mom has a ditch," says Tim, who has seniority in this group, "and your dad has a bike. Sometimes your dad rides his bike into your mom's ditch. Silas told me."

"My mom has a puntchina," Eric says, with authority, though the word he is aiming for is *vagina*, I think.

"My dad has a willie," Louis says.

"Boys," I say, leaning into the room, "why don't you go outside and play? The sun is shining."

Louis and Eric fly off, like birds flushed from a bush. Tim, oddly, remains, his eyes on me. Tim is an uneasy child, rabbity around the mouth, watchful. He is prone to colds and funks. He is heavier than Eric, built like his father.

"Everything all right, Tim?" I know there is trouble at the Wunsches', though the extent of it is unclear. For a while, it seemed that Liz was having an affair. Then it seemed that the affair had ended. Or so I thought after seeing the whole family drive off one sunny Saturday with a canoe strapped to the top of the van. Now I hear that Liz has gone away. She told her children that she was going to visit her sister in South Dakota. According to my neighbor, who keeps her eyes peeled for rents in the fabric of family life in our little neighborhood, Liz went to her sister's house with a man named Lance.

"My foot's asleep," Tim says. He is sitting with his feet under his rump.

"Whenever my foot falls asleep," I say, "I tickle it with the turkey feather I keep in my hair." I have the kind of hair—dark, curly, flighty—in which you could hide a turkey feather.

Tim looks at me as if I might be a witch, then manages to get his bare feet moving. "I have to go see if my dad's home," he says. "He went to look for Vukie."

"Vukie's missing?"

Tim doesn't answer. He hurries out the door and trots down the street toward his house, which on this particular Saturday, in the gauzy spring light, looks abandoned. I scout the block for Eric and Louis. I see Tom Heckman puttering around in his cathedral of a garage, to the accompaniment of heroic music—Beethoven, I think. Tom has hung speakers on the rafters.

I walk toward the grove of firs at the end of the block, where the boys sometimes play. I find no children, only a cairn constructed of pine cones and sticks.

I walk back to the Wunsches' and open the storm door. (It has been rehinged, but now the glass panel is missing.) I knock on the inner door and then push it open. I hear what sounds like someone moaning during sexual climax. "Hello?" I say. The moans fade.

I walk into the kitchen. Sunlight passes through the window above the sink, shining on breakfast litter, a pizza box, an open jar of Skippy. I call out a succession of boy's names.

I hear what sounds like a fart, and track it to the TV room, where Silas sits on the couch. He is wearing a black stocking cap pulled down to the bridge of his nose. No shirt. The iguana squats on his thigh, its long tail curled against its master's belly. The African parrot perches on the back of the sofa; its face and throat are peach-colored, its chest a comely shade of green. Silas has the TV remote in his hand. He has clicked off whatever he was watching.

"I thought I saw Tim come in," I say. "I thought Louis and Eric might be here." Silas makes me more nervous than a thirteen-year-old boy in a stocking cap should. I scan the room for his pet snake, an obscure north woods species. Louis has told me the snake is shy but friendly.

"Wrong," Silas says. The parrot flies off the sofa, making the air tremble, and then settles on the La-Z-Boy in the corner.

"When's your mother coming back? From South Dakota, I mean?"

"Maybe when she gets tired of fucking with her boyfriend," he replies. "How should I know?"

"You shouldn't talk like that, Silas."

"Who are you? My guidance counselor?" He points the re-mote at the TV—my cue to depart. I go out through the kitchen, taking the pizza box with me after failing to fit it into the overflowing can under the sink. At home, I find nobody, not even Cassius. There is a note on the kitchen counter: "Gone to take another look for my bike. Boys are at the school playground." This is something else that Peter does with his hands: leaves me messages in small, slanting script that makes me think of people walking into high winds, leaning forward so as not to be blown backward.

EARLY ONE MORNING IN JULY, I'm in the garden when Peter appears at my side and says without preamble that he has been seeing this person named Jamie. This strikes me as an odd locution—*this person named Jamie*—and for a moment I wonder if Jamie is a man. I've seen gay men look my husband over, as if he might be a prospect, and I've sometimes thought that the sex might appeal to him, that he would enjoy being ravished by a man. His hands are in the pockets of his shorts. His eyes are behind sunglasses—prescription sunglasses, though the prescription is long out of date.

A moment later, he clears up my confusion by saying that he is going to drive out West with her tomorrow. "I'll be back in two weeks and then we can decide what to do."

I'm on my knees among leggy veronica and baby meadow-sweet, a forked weed extractor in my hand. In order to fully see Peter, who is standing with the sun at his back, I have to turn and look over my shoulder. As I do, I'm aware of a rushing sound in my head, like blood cycling through me too quickly.

I say, "It seems too easy, your walking out like this. Like you're just stepping out for a jug of milk, see you in a bit. It's like what some cold-hearted bastard might do." I chip at the rich Wisconsin dirt with my weed extractor. "I don't think you're a cold-hearted bastard, Peter. Lacking in self-esteem, perhaps, if you'll forgive the phrase. But not by nature cold-hearted. Or a bastard. By nature."

He doesn't say anything, he doesn't defend himself. His hands move in his pockets. I can feel a mosquito sucking at my cheek and another one on my forearm. The spikelets on the veronica seem too purple to be real.

"What about Louis?" I ask. "Are you going to wreck his life so you can satisfy some need you have for I don't know what? A better blow job? Cannonball tits?"

"I'm not going to wreck his life." A hand emerges from his pocket and moves toward me. "You have a mosquito on your cheek."

"I'm aware of that," I say.

FOUR MORNINGS LATER, I'm taking the garbage out to the curb when Dennis pulls up in his truck. He has shaved off his beard. From ten paces, where I've halted with the can, he looks ten years younger.

"How you getting along?" he asks, more cheer in his voice than I expect from a man whose wife has moved out on him, leaving him to mind three boys.

"Fine." Inside the can, along with the week's debris, is the hedgehog boot scraper, that ponderous symbol of my husband's infidelity, which I twice screwed into the porch floor and then permanently unscrewed. Isn't it the hedgehog that knows one thing deeply, according to Aesop? One thing I know is that a hedgehog boot scraper makes me want to toss things.

"I was wondering if you and Pete and Louis want to come over for a cookout tonight. I'm going to grill some venison burgers."

"Peter's out of town," I say. The story he told Louis was that he was going to New Mexico to visit a college friend who has Hodgkin's. Louis carried one of his father's suitcases out to the car, and then he offered to lend him his plastic Army canteen, in case Peter got stuck in the desert.

"We'd be happy to have you and Louis," Dennis says. "You like venison?"

"Yeah, sure." This isn't quite accurate.

"Seven OK?"

"Yeah, sure." I press down on the lid of the garbage can; it's not secure.

"Nice robe," he says, and puts his truck in gear. The robe, which is sateen, has a bee-and-flower motif. I bought it this spring.

"Thanks." I don't say anything about his clean cheeks. I'm not up to trading compliments with a man in a truck at six-thirty in the morning.

AROUND NOON, LOUIS and I pedal our bicycles to the lake. Louis leads, shouting *"Avanti! Avanti!"* In my basket, I have his fishing pole and the worms he dug out of the garden. In my backpack, I have lunch and a *libro giallo*. A little Italian flag taped to the handlebars of Louis's bike flaps in the breeze he stirs up. He's a gonfalonier for a party of two.

It's a hot day, the air so thick and humid that it feels like we're tunneling through it. We take a trail that runs along a finger of wooded land that juts into the lake, and stop at a swimming beach halfway out. The beach looks southeast across the lake, toward campus—the old stone boathouse, the tile-roofed dorms among oaks. Poking up above everything is a red-brick campanile, which clever undergraduates sheathe in a prophylactic every so often.

Louis fishes from a rock shaded by a clump of white birches. I lie back on my towel and read five pages of my mystery before putting it aside. I'm sweating through my T-shirt. The leaves at the top of the birches are moving, flickering, but there is no breeze down here. I sit up with a desire for a cigarette. I haven't had one in almost eight years, since shortly before I became pregnant with Louis. The afternoon of the day I quit, I went to Central Park with a book and ate a gelato and then a hot pretzel and then blades of New York City grass, one by one.

I see a couple sharing a cigarette on the other side of the beach. He puts the cigarette in her mouth, and then she, laughing, puts it in his mouth. His, I'm afraid, is the ripe *bocca* of my ex-student Adrian.

I lie back down and shut my eyes. I remember Adrian leaning against the Bally, asking me the Italian word for *pinball*, telling me that if it wasn't his last semester at school he'd take more Italian. A ball shot past the flippers. Then I flubbed a rebound and another ball slipped down the run-out slot. I let him buy me a glass of wine. It was four in the afternoon and it was raining. I re-

moved my wire-rimmed no-line bifocals and put them in my bag.
My field of vision was reduced to Adrian's mouth, which seemed
to glisten in the subaqueous light of the bar. He told me he'd been
reading Calvino. "This dude I know told me about him," he said.
Adrian's hand grazed my arm as he reached for a bowl of peanuts,
and I thought for a moment that I'd be willing to pay fifty dollars
for a room at the Badger Motor Court, three blocks away. But I
left, saying I had a department function to attend, and bicycled
home, the cold late-April drizzle stinging my face, fogging my
glasses. Was I really that close to sleeping with a boy half my age?
I couldn't decide whether I felt virtuous or regretful for having re-
sisted Adrian, but the rain got into my bones and brought on a
fever that laid me low for several days.

"I need to go pee." Louis is standing beside me, dangling the
worm on his fishing line near my nose. He thinks he is being
rascally.

"Get it out of my face, please." There is an outhouse in the
woods, on the other side of the beach. I can lead Louis past Adrian
and his companion—the direct route—or we can circumnavigate
them. We take the direct route.

"*Buon giorno,*" I say. After the encounter in the College Avenue
pub, I saw Adrian only in the classroom, and only irregularly. The
absences were the reason he didn't get an A.

"Hey." On his smooth chest, above his left nipple, is a tattoo,
some sort of crested, long-tailed bird. Below the nipple is an in-
scription I can't make out, even with my glasses. His girlfriend is
tattooless, as far as I can tell.

"How's life after college?" I ask. I had him on the line for that
moment, the thrill of it shooting up my arm, and then I let him
go. Or he had me, I should say.

"It's all work and no pinball." He says "peen-ball," as an Italian
might, and grins.

Louis tugs at my hand. "Ciao," I say to Adrian.

Before we reach the outhouse, Louis stops and pulls down his bathing suit. "Can I get a Road Runner tattoo like that man?" He attempts to cast his pee widely. It patters on ferns.

"Maybe when you get to college." I put my hand on his head and let it slide over the occipital ridge down to his soft, damp nape. He pulls up his swimsuit. "I kind of like your skin the way it is."

He ignores me. He's looking toward Adrian. "It's so cool. It says 'Beep! Beep!' right here." He thumps his chest.

BEFORE TRYING ONE of Dennis's venison burgers, I fortify myself with a half bottle of wine, which I've brought along for the occasion. Dennis drinks a can of Diet Coke. He tells me he is trying to lay off the sauce. "Hoping to slim down a little here," he says, patting his stomach. "Got to make myself lean and mean for the divorce negotiations."

"I thought divorce was no-fault in Wisconsin."

"It is, but we still got a few kinks to work out," Dennis says. "Custody arrangements, that sort of thing." He touches his bare cheek, then his upper lip, as if in search of his missing beard. Close up, Dennis looks a bit raw without his beard—youthful in the way an overgrown boy is youthful, and yet harder, too.

"Yeah," he says, shifting in his lawn chair, setting an ankle on top of a knee. "Liz wants to blame me for the fact that she ran off with some hair stylist." Dennis makes a kind of *pish* sound, like a tire leaking. "A hair stylist who's supposedly not a fairy, who's got to be weird if he isn't. Who's got black hair down to his ass like what'shername, Rapunzel, speaking of fairy tales."

I don't know what Peter's girlfriend looks like. Not that I care too much. It seems enough to know her name and occupation. I scored one of her business cards while snooping around Peter's desk the day he left. She's a clown/magician/ balloon artist. (The virgules are hers.) She does kids' birthday parties and the like. Louis has probably watched her turn balloons into dachshunds.

I sip my wine and look at Dennis's bare, wagging foot. I want to ask him about the black nail on his big toe. What fell on it? What did he bump into in the dead of night? But Dennis wants to talk about Liz.

"You remember that day you were over here? I'd been fishing over by Racine, I think. That was when I finally figured out Liz was seeing this guy. It'd been going on for a while. Silas knew somehow. My thirteen-year-old son knew before I did. I guess I'd been too busy tying flies or something. I think it must've started the weekend I went up to Fond du Lac for that sturgeon-spearing deal. She shipped the kids out to my mom's house, and then she and the hair stylist had their fun."

"Well." I slap a mosquito on my leg and brush away the bloody remains. I'm ready for another glass of wine, almost ready for Dennis's venison.

"I sat in this shack on the ice and drank beer and watched through a hole for these big, ugly fish," Dennis says. "Whenever I told Liz I was going fishing or hunting, she always said, 'Sure, be my guest,' but what she meant was, 'Sure, be a bum and leave me with three children.'"

He falls silent. I can see him chewing the inside of his mouth, trying to get his failures and Liz's betrayal to add up, trying to make an equation out of it.

"Should we feed the kids?" I ask.

"Sure, sure," Dennis says, rising from his chair all of a sudden, like he is scurrying up out of a dream. "Let's do some cooking." Vukie, who is on a leash attached to a clothesline, sits up to watch. Dennis walks over to the grill and squirts several ounces of fire starter on the charcoal. And then, for good measure, he gives it another dousing. When he drops a match in, flames leap up, enlivening the dusk. "The magic of chemicals," he says.

I go over to the picnic table and pour myself more wine.

"What's Pete doing in New Mexico?" Dennis takes a hunk of ground venison out of butcher's paper and shapes it into a patty.

"Visiting a friend," I say. I don't say that Peter left a message on the machine this afternoon, telling Louis that he'd seen a herd of elk in the moutains near Santa Fe, telling Louis that he missed and loved him. I don't say that I erased the message and gave Louis a paraphrase: his father had called to say hi.

Dennis looks at me sideways, as if he might have some inkling of my situation, as if there is something in my voice or posture that suggests a fellow victim of a homewrecking. I stand up straighter.

"I went out West once, after college," Dennis says. He doesn't know. "I went with this girl, but she hopped off the wagon before we got too far. I camped out one night on the edge of a mesa in Utah. Got stoned, watched the sunset, and then just as I was closing my eyes, I heard this *whoosh*, like the air was being parted right above my nose. This happened four or five times. It was a big bird, an owl, probably, telling me to move, letting me know I was in its space. It was flying so close I could damn near smell its breath. It was all revved up for a night of hunting."

"What'd you do?"

"I moved my sleeping bag," Dennis says, setting the patty on a plate and grabbing another chunk of meat. "I'm a little slow sometimes, but I'm not dumb."

Even though he gives me a knowing grin, I still think he doesn't know about me. I take a handful of venison and shape it into a burger. The meat is dark brown, cool to the touch.

"I do most of the deer hunting in the family, but Liz got this one," Dennis says, tossing meat from palm to palm. "She hit it with my truck one night last winter out on County S. Some farmer driving by helped her get it into the truck. A nice little doe. Provided by my ex-wife." He touches my arm in what I assume is meant to be a reassuring way. "I'll go get the fixings."

SILAS RIDES HIS BIKE through the gate and up to the picnic table. His stocking cap is pulled low, but blond tendrils escape out the sides. He is wearing shorts that fall to his shins. He gazes at me as I bite into my burger.

"You going to join us, Silas?" Dennis asks.

Silas doesn't answer. To me he says, "You're eating roadkill, you know."

I try to smile, but my mouth is full. Even though I've dressed the burger with onion and relish, even though I've drunk a good bit of wine, the taste of the deer occupies most of my brain. A doe leaping through some dark wood is in my mouth; so is a doe straying out onto County S.

"I told her about it," Dennis says. He calls to Eric, who is eating dinner with Louis and Tim in a pup tent. "Hey, Eric, how's your Bambiburger?"

"Good," says Eric, who has put mayonnaise and ketchup on his. Louis and Tim are eating peanut butter sandwiches.

"Eric would eat a rat if you put it between buns," Silas says, taking a handful of potato chips out of the bag on the table.

"Did you find your snake?" I ask Silas. I learned from Louis today that the snake has gotten loose.

"No." Silas's blond eyebrows, just visible below the stocking cap, are faint brushstrokes; his eyes are smoky-blue faraway things. "He got tired of hanging out with a bunch of losers."

"Hey," Dennis says, sharply.

Silas edges backward on his bike. It's an old one-speed, a yard-saler—just a frame and two fat tires, though the handlebars are bent upward in a funky way. The bike is way too small for him, but some adolescent boys prefer things to be the wrong size, clownishly wrong, if possible.

"How come Louis's father isn't eating here?" Silas's question seems to be addressed to Dennis, but I answer it.

"He's out of town." Thirty minutes of light are left in the day. The first fireflies are out now, doing their glide-and-blink.

Silas makes a snorting sound. "How come I saw him with, like, this girl in the parking lot at Walgreens?"

"When was this, Silas?" I can taste the impact of deer and truck now. I reach for more relish.

"I don't know," he says. "Sometime. He was feeling her up." He snorts again.

"You must be mistaken, Silas." Probably he saw something. Whether he has made up the details to taunt me hardly matters.

Dennis swings his legs out from under the picnic table, brushing my shin with his foot in the process. "Silas, you and I are going inside to have a talk."

Silas, who has dismounted from his bike, holds it between himself and his father. "Forget you, man."

"Silas," Dennis says softly but firmly, as if he were talking to a jumpy horse. From behind, in his T-shirt and basketball shorts, Dennis seems scarily large. He disappears into his bulk. Is this what Liz saw when he headed out the door into the wilds of Wisconsin?

"Forget you, man." Silas thrusts the bike toward Dennis and sprints toward the gate. Dennis catches the bike before it hits him, and then takes off after his son.

Some moments later, I'm running, too. I'm yelling at Louis and the two younger Wunsch boys, who have beaten me out the gate. I'm yelling at Dennis, who is running under a full head of steam, who is going to reel in Silas in about five seconds. "Stop, you all! Stop, Dennis! Don't hurt him!" Even when I'm not top-heavy with wine and not wearing pool sandals, I'm slow on my feet. I have slender legs—I'm proud of them, I take them to the natatorium three times a week—but I run like a clod. Nevertheless, it's not me who trips on the whirlybird sprinkler in Tom Heckman's yard.

By the time Dennis pulls himself up out of Tom's wet grass, Silas is halfway down the next block. "Silas," he shouts, "I want you home now!"

Silas keeps going, into the gathering dark. The sky will be clear tonight, I notice, lots of stars.

"Daddy," Eric says. "What did Silas do?"

"He made me lose my temper," Dennis says, brushing clippings off his knees. "You boys go back home now."

"Silas is a big jerk," Tim says, turning away from us. Louis and Eric follow him over to the birch at the corner of Tom's lot.

Tom himself is in his garage, oblivious of the fact that there are five people on his lawn. He's got his table saw going.

"Are you OK?" I ask. "Your toe—is it all right?"

"My toe?" Dennis glances at me, then looks down at his feet —big white things ropy with veins, half-submerged in Tom's lush lawn. "Oh, that. It's just a dead nail dying. I dropped a drawer on my foot when I was cleaning out some of Liz's stuff." He looks down the street, in the direction Silas has gone. "I wasn't going to hurt him, you know." I'm not sure he has convinced himself of that yet, though maybe it's more humiliation than anger that burns in his cheeks. "I love him, even if he is a little prick half the time."

"Would you like coffee?" I ask. My head is pounding, I realize.

"I better take a rain check," he says. He looks over at Tom's birch, which Eric is climbing. Tim and Louis are circling it, chanting that caveman's rhyme about beans, the musical fruit.

"There was a while there when I thought I should leave the

door open for Liz, in case she wanted to come back," Dennis says, shuffling his feet, doing a dance with himself. "For the kids, you know. So they wouldn't have to commute between me and the hair guy's place. But things are screwed up beyond repair now. I can't see her knocking on the door, and I can't see me keeping it open any longer."

I look over at Louis, who continues to circle the tree with Tim, quietly now, like a philosopher mulling. Eric is way out on a limb, tempting fate. The dark is still coming down—faster, it seems, than a child could color it in. In a few more minutes, the stars will be out, pinpricks in all that velvety vastness. I imagine sipping black coffee in the silence after I've put Louis to bed, a silence that is contingent on Tom having put away his power tools.

"How about you?" Dennis asks. "You going to be all right?" He knows.

"Sure." I have Louis. I'll have him until he flees into the night, his head covered by a stocking cap pulled low.

I call to Louis. And after I thank Dennis for dinner, going so far as to touch him on the elbow, and after tall, bowlegged Tom Heckman, wearing protective goggles, comes out of his garage to tell Dennis about the snake he killed that afternoon in his breezeway, I take my son's hand and lead him home and shut the door behind us.

Not Renata

NOW AND THEN, he'd come into my head, unbidden, unconjured, the way long-ago boyfriends will do, if you aren't careful. I'd be chewing on my pencil or fingernail, say, or looking at the blue California sky while pumping gas into my car, and there he'd be, lying on a three-legged, rummage-sale couch in our graduate school apartment of twenty years before. (The fourth leg was a cookbook my mother had given me. "Hope this will inspire you," she'd said.) In this picture he's as still as a painter's model, cigarette smoke veiling him like stage fog. I peer at him, this secretive, cowardly boy I once loved, and then the picture dissolves and I'm inhaling gasoline fumes or listening to Mrs. Ramirez or Mr. Kuhn or someone else at the senior center tell me a story. I work with the elderly. With the crabby and unpopular Mr. Kuhn, I sometimes play checkers, waiting for the moment he says, "King me!" and stirs me from my daydreams.

The last time my former boyfriend appeared before me, I was in an oral surgeon's office. The doctor, who was rather cheerful for having to work on a Saturday, was removing a nugget of something from my upper gum, what he was ninety-eight percent certain was an accessory salivary gland that had calcified. But he was going to biopsy it just to be on the safe side. He shot me up with anesthetic. As I lay in the chair, waiting for my mouth to go numb, I thought about Chile, that root-shaped country at the bottom of the world. I was planning a trip there in December. ("Chile?" the querulous Mr. Kuhn asked. "What's so great about Chile?") After the doctor finished with me, I thought I might go buy a new pair of hiking boots. Then my ex-boyfriend floated into view, like a ghost on a litter, his big toe poking through a hole in his sock.

An hour or so later, my mouth still puffy with anesthetic, I was in a bookstore on Point Loma, looking for a guidebook on Chile. I found one and took it into the reading nook. A man in a soiled sea captain's cap occupied the couch, his head dipping and rising as he drifted in and out of sleep. I sat down in a wing chair and read about Chile's lake district, the volcanic craters and glacial *lagos* and waterfalls like wizards' beards. The man in the sea captain's cap began to snore; I saw that he had a welt under his chin. I picked up a quarterly that lay on the table next to me. I was attracted by the photograph on the cover: two pairs of dancing legs, one bare and female, the other blue-jeaned and male. On the back, among the list of contributors, was my ex-boyfriend's name, Peter Sackrider.

I read Peter's contribution, a long, quasi-autobiographical story called "The Hazeletts' Dog." It's set in the late seventies, around the time Peter and I were graduate students in Ann Arbor. It takes place in a leafy suburb of Louisville, where the actual Peter grew up, and it recounts the quasi-fictional Peter's relationship with his contemporaries Hal and Mary Lee Hazelett, who live down the road from Peter's parents. When this Peter arrives home from Ann Arbor, we learn from a conversation he has with Mary Lee (a well-bred tease who rejected him some years ago for the bolder Hal) that Peter has recently broken up with a certain Renata. The breakup was precipitated by events of the previous Christmas, which Renata, a Jew whose other identifying marks (if any) go unnoted, spent in Kentucky with Peter. Renata, it seems, took offense at an anti-Semitic remark made by Peter's potted aunt at a family gathering; she took further offense when Peter didn't respond to his aunt, and eventually—which is to say, in the next line—she dumped him.

The story goes on, exploring triangles (Peter, Hal, Mary Lee; Peter, his mother, Hal), Peter's moral shortcomings, his doggish longings to be liked, petted, caressed. Renata receives no further direct mention, though the reader recalls her when the narrator recounts an instance of anti-Semitism from Peter's high school days.

Renata is me, of course, though there are ways in which I'm not Renata, starting with my name. Peter was right to change it. Who would believe a Jewish character called Nora Sue? But it is a fact, as the story reports, that Peter and I lived together in Ann Arbor for several months, in an apartment above an adult bookstore. He read Keats and swarms of commentators, often while stretched out on that broken-down sofa, and I read William Blake, he who, at the age of four, saw God press his face against a windowpane. It's a fact, too, that Peter took me to meet his parents at Christmas. He didn't make up the stuff about his aunt's anti-Semitic comment—a rather mild one, as such things go—but his failure to respond to her wasn't the only reason we parted.

Sensation had returned to my mouth; my tongue found the single stitch in my gum, where once there had been that nugget of whatever. I put the quarterly that contained Peter's story back on the table and got up from my chair. The old sea captain, eyes now at half-mast, said, unnautically, "Happy trails, missy." I paid for the guidebook and left the shop. Sunshine flowed down the street, like something poured out of a bottomless bottle. A dry fall breeze rattled the fronds of the palms in the sidewalk planters. Unease nipped at me. I'd lived in California for a decade, but I felt about as permanent as tumbleweed. The stitched-up hole in my gum pulsed.

I TOOK TWO ADVILS, put on my bathing suit, and toted my Keowee half a block down the hill to the bay. The tide was out. A lady and her mannerly dog walked briskly along the beach. Sandpipers skittered away from them.

I set the boat down twenty feet from a young man who sat motionless on a rock, like a gull weighing its options. I fitted the paddle halves together, stowed my fanny pack, removed and stowed my sandals.

"That like a kayak or something?" the young man said, pointing at the Keowee with his head. His hair was cut close to the skull and he had long, narrow sideburns, like stripes on a hot car. He wore camouflage pants and a fatigue-green T-shirt. A tattoo decorated his right biceps. He looked about college age. Or maybe he'd gotten loose from one of the military reservations nearby. I smelled reefer but I didn't see any smoke.

"Yes," I said, feeling the bay lapping at my shins. I zipped my life vest, pulled my baseball cap lower.

"Like for beginners," he said. The Keowee was more stable than a regular kayak—and cheaper, too. My former husband gave it to me some years ago.

"Yes," I said, gripping the paddle, stowing myself in the cockpit.

"Yes, yes, she said yes," the young man said, looking out at the blue bay as if it were his true and only audience. "Have a nice day, Molly Bloom."

All kinds of people live in California. Why not a skinhead with a minor in literature? Or an AWOL soldier who reads the classics in his spare time?

Or maybe he was alluding to a pop song about a Molly Bloom. Pop music was full of yea-saying Mollys, wasn't it?

"Have a nice day, too," I said, sticking my paddle in the water, wondering if he'd be there when I came back. It wasn't my wish to see him again, but I wasn't afraid of him, either. He was just a boy who'd washed up on a public beach, like driftwood, all his complicated feelings worn smooth.

The spot where I'd put in is on an arm of the bay, an inlet staked out by yacht clubs whose members sail in and out on arks made of silk and mahogany. I headed out into the bay proper. A following breeze sent me skimming along. The sky was hazy blue, an indolent shade. I drifted, and thought of the autumn skies in the Midwest, where I grew up, and of how sharp the blue became when the temperature dipped; the color was like a shock to the skin.

I got the bottle of Dos Equis out of my pack—something to supplement the Advil. I drank it with my eyes half-closed, hearing the planes taking off from the naval air station on Coronado, the harbor seals barking near the piers of the naval research facility on Point Loma. When I first moved here, a year or so after I divorced, I had trouble sleeping. The constant buzz of aircraft I quickly got used to. It was the seals, with their urpy cries, like cute children in need of attention, that kept me awake. I'd lie in bed, imagining myself an Inuit with a club; I whacked pups and adults alike. I counted slaughtered seals, thousands of them. When I got tired of counting seals, I counted old boyfriends, going back to Billy Leach in fifth grade, shy Billy, who on Talent Day played an almost inaudible version of "When the Saints" on a pocket comb wrapped in Kleenex.

I drifted, trailing my hand in the bay, seeing my hand on Peter Sackrider's blue-jeaned knee as we sat in his idling Volkswagen, on the narrow, sinuous road that led to his parents' house in Kentucky. Peter had stopped—jammed on the brakes—to avoid hitting a deer and the dog chasing it. They'd shot through the headlight beams like cartoon sketches, almost too fast to be named deer and dog. We'd been driving all day from Ann Arbor. Peter had been tense, untalkative, smoking one cigarette after another. He *smelled* cranky. I put my hand on his knee and said, "The moment after you nearly get squished by a deer is pleasant, don't you think?" I understood his grumbled "Yes" to be something less than assent.

I was put in the guest bedroom, a floor below Peter's bedroom and that of his sister, who wasn't coming home until after Christmas. "You'll have your own bathroom," Mrs. Sackrider said. The guest room had twin four-poster beds with extrafirm mattresses. On the table between the beds was a glass-bottomed lamp with a frilly shade, a bowl of dried rose petals, and a 1928 edition of *The Book of Common Prayer*. When I opened the book, the thin pages released a sweet, genteel smell, like ardor sublimated.

That night, we went caroling. Peter said, "I hope this won't be too weird for you. You're not required to sing, you know."

I doubted I'd find it "weird," unless there was some Southern twist to caroling I didn't know about. I'd been before, with my friends in Belle Plaine, the northern Illinois town where I was born and raised. I liked those sweet, *lento* songs about a baby being born in the dead of winter.

I was, and am, a Jew, but hardly an observant one. Now and then, my mother, who grew up among Jews in Chicago, took me to the nearest temple, a forty-five-minute ride. But at an early age I sided with my father, an unbelieving Irishman who, if he was home on Christmas Eve, took me to church to hear the music. I sometimes thought that Peter, whose interest in practicing his own faith was well hidden, hoped that I, a pert-nosed reddish-blonde with an Irish-bumpkin name, would be more "Jewish" than I gave the impression of being. I was his first Jewish girl, and perhaps he thought he wasn't getting the full experience.

"I could mumble the words, if you liked," I said, pulling Peter toward me. We were in the Sackriders' front hall, getting on our coats. He smelled better; he'd taken a shower and changed.

After the caroling, we went to the house of a neighbor called (in Peter's story) Colonel Willborn. There was food in chafing dishes tended by a cocoa-colored man in a white jacket whom Peter seemed to know. Anyhow, they had a conversation. I drank the Colonel's spiked eggnog and talked to Peter's father. Judge Sackrider was thin, modest, unjudgelike. A clump of unkempt gray hair lay on his forehead; white hairs bloomed in his nostrils. When somebody called out to him from across the room—"It's the hanging judge!"—Peter's father touched me on the elbow and said, "Don't tell him my court is a civil one, where hanging is not permitted." Then he went to refill my cup and get himself some nonalcoholic cider.

I talked to the man who had accompanied the carolers with his wheezy accordion, and to a lady whose sweater was crewelworked with leaping harts, and to a bald-headed man who told me that he was one of the Wise Men in a church Christmas pageant. He was the king who brought the Christ child myrrh. He tried to shake the foam at the bottom of his eggnog cup into his gullet. Could you imagine crossing all those deserts on your camel, he said, with a box of gum resin as a baby gift?

The man who had called Peter's father "the hanging judge" put his hand on my back as he passed me in the hall, and said, "Excuse me, precious." I talked to a guy who wore a rumpled cord jacket and had a big, late-seventies mustache and drank beer from a can. This was Hal Hazelett (or the model for him), Peter's old school buddy, who was now a newspaper reporter. He seemed to regret his presence at the party. He hadn't gone caroling. He said he loathed Christmas. Didn't I hate the season, all that piety mixed with greed?

"As a Jew, you mean?" I said.

"You're Jewish?" He squeezed his beer can and made the metal pop.

I confessed that I was, more or less, but that I didn't mind Christmas. In fact, I liked its pagan excesses, all the drinking and eating and sentimentalism, its anti-Puritanism.

At some point late in the evening, the Colonel took me into his study to show me an 1885 edition of *The Works of Alfred Lord Tennyson*, which he thought I, as a student of English literature, would appreciate. The Colonel, whose title had come to him courtesy of some local honor society, had beautiful white eyebrows that looked as if they'd been licked into peaks by a cat. The silver buttons on his red vest gleamed. Tennyson, the subject of few dissertations where Peter and I went to school, was the Colonel's favorite poet; he knew a number of the poems by heart. To prove it, he recited "The Charge of the Light Brigade," clippety-clop, and then he read one called "Fatima," a love poem full of throbbing and swooning and shuddering. The Colonel was half in the bag and he read with fervor, closing his eyes as he came down on the end rhymes. Peter, long-lost, found me leaning against the Colonel's desk, grinning stupidly. I was half in the bag, too.

On the way home—we walked—I turned to Peter and said, "Kiss me, Pierre. Put your tongue in my mouth." We were near the spot where the deer had come bounding across the road.

"Now?" he said, as if a dark road might be an inappropriate place. There was no moon, only stars blinking in the cold, Christmas lights twinkling on bushes up ahead.

"Now would be a good time," I said. I had my hands inside his coat. I felt the baby rolls of flesh above his hips. I slid my hands up to his ribs, placed my thumbs on his nipples. He kept his hands at his sides, as if I were frisking him. "I barely saw you all night."

"I had to talk to my parents' friends," he said. "They wanted to know if I'm going to be a professor when I grow up."

"And you said?"

"I hemmed and hawed."

"You're slouching," I said, moving my hands around to his lower back. I untucked his shirt and put my fingers on his skin.

"Whew," he said, straightening. He placed his hands on my shoulders, as if to balance himself. We looked almost like a boy and a girl at their first boy-girl dance.

"Now's the time to kiss me," I said, sliding fingers under his belt, onto his warm hips. When my father went out the door with his saxophone under his arm and his Thelonious Monk beret on his head, on his way to a gig in Elgin or Champaign or Moline, he always said, "Now's the time to kiss me." It was an inside jazz joke—"Now's the Time" being a Charlie Parker tune—as well as a dart aimed at my mother, who was not a kisser and hugger. I compensated for my mother. To me, my dad would say, "Thank you for laying your salty peanuts on me."

"I don't think I'm really professorial timber," Peter said, the steam from his mouth almost warming my face. His hands fell from my shoulders, caught on the belt of my coat. "Flipping burgers might be more my level."

I figured this was one of his feints, self-pity rearing (or lowering, I guess) its shaggy head; he wanted me to tell him that he was a good student, that he should stick it out, finish his Ph.D., put elbow patches on his sports jacket, which did in fact have holes in it. I'd said something like this to him before, without quite believing it. The truth was, he was only a decent student. He was diligent, he wrote well enough, but he lacked presence, he wasn't quick on his feet, and he was frightened by audiences larger than one or two. I thought he would be lucky to get a job at a branch of some state college. Still, I was ready to hitch my wagon to his flickery star, follow him to west Texas or wherever, unless of course he preferred to follow me, crackerjack Blake scholar that I was. He was this weakness I had. It was not only the sight of him—the small, delicate hands, for instance, or the toe poking through his sock as he lay on our three-legged couch. Nor was it the fact that he regularly packed a lunch for me to carry to campus—fruit, hard-boiled egg, sometimes a cucumber-and-cream-cheese number that he called an Oscar Wildewich.

"Stay in school," I said. My hands were on his bottom. He was vulnerable there. "I don't want to sleep with a fry cook."

But he was looking away, toward the constellations that spun above big old Southern trees on which mistletoe actually grew. I saw that pictures were popping up in his head, slides of the future, and that I was a shadowy figure he didn't know what to do with. Even with my hands on him, I couldn't keep him near me.

"You still haven't kissed me," I said, "even though we're standing right under the aerial parasite that the Druids were so fond of."

"Huh?" he said, reaching into his coat for his cigarettes.

"Mistletoe." I took away his cigarettes.

He kissed me. A dog barked three times, and then it was over.

"Thank you for laying your salty peanuts on me," I said.

I DRANK THE LAST of the Dos Equis and pointed the Keowee toward home. I'd drifted while sipping my beer, pulled by the current toward the ocean, and I was now a good two miles from where I'd put in. ("Your mind wanders," Mr. Kuhn has said. "I could beat you blindfolded. King me again.") I paddled toward the shore, where I thought the breeze and chop might be lighter. My arms felt heavy, but I paddled like a regular Trojan for a while. I tried to remember what I had in my refrigerator that I could eat for dinner, but nothing came to mind. A pelican flew overhead, slowly, like something prehistoric.

Christmas Eve, 1978. Peter and I went to the midnight service at his parents' church. Peter hadn't wanted to go, but I'd asked him to take me, and his mother had said, "It wouldn't hurt to go once a year, would it?" The church, an Episcopal one, smelled of pine boughs and women's furs and candle wax. Peter mumbled the words of the prayers and rolled his eyes at me during the homily, but he went to the Communion rail with his parents. When he returned to the pew, I checked his face for signs of change. He looked slightly flushed and his lower lip seemed to glisten, though perhaps that was only the effect of the lights. I touched his wrist, to see if consuming the body and blood of Christ had altered his pulse. He pulled away before I could get a clear reading.

I didn't know what exactly it was that he wanted to withhold from me, what sore part of him he didn't want me touch. Unless he thought he was saving himself, tender spot and all, for some future lover. He was like that deer trying to outrun the dog.

That night, after Mrs. Sackrider had filled all the stockings (including one for me) and unplugged the lights on the Christmas tree and drunk her protein drink and set out the breakfast dishes, I went upstairs to Peter's room. I'd not come up the previous night because Peter had discouraged me; he'd said his mother was a night owl and would hear us. He was afraid of his mother. But I got lonely on my narrow guest bed reading my daily dose of Blake scholarship. When I tiptoed past Judge and Mrs. Sackrider's room and mounted the stairs, it had officially been Christmas for two hours.

Peter was still in his church clothes. He'd been wrapping presents. There was a small pile of them on the extra bed. He was smoking a cigarette — Santa's helper on a break. When I entered the room, he said, "How'd you slip past the sentry?"

"I'm a tricky little vixen." I sat down on the bed with the presents. "Which one is for me?"

"You can't open them until morning," he said. "It's a rule." He stubbed out his cigarette.

"'He who desires,'" I said, "'but acts not, breeds pestilence.'" I shook a box wrapped in green paper.

"I have to write my notes—as Willie Blake said to his girlfriend when she came busting into his room."

"Your Merry Christmas notes?"

"Everybody in my family writes these long notes to go with the presents. They're like testimonials and end-of-the-year requests for forgiveness rolled into one. If you've been a bad boy—if you haven't been a dutiful son or husband or whatever—you say you'll try to be more loving next year. You thank the recipient for her kindness and generosity and forbearance. You downplay the gift it-self, because even though it was carefully chosen, it can't stack up to the feelings you have for this person."

He lay back, putting his hands behind his head, and gazed upward. He was twenty-seven, but he could have passed for sev-enteen, a lonesome boy bouncing lonesome thoughts off the ceil-ing. It was this that had attracted me to him initially, though I'd mistaken it for detachment, grad student cool. It turned out that I had to do all the seducing, but this was less work than you might imagine. And for a while he seemed ravenous for me, like a desert saint who'd decided that he no longer wanted to live on bugs and thistles. I'd drawn him out, and he seemed happy about it. There'd been that weekend in a motel on Lake Michigan; the weather was rotten, perfect for our purposes. And then there were those after-noons in our apartment—pluperfect Midwestern fall afternoons, the skies radiantly blue even through our filmy windows—which we spent on our frameless mattress, reading, fornicating, reading. We'd hear the belled door of the porn shop downstairs open and shut, and I'd say, "May I help you, monsieur?" and he'd say, "S'il vous plait, do you carry Standing Proud, by I. M. A. Dick?" We read and napped and listened to jazz, like a grad school couple with a future. Then, early one evening, I awakened alone in the dark. He came back three hours later, stoned, with half a Dagwood sandwich for me, unable to say where he'd been. When the weather turned and the snow started to fall, he began to retreat from me to his library carrel, to the gym where he shot baskets, to a bar called the Idlewild. Though he continued to pack my lunch and kiss me (but only in the dark), he was remote, fretful about his schoolwork, difficult to stir from his sullenness. I minded that I had to wheedle and tease, but I did it.

"So," I said, touching a box wrapped in shiny red paper, "the gifts and notes are like expiation for the year's sins, not straightforward expressions of Christmas joy."

"Yeah."

I moved over to his bed. "I have a question," I said. "When you eat the Communion wafer and drink the wine, do you feel like a cannibal? Happy? Sated?" I undid the knot of his tie.

"It's a secret," he said, though he was blushing. I pulled off his tie, unbuttoned his shirt, and kissed his belly button, an inny with dark hairs swirling around it. He kept his eyes on the ceiling, his hands under his head. He swallowed a couple times, a sound like water lapping against the side of a boat. He wanted to resist me, but he couldn't muster the will. I unzipped his pants. I stood up and took my nightgown off. I said, "'The nakedness of woman is the work of God.'"

"Could you close the door all the way?" he said. "S'il vous plaît."

"You're supposed to say, 'The lust of the goat is the bounty of God.'" I closed the door. There was an old Cincinnati Reds pennant on the back of it. "Boo, Reds," I said. I was a Cubs fan.

He didn't laugh. "And maybe turn off the light, too."

I did as he asked. The dark was thick. I took everything off him. He was naked as a fish in black water, there but not there.

At some point, I said, "I'll stifle my cries of pleasure, so your mom won't hear us." He didn't laugh.

Later, when I said, "Merry Christmas," he said, "I need to tell you something." He had on his most solemn voice.

"You could put it in your Christmas note to me," I said, "if it's not too terrible. You didn't go cow-tipping with old Barnes, did you?" Old Barnes was his adviser.

He didn't laugh. "I slept with this guy, this biologist, a post-doc, he's studying bioluminescence in fungi or something. He's British—I mean, from England. Durham. It was a one-night stand. Or briefer than that, really. So 'slept' would be inaccurate, I guess."

I laughed a little. I couldn't help myself. Perhaps it was the way he described the man, citing his academic credentials and nationality, as if it mattered that he studied fungi instead of quarks, as if it mattered that he was English instead of Filipino. Or maybe it was the punctilious way he qualified the experience, as if he were saying that the meal he'd just eaten was only a snack, if looked at properly. Anyway, laughter seemed more appropriate than shock or hurt, though I was of course hurt, if not shocked. I meant to sound only curious when I said, "Did you fuck him or did he fuck you?" I pictured something hasty and untender—the biologist screwing Peter and then hurrying back to his lab to check his light-emitting fungi.

Peter was silent. I kept my head on his shoulder. He was warm, blood was being supplied to his head via his ticking carotid, but nothing issued from his mouth.

"So, what's he like? Is he a mesomorph, ectomorph? What are his hobbies?" I touched Peter's earlobe; it was soft, like baby's flesh.

"I don't know, Nora Sue." It always surprised me when he said my name; something in me sprung to attention. "He was just this guy I met at the Idlewild."

"What's his name?"

"Martin."

"Will you be making sandwiches for Martin next semester?"

"No." But he didn't sound positive. Maybe he'd lied about the number of times he'd slept with Martin. I turned on the night-table lamp so I could see him better. "Queer men come on to me sometimes. And I was drunk. And I guess I'd always wanted to know what it felt like."

"It must be hard to tell what it feels like when you're drunk."

"I wasn't totally drunk, actually." He gazed at me. His eyes, greenish-brown, like the woods in early spring, were clear about his desires: he wanted me to understand and comfort him, and he wanted to be released from whatever obligations he thought he had to me.

"I can move out of the apartment, if you want," he said. "I'll sign the lease over."

"Our beautiful apartment above the porn store?" I felt a rush of adrenaline, anger, and I rolled on top of him, like a wrestler, a lady wrestler with hard little tits and chewed-down fingernails. "I don't know why I don't want you to move out. I must be stupid."

"I'm sorry," he said, searching for his breath as I pressed on his chest.

"You can go write your notes now," I said, rolling off.

ON CHRISTMAS MORNING, Peter thought he saw a blue-bird flying across the yard. His mother said she hadn't seen a blue-bird in years; DDT had killed most of them off. Probably what he saw was an indigo bunting. Peter found a bird guide in his parents' library, and, after studying the pictures, said, "I think I'm right, but I don't want to argue with her."

"Save your breath for the important issues," I said.

We ate brunch and opened presents. I gave Peter four pairs of socks and a book. He gave me a black cashmere scarf. In his note he joked about the multiple uses of a scarf—neckwear, gag, blindfold, garrote, magician's prop—but he didn't thank me for my forbearance or compare me to a rose or say that the scarf was a trifling representation of his feelings for me.

I called my father in Chicago (he'd divorced my mother after I went off to college) and my mother in Belle Plaine. She said I didn't sound good, as if I hadn't been eating. I said I had—at brunch I'd eaten cheese grits and sweetbreads, a Christmas tradition at the Sackriders'. She asked if I was ever going to come home again—I'd seen her only that summer—and I said I would. She said I could bring my boyfriend.

A half hour later, I threw up the grits and sweetbreads. Peter smoothed my hair. He kissed me on the corner of my mouth. He was trying to be noble. He brought me crackers and ginger ale. He said I could skip his aunt's party if I wanted to.

If I had skipped the party, I wouldn't have heard the anti-Semitic remark that Peter failed to respond to, and Peter and I might have survived awhile longer as a couple. Into the next day, at least. But I had an anthropological curiosity about Peter's world, and so I went, woozily, into the bush, to Aunt Helen's house.

Aunt Helen lived in a large brick house on a bluff above the river, where she and Judge Sackrider, her brother, had grown up. There were two stone dogs flanking the steps to the front porch; they had iron rings in their mouths, which you could hitch your horse to, if you happened to ride up on one. Inside, there were four real dogs, including two Irish wolfhounds whose collars were trimmed with bells and Christmas ribbon. The wolfhounds and a dachshund and a small, ungroomed ball of hair barked ferociously when we entered. "I see you have the welcome committee out," Peter's father said to Aunt Helen.

"I let the wolfies out of their cages for Christmas," she said, taking a cigarette from her mouth. "Come in, come in." She was tall and bosomy and had the long Sackrider nose. Her voice was a nasal cackle, tobaccoey. She owned a gift shop—jewelry boxes, angels hand-carved in Italy, high-end baubles—but the shop was mostly a lark. She lived on the money her parents and late husband had left her.

The living room was vast, with fifteen-foot ceilings. The furniture was old and European, the Orientals thin and frayed. The Steinway, which a little girl dressed in red velvet was playing, was out of tune. The room was cold, except near the fireplace, which was large enough to roast an elk in. I stood next to the fireplace with Peter and a wolfhound named Seamus, who seemed to have been assigned to me. When Peter went to get some food, Seamus stayed at my side, his gray head pressed against my hip.

Seamus and I wandered over to the piano. Judge Sackrider was there, along with his sister and the man who had played the accordion at the caroling party. (He was a cousin of some sort.) Colonel Willborn, who had taken over at the piano, was attempting to play what sounded like "Good King Wenceslas," but a dead key and several flat ones crossed him up.

"You need to get this thing fixed," Colonel Willborn said to Aunt Helen.

Peter appeared at my side, with a plate of ham and biscuits. "My aunt makes these herself," he said, placing a biscuit in my palm; it was a hard little wafer with two rows of fork-tine perforations in the top. "They're called beaten biscuits. You have to beat the hell out of the dough before you bake it. My aunt has a special beaten-biscuit table that has these medieval-looking steel rollers on it, and you have to put the dough through the rollers about a hundred times, until it pops and screams for mercy."

"I need to get the whole damn house fixed," Aunt Helen said to Colonel Willborn. She brushed something off the front of her ski sweater, adjusted her bifocals. "I had the furnace man out here the other day, and he told me I was making all the sheiks in Arabia happy with the way my furnace sucks up oil." She took a swallow of whatever was in her tall glass. "And I got that old Jew plumber practically on retainer. I don't know how many shekels I've given him over the years. And somebody wants a couple thousand to shoot insulation into the damn walls."

Peter's mouth was full of ham and biscuit when his aunt made the comment. He stopped chewing and glanced at me. His glance contained embarrassment, but I knew that he wasn't going to say anything to his aunt. It wasn't his style to make a stink, or even file an objection of the mildest sort. (In a restaurant, he'd eat what he hadn't ordered rather than send it back.) And at least she hadn't said "old kike plumber" or something. He resumed chewing; he had to finish what was in his mouth. Life was going on. Peter's father and the accordionist were talking about Jimmy Carter's brother, Billy, and his beer label. Over by the buffet, a woman was laughing. Colonel Willborn was telling Aunt Helen that Mrs. Willborn used a blind fellow to tune their piano; the blind fellow was inexpensive and good. The Colonel winked at me, his white eyebrow descending.

I gave Seamus my biscuit.

"THE GODDAMN DEFROSTER ISN'T WORKING," Peter said, wiping the windshield with his forearm. We were on a road that ran alongside the river, though the river wasn't visible. Fog had erased from view nearly everything beyond the front bumper. "I feel like a pilot flying on instruments. Except there are no instruments on this car." He was hunched forward, his nose near the glass, both hands squeezing the wheel. I saw him fifty years hence, an old man, peeping through small, round spectacles, his hair still hiding the rims of his ears, his mouth a slot into which you could put a dollar and get a grunt in exchange. The woman in the passenger seat—he'd marry once or twice, keep his homosexual side secret, believing it to be shameful—would try to humor him and fail.

"Here." I turned the dial one notch, and air flowed out of the windshield vent. "You didn't have it on the right thing."

He muttered something and pulled his face back from the glass. Hanging from the edge of his nostril was a bead of moisture, the beginning of a cold perhaps. We traveled through clouds of vapor, the silence disturbed only by the sound of the VW's toy engine. We might have been aloft. Finally Peter said, "What time did you say your bus left?"

"There's one at one, and one at two-thirty. The one o'clock is an express." I was going to Chicago to see my father, and then I was going to Ann Arbor to clean my stuff out of the apartment.

"I don't think we'll make the express at this rate," he said. It was twelve-fifty. The bead of moisture clung to his nose, defying gravity.

I wondered whether I should leave in the apartment the cookbook my mother had given me, the one that served as a sofa leg. Peter would have more use for it than I would, surely. I thought I'd take the toaster, one of our few mutual purchases. We'd gotten it at a yard sale. Toast flew out of it as if launched by a catapult— perfect toast.

Peter said, "I can't see diddly." He downshifted and pulled off the road. Did he want to talk?

The fog was denser here, billowy. The river had to be close. I made out a tree, its branches drooping—a weeping willow? Peter turned off the car and lit a cigarette. He said, "Once I parked here with this girl who ate my draft card. The summer before my sophomore year in college. We were sitting right here, in the grass, talking, and she asked to see my wallet. I gave it to her, and she took my draft card out and wadded it up and stuck it in her mouth like it was a piece of gum." He wiped the drip from his nose, tipped ash into the overflowing ashtray.

"And then what happened? Is that the end of the story?" It exasperated me the way he told things in bits.

"She gave it back to me. Soaked with her spit."

"She was making a statement about boys who carried draft cards?"

"Me in particular, I think." He smiled wanly.

I got out of the car. I wanted to see the river. I thought seeing it would clarify my mind somehow. I walked across what seemed to be a picnic ground. The fog licked at me. I smelled the river, its cold basement odors. I descended a bank littered with cans and tree branches. I stood at the water's edge in my Michigan Avenue shitkickers, my traveling shoes, and watched the debris on the river's muddy back go by. I waited for Peter to come stand beside me.

I went back up. He was sitting on the car bumper, hunched forward, watching me. I tightened my scarf, his scarf. His face, as far as I could make it out, said, *Don't hate me for being weak.*

But all I could say was, "Some fog!"

WHEN I LANDED THE KEOWEE, my skinhead friend had abandoned his rock and was lying in the sand, up near the entrance to the beach. He'd stripped down to his boxers, and was deep into a reefer. I had to walk past him to get to the path that led to the road up to my apartment house. A rose tattoo bloomed on his flat, hairless belly; the rose was crimson, its innermost petals puckered like a tight little mouth and the crimped outer petals flowing away in waves. The stem seemed to begin below the waistband of his shorts. I got a close look because I'd tripped on my sea legs and lost my handle on the Keowee. The boat weighed less than fifty pounds, but after a beer it felt like double that.

"You want a hit?" he said, holding out the reefer, which was on an expensive-looking (ivory?) roach clip. His head was resting against a sea-scoured log. "It'll smooth you out."

"No, thanks. It's not my cup of tea."

He lifted himself up on his elbows. The rose rippled, folded in on itself. I thought of Blake's rose, the worm landing in it, fouling it. "That was a joke, right? Dopehead humor?"

I managed a shrug. Then I noticed the tattoos on his upper arm. By comparison with the rose, these were dull, the work of a bathroom-stall artist. One, enclosed in a heart, said "Mom," in Gothic letters. The other, up near his shoulder, was a mug shot of Hitler.

"I got the munchies. Maybe I'll order out," he said, tipping his head toward the cell phone in his basketball shoe. Perhaps he ran a business out of his shoe. "There's this yuppie pizza place down on Cabrillo. You know the name?"

"No," I said, lying, hoisting the Keowee. "Have you shown your mom your Hitler tattoo?" Hitler's oddly cropped bangs and square doodad of a mustache were, I had to admit, nicely rendered.

"Everything you see is my mom's work. And what you can't see is hers, too. She has her own shop. I'm her accountant." He grinned. "You like it, Miss Molly Bloom?"

I started away. What had I been trying to prove to myself by talking to this person, this gaudy anti-Semite lying here at the edge of the continent in his underwear, a boy who had possibly read Joyce, at least the dirty parts?

"Don't be a stranger," he said. "Don't forget to write. Or call. I got an eight hundred number. One eight hundred SAY-YESS. Two S's, like in S.S."

I hauled the Keowee up the hill to my building, put it in my storage space in the underground garage, and took the elevator to my third-floor apartment. I listened to my phone messages (Mr.

Kuhn: "If you take me someplace good to eat, I'll play checkers with you again. P.S. The food here stinks."), changed out of my swimsuit, got another beer and a jar of olives out of the refrigerator, and sat on the balcony. The tattooed boy was gone from the beach. A dog was running loose, scattering gulls. I nibbled a salty olive, waiting for the incision in my gum to react, but it didn't. A military plane took off, its wings flashing in the late sunlight. To the east, toward downtown San Diego, the air was a smoky southern California brew. Below me, a woman puttered in her garden—bougainvillea, pomegranate, oleander, a lemon tree, other things I'd never dreamed about as a girl in the Midwest and still don't know the names of. Sometimes at night, in between seal barks and planes ascending, I hear fruit fall to the earth. *Thump. Thump.* The tree gives up its burden, and then, a few months later, starts over.

Goat on a Hill

THE NIGHT BEFORE my daughter comes for a visit, I drink two drops of sherry and burn my supper. I give Digger what I don't eat of the scorched cod and then put on my gardening gloves. There's light left in the day, even if it's all squirrelly, flickering in the crowns of the trees. It calms me to put my nose in the anemones that I didn't think were going to make it through last summer's drought. I weed around the Stellas, then sprinkle them with a cayenne pepper solution to keep the deer away. I give a dose of bone meal to this and that. I linger near the clematis, its blossoms as purple as the moment before dark; it climbs the trellis I fixed to the side of the house too many years ago to count. (Henry, my late husband, couldn't hammer a nail straight to save his soul.) It thunders while I'm pulling up a clot of lemon balm that grows like Topsy, which I planted because I couldn't resist the smell. It's far-off thunder, just a rumble from another world. Usually when a storm is coming, my body tells me; a blaze spreads down into my hip. But I don't feel anything there now. So I go around the side of the house with my clippers, thinking I'll cut back the barberry that grows near the basement door. I snagged myself on it yesterday morning. Digger comes with me. The other evening, he got into my neighbor Vern Seybold's compost pile and looked like a sausage about to burst its casing when he was finished. He lies in the grass as I clip the barberry, a Japanese variety that I planted—Lord!—over twenty years ago. Henry was sitting on a lower-court bench then, looking almost holy in his black robes, and the children were stumbling around in search of occupations and mates and themselves, too, of course. What else was true in 1976? I drank a cup of instant coffee in the morning. The tumor in my breast had not been detected. Vern Seybold bought a pair of peacocks and let them have the run of the place; they strutted and screeched in their hair-raising way, vexing everybody's sleep, until the Stringhams' dog put an end to them.

But I have digressed, as Alex, my daughter, would surely point out. "Mom," she'd say, not without an edge to her voice, "what's the story?" Well, the story is that before I can finish trimming the barberry, the air has turned cool and the sky has gone black. Darkness has sneaked up on me. "Like a thief in the night," I say to Digger, who does not lift his head from the grass. A moment later, there is thunder and lightning all around, and the old beech down the hill is twitching like it's got Saint Vitus's. The wind picks up the hat I left on the patio and blows it clear across the yard, almost to Vern Seybold's lilac hedge. I let it go, and take Digger inside just before it begins to pour. I go to check that the windows in the upstairs bedrooms are shut. I stand in Alex's room and listen to the rain beating on the roof. It's a new roof. I had it redone two years ago, not long after Henry died. I remember the workmen— bare-chested young men flinging shingles into a Dumpster, laughing, teasing each other about their girlfriends, swearing, as if to prove to themselves how much they'd lived.

The lights sputter. I go back downstairs and turn on the television. It goes blank before I can find a weather report. The furniture vanishes, then leaps into view with a stroke of lightning. I get candles off the dining room table and sit down in Henry's old wing chair in the den. It's an awful-looking piece—a mustardy color, the fabric unraveling on the arms—but comfortable. A bit like Henry, who wasn't the handsomest of men. He wasn't the first man you'd choose to go to the dance with, and yet how much of life is dancing?

I read Paul, the First Epistle to the Thessalonians. The Bible is what I read, even when thunder isn't rolling around the house—it and gardening catalogs. I read in the evenings—most evenings, anyway, if there's nothing on TV. I have to regird myself at night, when I've come loose from my promises. "But let us, who are of the day, be sober, putting on the breastplate of faith and love; and for an helmet, the hope of salvation."

I am reading in candlelight, with Digger's nose on my foot, and then I'm dreaming a dumb dream: there's a deer in my kitchen, a buck with antlers up to the ceiling, and when I speak to it, tell it to move along, it gives me an indignant look. When I wake, the lights are back on, the TV blaring. Rain is still falling, but most of the storm has passed over. I feel as if some portion of the time allotted to me has just been scratched off the calendar. Time is like water when you try to hold it in your hands, isn't it? I haul myself into the kitchen and look at my datebook. It's June 19th. Today I had lunch with Virginia Durham at that noisy new place down by the river—so noisy I could barely hear her stories about her trip to Greece—and then I went to church to see about the altar flowers.

Tomorrow afternoon, Alex arrives from Oregon with my grandson. I need to order fish for dinner and buy John Henry some of that ice cream he likes. Ben & Larry's? Oh! And then on June 21st, Alex's friend Rose Hodelik is getting remarried. The wedding is the chief reason for Alex's visit. I wonder if my daughter will take the leap again—for the third time, I should say. The last I heard, she's seeing somebody nearly twenty years her senior, a man who sells electronic gadgets—beepers, I think. In the space under June 20—tomorrow—next to "Ice Cream!" I write, "Press striped dress. Pray without ceasing."

ON THE WAY HOME from the airport, Alex barks at me when I merge onto the expressway too slowly for her taste. They just widened the doggoned road and now every hot-rodder in Jefferson County thinks it's his own private drag strip. "If you hesitate, Mom," she says, "we're going to be roadkill."

"I think we're going to live," I say, though no more than ten feet from my bumper is one of those jacked-up pickups with tires taller than I am.

"Hoppy got killed in a car," John Henry says from the back seat. Alex turns to look at him. She's as tense as a piano wire.

"Your grandfather fell asleep at the wheel," I say. This is how I generally put it to myself. I try not to let myself picture Henry out on the interstate in that clanky old Cavalier—he was coming home from a rail-fan gathering in Chattanooga—or imagine the jolt when his car struck the abutment, the instant when he must have opened his eyes and felt death seize him. If I imagine anything, it's the moment before the accident, the moment he began to drift off into sleep, the pleasant tingling he must have felt in his limbs, like seltzer bubbling, the sound of the tires on the highway fading.

"And then the Lord took him up into His arms," I say, as that pent-up truck goes around me, honking, gleaming. "Into His kingdom."

"What kingdom?" John Henry asks. Alex takes John Henry to church only now and then. When she had him christened, she said, "I'm doing this for you, Mom." Her second ex-husband-to-be sat in a corner sullen and outraged.

"Jesus's kingdom," Alex says hastily. "Heaven." She rolls down her window and we ride without talking, the wind and the sound of the traffic filling the car. John Henry asks his mother for his drawing pad; at the airport he gave me a picture he did on the plane of Pickle Boy fighting a Martian. Pickle Boy wears a tri-cornered hat, like Paul Revere, and is half sweet, half dill, with ob-long eyes.

I get off the expressway without incident and onto River Road. I point out the new Islamic Culture Center, a white, lacy building set among hackberries and honeysuckle, where once there was a shack on cinder blocks. Farther along, where there used to be a marina and some summer cabins, condominiums are being built on huge concrete pilings, so that when the river floods, as it regu-larly does, millions of dollars won't float off with it.

"The world is passing me by," I say. "Did I tell you they're think-ing of building a new bridge over to Indiana out this way?"

"Time marches on, Mom," Alex says, as if to set me straight. Then she says, "Well, the swamp's still here." She indicates a patch of watery land, thick with viny trees and cottonmouths, which the owner is always threatening to sell to a developer if the county won't buy it and turn it into a bird sanctuary.

"I used to go skating there, John Henry," Alex says. "Me and your Uncle Peter and our friends."

"You told me that the last time we came to Kentucky," says John Henry, whose memory has no holes in it.

"Do you remember when they found that body in there?" Alex says to me. She sounds almost cheerful at the recollection.

"Yes, I do." Alex was seven then, just about John Henry's age, blond, gap-toothed, wound up like a top and in a hurry to spin out the door. The swamp is less than a mile down the hill from us. When they found the body, a young woman's, I told Henry that we should buy a pistol for protection, but he refused.

"What body?" John Henry says, as we turn onto our street. "What body?"

"WELL," I SAY TO ALEX, "are you still seeing that fellow, the electronics merchant?" We're sitting on the patio. The air is dry, almost cool. The storm gave it a good scouring last night. It tore a limb off the beech, too. "Clyde?" I'm not sure of his name.

"Clive," Alex says, grinning. She's on her second glass of wine.

"He's English?"

"He's from California, originally. Didn't go to college. He's one of those self-made millionaires. I made him a banana-cream pie for his fifty-ninth birthday last week. He loves mushy foods." She laughs. Henry loved to hear Alex laugh. It reassured him.

I can't decide whether I like the way she's done her hair. It's short, though not as short or bristly as it was the last time she came for a visit. It looked then as if she'd put a picket fence around herself and hung a "Beware of Dog" sign on the gate. She'd just gotten herself out of some mess with this part-Chinese lady-killer, a married man.

"It's not serious, then," I say. "This relationship."

"Don't worry, Mom, I'm not going to marry him." She tells me that Clive acquired his last girlfriend through the personals. "She got him to pay for breast implants and then she dropped him. After she left, he couldn't do anything except eat peanut-butter-and-banana sandwiches and stare at his fifty-inch TV screen. So far he hasn't bought me anything except a car phone." She takes a gulp of her wine. "So he can keep track of me."

I sip my mineral water. I see John Henry disappearing under the skirts of the magnolia with Digger, and then I recall Alex at nine or ten running off into the snowy woods with I forget which dachshund (Hugo, perhaps), following an argument in which she declared me the worst mother who ever lived. A couple years later, she and another girl were in the basement, ironing their hair, trying to make it as straight as some pop singer's they worshiped. (Was the other girl Rose Hodelik, with her unironable head of black curls?)

The next thing I knew, Alex was going out with boys who were one and two years older than she was. She had a woman's bust before her fifteenth birthday. And the boys came calling in their fathers' Fairlanes, with nothing on their minds that you could really talk to them about. Peter's friend Mac McRae was one of them, with his sleepy eyes and wrinkled khakis and loafers that looked as if a truck had run them over. I lay awake at night waiting for Alex to come home—Peter, too—praying for them to come home in one piece. And one night Alex turned up soaked to the bone, with her big-girl slingbacks in her hand; she'd walked two miles through the rain after Mac had put the car in a ditch and then fallen asleep while thinking about how to get it out. That was Alex's story, anyway. "They're all so stupid," she'd said of boys, with unshakable conviction. A week later, she was going out with one that made Mac look like a mother's dream. (Mac has righted himself now; you can see the Lord shining through him.) And I let her go, maybe because I'd gone out with some unusual ones in my day—like that Irishman who worked in the record store, whose hair was brilliantined, whose accent could make the simplest declaration sound like music—before winding up with Henry and his money and his hair that wouldn't sit down flat.

"Anyway," Alex says, "how are you doing, Mom? Everything OK?" If memory doesn't fail, she asked me this question just the other day, on her car phone, while she was stuck in traffic somewhere. And I said I was getting by, except for the flare-ups in my back and some bursitis. Peter asked, too, when he called last week. What I think they really want to know is whether I'm afraid of dying. Well, I've been getting used to the idea for some time now.

"Don't worry about me," I say, more sharply than I intend.

"I'm not worrying," Alex says. She puffs her cheeks in exasperation. "I was just wondering if you ever felt this house was too big for you, with Dad being gone."

I do sometimes think about moving into a condominium, like the one Virginia Durham has out at Duncan's Landing, with a balcony big enough for two lawn chairs and a plant trolley. "I'm getting ready for the day they cart me off to someplace smaller," Virginia likes to say. But I'd miss my garden too much. I'd even miss the blasted deer that come out of the woods to feast on my lilies.

"Well," I say, "sometimes Dad wasn't here even when he was, if you see what I mean. He'd be down in the basement reading his railroad books, and then he'd be gone on those rail-fan jaunts with his odd friends. Or he'd be at court or playing bridge with Vern Seybold and that crowd or watching basketball on TV with the volume so high you'd think he was deaf. Which he practically was, I don't have to tell you." I stop. I feel my face start to flush. "But I'm managing. Don't worry about me, honey."

"You don't need somebody to help you out now and then? You don't miss having Willie to talk to?"

"Sure I miss her." There are rooms that haven't been dusted since she left me, a year ago. But she was never the same after Walter went away on that spree. She was cross with me all the time. And then Walter had a stroke—just deserts, I thought, uncharitably—and Willie was spending every minute looking after him, spooning food into him, bathing him, changing the TV channels for him. "I haven't found anybody to take her place yet. But I'm managing. Don't worry about me."

Before Alex can tell me she isn't worrying, we see Vern Seybold coming across the lawn. He's wearing green slacks and a cranberry-red golf shirt and a cap to cover his dome, which has been bare since he turned thirty, back around the time we started shooting monkeys into space. When Louise was alive, she had some influence on him, though not in the clothes department.

"Here's a man who's enjoying widowerhood," I say to Alex, as Vern pauses at the magnolia. Digger, barking like a watchdog, has waylaid him. Vern scratches Digger's head and then peers through the branches. There are a few last blossoms on the tree. I should cut one and put it on the kitchen table.

"I always liked Vern," Alex says, trying to suggest, I think, that she's more liberal-minded than me. "You remember when he climbed that tree to get some mistletoe and he got up so high we had to call the fire department to get him down?"

What I remember is Vern on a raft in his pool, unclothed, his privates baking in the July sun. I'd gone to borrow a jigger of bourbon for a pecan pie. Louise had been dead for about two weeks. I watched him for an indecent period of time, felt the late afternoon heat on my neck, and then went home and made the pie without the bourbon.

Vern walks up the slope to the patio. He has a plastic bag of something in his hand. He puts a bronzed arm around Alex's shoulder, compliments her on John Henry and herself, and then hands me the bag.

"Hot off the vine, Libby. My first crop of the season." Vern brings me cherry tomatoes every summer, even though he has forgotten— or perhaps never knew—that I'm allergic to them. Henry used to eat them. He liked them refrigerator-cold, dipped in salt.

"They're lovely looking, Vern," I say.

"I pulled out all the stops this year, Libby, and fertilized with some of that South American bat poop. Paid an arm and a leg for it." He scratches the V of mottled-pink flesh where his shirt is open. He has a paunch, but he is otherwise quite healthy looking for a man of seventy-plus who drinks more than the occasional cup of cheer. He had some glad-handing job with a tobacco company, which seemed to have no adverse effect on his sense of well-being. Once, when I asked him if he wasn't just a merchant of death—I was kidding him only a little—he said, "Oh, now, Libby, I'm just a salesman for an agricultural product that the Virginia colonists cultivated over three hundred and fifty years ago." Guilt's purchase on Vern is always slippery.

Alex takes a tomato from the bag and pops it in her mouth. She makes a circle with forefinger and thumb. "Bravo, Vern. I could be happy eating these until my teeth turned pink."

"Alex is a chef," I tell Vern. "She owns a catering business." I can't remember what I've told him about my children. Sometimes I'm unsure myself about what's going on with them. Alex lives two thousand miles away, and Peter is up in Wisconsin.

"Well, it's good to have the experts on your side," Vern says. Alex's praises crinkle the lines of his tanned face.

"Would you like a drink, Vern?" I ask. "Alex brought some wine from Oregon. Just in time, too. My cupboard's close to bare." The sherry I drank last night was the dregs.

"I have to run." Vern adjusts his cap. It's pale yellow and has the name of a resort on it. "I played in a mixed fourball at the club to-day, and I'm due back there for a pig roast."

"Will we see you at Rose's wedding tomorrow?" Rose's father was in the tobacco business with Vern.

"You will," he says. "Unless I die from eating too much pig."

Alex and I watch him recross the yard, a blaze of color fading. "The reason I wouldn't marry Clive," Alex says, "is not that he's sixteen years older than me or that he'd rather eat at Popeye's than try a Thai curry it takes hours to prepare. It's that I know he'd drop me as soon as something better came along. A firmer piece of ass—excuse me, Mom. The other day, he told me I could get this lasered right off." She shows me a mulberry-colored blotch on her thigh.

"I wouldn't fool with him, honey. I'd let him go back to shopping in the personals."

"John Henry likes him. He takes him to see the Blazers." She swallows the last of her wine. "But I've started to see this other guy, too."

A THREE-QUARTER MOON lights my way from the patio to the magnolia—that old gibbering moon, Daddy called it, long before he went into decline. It is past eleven. Alex and John Henry have gone up to bed, though it is only eight by their bodies' clocks. Alex claimed to be bushed, as well she might be after polishing off all but an inch of her bottle, though this didn't keep her from taking a call from her new beau, the heir apparent to Clive. He is a building contractor—not a breed, it's been my experience, in which virtue runs rampant.

The perfume from the magnolia is faint. I practically have my nose in the tree before I smell it. Three weeks ago, when the blossoms were peaking, I could smell it from the patio. The scent would arouse even Henry, who wasn't normally susceptible to such things. I remember him rising from his chair one spring evening several years ago, saying he was going to take Digger for a walk. An hour later, Digger came home dragging his leash. I thought Henry must have had a stroke or something. When I went outdoors to look for him, my heart pounding, I found him and Vern by the magnolia. They both told me how sweet the tree smelled, how beautiful the evening was. They seemed nervous and fluttery—or Henry did, anyway.

Beyond the magnolia, from over near Vern's lilac hedge, comes a voice singing "Makin' Whoopee"—that hoary Ziegfeld tune that Daddy would sing to annoy Mother. The voice is Vern's—the same large one that he used to bring to church. (Louise dragged him there by the scruff of his neck.) For several years, he sang the role of one of the Wise Men in the Christmas Eve pageant—Balthazar I think it was, the one who brings myrrh. Vern wasn't exactly a natural for this role, and in fact one year he failed to show up. Louise said he fell asleep at a men's club downtown after having one too many.

I stand in the dewy grass with my clippers and listen to Vern belt out "another sunny/honey-/moon" like some pickled saloon singer. And then I hear a second voice, which is also male, though younger. "Come on now, Mr. Seybold," this voice says.

I creep forward to a spot behind Vern's bloomed-out lilacs. The floodlight above his garage is on. It shines on his snazzy new coupe and on another car that must belong to the person who is leaning over him, trying to get him to rise from the pavement. In his outstretched hand, Vern holds a wide-brimmed hat. It looks like the one the storm blew off my patio last night.

Bugs swirl in the light that shines on Vern's skull as he sings of a newly wed man, soon to be an adulterer, performing household chores. "I should be on the straw-hat circuit, don't you think, Eddie?"

Eddie is tall and slender, his hair crew-cut. He looks to be no more than twenty-five. "Time for you to hit the sack, Mr. Seybold," he says, trying to lift Vern from behind.

Vern wobbles upward to a sitting position and puts on my hat— I'm sure it's mine—tugging at the brim to get it to sit properly. "For an assistant golf pro," Vern says, "you're a pretty good-looking boy, Eddie."

"I got you this far, Mr. Seybold." Eddie stands up straight. "I bet you can make it the rest of the way yourself."

"You like Long Dong Silver, Eddie? I've got more of his movies than I know what to do with." Vern's face is tilted upward, like a supplicant's.

I turn and walk back toward the house. I remember Vern in crown and robe, black wing tips peeking out beneath, bearing his gift of bitter perfume up the church aisle, singing in his strong baritone. I remember him in his cups, too, being dragged home by Louise from this or that party. I walk past the magnolia, feeling my age. It is too late to cut the blossoms, I realize. They're past their prime, and would go brown almost before I could get them in water.

ON THE WAY to Rose Hodelik's wedding, which is at the groom's farm out near Goshen, Alex says to me, "Now, don't go saying anything about Rose's big belly." Rose is six months pregnant.

"I wouldn't think of saying anything, even if Rose has put the cart in front of the horse."

When I see Rose, I have to admit that she looks as pretty as any bride who is three months shy of delivering. She is wearing a long, floral-pattern dress and has a wreath of buttercups in her black, curly hair. I can still see in her face, in that candy heart of a mouth, the little girl who played hours of dress-up with Alex, as well as the slightly older girl who, with Alex, shoplifted blush and lip gloss from Moyer's Drug.

"I do hope this one will stick," I say, as the father-to-be, Doug, removes his silk hat and kisses Rose. His dark hair is tied back in a ponytail. He is a musician; he teaches strings at one of the high schools. Rose's first husband was also a musician, though not a very good one, according to Alex.

"Oh, Mom," Alex says. "Please." She walks off in the direction of the married couple, her head held in a proud, stiff way. Then she turns back, the sun catching her full in the face. She seems spun of some glinty material. Perhaps it's the sunglasses. "Come on, John Henry. Let's go see my friend Rose."

"I want to see the horse," John Henry says. Rose's husband has two horses. One of them, a pretty little bay, watched the marriage ceremony from the pasture fence, close enough that I could hear it swish its tail.

"You go with your mother," I say, putting my hand on his head. "I'll tell the horse you're coming."

I stand under a tree by the fence, smelling horse and creosote and the pasture cooking in the midday sun. It is a good deal warmer today, with swirly winds turning up the undersides of the leaves. I see Alex and John Henry among the well-wishers around

Rose. Alex is laughing, back to being the convivial person she seems always able to muster for social affairs. She busses Doug and then tries on his top hat, which is black and shiny as a beetle's shell.

Coming out of the tent where the bar and food tables are set up is Vern Seybold. He has a drink in his hand and a panama on his head. Given his performance of last night, he looks surprisingly steady. I didn't mention to Alex what I saw, though I was tempted. It took me forever to fall asleep. I was so restless I went into the basement and pedaled Henry's Exercycle for fifteen minutes and all the while tried to imagine what my late husband would have said about his neighbor friend. Henry was kinder than me, less harsh in his judgment of others, and I think he would have apologized for Vern, or would not have condemned him at least. "Vern is a lonely old goat," he might have said, as if he were also noting something about himself, something that I was unable to tend to.

Vern steers himself around a knot of people and walks my way. In his panama and light blue summer suit, he looks almost jaunty, though his trousers are too long and puddle around his shoes. He seems to have scrubbed last night from his face. On closer inspection, I can see sweat standing out on his forehead.

" 'Another bride, another June,' eh, Vern?" There is a part of me —a disagreeable part, I admit—which wants to lecture Vern, to tell him how disgraceful it is for a man to be drunk on his bottom in his own driveway, propositioning a boy who has helped him home and kept him from breaking his neck in a ditch.

Vern blinks. Some recollection of last night's performance seems to bobble to the surface of his face and settle in the folds beneath his eyes. Then it vanishes. They say it's the short-term memory that goes first—a blessing, I suppose.

"I hope Rose has found a good one this time around," he says.

"That last boy was a bit of a hell-raiser." He sips what I assume is not a Virgin Mary.

"It's always interesting to see who ends up with whom, isn't it?" I notice Alex introducing John Henry to our vet, a man known to be less interested in dogs than in the women who bring them to see him.

"Yes," Vern says, placing a shoe on the fence rail. "The world seems to be full of odd couples trying to prove they didn't make a wrong decision." He clicks his tongue to draw the horse over. The horse pricks up its ears, but doesn't move from its position.

Vern gazes across the unmowed pasture. "I'm trying to picture Henry on a horse, speaking of unlikely combinations. Did you ever see him on one?"

"Horses weren't among his friends." I recall him at a dude ranch in Colorado, where we took the children one summer, saying "Giddyup" to an antique piebald who wanted to eat everything that grew by the side of the trail. Henry was overmatched.

"I miss the old bean," Vern says. I don't doubt him, even though he managed to miss the memorial service for Henry. He sent me a note, saying he'd contributed to the Historical Railway Society in Henry's honor.

Vern sets his drink on the fence post and leans down and pulls up a clump of grass. He clicks his tongue again and holds the grass out. It seems to me that Vern's hand shakes a little. The horse is unmoved; he keeps his big glassy eyes on the party.

"I can't say I really miss Louise, to be honest," Vern says. "She was the very soul of decency, but we were basically incompatible, as you must have noticed, Libby."

"I'm sorry, Vern." I remember at a wedding some years ago—Eisenhower was president, I think—a man I scarcely knew telling me how annoyed he had become by his wife's loud, jolly voice and by the way she sopped up spaghetti sauce with her bread. Weddings rile people up—us bystanders, I mean.

"You're a good Christian woman, Libby," Vern says.

"Sometimes I'm not." I feel suddenly hot. I don't know what possessed me to wear stockings.

"Yes, well." Vern gathers himself, pulls his shoulders up, as if he is about to unburden himself. "I hope you won't be offended if I ask your daughter out for a date." He turns toward me, closing his hand on the grass.

"Oh, Vernon. For goodness sakes."

"I'm not quite as old as Strom Thurmond, Libby. And I still have my teeth." On the loose skin of his throat I see a red dot, where he must have nicked himself shaving. Henry was always coming to breakfast with bits of Kleenex stuck to his face.

Vern puts the hand that holds the grass in his jacket pocket. He is smiling at me in a vague way. I think what he most wants to do right now is finish his drink and order up another.

"You don't have to clear your plans with me, Vern." I see John Henry come loose from his mother, who is drinking beer out of a bottle, and walk toward us. I go to meet him.

THE GROOM IS playing fiddle and Rose is singing, one hand on her belly, the other on the microphone. There is a man playing a washboard and a bearded guitarist who looks like he is still waking up from the night before. I don't recognize the song, a slow one about lying in someone's strong arms. The microphone screeches like a cat underfoot when Rose puts her mouth too close to it.

"I didn't know Rose could sing," I say to Alex, who has brought her plate of food over to my table.

"She was hoping to be Laura Nyro when she grew up." Alex takes a bite of succotash, which Rose has served with barbecued chicken and corn bread. "You know, a rock singer. But reality intervened."

I look around for John Henry. A while ago, he and another

child climbed the fence and went to search for the bay's mate. They took carrots along.

"Last night," I say, "I saw Vern in his driveway with a young man. He was drunk as a sailor. And then today he tells me he'd like to ask you for a date. I didn't know whether to laugh or die."

Alex sips champagne from a long-stemmed plastic glass. I don't think she has stopped drinking since her plane landed.

"Vern is one of those gay men who can't admit it," she says. "It's not uncommon among men of your generation, you know." She gives me a look that the knowing tend to confer on the ignorant— or daughters on their aged mothers. "Sexuality doesn't tell you much about who someone is," she adds.

"Thank you, dearie." An older couple is waltzing up front to Rose's slow song. The man is leaning forward, his ear within a hair of the woman's mouth.

Alex taps her fork on the table, not in time to the music. I can see that she wants to pursue the subject and enlighten me further about men's hungers.

"Have you thought about the possibility that Dad was maybe not totally a straight arrow?" She turns away and looks at Rose, who smiles at her new husband as he pulls a high note out of his fiddle.

"I've thought about a lot of things. But whatever your father may have done, he didn't go to pig roasts and get falling-down drunk and try to get boys to go to bed with him." I hear my voice start to flutter as it rises; I fear it will leave me behind, like a husk, as it veers wildly about. "And when I was sick with cancer, he held my hand. We read the Bible together. You don't know what our life was like. You were gone all those years."

"I was out in the world, Mom, making my way," she says, trying to be calm.

Curtis Price, the vet, pulls up a chair between Alex and me. His hair is the color of straw, a dye job if I ever saw one.

"Could I talk one of you ladies into dancing with me?"

Alex volunteers.

"I'M HOLDING MY BREATH, Grandmom," John Henry says, as we pass a cemetery on U.S. 42. In the rearview mirror, I see his cheeks bulging with air, like a frog's, a dark spot at the corner of his mouth. Rose's cake was chocolate.

"We're past now," I say. "You can breathe." I press my finger against my temple. I have a headache from drinking two drops of champagne.

After another moment, John Henry loudly blows out air. "When you go to heaven," he says, "you'll get to see Hoppy again."

"I'll be with your grandfather's spirit." Some days I truly believe this, believe that I'll be taken up into the presence of the Lord, into light purer than the clearest water, and other days I feel that only the casket awaits me. There are a million ways to come loose from faith.

John Henry is quiet. I can almost hear him mulling things over, even as the wind and the countryside pour in the window. The car seems like no more than a layer of skin, barely anything between us and the space we're hurtling through. I slow down, even though a car stuffed with boys is breathing down my neck.

"Maybe you and Hoppy's spirit can play Uno when you go to heaven." When John Henry played this game with his grandfather, he wept when he lost. His grandfather would explain to him that Uno was a game of chance, of luck, but this didn't console John Henry, who considered a loss a loss.

Through the blur of my headache, I see a goat on a hillside, a smudgy-white creature idling in the sunlight without a thought in its head, no fear of death, no grasping after love, no need to be saved from itself. Who would not want to be that goat now and then? And yet how lonely it looks in its mindless browsing!

The car with the boys shoots by as we round a curve down into a hollow. Those boys are going to be in flames when I see them again, I think, but there they are, cresting the hill, sailing along, beer cans bouncing in their wake.

JOHN HENRY IS lying on my bed in his pajamas, drawing pictures of his space creature. It is getting on toward ten, past the time when Alex said she would be home. The last I saw of her, she was dancing with Vern. They were jitterbugging, swinging around the yard like they were having the time of their lives. Vern had removed his coat and tie but had kept his panama on. Alex had taken off her flats.

I'm reading Saint Mark out loud—chapter 6. I skip over the verses about John the Baptist's beheading, even though I think John Henry would probably be thrilled by the idea of the Baptist's head on a meat platter, or charger, as the King James calls it. I read the verses about the miracle of the loaves and fishes, multitudes being filled by scraps, and then about Christ walking upon the sea, amazing his disciples as they toiled in their little boat, confounded by the wind.

"Was He wearing shoes? Maybe like those Nike water shoes?"

"It doesn't say. His disciples thought He was a spirit or ghost, at first."

"Oh." John Henry has given his Martian a pair of feet that look like crookneck squashes and put a plume on the helmet. He resembles a Roman centurion.

"Where is Pickle Boy?" I ask.

"I haven't drawn him yet." His pen hovers above the pad. "Maybe I'll put Jesus in, too. He can bonk the Martian on the head with His cross."

"Maybe He could just tap him lightly," I say.

"I don't think so," John Henry says.

Digger barks. It is his sharp-eared-watchdog bark.

"Digger must see a deer," I say. John Henry keeps drawing; his Jesus is a quivery, wraithlike figure with big paddle-shaped feet.

I go out to the kitchen. Digger is by the sliding screen door in the breakfast room, his dachshund's nose aimed at the darkness. If I open the door, he'll shoot out like a torpedo.

I hold him back with my foot and slip out sideways. I walk into the yard, beyond where the light from the house falls, past the garden, past my smoke tree with its pink cotton-candy blooms, and down toward the woods. About halfway down the slope, I halt. I try to make my old eyes sort through the jumble of things. I see fireflies dancing, soft little blips in the blackness. I listen to cicadas vibrate shrilly, beat on their chests to attract the female of the species. I feel the cool, damp grass on my toes. I remember that when I was ill with cancer, Henry would massage my feet, corns and all, while I sucked on an ice cube. Digger barks again. Then I think I see something move near where the beech limb that the storm tore off lies.

"Henry?" I say, more to myself than to the figure I see by the limb. It has Henry's less than elegant posture, the figure does, the tipped-forward posture Henry had in his later years. But it is also wearing a hat, and Henry didn't often wear hats, except in the winter, when he wore that absurd rabbit-fur thing with the flaps that made him look like a Russian bomber pilot.

"Henry?"

"No," the figure says, chuckling way down in its throat. "It's your neighbor Vern Seybold, the merchant of death."

"What are you doing here, Vern?" I can see now that his hat, his partygoing panama, is askew. I note also that his arms and legs appear to be bare.

"I'm out for a stroll, Libby, bathing myself in all this supernatural moonglow." At the moment, the moon is buried behind clouds. "Did you really think I was Henry? The specter of him, I mean?"

"I made a mistake." All that Vern is wearing, I'm now able to see, is a sleeveless T-shirt and boxer shorts. And the panama, of course. When Daddy was in the nursing home, he would occasionally walk the halls in his underwear; sometimes he would spiff himself up and add an ascot or socks with garters. But Daddy had an excuse: he was coming loose from his senses.

"What did you do with Alex, Vern?"

"I left her at the party. She was dancing with some young buck. She's a very attractive woman, Libby. She must have lots of swooters."

He seems to have tripped over the word *suitor*—or was he shooting for *wooer?*—and I say, "Yes, she has flocks." Then I say, "Vern, what are you doing in my yard without any clothes on?"

"I was restless, Libby. So I went out for a stroll. And for some reason I started remembering the day I had to recite 'The Chambered Nautilus' at Clay Elementary. I was in fifth grade—1937, I think." Vern staggers a bit, then rights himself. "Monday morning assembly. I wore a V-necked sweater that Grandma Seybold knitted for me. I froze, I couldn't remember a single line. But tonight it all came back—'The venturous bark that flings on the sweet summer wind its purpled wings.' It's peculiar what one remembers from long ago, isn't it, Libby?"

"Yes." I feel a stab of pain in my hip. Is it going to storm? And then the thought occurs to me, like some long-submerged, waterlogged thing floating to the surface, that Henry and Vern were lovers. I have no proof of this, of course, and the picture that has arisen in my mind, of Vern and Henry locked in an embrace, seems implausible. I turn it around in my head, as if it possessed a fore and aft, trying to get a better view. I can't get it into focus. But is it any more implausible than the image of me, fifty-odd years ago, kissing the Irish record salesman with the brilliantine hair, hair so shiny that I could nearly see my own love-starved reflection in it?

"Vern," I say, "I think you should go home and drink lots of water and go to bed."

"Would you dance with me, Libby, before I go?" He doffs his hat and stands before me, a swooter in his underwear.

I can think of a dozen reasons to turn my back on him and haul my hundred pounds of pride back up the hill. But instead, after listening to every cicada in the neighborhood announce its presence, I say, "Well, if it will help you go to sleep."

I give Vern my left hand and put my right on his fleshy shoulder, and we move around the damp grass in a slow, nearly steady waltz. The moon remains under clouds. Vern hums something I can't identify, his own private music. I look up at his ear, in the shadow beneath the brim of his hat, and I think of telling him how Henry massaged my feet when I was ill. But I don't.

And then Vern lets go of me. "Thanks for the dance, Libby," he says, kissing me on the forehead, up near the hairline. I think he may have been aiming lower, but I accept it where it lands. I watch him stumble through the dark toward his house. What will he remember in the morning? That he dreamed he danced with Henry's widow in the dewy grass, he in his underwear and she in her nightgown?

I walk up the hill, and as I do, I hear voices coming from the house. Everybody is home, it seems. Or almost.

"Mom?" Alex says.

"I'm here," I say, stopping at the edge of the garden, where a tangle of prostrate veronica grows, crowding the anemones. I should do something about that. Tomorrow, after church.

III.

A Bed of Ice

FROM THE BACK SEAT, Peter Sackrider watched his onetime mentor, Harvey Blum, shoot his Mitsubishi toward a gap in the Saturday morning traffic. A truck in the outer lane, a wrecker, didn't give way. Sackrider pulled at the skin going slack at his throat but kept his eyes open. He saw a patch of snowy-gray northern Wisconsin sky. He thought of all the birds that had flown south months ago. He heard the blast of a horn, he heard Harvey's wife, Eleanor, say, "Jesus." Then the Mitsubishi was in the clear, eating up pavement, pointed toward some breakfast place that Harvey had claimed would be worth the drive.

Harvey drove with one hand; his other wandered in the vicinity of Eleanor's hair, which, despite being pinned and bunned, spilled down her neck onto the collar of her coat. Eleanor's hair was an interesting shade—it was blond going white—but Sackrider wouldn't have been tempted to reach for it in traffic. At the wheel, Sackrider was all caution. Which wasn't to say that he didn't admire his former professor's gift for being able to do two or three things simultaneously.

As it happened, Harvey had been holding forth on the corruption of the teaching of literature when he cut in front of the wrecker. Sackrider had heard Harvey on this topic last night at the dinner table and, later, in the living room as they listened to dead R&B singers who were available only on obscure British labels. Fueled by wine and reefer (an old habit, hard to break), Harvey had rambled on about genderists and other "sensitive souls" at the college where he taught. This morning, he seemed less grouchy; he said that he and a colleague were thinking of forming a campus group called the Literary Old Farts Association, or LOFA (rhymed with *sofa*). They would drink grog and tell stories about old white men who'd been dropped from the syllabus.

Sackrider, who was sitting alongside his girlfriend, Rachel, laughed at his ex-professor's jokes, though he was the only person in the car who did. Eleanor didn't laugh, perhaps because she'd heard it all before and perhaps also because she didn't approve of Harvey's views. Rachel didn't laugh because she was hung over, though Sackrider had observed that she'd raised her dark eyebrows once or twice, slowly, possibly in reaction to something Harvey had said, or more probably in reaction to a chemical disturbance within her head. Rachel's eyebrows had been among the first things Sackrider had noticed about her when they'd met, a few months before, because the brow above her left eye was pierced twice; Sackrider, who was seventeen years older than Rachel, had to that point never kissed a woman who was pierced anywhere but in the lobe of the ear. Jamie, the woman who preceded Rachel, the woman with whom he had committed his initial, home-wrecking adultery, had been completely unpierced.

One reason Sackrider laughed at Harvey's jokes was that he was afraid that if he didn't, Harvey would take his eyes off the road and turn to look at him. Twenty-five years before, when Sackrider was an undergraduate at his all-boys' college in Tennessee and Harvey was a plump, bearded, untenured professor of English, Harvey occasionally turned toward Sackrider in the classroom, in the hope that he would say something in support of Harvey's theories. Sackrider gave the impression of being different from his classmates—short-haired Southern boys who'd been confirmed in the Episcopal Church and drank immoderately. Sackrider had been raised Episcopalian and had also liked to drink, but he wore his hair long, and subscribed, at least on paper, to Harvey's belief that the reading of literature (and the writing of it, which he taught periodically) could result in pleasure that was close to sexual in its intensity and yet last (as Harvey put it) beyond the moment of climax. Sackrider had done his best when Harvey called on him, though his best was halting and nervous, Harvey's own thoughts, mostly, as if spoken by someone new to the language. Harvey appreciated the effort, however, and was kind to Sackrider's writing, which seemed to have been composed by another, more lucid being.

Sackrider had apparently not laughed as loud as he thought he had, for Harvey turned his head toward him for what seemed like a long moment—long enough, anyway, for him to study Harvey's face, which no longer featured the black, unkempt, guru's beard that he'd worn with such authority on that mountaintop in Tennessee. All that was left of the beard was a brushy, graying mustache. Exposed was Harvey's melancholy lower lip and extra chin and dark cheeks that age had begun to crease and fold. Visible through his small, scholarly glasses (a new addition) were what the narrator of Harvey's first novel (Theodore Shook, in *The Shape of Shook*) called his "gloomy, unsightly literary baggage," though Harvey's bags seemed more like bruises. But he still had a full head of hair and those thick black eyebrows that were so active whenever he talked.

"Isn't this it?" Eleanor said. "The exit?"

Harvey faced forward again, but not before his former student, now a jobless middle-aged man, had acknowledged Harvey's good humor in the face of academic rigidity.

"It would be a pleasure to break wind with you," Sackrider said, obligingly. Sackrider wondered if Harvey would oblige him and read his contribution to a quarterly called *Mid-South*. He'd given Harvey the magazine last night. Probably it was too early to worry that Harvey might not read it, but Sackrider worried anyway.

"You need to get off up here," Eleanor said, and Harvey shot the Mitsubishi across the inner lane, cutting off a gray county-agency-type van, transportation for the institutionalized. As Harvey sped by, Sackrider saw the head of a passenger leaned against the van's window, the mouth ajar. Did the person have Down's, maybe? Sackrider kept on seeing this placid face, like an afterimage, until they reached the bottom of the exit ramp, where Harvey hit the brakes hard, shattering the image. The face had been trying to tell Sackrider something. That he should count his blessings? That he should kiss his child today, tomorrow, as soon as possible?

Eleanor said, "Do you need to drive so fast?"

Harvey turned right and pulled a cigarette from the pack in his pocket. "I was hoping to beat the crowd, dear," he said. "There'll be a hundred fatties lined up out the door if we don't get there by nine." The clock on the dashboard said 8:59.

"I don't think you're in a position to call other people fat," Eleanor said. She herself was on the robust side—bosomy, pink-skinned, round-cheeked—plumper than she'd been when Sackrider had first met her. Sackrider liked her more now, for some reason. Perhaps it was the ghostly hair or the prideful way she held her soft chin.

"I was identifying with them, dear," Harvey said. "My cholesterol-challenged brothers and sisters of the upper Midwest."

They headed east on a four-lane arterial that ran past franchise restaurants and outlets for Jet Skis and Arctic Cats and shopping centers whose parking lots contained mountains of dirty snow. Harvey lit his cigarette.

"Could I bum one?" Rachel said, perking up, putting her hand on Harvey's headrest.

Sackrider had given up smoking ten years ago, before Louis, his son, was born. Claire, Louis's mother, had quit, too, and Sackrider had become accustomed to sleeping with somebody who smelled lemony and bookish. Then, following his affair with the nonsmoking Jamie, Sackrider had met Rachel, whose mouth often smelled like a tavern in full swing. Not that this had diminished his desire for her. Unfortunately for him, Rachel's interest in his small, tobacco-free mouth had not kept pace. Last night, he decided that one reason she was drinking so much—aside from the fact that she was upset about getting only a bit part in a local production of *Marat/Sade*—was that she didn't want to have to feel anything when it came time to admit him to her body. If she did. When they'd retired last night, Rachel was unconscious before Sackrider had brushed his teeth. He'd sat on the edge of her bed—the room, which Harvey's son had once occupied, had two singles—and touched her lower lip. But her mouth hadn't opened; she'd breathed through her nose, filling the room with a lonesome, whistling sound.

Harvey passed back a Benson & Hedges and his own burning cigarette to light it with. Sackrider noticed how Rachel held the tip of Harvey's cigarette to her own, as if something more than fire was being transferred. He noticed how, as she sucked in her cheeks, pulling in smoke, she rotated Harvey's cigarette a hundred and eighty degrees, as if to experience it in the round. He noticed how Rachel returned Harvey's cigarette, slipping the filtered end between the V Harvey made of his fore- and middle finger. And then he noticed how, just after this exchange, Harvey adjusted the rearview mirror so that he could see her.

Sackrider cracked the window. The frigid air nipped at his forehead. He thought he might go running after breakfast. He'd brought along his winter running gear—his polypropylene tights, the shirt that wicked up sweat. It would be cleansing to be in the cold.

Harvey took a right. Sackrider saw a lube shop and, across from it, a small squat building with a pagoda-style roof.

"*Hier ist der Fressenhaus*," Harvey said, turning into a parking lot. "It used to be a bad Chinese restaurant. Now it's owned by a frau who yells at you if you don't order fast enough. It's the Wisconsin version of the Carnegie Deli."

Once, a number of years ago, Sackrider had had lunch with Harvey at the Carnegie. (This must have been in the early eighties, after Sackrider had left Ann Arbor and returned to New York with Claire and a box containing some notes for the dissertation he would never write; he had a job at a magazine that told doctors how to dispose of their disposable income.) Harvey, who still had his beard then, had been happy, even buoyant. He'd come to town for the publication of his third (and next-to-last) book, which was a novel about his childhood in Scranton, Pennsylvania. He'd sparred with the sour-faced waiter. "What an actor," Harvey had said, leaving a large tip. "The Buster Keaton of deli men!"

Harvey waited for a van flying a Packers flag to vacate a slot. It was 9:03, and, as predicted, there was a line out the door. Presiding over the line, flashing a yard-long broadsword, was a man dressed as a Viking. He wore a helmet with a pair of horns sticking up like pregnant parentheses and an oatmeal-colored skirt that stopped above his bare knees.

"When did they get him?" Eleanor asked.

"He's the Wisconsin touch," Harvey said. "Every former Chinese restaurant with a mouthy New York–style waitress needs a Viking. To control the crowds."

"I wonder if he's wearing underwear," Rachel said. The nicotine seemed to have nudged her further in the direction of consciousness. She adjusted her hat, a fezlike thing that couldn't have kept a single hair on her head warm. "You know, like those Scotch guys in kilts."

Sackrider climbed out of the car, recollecting that some small part of him was of Scotch descent.

"We could ask," Harvey said, winding a muffler around his throat. Sackrider tried to imagine standing in five-degree weather with his genitals all but exposed. He shivered.

"I don't think that would be prudent," Eleanor said.

"'Dear Prudence,'" Harvey sang softly, mockingly, then put a hand on Sackrider's shoulder and said, "The portions here are obscenely large. I guarantee you won't emerge a thinner, healthier man."

ONE PIECE OF running equipment Sackrider had failed to pack was his fleece neck warmer, so he had to make do with Rachel's scarf, which wasn't much bigger than a hanky. Rachel was one of those people who thumbed their noses at the cold. "Please," she would say to Sackrider when he complained of the weather in southern Wisconsin. "Give me a break." She'd grown up in Ashland, on Lake Superior. She'd walk out of Sackrider's apartment into a north wind with her pea jacket unbuttoned and her head uncovered and her strip of scarf dangling uselessly. She wore her hair short and had a long neck.

Sackrider knotted the scarf as he jogged past the ranch houses in Harvey's neighborhood. Perhaps it was the absence of any large trees that made the houses seem so naked and vulnerable. He turned out of Harvey's neighborhood and headed toward town. He went by a Lutheran church that commanded a view of the river below—the river in which some Houdini-era magician, a local boy made good, had allegedly been saved from drowning when he was a child. (Sackrider paused to read the sign affixed to the bridge.) On the far side of the river was the college where Harvey taught and on the near side were paper mills that had kept the town and college going through thick and thin. "The throne I sit on at school is funded by toilet paper," Harvey had said last night, lighting a second reefer. "God bless toilet paper, one-ply and two-ply both! And God bless its makers! And God bless Wisconsin, what the hell!"

Sackrider had laughed, more than obligingly. He hadn't worked up a lot of affection for the state in which he'd lived for the last seven years, but then he hadn't really cared for New York, either, though it did have the advantage of being near an ocean. Once in a while when he was living in Manhattan, he would round a corner and inexplicably catch a whiff of the salty sea. That the ocean had somehow penetrated into darkest Manhattan made him feel as if longings he couldn't name might somehow be satisfied. Later, in the subway or his office, his nose no longer full of the sea, he'd conclude that the hopefulness he'd felt was just a lucky stroke, not a state of mind he could will or one that was likely to overtake him on a consistent basis.

Sackrider crossed the bridge. The wind caromed off the frozen river and attacked him in the neck, nose, under the rims of his glasses, even in the legs, which were sheathed in supposedly impenetrable electric-blue polypropylene tights. When Rachel had seen him in his winter running costume for the first time, she'd said he looked sexy. But that was a couple months ago. In what was possibly an attempt to be more Viking-like, Sackrider hadn't put on underwear beneath his tights today. But Rachel, who had been in the room when he was dressing, hadn't noticed. She'd been reading.

Sackrider knew it was a mistake not to have worn underwear. He'd wished only to divert Rachel, and now his loins were cold. Well, how could you compete with *Lolita*, the book Harvey had given her? (She'd asked him for recommendations.) Or was it Harvey he was competing with? On the drive back from the breakfast place, Rachel had sat in front with Harvey, in the smoking section. Eleanor didn't object. She referred to the spot next to Harvey as the "death seat."

Sackrider ran up the hill toward the campus. The slope was steep and he labored; the pancakes and breakfast sausage weighed on him like a gravitational force. As he neared the top, a black Mitsubishi flew by. It was Eleanor; he saw her ghostly hair. (Speeding ran in the family, it seemed.) He recalled seeing her push a baby stroller around that Tennessee mountain, a tall blond woman alone with her thoughts and her infant. (She was from Boston, raised Catholic. She'd eloped with Harvey when she was an undergraduate and he was a graduate assistant.) Harvey said she'd been happy when he'd been denied tenure. They could go north again, to where people wouldn't pretend to like you if they didn't. But Harvey's appointment at a college back East was temporary, and a couple years later they'd landed among Midwestern papermakers.

Eleanor gave no indication that she'd noticed Sackrider, but he waved anyway, like the polite Southerner he'd been brought up to be. He turned onto a path that led across campus. He ran past a premodern yellow-limestone building with tall windows through which sunshine would have flowed, had there been any. He didn't see any students—only mounds of old snow and a murder of crows in the limbs of an oak. The students weren't on vacation, were they? No, Sackrider remembered Harvey saying he had to meet one at his office before going off to the campus radio station to do his Saturday afternoon show. He also had a Monday night show and a Thursday night show. He played mostly R&B, a little jazz, a little Mozart, no authentic sea chanteys, no rap, no Tibetan monk music; he talked, read from books, did a

Guess Who Wrote This? segment. He'd taken up radio as a kind of substitute for the fact that he no longer wrote novels. It wasn't quite a second career, but it did get him out of the house and out of the English department.

Sackrider could have used a second career. The sums of money he got for the stories he wrote ranged from the low to mid two figures to the low to mid three figures—numbers that Rachel, for one, found hilarious. "That's not even beer money," she'd said. When she asked how he paid for everything—his apartment, Louis's needs, the repairs on his rickety Toyota—he'd tried to think of a plausible lie but could not. Anway, Sackrider wasn't capable of lying directly to somebody's face. And when Rachel had asked him about the sources of his income, they'd been in bed. Unlike Sackrider, Rachel liked to talk during sex. And like Harvey, she was able to pull off at least two somewhat complicated tasks at once. In this case, she'd been able to draw the truth out of him—his money had been inherited—and, a moment later, cause him to shudder and fill his just-emptied mouth with her breast.

Sackrider reached the northern limits of campus. Across the avenue that ran through the center of town was a limestone chapel with a red door and narrow neo-Gothic windows. Sackrider was an irregular churchgoer. Years of required churchgoing—at home in Kentucky, at the mountaintop Episcopal college in Tennessee— had not quite sapped him of all spiritual longing, or of a desire to escape from secular life. Sometimes he went to church with Louis, who asked questions about the crucifixion and always chewed the wafer slowly, as if he were analyzing its contents. Rachel was amused at Sackrider's religious streak. "You probably just feel guilty," she said, "and think your mother would like you less if she knew you didn't go." There was some truth in that, but not enough.

Sackrider jogged in place while waiting for the light to change.

He'd come about two miles so far, but he'd not warmed up at all. His penis, which had shrunk to the size of a small tumor, seemed to want to take up residence inside him. The wind needled his cleanly shaven face, sought out his nostrils and the unpierced lobes of his ears.

His head was covered only by a watch cap. It was against his principles to wear one of those wool masks from which eyes and lips popped out lasciviously. He was vain, or perhaps merely fearful of the image he would present if his still boyish countenance were hidden from view. A mask would have limited his vision, too. He would have noticed the woman with the cello walking on the other side of the avenue, but he might have missed the gray county-agency-type van parked catercorner from him. Wasn't it just like the vehicle that Harvey had so narrowly missed hitting that morning, the one containing the Down's people or whoever they were?

Sackrider jogged across the avenue and then turned left against the light. He was curious about the van. He felt it must mean something that he'd twice encountered it—assuming, of course, that it was the same one. The van was running, emitting pollutants, but nobody was in it except the driver. Sackrider ran on, past a tavern, a tae kwon do parlor, the college bookstore, where Harvey had said you couldn't find any of his books. (They were all out of print.) Sackrider took a right, down a street that featured a Christian Science reading room and another tavern and, farther on (a sign indicated), the historical society, which was having an exhibit featuring the town's own Houdini-era magician. Sackrider could go look at manacles, trunks, scarves, capes, the boxes used for cutting people in half. But he went into the tavern, a place called Czink's, which no sunlight would ever penetrate.

Sackrider drank only moderately nowadays and rarely before

dinner, but it was not drink he was after. What he wanted, aside from warmth, was to telephone his son. Often while running, Sackrider developed a need to talk to somebody. Sometimes the need would be so strong that it would halt him in his tracks.

In case he ever decided to make a phone call, Sackrider wore around his neck a beaded leather pouch that held coins and his credit card. The pouch had been given to him by his son. Sackrider thought of it as a medicine bag. It also contained lip balm, a couple of Advils, and scraps of paper and a pencil stub.

Czink's pay phone was in an unwarm foyer separated from the barroom by a door that had suffered some violence. Through a window in the door Sackrider observed the interior, with its twinkling Christmas lights and neon beer signs and handful of noontime drinkers. The patron sitting nearest to the door was large and bearded, and strongly resembled the breakfast-place Viking. Instead of the helmet and skirt, the man was wearing a T-shirt and Packers cap.

Sackrider punched in a string of numbers and was transmitted to his son's mother's house, where Sackrider had lived until he'd left for Jamie. The phone was answered by Claire's boyfriend, a carpenter-painter named Jonas, who had persuaded Claire that the house, a whitish two-story frame, ought to be painted a "New Orleans blue," which turned out to be something like turquoise. In Sackrider's opinion, the house now stood out like a brothel. Claire said it looked cheerful. Louis said he would have painted it black. Black was his favorite color.

Jonas turned Sackrider over to Claire. Louis wasn't home.

"Where is he?" Sackrider sounded more urgent than he meant to be. He was still catching his breath.

"He went skating," she said. "Should I have him call you when he comes back? Will you be at your apartment all day?" Claire was careful to be formal with Sackrider.

"I'm up north. I went away for the weekend. I told you I was going, didn't I?" Sackrider couldn't remember if he had. "I'm staying with Harvey Blum, this guy who was kind of my mentor in college. Did you meet him when we were in New York?"

"I don't think so," Claire said.

Sackrider gazed at the Viking look-alike on the barstool, the band of flesh between where his T-shirt stopped and his crack started. "I've been out running," he said, explaining his circumstances. "Now I'm in this tavern—or not quite in it—trying to get warm. There's an exhibit about some magician here, down the street."

Claire said, "Oh." Sackrider must have sounded more confused than he actually was.

He plodded on. "Rachel came with me. She's back at Harvey's house now. Reading *Lolita*. Harvey gave it to her. I think I'm going to be history pretty soon." Sackrider had a vision of himself with his head on the guillotine, a victim of his own revolution.

He said "Sorry," but she didn't respond. She asked if Louis should call him at Harvey's.

He looked up Harvey's number in the book dangling from the phone box and gave it to Claire. Then he went out into the street, into a flock of adults in parkas and stocking caps. Their voices were excited and like children's. It must have been the people from the gray van, the Down's group. They didn't make way for him. They shuffled around him, enclosed him in their puffy clothing and chromosomally aberrant babble. Their faces were welcoming, as if they imagined him to be as pleasant as a puppy. Sackrider smiled, saying "Excuse me, excuse me," but when he saw no gap among the clumpy bodies through which he might exit, he felt a touch of panic. He feared he might be borne away, carried off; the current produced by these people with their flattened occiputs and slanting eyes was as strong as any river's. Finally he heard a voice, firm and female, say, "Let the man through, please."

He jogged up the sidewalk, two long miles from Harvey's house.

BY ONE-THIRTY, Sackrider was in the hot tub on Harvey's deck. He'd returned to an empty house. Harvey and Rachel had gone off, taking Harvey's second car. Harvey had left a note: they were going to do some errands and then head over to the campus radio station. Sackrider was invited to join them there. After Sackrider had read the note, he'd gone upstairs to the room Harvey used as an office and poked around. The room smelled profoundly of cigarette smoke. Sackrider considered booting up Harvey's Macintosh to see if his files contained anything interesting. Love letters? Had Harvey had lovers? Would his letters reflect the ironic, jocular Harvey, or would they reveal some other being, a sentimentalist or a fetishist, perhaps? Sackrider decided that Harvey wouldn't have saved his letters, assuming he'd written any. He sat down on the daybed and picked up the quarterly he'd brought his old professor. It looked unthumbed, unread.

He'd then slumped off to the guest room and undressed. On the bed in which Rachel had slept last night was the copy of *Lolita*, open and facedown, along with the shirt and jeans she'd worn that morning. She'd changed before going off with Harvey. Sackrider sat naked on the edge of Rachel's bed and looked at the stuff spilling out of the maw of her carryall: socks, underwear, flannel shirt, hair dryer. When she stayed at his apartment, she lived out of suitcases, though he'd offered bureau drawers. Most of her few belongings, except for a bike and a jumbo beanbag chair, she kept at a girlfriend's apartment. Sackrider cooked for her—she claimed not to be able to scramble an egg—and did her laundry. He folded everything, the skimpy pieces of underwear and the jeans torn in the thigh, and stacked them in her bags. A day or two later, her clothes would be scattered like storm debris. It was a bit like having an adolescent around. The first time they slept together, she said, "It's nice to make out with somebody who isn't a macho bullshit artist, even if it was kind of fast." Probably the relationship started to go downhill at that point, though she would sometimes kiss him in the morning when she went off to her job at the mall photo shop, and in the evening she would sometimes hold his hand while they lay on the beanbag chair and watched sitcoms that Sackrider had never watched before. One night a couple weeks ago, while she drank the fumé blanc he'd bought to go with a mushroom pasta, she accused him of being "like some whack passive-aggressive dude." She told him to "get a job, at least." She said, "I don't want a fifties housewife for a boyfriend. I don't like asparagus sauteed in ginger. It makes my pee stink." A few days later, she brought him a feather duster as a joke, and apologized.

The hot tub bubbled, lulled him. He thought of the Down's people with their bobbing heads. He felt sleepy; the sun was sinking on the island of his self. The sky above was snowy gray, a give-up-the-ghost color. All but his head was under the water. He was cooking in Harvey's vat, softening, puckering, while Harvey was driving around town with Rachel, flitting in and out of traffic, shooting the breeze with her about music or Nabokov.

Sackrider heard a distant chirping, some hearty northern backwater bird, maybe. A moment later, he realized that the chirping was Harvey's telephone and decided that he should answer it. What if the caller was his son? He got out of the tub and grabbed his towel and shirt and entered the house through a sliding door. He picked up the phone on what must have been the ninth or tenth ring—the caller was either patient or desperate. Sackrider uttered a hasty hello.

"Professor Blum, this is Tara in your writing class?" She said it as if she didn't quite believe it herself, and then went on. Sackrider didn't stop her. "I can't write anything, not even crap, like you said it was OK to do. Not even about like how I want to put my roommate's budgie in the microwave and push "Cook" because it won't shut up. You know how you said sometimes a good medicine for writer's constipation is getting blasted? Stoned? So last night I got stoned and went down to the river and walked out on the ice. Every step I thought I was going to fall through. I mean, I was hoping I was going to fall through. Professor Blum?"

"This isn't him," Sackrider said. "I'm a houseguest. Should I have him call you?" He wondered if he should offer advice. Was she suicidal or was she just being theatrical?

Tara was silent.

"Hang in there," Sackrider said, with what he intended as conviction. But Tara clicked off.

Sackrider stood naked at the kitchen counter with the receiver to his ear and his shirt in his hand. He'd never quite secured the towel around his waist, and now it lay at his feet. He put the receiver back, and then, hearing a noise like paper ripping, spun on his heels. He saw nobody. On the other hand, he wasn't wearing his glasses. Distant things threatened to dissolve into essences.

He wrapped himself in the towel and walked out of the kitchen and down a hall, into the living room. He came to a stop on a throw rug, not far from Eleanor, who was sitting on the couch, a pile of mail in her lap. She had her coat on, over sweatpants and sweatshirt. Perhaps she'd just returned from the health club. That might account for the extra color in her cheeks and throat, which Sackrider could see even without his glasses.

"You beat me to the phone," she said. "Anything I need to worry about?"

"It was one of Harvey's students. She sounded kind of desperate." Sackrider felt the towel loosen. He clutched at it. His shirt was still in his hand.

"They're all desperate for good grades," Eleanor said. She took a clip out of her hair and it tumbled to her shoulders and beyond. "They used to be desperate for good grades and sack time with the professor, but most professors nowadays are smart enough to keep their zippers zipped."

Eleanor looked at Sackrider in a way that made him want to search the room for something to pet. But the Blums had no pets.

Eleanor said, "Did Harvey ever tell you why he didn't get tenure in Tennessee?"

"I assumed he had enemies."

"A few," Eleanor said. She opened an envelope and extracted the contents. A bill, it looked like. "I always felt sorry for you boys having no girls to keep you alert in class, but it was mostly a blessing for us faculty wives—the absence of girls, I mean. And if you were inclined to it, you could have a nice little Episcopal boy to comfort you on those afternoons when that mountain felt like Mars." Eleanor looked at the bill. Had she had one, a nice little Episcopal boy? "Among Harvey's mistakes was the fact that he chose to sleep with the seventeen-year-old daughter of the Dean of Pieties, as Harvey liked to call him."

The dean's daughter—May?—walked splay-footed through Sackrider's head in plaid kilt and cable-stitched sweater. She was said to have flunked out of a couple of overseas prep schools.

"It was a summer romance—brief but upsetting to May's daddy. Tenure wasn't in the cards."

Sackrider rubbed his damp neck with his shirt, while keeping a firm grip on his towel. "I'm sorry," he said, pointlessly.

"And then," Eleanor said, laying the mail aside, pulling a cross-trainer under a thigh, "there were the others—the actual undergraduate at the college in upstate New York, and the one here, back before the P.C. stuff that Harvey likes to rail about caught on."

"Why didn't you leave him?" Sackrider was becoming chilled. He needed to get dressed or get back in the hot tub.

"We had Daniel." The Blums' son was out in the world now, working for some dot-com concern. "I wasn't going to let Harvey off so easily."

Sackrider said, "I have a child." She knew he had a child; he didn't need to tell her, but she looked motherly, willing to listen. "I messed up his life so I could sleep with Rachel—and this other woman before that. It seems so pathetic now. But Rachel sparked something in me. I used to pick her up for lunch at this photo shop where she works. I made sandwiches for her—crabmeat and avocado, crayfish and peppers, fancy stuff. I wanted her to fall all over me in thanks, but she wasn't very interested in food. So we ended up going to McDonald's. She likes the McChickenwich or whatever it's called."

"I thought she was an actress."

"Aspiring, mostly."

"I'm sure Harvey is glad to have her under our roof, but I wouldn't worry about him screwing her, if you are. He's kind of lost the hang of it."

"They went off together," Sackrider said, only now, a moment late, hearing what Eleanor had just said. "To the radio station. Harvey's doing a whole show on Frankie Ford, I think he said. The guy who did 'Sea Cruise.'" He was babbling. He was beginning to shiver, too.

"We could turn on the radio," Eleanor said. She moved a pillow from one side of her to the other. Was she making room for Sackrider on the couch or simply occupying her hands? Without his glasses, he couldn't clearly read her face. But her large bosoms looked so appealing, more than essences. He could cry on them. It had been a long time since he'd cried on anybody's bosoms.

"Maybe Harvey will put Rachel on," she said. She patted the couch and he sat down. He lay his head on her padded shoulder. She stroked the goose-pimpled flesh on his ribs, and offered advice. "Don't be a jackass like Harvey," she said. "You need to choose who or what you can't live without. And stick to it."

The urge to cry was fading. He was thinking of geese V'ing southward before the snow flew. In a couple months, they'd return to northern lakes and fairways, bringing spring with them. He was thinking of migrating geese—how did you get to be the head goose, the one at the point of the V, or was the job rotated?—and trying to ignore his rising dick.

SHORTLY BEFORE DINNER, Sackrider volunteered to make a liquor run. He needed to get out of the house. He almost couldn't bear to look at Eleanor, who kept peering at him, as if she hoped to see all the way to whatever lay at the bottom of him. This she did while slicing things for a Thai fish stew. She used a large, professional-looking knife and managed not to cut herself. Sackrider peeled shrimp that looked as if they'd traveled for days before reaching Wisconsin. He imagined the shrimp not long off the boat, their pink feelers still twitching and their shells still lustrous as they stood alongside some Louisana highway, trying to catch a ride north. "Wisconsin or Bust," their sign said.

Harvey wandered the kitchen, sliding the last of the wine down his throat, talking about a phone call he got at the radio station from a man who wanted him to play Tennessee Ernie Ford. And then he'd said, "I should go get us something to drink with dinner."

Sackrider said, "Let me go. I don't mind."

"You might want to devein those," Eleanor said, looking at the shrimp and then at him. He met her eyes for a second. She'd held him on the couch, but now he was moving away.

"We'll both go," Harvey said.

Eleanor released Sackrider with a shrug. He went and knocked on the door of the sauna, where Rachel was burning off poisons to make room for new ones, and told her his plans.

"See ya," she said.

Harvey declined Sackrider's offer to drive. "I know the way. Hop in."

Snow was falling. It swirled in Harvey's high beams and, farther up, in the light cast by street lamps. The snow had begun to stick to the roads, but Harvey drove as if it were pure ephemera. He followed the route Sackrider had taken when he went jogging. He zoomed across the river and up the hill toward campus.

Sackrider thought about those moments with Eleanor on the couch. It hadn't been an accident that he'd had an erection, but it was (sort of) an accident that his towel had come undone and that he appeared to be making an offering to her, like a suitor with a flower. But despite the evidence, the offering wasn't wholehearted. He wasn't sure he wanted to add to the betrayals that he carried around with him, like original sins. His mouth had been among the fine hairs on Eleanor's coat collar, not far from her pink neck, but he hadn't kissed it, and then the phone rang, and he'd jumped up, attempting to reswathe himself, saying, "Maybe it's my son. I'll get it." If it was his son—and it was him, all chattery with news about his weekend—Louis would save his father from drowning in the puddle of his desire. Temporarily, at least.

At the top of the hill, Harvey hit the brakes in his customary fashion and slid partway into the intersection, nearly striking a student and her dog. The student glared, and Harvey conveyed apologies through glass and snow. Then, before Harvey could speed off, the young woman walked over to the passenger door and knocked on the window.

"Oh, shit," Harvey said. "It's one of mine."

Sackrider rolled down the window, and snow and the woman's

face and her dog's snout came in all at once. "Professor Blum?" she said.

Sackrider thought he recognized the voice, though it was less anxious than the one he'd heard on the phone that afternoon. He'd forgotten to tell Harvey about the call. He couldn't keep up with what he had to remember. What was it his son had told him this afternoon about Zeus? (Louis and his mother had been reading a book of myths.) Sackrider had vowed to remember this bit of wisdom, but it was gone, at least for the moment.

"Hello, Tara," Harvey said. Red hair escaped from her knit cap. She wore glasses with small oval lenses. The glasses were starting to fog up, but Sackrider could see the lights burning behind them. They were all-night lights.

"I was hoping to talk to you about my writing?" There again was the simple declarative sentence slipping its mooring, becoming a question. "You're hard to get hold of." She looked at Sackrider, as if wondering if it was him to whom she'd confessed her anguish. Sackrider petted the dog, whose muzzle sparkled with snow.

"How about you come see me Monday morning?" Harvey jiggled the stick shift.

"OK," she said, pulling herself and the dog out of the window. Sackrider thought she was disappointed that she'd not been invited to get in.

Harvey fishtailed away. Sackrider said, "I forgot to tell you she called earlier."

"I'm supposed to be her therapist," Harvey said. "A few years ago, we could've necked on my office sofa and she could've gotten a couple stories out of the experience and everything would've been fine."

"With Eleanor, too?" Sackrider asked, remembering now what Louis had said about Zeus: that just because he could turn himself into a bull with a silver circle on his brow and horns like the crescent of a young moon—as he had when he kidnapped Europa—didn't mean that he was any better than a regular bull.

"She knows I'm incorrigible. Or was. I'm basically dysfunctional now. That's my punishment." Harvey turned to smile at Sackrider, the way he had sometimes done in class, following a remark meant to put everything in perspective. Then he said, almost jovially, "So how's your writing?"

Sackrider said, "It's OK"

"Don't take it too seriously," Harvey said. "It ain't the end of the world if everybody but your mom would prefer to see the latest horseshit from Hollywood for the third time rather than even glance at your stuff. Hey, I know all about it. That's why I quit writing. Hardly anybody wanted to read my novels, and in the case of the fifth one, nobody wanted to publish it."

Harvey pulled into the liquor store parking lot, into a space reserved for the disabled. The whirling snow made the store seem like an imaginary place, its neon soothingly fanciful.

"Rachel worries about you," Harvey said.

Sackrider found this hard to believe. Out loud, she worried about her next stage role, her next drink, her dork of a boss at the photo shop, the way she looked in skirts. She worried about Sackrider less than she worried about all the plays of Shakespeare she hadn't read.

Harvey said, "Now hear this. This is your therapist talking, formerly your professor." He turned off the motor. "There's more to life than writing and therapy. There's Ivory Joe Hunter and Irma Thomas and high-cholesterol breakfasts. And midafternoon naps if you can squeeze them into your schedule."

Sackrider thought of things he might add to Harvey's list, but he didn't bring them up, out of fear of appearing sentimental. "I suppose you're right," he said, a bit glumly. He would have liked to discuss with Harvey his position at the margins of the literary world, ask about the chances of his turning out to be a late bloomer, like, say, Joseph Conrad. Harvey probably would have taken a stab at answering that question, if Sackrider had been able to pose it. What Sackrider asked instead, as the snow tumbled and coated the hard world, as silence seemed to suck the air right out of Harvey's car, was, "May I buy the wine tonight?"

SACKRIDER COULD HEAR Eleanor snoring from halfway down the hall. She snored throatily, irregularly, not peacefully, as if struggling with a difficult idea. Rachel didn't hear her. She'd drunk her usual quantity and had shared a joint with Harvey and then had fallen into unconsciousness, though not without first telling Sackrider that maybe they ought to "bag it"—"it" being their relationship. Sackrider, who had limited himself to two glasses of merlot, said that maybe they could talk about it tomorrow, when Rachel was less tottery. He had tried to keep anxiety out of his voice. He would miss her, or miss sleeping with her, or, rather, miss sleeping with her when she was sober. She liked to be on top on those occasions, and he didn't mind; it was easier to see the gold rings in her eyebrow as well as her unpierced mouth and nose and breasts and the long stalk of her neck that made her seem foreign and remote and yet childlike, too. He hadn't imagined that he had all of her during those moments, or even very much of her, just a handful, something to keep him going until the next time.

Now he sat on his bed, with *Anna Karenina* in his lap, watching Rachel sleep, listening to Eleanor snore. Harvey was still awake, too. Sackrider had seen the light under the office door. Harvey had said he was going to read Sackrider's story tonight, before he went to bed, but when Sackrider had paused outside of his ex-mentor's study on the way to the bathroom, he'd heard a burst of typing on the computer keyboard, not the sound of a newspaper-thin journal page being turned. Probably Harvey had gone into the one of the chat rooms he frequented. Of course there was a chance that Harvey was reading and typing simultaneously, but it was an awfully slim one, even for someone as clever as Harvey.

Sackrider got dressed, packed his suitcase, put twenty dollars in *Lolita* for Rachel (enough for bus fare and maybe some Tic-Tacs), and went downstairs in his stocking feet. He found his shoes and coat, wrapped Rachel's scrap of a scarf around his neck (she wouldn't miss it), and went outside, gently pulling the door to. The snow on Harvey's walk was a half foot deep, but the storm seemed to have blown itself out. The snow that fell now was wispy, the last of the confectioner's powder. Sackrider walked out to his car, put his bag inside, found the ice scraper in the back seat, and began to clear the windows. He could drive home in two or three hours, if the roads weren't bad. That would put him at his apartment at around three. Then, a few hours later, he could pick up his son and take him out to breakfast and, if time permitted, to the late service at St. George's. At church, Sackrider would pray for miracles—the restoration of his marriage, for instance, or answers to those questions he couldn't bring himself to ask Harvey.

When Sackrider turned the key, his Corolla moaned but could not be roused. He tried several more times and got the same result. The car was thirteen years old. He and Claire had bought it in New York. It had been silver then, and now it was pitted and scarred, a battleship gray. Sackrider climbed out. He could go back inside the house and return to bed—easily managed, if the door he'd shut behind him wasn't locked. Or he could go off in search of a phone and an all-night wrecker. He was still consider-ing his options when he glanced up and saw Harvey standing at his study window, looking down at him. At least Harvey appeared to be looking down at him, though whether he could actually see his former student on the snow-lighted street was another question. Harvey lived apart from him, Sackrider understood, in a world in which he had only briefly figured. Sackrider gave a little wave, but Harvey didn't wave back. Well, it was difficult to see into the dark from a lighted place, wasn't it?

Sackrider went off, taking the route he'd jogged that afternoon and later driven with Harvey. He walked in the middle of the road, in fresh car tracks. He thought of the Down's people, safe in their beds, dreaming whatever they dreamed. (Did someone read to them before they went to sleep?) He heard no sounds except the crunch of his waffle-bottomed shoes on the snow and a muffled, headachy knocking at his temples. Even if he found a phone and a wrecker service before he froze to death, even if his car could be started, even if the roads were clear enough to drive on, he now wouldn't get back to his apartment much before dawn, his carpeted, beige one-bedroom that smelled of Rachel's smoke and his own fizzling life, and he wouldn't be much of a companion for his son on Sunday morning. He walked past the Lutheran church and turned down the hill toward the river. The snow had ceased, and the dark vibrated with cold, ringing in Sackrider's ears. (He'd left his watch cap in his bag, unfortunately.) Halfway across the bridge, he stopped. He saw a figure out on the ice, a hunched shape. Circling it, as if trying to determine its identity, was a dog.

Sackrider wiped his glasses on Rachel's scarf, and looked again. He saw that the figure, which was perhaps fifty yards from where he was standing, was now supine, arms outflung. The dog had settled into a sentinel's position. Sackrider continued across the bridge. A snow plow, lights and blade flashing, rumbled past, shaking the bridge. When he reached the other side, Sackrider descended the bank to the river. He couldn't leave the person out there, could he?

He crossed the ice warily, keeping an eye on the dog, which looked German shepherdish. He remembered a passage in *Anna Karenina*, a hunting scene with Levin and his dog, in which Tolstoy writes from the dog's point of view. A line from this scene had stuck in Sackrider's head: "Laska ran joyfully and anxiously through the bog, which swayed beneath her."

Sackrider felt nothing swaying under his feet, but he felt anxious nonetheless. He stopped ten yards from the dog and its companion. It had occurred to Sackrider that the supine figure was likely to be a student—students tended to do insensible things on Saturday nights—and then it occurred to him that the student, if it was one, was likely to be Harvey's pupil Tara. It seemed to be Sackrider's fortune in this little mill-and-college town to keep running into the same people. It was easy to imagine that he would see the breakfast-place Viking again before the night was out. Probably the Viking moonlighted at the wrecker service.

"Hello," Sackrider said to the figure, who was wearing a greatcoat of some sort and a colorful woolen cap. The arms were still outflung, and the boots were pointed skyward.

The dog and its companion turned their heads toward Sackrider. A female voice said, "'Lo."

The dog abandoned its position and trotted across the ice to investigate. Sackrider recognized its muzzle; it had been in Harvey's car earlier that evening. Sackrider let the dog smell him, showing it both gloved hands, and said to the woman, "You're all right out here?"

"And whom may I say I'm speaking to?" she said, slowly, as if she might be stoned. "Die Polizei? Doctor Marvelous? Or the man who answers Professor Blum's phone?"

"The last," Sackrider said, petting the dog.

"Do I win a prize for hitting my head on the nail? Or vicious versus, I guess."

Sackrider said, "Sure. How about a cup of coffee, Tara?" Sackrider couldn't see much of her face — just her glasses, shining in the snowglow.

"Oh, so it's Tara now, is it? When I was in middle school, the boys called me Re-tar-da, because I was bad at sports. Did you know that, Mr. Coffee?"

Sackrider said he didn't. He would walk Tara back to wherever she lived. If she brought it up, he would talk to her about her writing, about her budgie story. He wouldn't discourage her. He might also suggest the possibility of writing a story about this guy she met while lying on a frozen river at midnight, a river in which a famous local magician had swam and nearly drowned, a night so cold that it shocked the eyes. She could make it up, she could invent what happened next. And then he would ask to use the dorm phone, and call the wrecker service. And if all went well, he'd be home before dawn. He'd pump himself full of coffee and be awake for his son.

"You ready to go home now?" Sackrider said, tightening Rachel's tatter of a scarf.

"I am home now," Tara said cheerfully. "And where is home for you, Mr. Man Who Answers Professor Blum's Phone?"

It wasn't here, on this ice, was it? No, it was elsewhere.

Invisible

ALEX AND I WALKED round and round in the rain. It was February in the Northwest. My sister wore a long wool coat and no hat. I wore a hooded slicker that I'd found in her closet. She didn't know who had left it there. Possibly it belonged to her second ex-husband, though it was short in the sleeves and snug in the shoulders, and her second ex-husband, who was taller than me, wouldn't have easily fit into it. It disturbed her that she couldn't remember whom the slicker belonged to. "It's not like I operate a flophouse," she said, "and have men coming and going."

The rain was a drizzle, a patter, a plague of tiny, nipping bugs. Clouds obscured the hills that hemmed in the city. Alex, fresh from an hour with Dr. Shoup, said, "These drugs aren't helping," and "My life is like this box that split open from all the junk inside."

As we started to circle the block again, it came to me that if we walked straight west, up Lovejoy and into the hills, we'd disappear into the vapor, each into his own personal cell. Alex could talk about her problems—or not—and I could nod or scowl unobserved.

But we turned left at Twentieth, and left again at St. Helen's. We passed the rose-colored Victorian house that had the glider on the porch and the woman in an upper window studying her computer screen. She had the profile of an icon. If I could have clicked on her, would she have waved, perhaps, or shimmied?

We passed the little Catholic church with the courtyard that in other weather might have been a contemplative's paradise, and then we passed the woman wearing the platform shoes who was talking to the man whose pug was wearing a roll-collar sweater but was shivering anyway. We passed the building where you could get massage therapy or acupuncture or buy a cheap airline ticket to Baja. Then, turning left again at Nineteenth, we passed the bakery where I'd spent the previous hour, waiting for my sister to emerge from Dr. Shoup's office. I'd sat at a window table, vacant now, drinking a tall double latte (whole milk: skim was what my mother had given me as a child when I was sick). A half hour into my vigil, I'd bought two snickerdoodles. I told myself that one was for Alex, even though she wasn't letting herself eat anything so frivolous these days. All she put in her mouth were pills and ginger ale and the grapefruit that I sectioned for her in the mornings.

As we went past the bakery, I saw myself in the window—a man in a yellow rubber slicker, such as children and fishermen wear, hood up, ill-humor in the smear of his face. I'd eaten half of the second snickerdoodle before Alex had appeared outside the bakery and signaled to me. I'd wrapped the remainder of the cookie in a napkin, put it in my pocket, and gone out into the drizzle, which was her element, after all, one she'd become accustomed to, certainly, after twenty winters in the Northwest. We'd had thirty minutes to kill before Alex's next appointment, at the gynecologist's. Now we were down to ten.

Alex walked with her hands in the pockets of her coat, her collar turned up, her nose pointed toward the pavement. The slant of her shoulders and the tilt of her head made her seem old, though she was only forty-five. Or perhaps it was the near shuffle at which we walked that made her seem old.

As we turned up Lovejoy, toward the hills veiled in clouds, Alex said, "I don't know how to put things back together again. I feel stupid. I'm a burden to you."

"You're not a burden," I said weakly, glancing away, feeling her eyes on me. Did she think I'd say that I was looking forward to flying back home, to Wisconsin, to winds that raced across the plains and smacked you in the face? I was nothing if not accommodating. When a friend of hers had called me, saying that Alex needed someone to stay with her, that it looked as if the wheels were coming off, I'd promptly booked a flight. At some point early in my life—even before the episode of twenty-five years ago, when Alex swallowed all those pills—it had been determined that I'd be the one who attended to my sister when she began to wobble and lurch.

"I am," she said, sidestepping a puddle, grazing me, then setting herself back on her separate course. I thought she was going to cry, but she lifted her head into the rain and didn't. "You need to get back to your things."

"Don't worry about it," I said. I didn't have a job to return to, only an apartment, a couple of African violets, and my son, who lived primarily with his mother.

I stopped to pet a cat that was crouched in a driveway, waiting for a slow, wet snack to happen by. The cat was black with a rakish slash of white across its face. It watched me through yellow eyes when I squatted and extended my hand.

I said to Alex, "Maybe we should give Julius a bath tonight." Julius was my sister's seventeen-year-old cat, a legacy of her first marriage. He was orange, and sometimes he was called Orange Julius and sometimes Julius Child because he liked rich, buttery foods. He was mostly fluff and bones now. His kidneys were shot. Litter clung to him and he smelled of urine. Usually he slept in my nephew's room, but last night, when John Henry went to stay at his father's house, Julius had somehow scaled the guest room bed and slept with me, until I woke and put him off.

"I bought some kitty cologne a while ago," Alex said. "We could use that if we can find it."

The black cat rose from its crouch and walked back up the drive, showing us its regal hindquarters and scepter of a tail. "Maybe I'll try a little shampoo on him," I said. Or, I thought, maybe we could just put him out in the rain for a while.

We walked on, turning left at Twentieth. I noticed that the young woman in the platform shoes was wearing purple lipstick. I said, "I'm guessing that I'll live my entire life without kissing a woman who wears purple lipstick."

Alex, who wasn't wearing lipstick, said, "Because you don't like it?"

"I like it. I was just making a prediction." I felt hot inside my hood and pushed it off my head.

Alex said, "Shoup was wearing a bow tie today. I told him he looked like Arthur Schlesinger. I think he was offended. At least I didn't say he looked like a ventriloquist's dummy."

"He's touchy?" Cars went by; the tires made a spattery sound on the pavement.

"Maybe he was hoping to be compared to somebody else. Shrinks have feelings."

"So, what did you get for your hundred dollars?"

"It's less than that. He gives me a reduced rate, since the insurance doesn't cover it anymore." She stopped and turned toward me. Thoughts, like a school of fish, moved beneath the damp, gray surface of her face. "He said maybe I wasn't loved for who I was as a child, so I created a false self that would make it possible for people to love me—the happy child instead of the one with all these dark impulses."

Up ahead was a tavern I thought I might duck into while Alex visited the gynecologist. "How does that relate to your situation now?"

"I don't know," she said. "Unless it means I need to be loved for being a depressive." The rain had darkened her hair; a couple of years ago it had been light brown, but now it was ash.

"There's something to be said for shrinks who practice silence," I said.

We were across the street from the clinic that housed the gynecologist. Sometimes she got the sweats, she'd said, and her heart raced, too. She wanted to get her hormone levels checked.

She took my hand. Hers—slender, bony, ringless, warmly moist from being in her pocket—seemed at first like somebody's maiden aunt's, but then I felt the roughness in the tips of her fingers. When she was a child, her hands were often inflamed with eczema, but she managed to play the piano, attract boys, excel in school. Later, when she lost her grip and landed in a hospital, she made ceramic dogs with expressive faces. And then for much of her adult life, until two months ago, in fact, when her catering business went bankrupt, she'd made her living with her hands—grinding, slicing, molding, stirring, making tarts and soufflés, steaming wild salmon in lemon grass and mint. Now she used her hands to open pill bottles or rub her temples. She had eye-blurring headaches.

She said, "Bear with me, please."

WHEN ALEX WAS A CHILD, she had an invisible friend named Gaylord—Gay, for short. (In the fifties and early sixties, Gay was just another name, if not a common one.) Though he spent a fair amount of time at our house, in the suburbs of Louisville, Gay also had a home in the country, at the corner of Burleytown Road and Frey's Hill Lane. We'd pass it on the way to my mother's parents' house. Gay's house was a crackerbox, with a tin roof that shone in the sun and a porch on which I never saw anybody sitting. The gutters sagged and the window shades were always pulled. There was a dirt drive with deep ruts and a weather-beaten shed against which a push mower always leaned and a tire swing nobody ever swung on. Once we saw a dog in the yard. My mother said, "I see Gay has a pet."

"It's not his," Alex said firmly, even though the dog looked friendly enough.

When Gay ate dinner at our house, he would be given a chair and silverware but no actual food or plate to eat it on. Alex talked to him solicitously, as if he were unable to do much for himself, but she sometimes forgot about him after placing a napkin in his lap, and would often leave him sitting there when she got up from the table. I pictured Gay as tall and homely, a man of few words, like Bristow, this person who took us fishing for bass and crappie down at Lake Cumberland. When my father asked Alex what Gay looked like, she said, "He's invisible. You can't see him. But he's very nice."

Gay was around for a couple of years, until Alex was eight or nine. He disappeared gradually. He came to dinner less frequently, and when we passed his house, Alex didn't always shout hello or wonder how he was holding up in the heat. He was in there alone, sweating, with only flies for companions, I wanted to say, but didn't.

Gay disappeared for good one weekend when Alex and I were staying with our grandparents. It was a slow weekend—I hit a baseball over the fence, into the neighbor's cow pasture, until I lost it; Alex and my grandmother gardened and listened to a recording of The King and I—and during some of the slower moments my sister and I picked at each other. At one point, Alex knocked down a structure I'd made with baseball cards, something like a ziggurat.

When I caught her, I tried to stick her hand in a floor fan, but her fingers, all crusty and red with eczema (the summer humidity made the condition worse), wouldn't fit through the slots.

After dinner, which Gay didn't attend, my grandmother played a recording of birdsongs to see how many we could identify. Alex won easily, having heard the recording more often than I had. My grandfather read the paper, whistled at stock prices, told my grandmother that somebody had gotten loose from O'Dell, a state mental hospital that was a mile away. "What a thing to say in front of the children," my grandmother said, as a bird that was not a scarlet tanager (my guess) trilled.

Alex and I slept in an upstairs room that had twin beds and a closet full of hatboxes and dresses in mothballs. The darkness at my grandparents' house was thick and heavy, a well you could never see to the bottom of. It wasn't like the dark at home, which didn't swirl, which contained shapes I knew the meanings of: there, on the dresser, was the plastic figure of Willie Mays making a basket catch, and there the gooseneck desk lamp. At my grandparents' house, I didn't fall asleep until I'd exhausted myself trying to determine the identity of everything the dark concealed.

I heard someone or something breathing, through the nose, in a strained kind of way. It came from outside. Alex said, "I'm scared."

I didn't say anything. The breathing continued, labored but persistent. It was the only sound in the world; even the insects were quiet in the face of it. Finally I said, "Why don't you make Gaylord come? If you're scared."

"He's asleep. Anyway, he's not a genie."

"He's going to die in that house," I said. "From heat prostration." This was a phrase I'd heard my mother and grandmother use, as they dabbed at their necks with hankies.

Alex was silent. I took this to mean that she wasn't worried about Gay dying. Or perhaps it meant that the Gay I was talking about wasn't hers. Anyway, what good was he in a pinch like this?

Alex appeared beside my bed. "Can I get in?"

"Only for a minute," I said, moving over and turning away, onto my side. She wanted to talk, but I told her to be quiet. I lay on the edge of the bed, listening for the escapee from O'Dell, feeling Alex's breath on my neck. Eventually she fell asleep, her hand pressed into my back, as if she needed to brace herself while she negotiated her descent. Later, when she started to mumble and kick her legs, I made the treacherous trip from my bed to hers, where I dozed until I felt the sun on my face.

When my grandmother drove us home the next afternoon, we passed Gay's house. A girl was riding the tire swing and a man was taking a box out of the trunk of a car. The shades had been raised and the windows opened. Gay had slipped out during the night, if not the previous day, along with the flies and the odors. Alex didn't wonder about his whereabouts. She was reading a book and she was going to make do without him.

ON THE WAY HOME from the gynecologist, Alex braked late at an intersection and slid her old Subaru with the balding tires into the crosswalk, nearly striking two pedestrians. Each was wearing a swallow-tailed coat and a bowler and a black mask like the Lone Ranger's. Alex cowered while one of them, a person with a buzz cut and dark lipstick, swore at her, calling her a "dumb bitch." A minute later, Alex pulled over and said, "You drive, please."

When we got back to her house, the only one on the street painted a tropical pink, I said, "Maybe those two people in the butler's costumes were going to a Mardi Gras party. I just remembered what day it is." I'd lost track of the calendar while staying with my sister.

"I shouldn't even leave the house," she said.

I turned on the kitchen lights. Julius, who was lying by the hot-air vent at the base of the counter, lifted his head. When Alex went on through the kitchen, he rose and wobbled after her; I could almost hear the bones in his hindquarters rubbing against each other.

I cooked dinner—Shrove Tuesday pancakes. Alex ate half of one. The rain continued to fall, picked up, even. A stream of it slid down the spout outside the dining room window. Alex's eyes were set way back in her face, as if she were staring out from a cave. Her long nose, so sharp at the tip, showed no interest in poking into anything beyond the clammy space she occupied.

With my fork, I pushed pieces of pancake through glistening puddles of syrup. I wanted to drink bourbon and listen to fast Mardi Gras music made by people playing frottoirs and accordions and electric guitars. Instead, I washed the dishes and then looked in cupboards for the kitty cologne. No luck.

Our mother called. She still lived alone in the house we'd grown up in in Kentucky. "Is she crying a lot?"

"Some." I'd taken the phone partway down the basement stairs, more or less out of earshot of Alex, who was in the kitchen, nursing a ginger ale.

"I wish she'd go get some valerian root. It helps with the crying. And at least give Saint-John's-wort a try."

"I'll tell her." Hanging on the pine-paneled stairs wall were photographs of my parents when they were young. Alex had arranged the pictures chronologically, so that when you got to the bottom of the stairs the children who were at the top were feeding each other wedding cake.

"Those drugs that doctor gives her are just poison."

Among the photographs was one of my father on a camel in front of the Pyramids. He is sitting with his father, a man who made large sums of money in the dry goods business. It is 1928. My father squints in the desert sunlight, looks mildly uncomfortable in the coat and cravat that his mother (riding sidesaddle on another camel) has put him into, but otherwise gives little sign that he is thousands of miles east of Kentucky, on a humpbacked beast that will carry him to the immense tombs of kings who have been dead for thousands of years. Perhaps my father is thinking of other things: the sweet tea he drank at the hotel in Cairo, the Howard Pyle book he has been reading, the boats and trains that have deposited him here, somehow.

I heard my mother talking about doctors, about all the things they didn't know, about the psychiatrist she'd been handed over to forty years ago, a stiff little undertaker of a man, about the healing properties of substances I'd never heard of, extracts of flowers that grew in meadows and ditches, and I thought that if my sister could sit on a camel in the desert, she'd feel a little better.

"Peter? You there?"

I said I was. I moved down the stairs, past the photograph of my mother in a college-girl sweater and bobby sox, past the wedding picture. I'd heard a noise, a strangulated sort of mewing, coming from the laundry room.

"What kind of drugs is he giving her now? Just those Prozacs?"

I switched on the light in the laundry room. The concrete floor gleamed, shimmered; water, seepage from outside, apparently, covered much of the room. In a corner, next to some storage shelves, Julius squatted in his litter pan. He seemed frozen there, as if he were waiting for the water to rise and wash him away.

"Prozac. Yeah," I said, though on Alex's dresser were a number of plastic pill containers, all of them tinted a pretty sunset color.

"Is she worse, do you think?"

"Than what?" Julius was still hunkered down in his pan. Perhaps he didn't have the strength to get himself out.

"Than yesterday. Than a week ago. Than when you got there."

"She was better yesterday. Sort of. She went to see John Henry play basketball." I held the phone between my ear and shoulder and lifted Julius out of the litter pan. He was as light as a box of cornflakes. As I set him on the floor, the phone slipped off my shoulder and fell into the pan. Upstairs, the doorbell rang.

I brushed the phone off and held it at a distance from my ear. My mother was saying, "I wish she would let me come out there and stay with her."

"Maybe she'll reconsider," I said, though I knew this was unlikely. Julius hadn't budged from the spot where I'd put him. He stared down at the skim of water on the floor.

"She's in God's hands," my mother said. "I'll just keep praying. You pray, too, dearie."

I carried Julius out of the laundry room and put him on the beanbag chair in the rec room. Then I headed upstairs. I heard laughter, a sound strange enough to cause me to halt my climb. The laughter—more like a chuckle, in truth—was male, chesty. Perhaps Alex had told a joke.

THE SOURCE OF THE LAUGHTER, possibly the inspiration for Alex's joke (if that's what it was), was a short, plump man who wore a white double-breasted tunic and gray-checked trousers beneath a raincoat. The tunic was spattered with colors—pink, yellow, green. On his head was a baseball cap and around his neck was a blue bandanna and from his ear hung a pirate's gold hoop. His beard was gray at the chin and black elsewhere. His skin was light brown, like a cashew. With him had come a scent, something sweet and tropical.

"This is my brother," Alex said to the man. "He's looking after me, making sure I don't stick my head in the oven or anything."

"Bernardo Astacio," the man said, extending a hand, ignoring

Alex's comment. "I am gratified to meet the brother of Alex." The way he said her name, with the *x* slightly lisped, stretched out like a sigh, made it sound exotic.

"Bernardo runs a restaurant," Alex said. She seemed to have come a few feet out of her cave, or to the threshold at least, where it was possible to hear a dog barking in the next valley, see the smoke from other people's fires. "Called Bernardo's." She pointed to his cap, where his name was, in florid script.

"I am only the chef," Bernardo said to me, as if explaining the fine print. "The bank owns it." He had a ready smile, one he could turn on for the tables of customers who insist he come out of the kitchen and accept their praises. But his eyes were glinty: wasn't that a critic hiding in the corner, behind the bird-of-paradise arrangement? I thought the pink on his tunic was probably from tomatoes and the yellow possibly from turmeric. The swipe of green might have been avocado.

"Bernardo is El Rey de Nuevo Latino cooking," Alex said. "Here in the lower Northwest." She grinned, to show she was only teasing him.

"It is a good place to be king of," Bernardo said. "Because you are my subject." He removed his cap and placed it on Alex's head. She submitted to this with another grin. "Now you must come work in my kitchen. It's an order. You'll no longer feel sad. We will make our guests fat with coconut prawns and *pollo* with pineapple *mojo* and you name it. You invent it and we will call it Sopa d'Alex, Mojo d'Alex."

Alex gave Bernardo a long look, like what a child might give a comedian who is perhaps not a comedian. The light in the room danced on his head, which was smoothly brown and bare except for a ruff of black hair his beard flowed out of. I assumed Bernardo had proposed the idea of Alex working for him before. "I'm not worth a shit as a cook anymore, Bernardo," she said.

"First you eat my plantain turnovers," he said, indicating a foil-covered dish on the coffee table. "Then you think about it again." He kissed her on both cheeks.

I went out with Bernardo to his car. "Fucking rain," he said. "Makes my bones ache."

I said I knew what he meant.

With a remote, he unlocked the door to his car, an SUV of some kind. "I know this guy, a *curandero*, who will help your sister," he said. "He works with herbs."

"My mother believes in herbs," I said.

"It's not all bullshit." He took a pair of glasses from a case in his trousers and put them on. The glasses, with their small round frames, gave the impression that he didn't take his own views lightly. I wondered if Bernardo, as El Rey de Nuevo Latino cooking in the lower Northwest, ruled his kitchen with an iron hand. "I love your sister. I'd do anything for her."

Did he mean that if I really loved Alex, I'd do anything for her? Or was he simply letting me know where he stood with respect to her?

I asked if he was missing a yellow slicker, and he said he wasn't.

When I got back inside, Alex had gone up to her bedroom. Julius lay in the middle of the kitchen floor, as if worn out by what it took to get there. I watched his chest rise and fall while I ate two plantain turnovers; they were filled with sweet, white, crumbly cheese and were still warm. When I finished, I climbed the stairs to Alex's room.

On the door was a drawing by John Henry that said "To Mom." It featured a helmeted alien whose feet were size 22 clown's shoes. I knocked and asked if she was OK.

"I have a headache. The kind that makes you want to jump off a bridge."

I didn't say anything. I gazed at the alien's ray gun with its mega-phonelike muzzle.

"Do you hate me for being like this?"

"No," I said, like a good soldier. "Can I get you anything?"

"A bridge to jump from."

"Sorry," I said. The alien's opponent was a figure whose torso was the shape of a pickle or a saguaro cactus, on top of which was a tricornered hat. "How about a turnover? Or a snickerdoodle?" The latter was in crumbs in the pocket of the slicker, but I'd bring it to her, if she wanted it.

"No. Nothing."

A YEAR OR SO after Gay disappeared, our parents took us to New Orleans for a vacation. I was about twelve, Alex ten. We rode a riverboat up the Mississippi, got on a bus and saw plantation houses and old cypresses bedecked with webs of moss. My mother spent an afternoon buying wrought-iron furniture for her patio. One night we ate dinner at a French Quarter restaurant full of mirrors and women whose shoulders were bare and waiters whose tuxedos made my father's seersucker suit look shabby. When I finished eating, I asked permission to go outside. "Stay by the door, under the canopy," my mother said. Alex was allowed to come with me, to my dismay.

We stayed by the door for a while, and then we crossed the street to watch a woman sing. She was large. Her purply-black arms shook like jelly and her feet spilled out the sides of her shoes and you couldn't stand too close to her or her voice would knock you back. It whooshed at you, hot and angry, like gas igniting. She sang about somebody who had left her. The light from the street lamps kept bouncing off her face, as if it couldn't find a soft spot to settle on.

One moment Alex was beside me, and the next she was gone. I went up and down the street looking for her. I thought I saw her standing with a tall man in front of a store that sold pralines, but that was another girl with dirty blond pigtails. I heard a man say, "You stuff 'em, we buff 'em," and I didn't know what he meant. I heard laughter, saw a red, beefy face with a cigar stuck in the middle of it. I looked again among the clump of people near the woman singer. I saw a coin in the pan in front of her and I heard her sing, "You can't do what my last man did." It was a threat. I checked in front of the restaurant, in the hope that Alex had come to her senses and gone back there. And then I saw her, a few paces beyond the edge of the canopy, talking to a man wearing a chef's toque. The toque had collapsed, like a cake that had risen and then fallen. He was sitting on a step, smoking, his chef's white tunic unbuttoned, his gray-checked trousers riding up his shins.

I stood under the restaurant canopy, watching Alex in her pale blue, puffy-shouldered dress and black Mary Janes, loathing her for having so easily strayed from me, hoping my parents would appear soon and see her and yell at her. But then I realized they'd yell at me even more, since I was supposed to be the responsible one. I went over to her, grabbed her wrist, and said, "Come on."

"Better mind the man," the chef said, grinning. He had a tooth rimmed in gold.

"He's my brother," Alex said. "Sometimes he beats me up." It gave her some satisfaction to say this.

"You do?" the chef asked, looking at me from behind a cloud of smoke.

"No." I'd ridden my sister down more than once, used my fists on her, hit her dead in the nose with a football, but done no serious harm.

"I'm thinking of taking this girl home with me," the chef said. "Keep her safe from trouble and wickedness." He giggled, and so did Alex.

"Come on," I said to Alex, pulling her away from the chef.

"Better mind your brother. Don't want to make him mad."

IN THE MORNING, the rain fell slantwise. The wind shook the shaggy fir in the back yard and the weeping cherry in front. Alex slept. I went into the basement and saw that the water in the utility room had deepened; it gurgled as it slid down the floor drain. I put Julius's litter pan in the rec room. I dialed my ex-wife in Wisconsin to remind her that I still planned on seeing my son that weekend, but the line had gone haywire and she kept saying, "I can't hear you." I sectioned a grapefruit for Alex, put it on a tray along with coffee and one of the plantain turnovers, and carried it upstairs. It was ten o'clock.

Alex was sitting up in bed. She'd been crying. Her face looked as if it had grown longer during the night, darkened as daylight— or graylight, the Northwest winter version—approached. The orange plastic pill containers on Alex's dresser—her childhood dresser, on which she had once arranged her collection of china dogs—were the brightest things in the room.

"You should try one of Bernardo's turnovers. They're good."

"Bernardo's nice." She eyed the food, then took a sip of coffee.

"He seems very fond of you." I sat on the edge of the bed, which was large, big enough for a giant and his wife and a couple of little giants. It had been built by Alex's first ex-husband. Alex looked like a castaway on it. She was wearing an old lady's shawl over her nightgown. "How come you never told me about him?"

"He's just a friend," she said, sighing. "I went out with him a few times. He's trying to divorce his wife, but she won't let him. Plus he's bisexual, I think."

"He told me he'd do anything for you. He wants you to get well."

Alex picked up the turnover and sniffed it. "*Queso blanco,*" she said. "Sometimes he puts crabmeat inside."

"How old is he?"

"Somewhere in his fifties. He's probably the only hot-shot chef in town who isn't thirty-seven. Chefs peak at thirty-seven, you know."

I said I didn't.

She didn't eat the turnover. She pulled the shawl more tightly around her shoulders. "When are you going back to Wisconsin?"

"This weekend, I hope—I mean, unless the weather socks me in."

"I keep thinking these drugs are going to kick in," she said. "It's like waiting for Godot."

WHILE ALEX WAS AT DR. SHOUP'S, I went to an Ash Wednesday service at the Catholic church we'd passed on our walk the day before. All the crucifixes, from the big one above the altar to the smaller ones in the nave, were wrapped in purple, gauzelike sheets. The priest dipped his index finger into a small jar containing a dark gray substance and drew a cross on my forehead. "From dust you came, and to dust you shall return," he said.

When I left the church, the rain had all but ceased and the clouds that milled about the hills to the west gave the impression they might lift. I walked toward Dr. Shoup's office, lightened by the information that I was dust. I came upon the rose-colored Victorian house where I'd seen the woman working at her computer, and there she was, sitting straight-backed before her screen, diligently typing. I wanted to lie on her daybed—she'd have one, for musing—and listen to the keyboard clattering under her fingers, to the mouse emitting its little clicks, to her sighs or groans (I couldn't decide which) when she thought to delete something. But I had to move on and fetch Alex from her hour of therapy.

We drove to the grocery to buy ginger ale, grapefruit, kitty litter, a few other essentials. In the snack foods aisle, she gazed at me for a long moment and said, "Hey, you have a smudge on your forehead." She pronounced it "far-id," the way we'd grown up saying it in Kentucky; she almost sounded like her old self. "You fall down in the mud?"

"It's ashes. I went to church. There were nineteen old ladies there and me."

"You're so secretive," she said, in a tone that was not quite accusatory. She took a bag of Ruffles off the shelf and opened it, holding her face close to it. "There's this rush of gas or something that comes out of these bags when you open them. It's so strange—stranger than airplane food at thirty-five thousand feet, if you think about it." She put potato chips in her mouth, one after the other. "Salt and grease. Yum!"

Something had happened. Maybe it was the lights in the store, thousands of watts shining on Alex's gray face, causing gates to open and information to flow along the twisting, jiggery pathways of her brain. Maybe it was as simple as that: light, artificial light. Or maybe it was the piped-in music—something country, hardly noticeable—that had tripped a wire in her head and induced this moment of well-being. I didn't ask. I bought a bottle of wine. From the white-coated fishmonger, who smiled when she praised his display case, Alex bought shrimp and mussels and translucent rings of squid.

BERNARDO KNOCKED ON THE DOOR. He was wearing a sports coat over his chef's tunic. No cap. It had stopped raining, though, according to the radio, it would start again later that night. He tipped his nose up and said, "I smell saffron. Have you been cooking, Alex?"

Alex admitted she had. She'd hummed while working at the stove, making a paella. She'd drunk a glass of wine, called her son at her second ex-husband's house (the line had been repaired), and told me a joke that John Henry had told her. Had I heard about the guy whose gravestone said "Pardon me for not getting up"?

Bernardo said he'd left his kitchen in the hands of his sous-chef.

"I said, 'OK, Mr. Hot Shit from the Happy Valley Institute of Culinary Rats, here's your chance.' You can have his job anytime you want, Alex."

She said, "Thanks, Bernardo, I'll think about it."

"You ate my plantain turnovers?"

"I smelled them. My brother ate them all." Alex smiled. It was the toothy smile that led men to hang their slickers in her closet.

Bernardo said, "I think we're making progress. Maybe we should go see a movie and eat a box of popcorn." The cell phone in his coat went off. He ignored it. "What's it going to be? Jackie Chan or one from France that has a little philosophy and a lot of sex?"

I would've liked to have seen a French sex movie, but not with Alex and Bernardo, so I didn't go. I drank the rest of the wine, cleaned up the kitchen, and talked to my mother on the phone.

She said, "Alex should get her blood sugar checked and go see an herbalist before she starts running around with these men again. Men are her downfall, you know. She just can't seem to find a good one. They prey on her, poor thing. And now her system's all toxic, and this psychiatrist is filling her head with ideas. I don't believe in those people. They never did me any good, I can tell you. They think they're gods. I've told you about how that doctor put me in that place and gave me all those shock treatments, haven't I?"

I said she had, not too long ago. Alex and I had been children when she'd been hospitalized, she'd said. I had no recollection of her absence, but I did remember a later period, after she'd come home, when I'd found her lying on her bed in the midafternoon, gazing at the ceiling, a Christian-life magazine that she subscribed to on her chest.

"Well, I won't bore you again. Does Alex need money? Is she paying her bills?"

I said Bernardo had offered her a job.

"I don't think that's such a good idea. How is she going to take care of John Henry if she's working in a restaurant at night?"

I said that maybe God would help out.

There was a moment of silence, during which I regretted my comment. Then my mother, furiously polite, signed off, saying she had to take Digger out for his walk.

I got a beer out of the refrigerator and searched the house for Julius. I found a puddle of pee in the doorway of the guest bedroom and a pink, liquidy glob of rejected food on the stairs leading to Alex's bedroom. Julius himself was lying at the foot of Alex's unmade bed, in a heap of clothes that Alex may have meant to put down the laundry chute.

I made the bed and lay down on it. Julius mewed weakly, pathetically, like a cat that had forgotten how to mew. I lifted him up on the bed and said, "We'll rest here for a while. Then I'll go see if I can find the kitty cologne."

When I was a boy, I would sometimes go into Alex's room when she wasn't around and lie on her bed. I would read there (usually her teen fashion magazines, later D. H. Lawrence, whom she discovered before I did) or listen to her AM-FM clock radio (identical to my own) or lie under the sun lamp that Alex kept borrowing from my mother until it became a fixture. Once, when I was fourteen or fifteen, Alex came upstairs from watching TV— our parents had gone out—and found me on her bed, the radio playing, the orange bulb of the lamp shining on my dick, which stood tall, like a sun-loving flower. It goes without saying that I wanted her to see me and my need, my depravity, but shame overtook me even before I saw the stunned look on her face. I begged her not to tell anybody; I said I'd do anything for her. She told me to get out of her room and never come back. I was a pervert. I knocked on her door and pleaded. I said she could wear my shirts whenever she wanted. She could listen to my records whenever she wanted. She could always have the bathroom first. I would always be nice to her.

After a silence, she said, "What does 'nice' mean?"

"It means I'll be nice. You know, your brother."

"You have to be better than that," she said. "All the time. Forever."

"I'll try." I felt the weight of the promise, and I didn't see how I could keep it.

"You better."

ALEX STOOD AT the foot of the bed. She'd gotten dressed up for Bernardo: gray skirt, black blouse, jewelry circling neck and wrist, pink lipstick.

"I fell asleep," I said. "I was keeping Julius company. He's not doing too well."

"I haven't been able to face it." She sat on the bed and ran her finger under Julius's chin. He hardly stirred. "I don't think I want to have him put down."

"He's still hobbling around," I said. "There's no reason to."

I sat up. The bedside clock said 11:19. My mother would be asleep in Kentucky, unless of course she was up, drinking her protein drink, complaining to the dog about my incivility. My son would be asleep in his mother's house in Wisconsin, snow falling outside his window, lining the limbs of the trees. Tomorrow was a school day; there were math problems to be solved, books to be read, songs to be memorized. I said, "I should go downstairs."

"Stay," she said, taking my hand. I felt the cracked skin on her fingertips as she stroked my palm. On the back of her hand, I saw three moles lined up like ellipsis marks. Then she leaned into me, pressing her head under my chin. In her hair I smelled movie-house popcorn and something like the scents of all the men who had ever put their noses there. I smelled myself—my beery breath, the thousand desires that hadn't left me during my nap. She said, "Baby-sit me a while longer."

"You want a beer or something?"

She lifted her head off my chest. "How about a ginger ale."

I went downstairs and got two cans of ginger ale and brought them back up. Alex had changed into her nightgown and wrapped her shoulders in her old lady's shawl. She said Bernardo had talked all during the movie. He wanted to take her to see a *curandero* tomorrow, an old Mexican guy who lived out in the country.

"He means well," she said, "but I don't think I need both a shrink and a shaman. Do you?"

"Probably not. Are you going to work for him?"

"I don't know if I want to work for somebody who wants to have a romance with me."

I sat on the edge of the bed, listening to the ginger ale in my can fizz. "I was thinking about that time we were sleeping at Grammy's house, and somebody had gotten loose from the mental hospital, and we thought we heard him outside the window breathing heavily. I figured out later it was the neighbors' cows. You remember?"

"I got in bed with you. My big, grouchy, horny, secretive brother. I was afraid of you, but I loved you, too." She went over to the dresser and opened one of the pill bottles. "Nowadays I have to take one of these numbers to get to sleep."

Rain was falling again, in torrents. It clattered against the roof, like thousands of little hoofed devils. Julius slit an eye open. I imagined walking in the rain, the force of it washing away some of my lesser sins.

Alex took a last swig of ginger ale, removed her shawl, and got under the covers. "Did I ever tell you about this place I had in Mom and Dad's attic? It was behind a pile of suitcases. It was my most secret place. I didn't take anybody there, except for Gay, my invisible friend. You remember him? The spot was right under the roof, you had to watch out for the shingle nails poking through. I liked to sit there when it rained. Gay and I would talk—he was quiet and serious, like you—and listen to the rain beat down. Sometimes, when there was a lot of thunder, I'd have to reassure him. He'd quiver and not say a word. Some of those storms we got in Kentucky were pretty scary. It was like everything was going to be tossed and thrashed until it was returned to what it originally was." She fiddled with her pillow, then settled her head on it. "Good night, Peter," she said. "I hope you sleep well."